Legend of the Blood Raven

D.C. McLaughlin

Year of the Book
135 Glen Avenue
Glen Rock, PA 17327

ISBN 13: 978-1-942430-47-6
ISBN 10: 1-942430-47-7

Library of Congress Control Number: 2015958015

DEDICATION

Since this book has quite a lot to do with horses, it seems I would be remiss not to dedicate it to the memories of those valiant steeds my husband and I have shared our lives with.

To Sonny Joe Dodger, Foxrun's Hamdan and Argo who are no longer with us but were all alive during its creation. They now run on Epona's ever green fields.

ABOUT THE BLOOD RAVEN

"Legend of the Blood Raven" was a complete surprise to me from the beginning.

I wasn't supposed to publish this story. I was supposed to write, complete and publish the third and final book in the Mykhalo (my vampire) series. But my muse was being frustratingly obstinate about gifting me with any ideas. I had fifty pages of story and then everything ran dry. I had the urge to write, I desperately needed to write but nothing was forthcoming on this particular tale. So out of complete desperation, I went down into "the vault."

"The vault" is a dungeon-like place on my computer where I store all my unfinished stories. It's full of cobwebs and smells like failed dreams. I rummaged through all my pathetic attempts at epic novels and found one special gem. This one showed unusual promise. I had written it in another house, in another place, in what seemed a lifetime ago although it was really only 2003. So for the better part of twelve years, it had been languishing, gathering dust, waiting for me to work on it. And better yet, it was nearly finished. All it needed was a climax scene, wrap up the story, and the first draft version would be done. It wouldn't take much to bang this one into shape and get it ready for publication within a few short months.

So I left the vampire world and stepped through the portal into the completely different world of fantasy. This was the sort of story I had been writing since I was eleven. It had everything I loved in a good fantasy: horses, unicorns, dragons, magic instead of science, medieval kingdoms, warring races and of course the epic struggle between good and evil. I found myself rediscovering characters I had long since forgotten. I found their joy was my joy and their tears my tears.

Twelve years after I had started the story, I wrote the next few words. These words turned into a flood and the end came pouring out like a secret which must be told. Along the way, the characters snapped me in directions I never expected. Luckily I now know enough about the way I craft stories to comprehend this is where the true magic happens and I just trusted them. It is now finished, polished and I couldn't be happier or more proud of my new baby.

So now enter the world of the Blood Raven.

PROLOGUE

"I will wipe them off the face of the earth! The infestation must be dealt with."

The air inside the spacious tent crackled in sinister energy.

Savas-Zev was in a foul mood. He stalked about the tent in anger, garments swirling in his wake—not precisely wizard's robes yet not a cape either. Dask, one of his many captains, shuddered in terror of his master and shrank against the tent wall, fearing to let even the hem of the wizard's fabric touch him. It was a strangely enchanted garment whose color fooled the eye. It was a dark shade of... something. Sometimes the fabric appeared midnight blue, sometimes green, sometimes velvet red. But it changed with the angle of its wearer and the brightness of the light. Constant observation of the robes usually gave the gazer a headache. Dask was now convinced they were sentient and changed in accord to the master's mood.

The robe/cape thing glimmered and flashed deep velvet red now. Dask knew this was never a good sign.

Savas-Zev was a thin, half-starved, rakish looking man with sharp features and limp black hair falling back from a quickly balding head. His black beard was cut to a point at his chin, which he liked to fondle and tug when upset, like now. His slanted, squint eyes almost disappeared into their sockets as he stalked, muttering and glowering to himself. Dask was glad indeed those beady, evil orbs weren't turned his way. The eyes of Savas-Zev unnerved him most of all. As pale and unhealthy as his skin, his eyes were paler still, the lightest shade of gray imaginable with tiny pinpoints instead of pupils. Dask thought they looked like some dead thing long buried. Those eyes didn't belong on someone still very much in the land of the living.

Dask caught the word "dwarves" muttered from time to time in his master's garbled speech.

"Maybe the dwarves will get word of our advance and will flee in fear before us. Surely the terrible fame of your troops has spread far and wide by now," Dask finally dared to say in a trembling voice.

"Not likely!" Savas-Zev said aloud.

Dask just heaved an immense sigh of relief the master's eyes had not accompanied the words.

"Besides, that would deprive me of all my fun," Savas-Zev returned maliciously.

The wizard then slew Dask's final hope and looked him full in the face with those demented eyes... eyes which should not be.

"No, if anyone exterminates the dwarves from this place then it should be me. And I want to be there to witness every tormented dwarf's soul as it screams its last pleas for mercy." Savas-Zev's words dripped with utter scorn and hatred.

Dask recovered somewhat when the hated gaze was turned away from him. He caught his breath briefly and then dared to ask a bold question.

"Why the dwarves? Why do you hate them so?"

Savas-Zev picked up a heavy dwarf-made axe, straining to do so. He admired and hated the workmanship, the perfect detail, the skill and care taken to craft the weapon, and more besides. Just by touching the axe the wizard could feel and see the face of the dwarf who had created it and those who had been around him although they had been dead many years.

His face twisted in an angry scowl of distaste and he spat his hatred on the axe as if to cleanse it from its emanations.

"The dwarf race are a plague on the land, on any land they inhabit," he replied. "They delight in making every other race seem lazy. They hate any magic but their own." Savas-Zev said his next words with a scornful snort. "As if theirs is all that great!"

"Any wizard with the most rudimentary training can overcome a dwarf-spelled weapon or trinket. It is a minor inconvenience. But it is more than that."

The wizard strode over to his scrying bowl.

"Every race has its weak spot where they can be bent, and molded. The humans are easy. Just offer them power or wealth beyond their mortal grasp. The elves can be cajoled with clever words and magic promises disguised as truth and justice. But dwarves! Dwarves cannot be bent, persuaded, perverted, beaten down or enslaved in any way. Once they've made up their minds, that's it. Pompous fools!"

"There's rumors the dwarves of Tor Ambroc may attempt to negotiate a truce with you," Dask suggested.

"They will offer but it is useless. They have already made up their minds. They will never bend," he spat. "But I will accept their truce. It will do them no good. Their end will be the same."

Savas-Zev turned his hated gaze on Dask and the man quailed and cowered fearfully under it. Seeing this reaction, the wizard smiled. He liked his subjects' fear. It assured him they were too afraid of him to do anything but obey without question.

"The dwarves are a plague on the land, as I said before. A plague they are, and a plague they will get. It shall be great fun to watch them suffer and die one by one. They deserve no less from me."

There was a commotion at the door of the tent. Two heavy, half-human guards bodily dragged in a kicking and struggling dwarf who was swearing and spluttering curses.

"Ah, this is the spy you found skulking about our little encampment!" Savas-Zev said cheerfully rubbing his spidery hands together in anticipation of his amusement. The wizard waved away the guards and they were more than happy to dump their prey and leave his hated yet feared presence.

Dask shivered and cowered further away knowing what was to come and dreading every bit, even though he knew he would not be the target.

"You will not need those here," Savas-Zev said and, as he waved a thin hand, the sturdy handcuffs and iron chains fell away.

The dwarf looked down at his freed bonds and back to the wizard in surprise. Then he stood up straight, proud and utterly defiant.

"I'll still not be tellin' ya nothin'!" he insisted.

"Oh but you shall, my little bristly friend." Savas-Zev waved his hand again, levitating the dwarf into the air before him. "You will tell me everything I wish to know and more besides. You will tell me the truth because you will have no choice. And then... maybe... I will release you to your dark, little holes."

Dask shuddered in terror. He knew it was an empty promise. Savas-Zev never released any dwarf except by death.

Dask crawled into the darkest corner of the tent and huddled there, eyes squeezed shut and rocking madly. He dreaded what was to come. He dared not leave for Savas-Zev would catch him and be very displeased indeed. And yet he was so relieved it was the dwarf and not himself in front of the cruel wizard now. He would still be alive tomorrow morning.

The dwarf would not.

CHAPTER 1

Life had been so different for Bran only a month before. Life had been wonderful. Her favorite uncle Daga had taken her to the human town of Kopa which was the nearest settlement to the dwarf kingdom of Tor Ambroc, Bran's home. The month-long celebration of Winterfest was about to commence, their last great feast before the bitter cold began. Daga knew the farrier in Kopa.

Daga had tried to prepare Bran for her first encounter with a large mass of humans.

"Now, Bran," he said patiently. "These humans aren't like us, they're quite different. Don't try to make sense of them. You can't. Just watch them and let them be."

"Well, I know they're bigger than us," Bran said.

"It's more than that," her uncle replied with a frustrated sigh. "I guess it's because their growth rate is all twisted. They don't fully mature 'til they are twenty. And even this is questionable! They're a lot weaker as children than a dwarf child... and more stupid. They're emotional all the time. They wear their feelings on their faces way too much so it's easy to tell what they're thinking." Her uncle exaggerated his facial expressions crazily until Bran nearly laughed out loud. Daga continued, "And their women don't grow beards."

"What?" exclaimed Bran in utter astonishment. "You must be joking!"

"I am not," her uncle assured. "I've seen them in every stage of life. Not one woman has a beard. And if they have a few stray hairs on their chins, they're teased."

Bran shook her head in amazement.

"I'm going to be the best looking female there!" she muttered scratching her healthy, young, bright red stubble.

Her uncle nodded, his black eyes flashing one of his famous smiles.

They arrived around midday. Kopa was a town of modest size, populated by mostly humans, a scattering of dwarves and on the rare occasion, an elf or two passing through on the way to more important or exotic locations.

It was the first time Bran had seen so many humans and she was slightly overwhelmed by the sheer numbers of them. And the smell. Dwarves always smelled of the forge—ash, smoke and half-smelted metal and sometimes burned leather apron. Humans smelled like everything!

She saw few women but they were as her uncle had said, without beards. The human women seemed to have a fixation with wearing dresses. In dwarf society only the religious leaders wore robes. All other dwarves, male or female usually wore trousers with a leather apron for protection from the sparks. Most dwarves wore it constantly as a racial uniform of necessity.

Conal, the farrier, ran a livery stable on the outskirts of town. He had a large barn with many stalls and enough land for a few paddocks. He also had a small cottage for special guests. But shoeing horses and running the stable were his main profession. Daga had rented the cart and horses from Conal so they stopped to check in with him first.

Bran didn't like the man the minute she saw him. She thought him too small in the torso to have any business working a forge, even a farrier's. Among the humans, though, Conal was considered quite stockily built. He had straight brown hair and a curly beard, which almost reached his chest. Bran supposed it was because humans barely lived a century that he didn't have a beard of proper length. Daga had a shiny blue-black beard and glittering black eyes. His beard was fastidiously groomed, braided and tucked into his belt, as was dwarf custom. He was considered quite fetching by the female dwarf community. The king of Tor Ambroc needed retainers to carry his beard braids or else he would have tripped over them, and he looked very distinguished indeed.

Conal strode boldly up to the cart, waving and smiling broadly so all his white teeth flashed.

"Daga!" he exclaimed cheerfully. "So nice of you to drop by on your way to the festival."

He clasped Daga's arm in a grip which was considered strong by human standards.

Bran almost curled her lip in distaste. Her uncle was right. These humans *were* an emotional lot!

Daga nodded in reply but did not smile back.

"And who is this fine strapping lad you have with you?" Conal asked peering up into the cart at the figure who sat beside Daga.

Daga snorted as if insulted and replied with some heat, "This 'lad' is my brother's daughter, my *niece*."

"Oh!" said Conal in surprise and his eyes immediately flew to Bran's as yet unsprouted chest. His gaze then shifted to peer narrowly at the hair on her cheeks noticing how fine and silky it was as compared to Daga's.

"Niece!" he stuttered in embarrassment. "Quite right! Of course! How silly of me to have made such a blunder!"

Bran's lip did curl at this. These human creatures certainly were rude!

Then the thing named Conal started to look her over with a more critical eye noticing her barrel frame and big arms.

"Can she work a forge yet?" Conal asked.

Daga harrumphed in disgust.

"Of course she can!" he assured heatedly. "Our children can work a hammer and anvil while your pink brats are still learning to walk and talk."

Conal flashed him an angry look but let the retort die on his lips.

"What plot are you hatching, human?"

"Well, it's just my eldest son, Drock, is in bed with the heaves and chills and can't help me with the forge. My second son is good with the beasts but he's useless with the forge. Could I borrow Bran while you're here? There are so many more people passing through Kopa because of the festival. I could really use her help. What do you say?"

Daga looked at Bran thoughtfully.

"What do you think, lass? It's easy and honest work even though it's not as glorious as forging swords. The decision is up to you."

Bran nodded wordlessly.

"Great! I'll have Vilmar, he's my second son, show you the ropes," Conal said in obvious relief.

He extended an arm to assist her as if she were a lady. But Bran gave him such a shocked look he soon pulled it back. Silently, she clambered down from the cart and took her bedroll and pack from her uncle.

Daga's eyes glittered at her as he said softly, "You'll do just fine, lass!"

Then he snapped the reins and drove away toward the center of town. The heavy throngs of tall, strangely dressed people quickly swallowed him up.

Bran followed Conal into his shop and strode up to the only other person who was there—a tall, lean, underfed looking teenager. He had sandy red hair, ice blue eyes and a smattering of freckles across his nose.

"I'm Bran," she told him without smiling. "You must be Vilmar."

He nodded staring at her and then hesitantly said, "Why do you have a beard?"

"Why don't you?" she shot back almost without thinking.

He stopped, startled by her reply and then slowly smiled.

Bran caught the corners of her mouth turning up in a return smile although she fought it. He looked as weak as water, but somehow she immediately liked him. Even if he did smell of magic.

Despite her first misgivings about them, she found herself quickly growing to like the humans, especially Vilmar. Bran was only seven years of age at the time. But this was considered the edge of adulthood to dwarves. Vilmar was much older than her at fourteen. In spite of this, they got along as if they were the same age.

Bran quickly learned how to forge horseshoes. She found the work easy compared to what she had done at home even though she had only forged tools, not weaponry yet. And yet as easy as it was for her to make shoes, she found the variety of them—made to treat certain problems in a horse's hooves—intriguing. It certainly kept her from getting bored.

But what she enjoyed most was working with and watching the horses. She had an insatiable fascination with the beasts, although she had so far not spoken of this passion. She knew no other dwarves with a love for horses so she assumed it was something which was not permitted among her people. So in true dwarf fashion she simply said nothing.

Bran pounded and shaped the metal, listening and learning in silence.

Vilmar was a fascinating character. Bran watched him carefully as her hammer rang and the sparks flew. It was true he had no forging talents. This would have been close to a crime in dwarf society. But Vilmar was not a dwarf and he seemed to have other talents which made him just as valuable to his own people.

The first day Bran saw a young colt dragged by force into the shop. The horse was accustomed to a whole lot of nothing, didn't even know how to be led and was confused and frightened. He was to have his first set of shoes put on. But being as he'd hardly ever been handled, he was fighting every step of the way, eyes rimmed white with fear and heels flying toward any person who approached. The colt's owner was only making the situation worse—shouting, moving quickly, and waving his fist threateningly. Vilmar told the man to put the colt in a box stall, which they finally managed to do with difficulty. Then Vilmar ordered everyone away and told them to come back at the end of the day. By the light in his eyes, Bran knew he meant to keep the owner away at all costs!

Conal began to trim a much more agreeable animal's feet, totally trusting in his son's talents. Bran forced her curiosity deep down for an hour. There was the sound of the colt's hooves hammering on the walls of the box and Vilmar's voice, soft and low. Then everything became quiet save for the song of Vilmar.

In about an hour Bran peeped into the box. The colt was almost asleep, his head in Vilmar's arms. The young man winked at Bran who was standing there aghast. Conal entered the stall and the colt woke up briefly. But then Vilmar started his song again and the colt relaxed, trusting him. Conal trimmed and shod the young horse. It didn't go perfectly but the colt also never panicked like before.

"Da, I think we better buy this one. I didn't do all this work just to have his master ruin him all over again," Vilmar chuckled.

"Sounds fair to me," Conal agreed. "He ought to let this one go easy in spite of its good breeding. All you have to do is wave enough coin under that man's nose and he'd sell you anything, even his own mother!"

"You drugged him!" Bran said.

"I did not!" Vilmar shot back. "My Da raised me better than that!"

Bran saw Conal's cheeks curve in a smile as he worked on the colt's foot.

"Then how'd you get him to quiet down so fast?" she asked more fascinated than doubting.

"I have the magic touch," Vilmar said with a big smile and massaged the colt's winter-furred neck with a wide hand.

Conal snorted. "Just as long as he uses that touch on horses and not women," he said and dropping the foot, straightened up. He flashed his son a certain look. "Horses pay better!"

"Now, Da, you know I'm not like that," Vilmar said quickly, his cheeks flushing in embarrassment. He looked sheepishly at Bran and muttered under his breath as his father walked out. "The women around here are about as interesting as cows."

This was Bran's first experience with Vilmar's 'magic touch'. She suspected there was much more to it than just being naturally gifted with horses. This reek of magic about him nagged at her. Dwarves are suspicious of anyone's magic but their own and this smell definitely wasn't dwarf magic. But she wisely kept her mouth shut until she could find out more.

Later that evening at dinner, Daga asked about her first day.

"So Conal tells me you did quite well," her uncle said as he slurped from his mug. "What do you think of him?"

She replied as she reached for a large wedge of cheese. "His talents may not be dwarf talents. But he seems to be masterful at what he does."

She tore off a mouthful of bread and considered while she chewed. "I have never known that shoeing horses could be so beneficial. It's almost like healing, shaping and adding support to the hoof to promote a more healthy growth."

Daga nodded as he cut a hunk of cheese Bran offered him with his dagger.

"The human horsemen have a saying, 'No foot, no horse.' "

"I'm beginning to see what it means," Bran replied with a tone of respect to her voice.

She thought a bit more. "Conal seems to be a good, honorable sort. He cares about the horses who come to him. Tries to improve or help them on their way. Others just use them like machines and discard them when they break down."

"He better care about them! They're his bread and butter!" Daga snorted. "He wouldn't get very far using them up like other people... although I've seen farriers with less soul do just that. I've seen others get a horse to work on who's lame in one foot, so they lame the poor beast in the others so they won't knock their knees, just to get paid and get them out the door for the next paying customer to arrive. Conal won't do it. He'll get the folks a useful animal and fix up the old. You saw this today. It's only fair. He's a good man, a genuine man. He won't lie or hurt a horse to make a profit."

They both were silent a bit while they ate.

"Were the human tools adequate for you?" Daga asked suddenly, looking up from his stew.

"They were not!" snorted Bran in scorn. "Conal gave me these things he had made especially for Drock when he was first learning the forge. He thought because of my size, they'd be easier for me because they were lighter and had more reach. They were awful! Nice reach but way too light. I felt like I was using toothpicks!"

Daga laughed, shaking his head and banging the table with the flat of his hand.

"These humans learn and grow much slower than dwarf children and are far weaker. You're seven years old. Near to being grown. At seven, a human child is just beginning to learn the forge. In another two years, Bran, you'll be marrying age if you so choose. Humans don't marry until they're eighteen or more."

Daga reached for the ale to refill his tankard.

"I'll see you get a set of tools made properly for your hands. No dwarf should travel without their own set of tools."

Bran stirred her quickly cooling stew absently, her thoughts elsewhere.

"How old is Vilmar?" she asked suddenly.

"Just a pup," Daga sniffed. "Barely fourteen years."

He looked at her with a narrow gaze sensing her interest.

"What do you think of Vilmar?" he asked suddenly.

"He's no dwarf!" she snorted and Daga nodded, smiling with just his eyes. "He's a good sort though. True enough like his father and he has a great touch with horses. He's terrible with a forge! Good thing he's a human then. Humans can overlook such things, I guess. I wouldn't want to marry him though. Too gentle and soft."

Daga nodded slowly, watching her face closely.

"Vilmar stinks of magic," she finally said.

"So you noticed, eh?" Daga said quietly.

"Oh yes," Bran replied "But I can't place what kind of magic. Is it human?"

"Not on that one! He's just lucky his parents can't tell!"

Daga sighed deeply and frowned, his brows knit in concern. "He started to stink like that a couple of years ago. I haven't quite been able to put my finger on exactly what kind of magic it is. Kinda seems like druid 'cause it smells like a forest in springtime, but not quite. Also kinda feels like wizard magic."

Bran stared at her uncle in shock. She spat on the floor in disgust.

"Damn wizards!" she growled.

Daga nodded grimly.

"Is he dangerous to us?" she asked gulping her drink nervously.

"I think not," her uncle replied slowly. "I think the lad is barely aware what kind of magic he has, although he *is* aware. He's awfully young to know those sorts of things without proper, full-time instruction. And his heart is still pure and good like his da's. I wouldn't worry yet. Something or someone's gotta twist his mind or heart to turn him dangerous. And he hasn't lived long enough for that yet, my dear."

Bran nodded but the glint in her eyes was suspicious. "But all the same, I'll watch him."

Daga nodded and winked. "You do that, lass."

The first week passed quickly with Bran learning more each day. Conal gave her new chores, from mucking stalls and currying, to harnessing and saddling the horses. Conal said he wanted her to have a good working knowledge of the animals she was caring for. He was a stern taskmaster but fair. Bran learned and Conal made sure she learned well. Next to working the forge, Bran liked harnessing the horses to the cart best. It was almost like assembling the pieces of a sword. She was also quickly designing ways in her brain of making the harness more efficient just by adding a buckle here or a strap there.

By the end of the first week they were starting to introduce her to the art of healing a horse's many ailments. They explained the mystery of salves and poultices, creams—which drew heat out—and herbs, which would fire a limb up, and the reasons for the use of each. They showed her the good a fast-moving, cold stream could do on a horse who could barely rest any weight on one leg. It was an art in and of itself. It was this healing art she felt the least confident of practicing. She was always worried about doing the opposite of what the animal needed and making it worse. But Vilmar was patient with her and Conal's instructions were precise. She learned the healing art.

One evening after all the shoes were made and fitted, the stalls mucked and the horses seen to, Bran went outside to watch Vilmar work. He was standing in the middle of a perfectly round pen herding a young horse around the outside at a fast-moving pace. She had seen him do this before but he'd always had the horse on a long tether before. This time the colt was free in the pen.

Bran looked admiringly at the young horse Vilmar was working. It was a colt, newly gelded and just settling down. The colt was a solid blood bay with no white markings. The setting sun touched the animal's flanks as it trotted calmly around the outside of the ring, turning its brown hide to burnished flame. The colt's eyes were bright and intelligent and showed no fear.

Vilmar pivoted in the center of the ring, always facing the animal, keeping his attention focused on the young horse. At a sudden word from him, the colt sat back on its haunches, spun and continued its passage in the other direction. Vilmar watched for a few passes before calling out another command. Instantly the colt stopped and spun to face him, waiting expectantly for the next command. Vilmar called the colt. Licking and chewing meekly, the bay strode easily up to him and stood with its head lowered to his hands. Vilmar spoke softly to the horse, stroking its face and neck. The colt's eyes were soft and gentle.

Vilmar's eyes went to Bran's face.

"Want me to teach you to ride?" he asked her with a small, mischievous smile.

Bran tried not to look as startled as she felt. "You're kidding, right?" she said.

"Not at all," he replied still smiling. "Well? How about it?"

Her breath caught in her throat. Then suddenly, without knowing exactly why she was doing it, she spun on her heel and left without answering. She knew she was being terribly rude. But Bran was too afraid to say what she really wanted.

She wanted to say yes.

CHAPTER 2

Daga noticed her pensive mood later that night at dinner. "Bran?" he asked her quietly.

It took a moment or two for her to realize she had been spoken to. She looked up guiltily.

"What troubles you, lass?" he asked and his voice was very gentle.

"Vilmar asked me if I wanted to learn to ride today," she said watching her uncle's face carefully.

"Ah," Daga replied tearing off a chunk of bread. "And your answer was...?"

"I didn't answer him," she said. "I just left."

Daga looked up in confusion. "Well that was certainly quite rude of you, child!" he snorted.

"I know," she said dismally. After a long silence, she continued. "Da would have fifteen fits."

Daga shot her a withering look. "Your Da is not here, lass."

She wrinkled her nose in confusion.

"Bran, you listen to me. Soon you will have to make decisions on your own and your Da will not approve of all of them. Do you really want to live your life according to what other people expect of you?"

"No," Bran replied. Her arms were folded on the table and her fuzzy chin rested on them. She couldn't look her uncle in the eye.

"Don't you want to learn to ride?" he asked.

Bran's eyes flashed up to meet his and now there was a spark of heat in them like the coals in a forge's fire.

"More than anything!" her voice was soft but fierce.

Daga pushed his plate and drink aside and punctuated his words with his dagger.

"I've watched you these past few days and so has Conal. You want to know what he says about you? He says for a dwarf, you have the makings of a great horseman. He wouldn't be teaching you his horse leech craft if he thought the knowledge would be wasted on you. He's only teaching you what he thinks you can handle—and from all reports, he thinks you can handle quite a bit! You're good. You have the talent for it."

"Dwarves delve," Bran replied and her voice echoed slightly as she buried her face in her mug. "They don't ride."

Daga took hold of her sideburns in his big hands.

"Look at me, brother's daughter!" he commanded sternly.

Her green eyes locked with his glittering black ones.

"Not all dwarves delve. Some do ride. Some very great dwarves ride. It is a tradition with highest honor. Don't you ever belittle it!"

Bran's face twisted in confusion. She didn't understand. She had never heard of any dwarves who lived above and chose to ride. She had no idea what her uncle was talking about.

Bran was quieter than usual the next day. She hammered her forge dutifully making horseshoes. She mucked stalls and she unharnessed horses coming in and saddled horses going out. She slathered fiery cream on one horse's legs and walked a lame horse on three legs down to the stream in the paddock to stand in the soothing, icy, winter flow. She brushed shaggy horses until their coats gleamed. Then she went out to the round pen to watch Vilmar work the colt.

Vilmar stopped and called the colt like the day before. But this time he grabbed a handful of mane and swung onto the sleek back. The colt stood placidly awaiting his commands. Bran watched in amazement as he worked the colt one way and then the other with no aide from a saddle or bridle. He trotted, then cantered the horse in small circles. Then they swung the other way and did the same in the opposite direction. Vilmar stopped the horse and somehow made him back up. She had seen this routine for the past few days but it was still such a mystery to her how anyone could get a horse to do these things, especially without a saddle or bridle.

When he was done, he rode the colt up to the fence where she was standing.

"Vilmar," she said quietly struggling to keep her voice from trembling.

"Yes?"

"Teach me how to do that," she finally said after taking a deep breath.

Vilmar grinned widely from ear to freckled ear. "Gladly!" he said in a quiet voice.

Daga noticed the difference immediately when Bran walked, or rather hobbled into the cottage that night.

"Ah!" he said cheerily. "First riding lesson, I see!"

Bran gave a pained smile and nodded.

Daga laughed loudly and slapped his knee as she tottered to the nearest chair and eased herself carefully onto its hard, wooden surface.

"I didn't think it would hurt this much," Bran said and hissed in pain when she shifted the wrong way. "Tomorrow I want a saddle."

"Oh, no you don't!" insisted Daga. "If he's teaching you with no saddle he's teaching you right."

"Wouldn't a saddle be more comfortable than backbone and hide to bounce on?" she nearly whined.

"Saddles aren't for comfort. They're for better grip to help you stay on. If you learn without a saddle, you'll learn to stick like glue. Your legs will be stronger. Stirrups are for lazy riders to rest their dangling feet on long rides. They're a crutch. You don't really need them."

"All the same, I think I'll skip tomorrow's lesson," she said.

"Oh, no you don't, Bran!" Daga lectured sternly. "You will hurt more tomorrow, and tomorrow you will ride longer than today. You've got to build up those inner leg muscles. Don't worry, they'll toughen up just like you."

Bran groaned and buried her head in her arms.

"Have you fallen off yet?" Daga inquired with sadistic eagerness.

Bran moaned again and raised a hand with two fingers uncurled.

Daga cackled with glee and gave her his tallest tankard.

"You're a little young to drink but tonight I think you need some ale, my dear. For medicinal purposes, of course. Here! Drink up, niece!

He filled her mug until the foam overflowed the top and then smacked her hard on the shoulder. She lurched and it took a great dwarven effort for her not to bellow in pain.

"Have a care, uncle!" she pleaded in a tiny voice. "That's where I landed!"

Daga roared in laughter and pulled out a flask of his better ale. She had never seen him laugh so much on a non-feast day. She growled at his glee of her obvious suffering.

"Cantankerous old mule!" she muttered not caring if he heard, and gulped her ale as if it were life-giving ambrosia.

He only shook his head and wagged his black beard in mirth.

CHAPTER 3

Vilmar had her riding a different horse every other day. He started her on a dead quiet old pony who had to be pushed with legs and seat to get going. But once moving, the pony wouldn't stop short of crashing into a wall. It took all of Bran's arm strength, toughened by hammering to haul this pony to a stop with the reins. The next mount was exactly the opposite, sensitive as an open wound. First time she kicked this one in the ribs, the pony reared straight up in the air and dumped her. She got up, dusting off her backside and anticipated more ale from her uncle, 'for medicinal purposes' of course.

"If this keeps up, I'll either be a great rider, or a drunk," she complained.

Daga squinted his eyes at her and taunted cheerfully, "Just wait until you're in your first pitched battle! You never know when you'll get a break. You either got to keep on fighting or die. You'll be just as sore the day after... if you live. Being sore means you're alive."

He refilled her tankard and she moaned again.

Gradually Bran got the hang of riding. Vilmar was a bit amazed with how quick she was to get back on after a fall. Many a human would have given up by now and he told her so. But she was determined to master this skill. Vilmar just shook his head and muttered, "Dwarves! Your kind is like pit-fighting dogs! Once you latch on, you don't let go."

"That's a good quality to have when in a fight, young Vilmar," barked Daga who had shown up.

Daga had come to watch several lessons. When Bran hit the dirt he said nothing, neither praised nor criticized, his face a blank shell. He waited until she was back on the horse before flashing her some sign of encouragement either in a gesture or word. Bran found she appreciated having him there. She liked having at least one family member who would support her.

She was also getting to know the different little details of riding. She learned how simply shifting her weight on her mount communicated signals to the animal. She could feel the horse beneath her tense when she leaned forward or took a more snug hold on the reins, anticipating her next command.

She also learned the tricks which worked with one animal didn't necessarily work with another. She learned some horses had nice smooth gaits and some were like bouncing on jagged rocks no matter what kind of saddle she put under herself, when Vilmar permitted it. She learned to watch their ears when going over a jump. The ears' position told her where the animal's mind was. She learned to adjust her riding skills to each particular animal.

And one day, Vilmar let her ride a horse who moved differently from all her other lesson horses. He told her this was a 'gaited horse'. She had no idea what that meant until she was on the animal's back and asked him to speed up from a walk. She prepared her legs for the jarring of the bouncy trot and was surprised by the smooth, rhythmic action the horse swung into.

"How do I sit to this?" she called out in panic.

Vilmar just laughed.

"It's easy!" he directed. "Sit up straight and tall and sway your hips in time with the motion."

It *was* easy! She kept waiting for the gait to get more complicated but it didn't. She was so relieved she wasn't bouncing anymore.

"Hey!" she called out in joy. "I could shoot arrows from this!"

Daga was watching and said quietly but loud enough to hear. "Many archers do."

Bran decided she liked the gaited horses best. Then Vilmar told her they were often picked to be a fine lady's mount. She screwed up her face in disgust at this.

"I prefer an 'archer's horse' to describe them," she muttered.

"Typical dwarf!" teased Vilmar. "Always thinking of fighting!"

Just when she got confident about her riding skills, Vilmar threw a new challenge her way. Now she was to learn to do an 'emergency dismount'. What it turned out to be was a controlled fall from a horse.

"Great! More bruises!" she muttered grimly.

"I'll have to buy more ale," replied Daga. "Blast it! The inferior human stuff will have to do."

Bran actually didn't do too badly this time. Emergency dismounts required more balance and timing than actually throwing oneself carelessly off a horse. She became rather skilled at landing in a roll—which took her out of harm's way—or landing on her feet. Daga approved mightily of this skill. He said it would come in handy in a fight. Vilmar just rolled his eyes and shook his head at this. Bran grinned. She didn't need him to say anything. She knew his thoughts.

'Damned dwarves!'

Bran was getting to be quite a good rider by the time Winterfest was over. She found she didn't want to go back to the horseless tunnels of Tor Ambroc. She liked Conal and Vilmar. The farrier's son had become a good friend. And she liked everything to do with horses, most especially the riding. It took a supreme dwarven effort for her to hide her regret of leaving them.

Conal told her to visit as often as she liked for she was always welcome in their house. Vilmar said he would visit Tor Ambroc and always bring a spare horse in case she wanted to ride.

This cheered her up a bit. She wondered if she would still remember how to ride when the time came, or would her inner leg muscles return to as before?

And then came the dinner talk with her mother and father, Yaffa and Varg. That's when everything went to crap in a basket!

CHAPTER 4

Their return was greeted with as much joy as dwarves tended to express. The family members gathered around her and Daga at the dinner table that evening asking about Winterfest and Bran's opinion of the great outside world. Bran was as brief as could be with her answers and dreaded the topic of horses coming up. At least the family approved of her learning to drink but no one asked why. They just assumed it was because of the month-long celebration.

Bran and Daga, along with her parents, stayed up long after the evening meal talking and smoking their pipes. Bran finally yawned and made to go to bed. Yaffa, her mother, pushed her back down into her chair.

"Not so fast, miss," she chastened sternly. "We have business to discuss."

Bran was instantly awake, her mind whirling in nervous wonder. Had they found out about the horses? Did they know she had spent her last month making horseshoes and learning to ride? Her Da would be furious!

Then something else even more frightening occurred to her. What if they planned on marrying her off? Arranged marriages were not a common custom among dwarves and she was just a bit young, but sometimes it was done especially if there was fear in the family of a young member going astray. Bran had no intention of marrying anybody!

Bran swallowed hard and, trying to keep her tone unassuming asked, "What business, Ma?"

"The business of your education, my dear," she said seriously sitting down across from her.

The wild fluttering of Bran's heart subsided somewhat but she was still nervous.

"What education?" Varg spouted in a huff. "The lass knows our history. She knows how to read and write, how to forge and a little of how to enchant a weapon. The rest will come with time. What more does she need to know?"

"You know exactly what I mean, husband," Yaffa said giving him a long look from her ice-blue eyes. "So does Daga. It's just you who doesn't see the sense in it."

"She needs to know more than just the world of dwarves," Daga said gravely. "She needs to be prepared for the world outside Tor Ambroc."

"She should learn to read and write and speak in other languages. She should learn the customs of elves and men," said Yaffa.

"Why?" bellowed Varg. "Is she gonna leave Tor Ambroc for good?"

Daga and Yaffa exchanged knowing glances.

"I have left these tunnels but once in me life and I'm still kicking!" he insisted. "Our whole lives revolve around forging and delving. We don't ever need to stick our noses out of the tunnels. Nothing but trouble comes from out there. Here is home."

Bran's heart sank when she heard his words. She suddenly felt the world was closing in about her and becoming very small. She didn't want to be like her father and spend her entire life underground away from the free air and away from horses altogether.

"My dear, misguided brother," Daga said with a patient sigh. "Do you remember what happened the last time we let you out to mingle with other races?"

Bran's ears perked with curiosity. She had never heard this tale. "What happened?" she spoke up.

"Your father insulted a human of some importance and nearly started a war!" Yaffa chuckled and Daga joined in her laughter.

"Bah!" Varg said throwing up his hands and stomping over to the fire. "He had it coming to 'im. Damn humans are too soft with their feelings!"

Bran snickered quietly trying not to let her father notice.

"King Garshan decreed the easiest way to smooth over the hurt feelings was to never let your father have anymore dealings with any of the races save his own kind. It seems Varg has some lousy people skills."

"So he banished me to the tunnels forever," Varg puffed stomping back, hands on his hips. "Where's the harm in that? The peoples who live above ground are strange and outlandish with barbaric customs. They're just not right in the head. Who would want to deal with them anyway?"

"I think your youngest daughter might," Yaffa said quietly.

Varg turned about slowly and trapped Bran with a deadly gaze.

"Bran already has two human friends she has so far managed not to drive away," Daga said slowly. "I think she might care to have some more non-dwarf friends."

"Bran, is this true?" her father asked slowly, glaring accusingly at her.

Bran fearfully met those dangerous eyes. She glanced in growing panic to her mother and Daga. She felt like an arrow's target.

"I met a farrier and his son in Kopa," she said finally after taking a deep breath. "They taught me how to make horseshoes and ride. They're my friends. I would very much like to see them again."

"You need no friends who are not dwarves," Varg said in a voice so quiet it sounded deadly. "Keep to your own people, Bran."

Bran listened to her father's words. Then she remembered Daga's advice to her not so long ago.

"Soon you will have to make decisions of your own and your Da will not approve of all of them."

Bran squeezed her eyes shut in pain.

"Muttlith," Varg said in a quiet but hostile tone of voice. "My daughter's a muttlith."

He turned and stomped out of the room, slamming the door behind him.

Bran felt herself begin to shudder with dread.

Her father had called her a muttlith. It was the greatest insult one dwarf could give another and this word had been delivered to her by her own father. She had been disgraced.

CHAPTER 5

After the outburst, Bran made herself scarce around her father. And it seemed that was just the way he wanted it. She buried herself in her work, hammering at the hot metal of her forge as if it were an enemy to be conquered and beaten. She turned her frustration into her work. If she met her father, she stood firm and tall, but never once did he look her in the eye. He ignored her completely.

"Bran, you need to deal with this issue between your Da and yourself," her mother counseled one day. "It's ruining your work."

Bran looked up in surprise from the sword she was about to finish.

"But I thought my blades were improving," she replied. "And it's better than sticking my Da with a hot one!"

Yaffa grinned but shook her head.

"Yes and no, child," she explained. "Your work has improved by far. But your expertly made weapons of late need to be cleansed by the cleric before they are used. It does no good to create a blade with anger and frustration. Your feelings go into the metal and will bite anyone who touches them. You need to settle this and soon. Or else only goblins will buy your blades."

Yaffa patted her reassuringly on the shoulder and left. Bran stared at the nearly completed short sword, her best by far. It was a weapon and a thing of beauty.

Yet her feelings had cursed this beautiful thing.

She threw it rudely down on the table and stormed out, not knowing where she was going, and now without any outlet for her pent-up emotions.

She found herself quite by accident in the upper levels of Tor Ambroc making for the outer gates. She stepped outside the tunnels and breathed deep the cold air clinging resolutely to winter's chill despite the threatening spring. Three deep breaths and she felt better though she still didn't know what to do. But at least out there in the free air, her problems felt a little further away.

There was a sudden horse's neigh and the guards at the gate looked up. Bran followed their gaze. A horse and rider were making their slow way up the mountain path. Then Bran saw the rider was leading a little pony behind him. The pony had no pack but a saddle and bridle. She recognized the rider in an instant.

"Vilmar!" she called in relief and ran up to him.

"Hullo, stranger!" he called back.

He looked her over closely from the saddle.

"You look like you could use a drink or a ride to clear your head," he said with a slow smile and led the pony up suggestively, eyes twinkling.

"I'm not thirsty," she smiled back getting his drift.

"Well, then let's see what I can do to make you thirsty, shall we?" There was an obvious hint of mischief to his voice.

She needed no prompting but vaulted onto the pony's saddle from the ground and spurred the little beast past Vilmar at a gallop scattering the dwarf guards.

She could hear him shout, "Not fair!" as he gave chase.

She wanted to be far away from Tor Ambroc. She knew her problems would still be there when she got back, but she wanted to put them at arm's length for a little while. She just wanted to be able to breathe.

So for the first hour, she kept her nimble little pony just ahead of Vilmar's big bay, weaving in and out of trees and skidding along rockslides, pressing the horse just as fast as she could safely take him. The wind combed her beard and branches tore at her hair, and all of it didn't matter. She was finally free!

She eventually slowed the pony to a walk and let Vilmar catch up. Both horses were breathing hard from the chase. They slowed the animals to cool them out in a wooded area where the trees weren't too close. Bran and Vilmar rode for a bit in silence just enjoying each other's company. Bran reveled in the moment and thought of nothing else but the wind on her face and hair, the soft sounds of a woodland in winter and the smell of the horse under her. She was at peace and wanted to stay that way.

Vilmar's words suddenly jolted her and brought her back to her problems.

"That was quite a display back there," he said. "When I came up here I didn't expect you to challenge me to a race."

Bran grunted but said nothing.

"You act like a horse who's been penned up too long in its stall."

Bran thought on this briefly.

"That's a very good comparison," she agreed.

"Well, would you like to tell me what you're running from?" he asked quietly.

She stopped her pony and looked hard at him. Their friendship thus far had been happy and full of fun. Could she now trust him with the darker side of her life? Would he forget about her if their relationship stopped being so carefree? She thought hard in those brief moments. She finally decided if she didn't like his answer, she could always run away with the pony until she could trust her emotions again.

"My father thinks I'm a muttlith," she said at last.

Vilmar blinked stupidly, not comprehending.

She sighed and patiently explained the meaning to him.

"Oh," was all Vilmar said at first.

She felt her heart sink at his reaction. She just might have to charge wildly away from him after all.

But she also saw him slowly mulling it over in his brain.

"I don't know much about your people," he said finally. "But you certainly don't seem like muttlith material to me. I'm sure you're much better with a real forge than you are at making horseshoes."

He fell in beside her with his horse towering over her little white pony. She felt somewhat better.

"Is it because of the whole horse thing?" he said.

"And the fact I'm associating with humans," she replied.

"Well, I know it is unusual for a dwarf to ride horses," he returned. "But dwarves do ride from time to time. Some do it quite well. Like you."

She stopped her pony again.

"I've never heard of such a thing," she said.

"Oh," he replied with some nervous concern. "Well then, maybe I shouldn't be saying anything. Your kind should be the ones to tell you the story, not a stupid human." His face suddenly brightened. "Wait, who did you say your father was?"

"I didn't," she replied not understanding. "His name's Varg. Why?"

"Ah! That explains everything!" he said quite cheerfully.

"Not to me," she was getting frustrated again.

"Varg the Raging Wolf!" Vilmar said with a dash of nobility to his voice and his horse began to trot. "Varg the Mouth of War whose words are dagger and swords to any but his own kind! Varg the Warmonger!"

"That's my father you're making fun of, flawed though he be," Bran said only slightly joking.

She gave Vilmar a warning shove which failed to unseat him.

"I'm sorry, my dear friend," Vilmar apologized, laughing. "But why didn't you tell me your father was Varg? He hates anyone who is not a dwarf! No wonder you're having family troubles! You're doing everything he hates."

He rode a circle around her poor little pony while she fumed at him.

"Peace, my friend!" he said with a little bow from the saddle. "I never meant to insult you. And I still do want you as my friend."

Bran bristled but rode on in silence. Vilmar pulled up alongside, looking quietly at her, smiling all the while.

"Would you like me to tell you something? A secret?"

Bran's eyes drifted his way, her curiosity piqued despite herself.

"Soon something will happen which will make all your family troubles seem oh so trivial to you," he said and now his voice was very serious.

"What will happen?"

"There's going to be a war, Bran," Vilmar said.

His voice was very grim and no longer jesting.

"It's been building for quite some time now, one little battle at a time, a skirmish here, an ambush there. I don't know what the real reason is but it's coming closer and closer to Kopa and Tor Ambroc every day. Soon the dwarves will have to join in. They have the wealth and the weapons to supply a war. Whoever controls the dwarves controls the tide of battle. They will either join willingly or be forced to join. War is coming."

Bran was silent for a long moment. She was aware Vilmar was watching her reaction to this revelation very closely.

"Can you fight, Bran?" he asked.

"Of course I can," she replied with a haughty tilt of her chin.

"Good!" he said levelly. "Because I sure can't."

Bran snorted in distaste.

"Well, don't look to me to protect your pink skin!" she said with some disdain. "Run down a hole and hide like a rabbit then."

"I never said I was a scared rabbit!" Vilmar replied and now it was his turn to get angry.

"You may be my comrade, Vilmar, but I want no helpless friends!" she shot back.

"Now wait just a minute!" he stormed and pulled his horse in front to stop her. "I just said I couldn't fight. I never said I didn't *want* to fight. I do have some skills."

"What skills? Will you sing to calm the enemy like a skittish horse? Or will you re-train them to be peaceful?" she retorted.

She thought briefly and a different choice occurred to her.

"I'm not teaching you to fight," she said suddenly.

"I never asked you to," he replied with some scorn. "I told you I have other skills."

His hand traveled up to the hollow of his throat and clasped his shirt. Something on a string bulged underneath. She also noticed the magical reek, which always emanated from him, became suddenly thick and heavy.

Bran's eyes narrowed in comprehension. She looked Vilmar straight in the face.

"Are you a wizard?" she asked quietly and slowly.

Vilmar winced as if in pain.

"No. I mean, I don't think so. I hope not."

"Why do you hope not?" she asked.

"Well, you wouldn't care too much for me if I was a wizard, would you?" his tone was curious as he fished for her reaction. "I don't really know. I'm still finding out," he replied and his hand left his throat. The magical reek dissipated somewhat.

"But you are magical," she stated.

"Yes, I am," he replied switching his horse to her other side.

"Were you born this way?"

"No," he replied. Then, after an uncomfortable silence, "It was a gift."

"A gift? From who?"

"A unicorn," he replied simply.

Bran pulled her horse to a stop and stared at him, mouth open in astonishment.

"A unicorn?" she repeated. "And how did you manage to pull that one off?"

"I helped her," he said somewhat sheepishly. "She was grateful."

"How does a human help a unicorn? Unicorns don't need anyone's help!"

"This one did," Vilmar replied. "She was giving birth and was having trouble. She was too weak to do anymore. She couldn't even heal herself. The baby was breached. I found her and figured out what she needed. I helped turn the baby around so she could give birth. When the fawn was born, both mother and baby were too exhausted to do any more. I milked the mother and fed the baby. I guarded them both until they recovered their strength. Now I'm the unicorn's 'champion', so she says. She gifted me with magic. The unicorn helps with the education, too. I see her and her fawn on a regular basis. She still teaches me things. I guess she's now my patron, you might say."

Bran was just sitting there on her pony, mouth wide open in surprise.

"Bran, please believe me. I'm not making any of this up. You're the only one I've told this to."

"What's that?" she finally said pointing to his throat.

He smiled and pulled out a strange object wrapped in silver wire and fastened to the leather string.

"It's what she gave me for helping her. The baby carries it in its mouth before it's born. It's called a hippomane by some and a foal's stone by others. It's my talisman."

Bran reached forward to touch it. He made no effort to stop her. It wasn't fired clay, or metal or a gemstone or carved wood. She couldn't quite figure out what kind of substance it was. It felt smooth and warm like flesh. The foal's stone tingled her fingers with energy and she snapped back her hand in surprise.

"Don't be afraid. It won't hurt you," Vilmar said and guided her hand back to it so she could investigate more.

This was where the magical sensation came from. Before she could only smell it. Now she could feel it as tangible as a horse's breath on her skin. It hummed softly in her hand, its magic treating her gentle curiosity with a friendly warmth.

But she could also feel the power within the hippomane. She knew if she or anyone else threatened Vilmar, it would suddenly blaze forth into the raw power of a unicorn enraged like the ferocity of a windstorm, leveling everything in its path. This thing could help Vilmar to heal, of this she was certain.

It could also help him to kill.

The only reason it accepted her touch was because it recognized her as a friend. No one would be able to take it from him.

"You have a powerful tool there, Vilmar, my friend," she said at last when she trusted her voice. "And I am very glad I am not its guardian."

Vilmar smiled a slow but grim smile. She knew he grasped the true depth of what she had said.

"What I said about the war? Remember it, Bran. Remember it well. Keep your eyes and ears open at all times. There will be rumbles coming and rumors. Say nothing but listen well. I know you're good at that."

"And what will you do when it comes?" she asked.

He shrugged distantly.

"I will do what the unicorn advises me to do, whatever it is. She is guarding me now. Her and her son."

They were silent on the way back to Tor Ambroc both deep in their own thoughts. They had a lot to think about.

But when they arrived at the trader's gates they found one extra person awaiting her return. Varg was standing there, arms crossed grimly over his burly chest and storms in his eyes. He didn't look very happy. It seemed her presence had been missed.

"This may not go well," Bran muttered softly to Vilmar.

"That your Da?" he asked in the same tone. She nodded wordlessly in return as she dismounted from the little white pony who had carried her so faithfully.

"Well, I can fix this!" Vilmar replied in a confident voice as he winked slyly.

Before she could stop him, he rode boldly up to her father.

"Excuse me, sir," he said in a voice dripping in politeness. "Are you Bran's father?"

Varg turned a withering look on Vilmar and grunted his affirmation.

"I am Vilmar, son of Conal the farrier," he said with a bow and a flourish. "Your Bran helped my family this Winterfest. We got to be friends. Let me just say I have the utmost respect for your son and I would rather have no one else beside me in a tight spot. Your son, Bran, is as a brother to me."

Bran struggled to keep from choking when Vilmar called her Varg's 'son'. With a supreme effort, she steeled her face from any emotion which might show. She wanted to let loose with a belly laugh but she dare not.

She saw Varg's mouth tip upwards for a split second and she saw the guards attempt to hide their snickers.

"A brother, eh?" Varg growled, his grumpy composure restored.

"Yes. Did I say something wrong?" Vilmar said innocently as he noticed the guards' reaction.

"Not at all. A brother, hmm?" he repeated. "Well, just keep it like that!"

Varg turned and stormed away.

Vilmar nodded and bowed again to his quickly retreating backside.

Bran flashed her friend a secretive smile.

"Thanks for bringing the pony for me to ride. And... well... just thanks," she whispered.

Vilmar nodded giving her one of his famous, aggravating smiles.

"Glad to help a friend," he replied and waving, rode away.

Bran saw the other dwarf guards let loose with their laughter when Vilmar got a safe distance away. She grinned happily.

Her father was waiting for her just inside the tunnel's entrance. His eyes were twinkling at his daughter but she couldn't tell whether it was with anger or mirth.

"Your friend, Vilmar, is that his name?" he said slowly.

"Yes?" Bran replied and steeled herself for anything which might come.

"He's a stupid fool!" Vary said. "But a very polite, stupid fool."

And Varg stumped away laughing loudly all the while.

"Stupid human can't tell the males from the females! 'My son', indeed!" he was heard to bellow in humor as he left.

Bran smiled and shook her head.

CHAPTER 6

Bran awoke later in the night to the sound of her parents arguing. She rolled over on her straw mattress and listened carefully hoping to hear something about the impending war. But they were talking about her.

"She needs training," Yaffa said, her tone pleading with her mate.

"She's got training!" Varg shot back.

"You know what I mean!" her mother's words were insistent.

"Why? I never needed to know any of that junk!"

"Yes, and just look where it's gotten you!" Yaffa scolded.

"I know, I know. Banished to the tunnels. Why is it so bad? I kind of prefer it."

"We're talking about your daughter Bran, not you!" Yaffa sighed and she heard the scraping sound of a wooden chair on stone as she sat down.

"We all know what she is. Everyone knows and accepts this but you. Your daughter is no muttlith. But she will also never be a tunnel dweller like you. This is not a bad thing."

"It's not a good thing either!" grumbled her father.

"We will be needing dwarves on the outside in the days to come, husband. Bran could be very useful out there," Yaffa patiently persuaded.

Bran's ears perked up just a bit.

"Nothing's decided yet. It might not even happen," Varg sighed hopefully.

"That's a lie and you know it! If you believe it, you're a fool! And I'm a fool for marrying you," Yaffa spat and Bran heard her slam her fist onto the table.

"War is coming," her mother said in a low voice full of dread. "Soon we will need every dwarf lass with Bran's qualities. Do you want them to catch her unprepared?"

Varg made no reply but to grumble.

"Shall I tell you what they would do to her? What *he* would do to her?" Yaffa's tone held a barely veiled threat.

"Do you so resent your decision to give all that up, to live here in the tunnels with me and bear my children?" Varg's tone was wounded.

Bran had never heard her father speak like this.

"I gave you five wonderful gems of children." Yaffa's words were gentle and at the same time ice cold. "I will never resent it. I only resent the fact I must play a silent and passive role in my people's defense. And I resent that the youngest and most promising of my children is being held back by a father who does not believe in her abilities."

"Bran was never like me," Varg muttered dismally.

"No," Yaffa agreed. "She's too much like her mother."

She stood up and stalked the room, her steps resolute and firm.

"At one time, the dwarves of Tor Ambroc called me a heroine."

"They still do," Varg muttered in awe of his wife. "That's how I fell in love with you."

"I will not have my youngest's talents wasted and forgotten. She must be prepared for what is to come. Her heart is of the Yazu."

Her father gasped in surprise.

"Are you sure?" he asked.

"I am certain of it," Yaffa said directly. "It takes one to know one. Bran is no muttlith. She is Yazu."

There was a long pause broken only by the cracks and pops from the fire pit.

"Then you're right, love," Varg said suddenly. "She must be trained."

Bran rolled over and stared at the stone ceiling. She didn't even have the foggiest notion what they were talking about. But one question nagged her more than any other.

"What's a Yazu?"

CHAPTER 7

Bran dreamed of the Yazu that night. Yes, it was true she had no idea what they were but she dreamed of them all the same. And in the morning when she awoke, she remembered nothing of it. But the word 'Yazu' was on her lips before she had opened her eyes. It haunted and harried her like hounds coursing a deer and yet she knew nothing. Although the word bothered her mightily she said naught of it to her parents.

They stopped her from going to the forge in the morning. Her mother had other plans for her, plans her father had grudgingly agreed to. She was to be trained in the language and customs of other races. She was to report to the dwarf king's scribe, Keld.

Now Keld *was* a muttlith. He was half human and half dwarf. But he took after the human side. Keld was too tall and lean for a normal dwarf's liking. His beard never reached proper braiding length; he had no talent for forging and the sight of blood made him weak in the knees. His eyes were bad and he needed spectacles. But the dwarf king kept him because he did have his uses.

Keld could read, write and speak in ten languages, even goblin. He knew the customs of many races intimately, was invaluable in negotiation, and was the king's trusted advisor and tactician. So he was kept in spite of being a muttlith for his many talents.

Bran was led into a room cluttered with scrolls and piles of dusty tomes, lit dimly here and there by candles which dripped wax in long streams. Next to the largest table was an enormous candelabrum to illuminate the most important books. Three huge tomes were open and the half-breed was busily pouring over them, scribbling something on his parchment as he squinted closely at the words.

"Ah! So this is the girl child I've heard so much about," Keld muttered as she sat down across from him. "The child who fancies herself a jockey."

"I just like to ride. I'm no jockey," she said simply.

"Humph!" grunted Keld. "I can't abide the creatures. Dirty, smelly, dangerous, unpredictable animals if you ask me. They can do a lot of damage to a good scribe's hands or skull if you get bucked off. Nope! Horses aren't worth the risk if you ask me."

"I didn't," replied Bran softly and Keld glanced up sharply over the rim of his glasses to glare at her.

"Humph!" he grunted again. "Still, to each his own. So my dear, what would you like to learn first? Elvish? Goblin? Perhaps you'd like to speak Dragon, eh? Fascinating language if you survive long enough to learn it or catch a dragon when he's in a particularly good mood—which is rare. But I know all the dragons' speech. So speak up, which one first?"

"If you please, sir," she said slowly and with some trepidation. "I'd like to know the meaning of just one word which I overheard."

"Easy enough. What word is it?" Keld quipped confidently.

"Please, what does 'Yazu' mean?"

Keld's hands exploded in shock, scattering papers and blowing out candles in the sudden motion. When the leaves settled in their wild fluttering, Keld was sitting ramrod straight, staring aghast at her, spectacles hanging crookedly on his face.

"Where did you hear *that* word, my dear?"

"My parents were talking..."

"When?" Keld barked abruptly.

"Uh, last night," Bran was starting to get worried. "They said I was Yazu."

"Oh really?" he replied.

He just sat there for a moment thinking hard, one finger tapping his pathetic excuse for a beard.

"If you are... what they say you are... then yes, you certainly do need my training because you won't be living underground. But first you must sit down and have a very long discussion with your mother. I am forbidden from saying the word or informing you what it is."

"Forbidden? Why?" Bran replied.

"The word has a spell on it. If any but a female dwarf speak it, bad things will happen. The word brings bad luck to males. It is a word of women's power and mystery. I am damned forever if I say it."

Bran sat quietly for a moment considering and blinking in surprise.

"My dear, it is your word and your luck. If you do not find out immediately what this word means it will kill you, eat at you like a tumor and twist you all up inside. You must go now to your mother."

Bran could only stare at him.

"Well?" he said to her. "Why are you still sitting here? Git!"

Bran bolted up from the chair and fled.

Yaffa was alone in her chambers save for her hounds when Bran burst into the room.

It startled the dogs, some of which jumped up and barked at her sudden entrance. Yaffa soothed them with a word.

"Bran! Whatever is the..." she started to question and then saw the stricken look on her daughter's face.

"Ah!" she murmured softly. "So you did hear us last night."

"Keld said the word would kill me if I didn't find out what it meant," Bran panted breathlessly. "And he said only you could tell me."

"Only a female dwarf could tell you, not just me," she corrected. "But Keld is right. You should hear this from a family member and no one else. And since I am the only family member which is a Yazu and your mother, it would be quite appropriate for me to do the honors."

"You're a Yazu?" Bran gasped.

Yaffa motioned her daughter to sit down. She sighed and was quiet for a moment thinking on times long past. Finally she began to speak.

"Ever since I was born, my sweet. Every Yazu is born this way. There are many dwarf women but only a select few are born with the qualities which make them a Yazu. And Keld wasn't trying to scare you, my dear. Knowing the word and not its meaning will curse you to die a horrible death just like a man who speaks the word. It is how we protect ourselves."

"What is a Yazu?"

"We are a secret society of dwarf women warriors trained to protect our race from the outside. We have many jobs, some are scouts, some are spies, some are even assassins. But we all protect the dwarf race from any threat. In peacetime we are normally scattered throughout the many dwarf kingdoms. But in war, we unify usually in a cavalry to fight for our people above ground."

"Cavalry? Then that's what Daga and Vilmar meant when they said some dwarves do ride!" Bran said suddenly understanding.

"Yes, and that's all they could dare to say," Yaffa explained.

"You can ride?" Bran questioned. It seemed impossible. She couldn't even imagine her mother on a horse.

"I can ride with the best of them, my dear," Yaffa replied with obvious pride. "I was known as Yaffa, the Archer of Fire. My burning arrows would put any enemy on the other side of life looking back in. There was no escape when I had a target lined up in my sights. It's no wonder why you are such a good archer!"

"It seems the blood breeds true, then," Bran answered with a smile.

Yaffa returned the smile and her eyes sparkled in fierce pride.

"I wish I could have seen it," Bran sighed wistfully.

"You may yet have a chance, daughter of mine," Yaffa replied in a low voice.

"Then it's true. War is coming."

"It most certainly is, Bran," Yaffa replied seriously.

Bran looked at the hounds curled up at her mother's feet. She knew her mother was the 'Lady of the Hounds' as the dwarves liked to call her. The hounds were used for the relaying of messages near and far. They commonly wore harnesses with little leather tubes on their backs to carry the notes from kingdom to kingdom. The letters themselves were also enchanted. If anyone other than the named recipient tried to read it, the words would vanish and the page would burst into flame. Yaffa was in charge of the messenger hounds and it was rumored she knew more secrets than any other dwarf in Tor Ambroc. If war was coming she would know the most information.

Yaffa's narrow gaze quickly told her what her daughter was thinking.

"When I was an active part of the Yazu, I did many heroic things. When I married, I took a more passive role in screening the messages which came and went from Tor Ambroc. I have never left the sisterhood. No one ever does. My role just became more... private."

Something frightening then occurred to Bran.

"What if the enemy caught you? What would they do to you?" she asked, fearing the answer.

Yaffa sighed deeply. *'And now we come to it,'* she thought to herself.

"I know way too much. Your mother is a treasure trove of secrets many would love to exploit. A powerful wizard could tap my information far too easily. If I was caught, I would have to kill myself to protect my people."

Bran stared at her mother in abject horror. Yaffa's gaze was fixed and unwavering. She held her daughter's eyes as if she had cast a spell—and in a way she had. She had to make her child understand the gravity of this charge. This was no fun hero's adventure where everybody ends up with a happy ending. Death was a very real possibility.

Bran noticed her mother's hand resting lightly on a small vial carried around her neck. Bran knew Yaffa went nowhere without this special vial. But now she didn't need to ask what its contents were. She knew the elixir had to be some very potent poison.

Yaffa's eyes narrowed as she noted her daughter's glance and guessed her thoughts. She nodded grimly.

"These are the sacrifices a Yazu is sometimes expected to endure. It was easier for me when I was a simple warrior. Fighters do battle face to face. Spies do battle in the silence of the mind. Mark this well, my child, and you may live a long life."

"Do I get to choose whether to be an open fighter or a secretive one?" Bran asked trying very hard to keep the tremble from her voice.

"Only sometimes," Yaffa answered truthfully. "Sometimes life chooses for you. We shall have to see where you fit in, my dear."

Soon after Bran had left, Yaffa turned to her writing desk. She silently took a magic quill and wrote for quite some time on a long parchment. The lean hounds reclined peacefully at her feet. When she finished, she waved her hand over the document speaking one word, which made the leaf glow for a moment. When the spell had faded, she immediately and noisily rolled up the parchment. At this sound, all of the hounds jumped up. She turned to them, carefully looking over each dog. They awaited her choice, tails slowly wagging in doubtful eagerness.

Finally she made her choice.

"Snow Crow," she called.

A tall, lean hound with long, white curling locks and large black eyes leapt eagerly to her side. The others whined and cried their disappointment and threw themselves back down on the stone next to the crackling hearth.

"It is time for my daughter to meet Dra-Oog, the one who taught me. Take this to her at once, my faithful Snow Crow. You know the way," she said softly as she threaded the scroll into the ensorcelled magic tube on the back of the dog's leather harness.

She patted the hound's smooth-coated, lean face and ran her hands lovingly through the animal's thick curls, which started behind her ears. The hound wailed her keenness to be off on the road.

Saying no more to the dog who stood nearly as high as Yaffa, she swung open the door to her chambers. Snow Crow bolted at once into the corridor of the main living quarters of Tor Ambroc and wound her way quickly among the maze of tunnels until she came to the traders' gates opening to the world above.

Few dwarves took notice of the white hound as she leaped away in her best traveling gait into the darkness of the night. It was snowing gently, one of the last wet snowfalls of a dying winter.

Snow Crow took no notice of the weather. Her legs were longer than most of the melting drifts and her coat was thick and warm. She had a job to do and she was happy. She had not gone this way in quite some time but she cared not. She knew the way well.

It was a much quieter, more somber Bran who returned to Keld. A quick glance from him told the scholar all he needed to know.

"So she told you, eh?" he asked.

Wordlessly she nodded in reply.

Keld grunted briefly and was silent for a long moment.

"And she told me war is coming," Bran said in an emotionless voice.

"It is," Keld said.

"How soon?"

Keld pursed his lips and hissed, shaking his head in doubt.

"I'm not sure exactly when, but soon. Very soon," he replied.

"Have the dwarves been approached about it yet?" she asked urgently.

Keld uttered a quick intake of breath and muttered somewhat sternly, "You're rather young to be asking the affairs of the state, my dear."

Bran lowered her eyes, not wanting to be disrespectful.

"Bran, look at me," Keld said.

Bran obeyed and met his stern, spectacled gaze.

"Soon you will be trusted with many secrets. A loose tongue can be extremely dangerous."

"I'm already aware of that, Keld," she returned quickly to his surprise.

"Are you really?" he questioned.

"Yes," she whispered. "A loose tongue could lose me my mother."

Keld considered her quietly over his glasses, the fingers of one hand tapping thoughtfully on the tabletop.

He finally nodded.

"The dwarves have not yet been approached about what role they are to play in this war. But it is coming. I, very likely, will handle the negotiations."

"Vilmar said whichever side controls the dwarves, controls the war."

Keld spun sharply on his heel at her remark.

"Vilmar said? And just who is this Vilmar? The name doesn't sound dwarvish at all."

Bran swallowed carefully.

"He's my friend, my human friend," she replied. "He's the first one who told me about the impending war."

Bran hoped she hadn't said too much.

Keld stalked up to her and put his face very close to hers, glaring disapprovingly over his specs at her.

"And just what rank is this Vilmar among the humans?" Keld demanded of her.

"Rank?" Bran stuttered in confusion. "No rank. No rank at all. He's a simple farrier's son."

She decided to leave out the part about him being of a magical persuasion. So far it was a secret to all but the two of them.

"A farrier's son, eh?" Keld muttered in distaste. "If even the commoners among the humans know war is coming, things could get very ugly indeed. People could flee instead of fight."

"Who are we going to be fighting?" she asked trying to guide the conversation in a different direction.

Keld turned his attention back to her.

"There are rumors a great warlord is rampaging over all the land, conquering any kingdom who stands in his way. The rumors say those who attempt to barter peace with him only get a slit throat and a gutted land."

"Those are only rumors and bad to rule a kingdom by," replied Bran. "What do our trusted sources say of this?"

Keld's lips twitched up in a quick smile for Bran's reply reminded him of something her mother, Yaffa, would have said.

"Our sources say there is no warlord at the head of this force but a very powerful wizard or sorcerer. He is quickly gathering to his side all manner of dark beings to fight for him—like goblins, ogres and gnolls. Not the species any force of dwarves would willingly call an ally. But it has also been discovered by our sources that negotiations are not very effective with this magic lord. He seems to revel in blood, destruction and the looting of his enemies' wealth."

"Negotiation may not always work but there are plenty of other instances in a war that you use words for," Bran said considering her plan carefully. "Maybe your best bet to prepare me for what is to come, is to teach me how to speak like a goblin, or a gnoll or an ogre."

Keld slowly smiled as his brain caught her thoughts. He nodded and at once began to rummage through his old tomes.

CHAPTER 8

A few days later was Bran's eighth birthday and her coming of age celebration. There was a big feast among the family in one of the minor feast halls. Yaffa and Varg dressed in their best war gear. Yaffa wore golden chains wound into her hair and beard.

The first time Bran saw this, she stared. Being the youngest, she had never seen her mother dressed in her war finery. She knew chains of gold and silver wound into the hair were for valor in battle. She noted at the feast table, her mother wore many more chains than anyone, even Varg her own mate. Yaffa's eyes glittered at Bran when she saw her daughter's gaze and Bran dropped her eyes in respect for her mother. She also noted the honor most of the other dwarves paid Yaffa. How could she have been so blind before? Bran hoped to one day wear gold chains in her beard as well.

She scratched her chin considering. Her sideburns were well grown in and thick. Her chin hairs were just starting to sprout. It wouldn't be long before she could start braiding her locks.

The mead flowed freely at Bran's feast. The roast cave boar was the largest she had seen in quite some time and the platter was set directly in front of her. Her father gave Bran her first pipe, beautifully made from white clay with dwarf runes carved into it. She and the whole family got a good laugh at her first attempts to smoke it.

Then her father bellowed for the family cleric.

"Today is my youngest daughter's coming of age party," he shouted to those gathered. "And I wish her fortune foretold. Tell me, cleric, how rich will my daughter become and how brave will she be?"

Bran grumbled at this. Divination should be private, she felt. Not something to be on public display in front of all her friends and relatives.

It was obvious to all Varg had had a bit too much mead. His speech was slurred and he was staggering and spitting when he spoke.

Bran leaned over to her mother as the cleric vigorously shook the runes he carried in a plain wooden cup.

"What if there is evil ahead of me this year?" she muttered. "I don't want that announced in front of everybody!"

Yaffa shushed her immediately.

"Kusa is too good at divining to do that to you. If there is evil, he will hide it in a rhyme or cleverly placed words. Never fear, my sweet."

The other dwarves pounded the tables and chanted Bran's name as the runes were shaken. Their voices rose to a crescendo and Kusa cast the runes on the floor. Then he held up his arms for silence.

They watched as his head waggled to and fro, scrutinizing the pattern of the stones. The room grew very quiet.

"The child's future is thus: This will be a year of immense change, growth and upheaval for you, my dear. A sword will strike the heart. The hammer will smite the anvil and hooves will trample all before them. A great wave shall sweep the land this year and you, Bran, will be at its center. Your people will need you most when you think all is already lost. You will carry vengeance on your shoulders and justice in your blade. Lightning will carry you from your purse. Strength you will have and strength you will need. And Bran," Kusa said these last few words as if he and Bran were the only ones in the room. "Never forget where you came from."

Kusa's slate-gray eyes held her for a long breathless moment. Bran suddenly grew very cold as if a chill winter's wind had gusted down the hallways from the gates above.

The prediction didn't sound like a good one.

"A sword will strike the heart..." Kusa's words echoed ominously in her head.

Bran suddenly felt closed in and cornered. She couldn't breathe.

"The hammer will smite the anvil and hooves will trample all before them."

She excused herself from the feast hall not caring how obvious she was being. Dimly she heard her father jest about her having drunk too much. The whole table erupted in laughter. She didn't care. She felt dizzy and lightheaded but not from the mead.

She needed space. She needed it now. She needed to breathe.

"A great wave shall sweep the land this year and you will be at its center."

Bran squeezed her eyes shut and shook her head, refusing to hear the words. But they spilled around her anyway.

"Your people will need you most when you think all is already lost."

When she was out of sight of everybody, she fled. She ran as hard as she could down the tunnels not caring where she would end up. She ran until she felt her feet complain through her thick-soled leather boots. She ran until her chest hurt for want of air.

The maddening prophecy kept babbling about her.

"You will carry vengeance on your shoulders and justice in your blade."

She felt a cold gust of air and followed it up a winding staircase. At its top was a room with a window overlooking the outside world. A cold, late winter breeze was blowing through it. Bran knew by speaking a simple dwarf rune she could shut the window and turn it into a blank stone wall again but she didn't. Cold though it was, the air helped to clear her head.

"Lightning will carry you from your purse."

The words faded slowly and she crumpled to the cold stone floor.

"Strength you will have and strength you will need."

Her fist slammed the floor. What did it mean? What did all of it mean?

"Bran, never forget where you came from."

Predictions with hammers and anvils in her culture were weighty ones better suited for heroes and royalty. They were some of the most difficult to decipher. And they always came true.

She wished Vilmar were here. He could make sense of all of this, him or his unicorn patron. She so wished he were here.

She took a deep breath and the air's icy coldness burned her soot-hardened lungs.

"That was a most interesting divination, my dear," said a voice behind her.

She gasped and spun about.

Daga, her uncle, stood there before her.

"That was the divination of a hero," he replied in a soft and gentle tone.

For the first time in all her short life, her uncle came forward and wrapped her in a bear hug. He had never hugged her before. She found she needed the gesture to keep her tears from falling. She clasped him tight and buried her eyes in the rabbit-skin fur about his neck.

"A twig seems harmless," Daga whispered cryptically to her. "But if picked up by a storm's gust, it can pierce through the largest oak with the force of an iron spike. The littlest actions can have the greatest of consequences."

Bran's face crinkled in confusion. "Daga," she almost sobbed. "I don't understand any of this."

Daga clapped her reassuringly on the back of her shoulders. "You'll understand it later. We all will. Don't fret too much about it, lass. It did not sound all bad. At least not to me." He pulled away and chucked her fondly under her jaw.

"Chin up, Bran. The future is not yet written. There's still time to change the parts you don't like. In any case, I have a present for you which might help you feel better."

Bran appreciated the distraction. She wanted to think about something else other than the horrible, confusing prediction.

"What is it?" she asked.

Daga felt clumsily about his baggy clothing. He finally clutched a leather bag tied to his belt.

"Ah! Here it is!" he said and untying it, handed her the pouch.

Bran felt the bag curiously and looked at her uncle.

"You just gonna feel it through the leather or are you going to look at it?" he muttered with a sly smile.

Bran loosened the drawstrings, spread the mouth of the pouch and turning it over, spilled out the contents onto the floor.

A wooden figure tumbled out and came to rest upright on its legs, staring toward Bran.

It was a little, carved wooden horse. It was fashioned out of a single piece of oak and had a smooth, buttery finish. Bran was amazed by how plain it was. It had no eyes and its mane and tail were so nondescript as to barely be there. But on the side of its right hindquarters was a swirl, a knot in the wood.

Bran looked at her uncle in confusion.

"Aren't I a little old for toys, Uncle?" she said to him.

Daga harrumphed grumpily.

"It is *not* a toy, Bran," he insisted. "It is a very useful tool and maybe a friend."

"Oh, so it's magic then?" she asked.

"Course it is!" Daga shot back. "Do you think I'd give my favorite niece a plain ole hunk of carved wood while making magic toys to sell to the human brats?"

Bran looked closely at the little horse sitting silently on the rock floor. She reached forward and picked it up. She expected it to be cold and hard. But it was strangely warm to the touch. It felt like living flesh, soft and breathing. She could almost feel the blood pulsating through the carving's veins. As plain as it was, the little horse was incredibly fascinating to her.

"How do I use it?" she asked slowly. Bran found herself unable to take her eyes off of it.

"For that, we shall need some room. Come with me, my dear," Daga said and led her quickly down the stairs through a network of tunnels to a large, naturally cavernous room with a swept dirt floor. Torches along the wall dimly lit the room. They were alone, totally alone.

"Now," Daga explained softly. "This horse will become a real horse anytime you want it to. But the first time it manifests is very important. It will only come to its name, so now you must name it."

Bran thought briefly.

"Val," she said after a time. "Short for Valynt."

The little horse suddenly grew quite heavy in her hands and she could feel it start to hum as a great magical power gathered.

Daga nodded and smiled.

"Valynt it shall be for all time," he replied. "Now listen carefully, niece of mine. Whatever gender you decide this little horse to be, it will be. But other than this, everything is up to change. You must place within your mind a picture of what you want this little horse to look like each time you call it. If you want it to be a piebald pony one time it will be a piebald pony. If you want it to be a gigantic, black plow horse the humans are so fond of, so be it. If this time you choose it to be a stallion, it will always appear as a stallion. If you want it to be a mare, it will always be a mare. If you want it to appear with a fancy saddle and bridle or no saddle and bridle, it will appear that way. But you must have the picture in your head."

Bran nodded carefully as her uncle told her this.

"And its drawbacks?"

"It will need to rest for an amount of time equal to the amount of usage. If you ride it for a day, rest it for a day. So, although I can understand your desire to keep this wonderful thing with you all the time, I wouldn't. You never know when you might really need Val for something important."

"Is it really a tool or does it have feelings?" she asked.

"It's as real as you or I, Bran, my dear," replied Daga. "Not only does it have feelings but it can feel pain both emotional and physical. The little horse is more resistant to wounds or sickness but in its horse form, it can be killed. If something threatens its immediate life, it must be sent back to its own plane to heal and recover."

"What about the wooden figure's strength?" she asked.

"The wood is magically protected. It cannot be broken, burned or hurt in any way. If you sat on it or fell on it, its legs would not break. It also cannot be lost from you, nor can it be stolen. In order to do any of these things to it you would need to remove all trace of magic spells from it. So keep Val away from very powerful wizards. They can take it and use it for themselves.

"Val will be bonded to you for the rest of your life. You may let someone else use this trinket with your permission but Val will never respond to them like it will to you. Valynt is yours only."

"What if I lose it in horse form?" Bran asked. "A horse will be a horse."

"Not this one. Val will seek you out and prefer your company to others. But if you do lose it, like in a herd of other horses with the same markings and color, look for a horse with a swirled marking on its right haunch. See the knot in the wood here? Val may not have this on its own plane but it will have this marking here no matter what color you picture it in. Val will always have the particular swirl on its haunch."

Bran nodded, taking it all in and committing the information to memory. Dwarf tools like this were very special as long as one never forgot their shortcomings.

"Well?" asked Daga. "Don't you want to see what your new horse looks and rides like?"

Bran smiled in agreement. She walked forward into the center of the cavernous room. She placed the little figure on the ground before her and backed up a few steps. Bran then cleared her head of all other thoughts. She tried to picture what the perfect horse would look like. She pictured a mare who was not quite a pony in size and yet not quite

46

a horse. She envisioned an animal dark red in color with a long blond mane, which hung down to her lower shoulders with a blonde tail, which swept the ground. Bran also imagined a simple functional saddle and bridle already on the horse.

She opened her eyes to the empty cavern and called in a firm voice, "Valynt, come to me."

A gust of wind, independent from all others, stirred up the dust right before her feet. It rose in a graceful twister and spun softly before her. A shape began to solidify within the dust. Bran reached for it without knowing she was doing so. As the dust settled into a horse form, she felt it create underneath her very hand.

And there was her horse, Val, alive and warm with her hand on its velvety black nose, its blonde foretop spilling through her forge-hardened fingers.

Valynt snorted and blew on her hand, absorbing Bran's unique scent.

She was beautiful! Her eyes sparkled a dark brown warmth toward Bran and her body rumbled gently as she nickered to her a sound, which was only for Val's bonded person. Val smelled like horse and magic dust all at once.

"Very nice!" Daga told her softly. "What a beautiful animal."

Bran walked slowly around the animal she had called, observing her from every angle. Valynt remained still but her eyes followed Bran curiously the entire time. Bran finally stood in front of her magical mount. She ran a hand lovingly over Val's chestnut face and the mare nuzzled her arm affectionately and nickered again.

She had never met this animal before. And yet, she felt as if she were being reunited with an old friend who had been dearly missed. She looked into Val's eyes and felt like she was falling into a deep and fathomless well. Time ceased to be. She did not want time to move. This feeling was far too personal and important. Bran felt everything the horse was feeling. It was as if they were one creature. Val was her mirror in animal form.

Bran could have stayed in this private place with her forever. But then Val snorted and shook her head, setting her mane dancing. The first spell of bonding was broken. The horse pawed in impatience and Bran sensed what it was she wanted.

She stepped to the side of this glorious animal and looked at the polished surface of the saddle. She suddenly realized she had created a horse who would be a little difficult for her to mount without a boost or a higher surface to swing up from. The saddle was way above her head.

Val immediately caught her thought and assisted. The horse dropped to its knees and nuzzled Bran's leg encouragingly with a velvet nose. Bran could now reach the swinging stirrup.

She placed her foot in the stirrup and swung her leg over. Val waited a moment for her to find the other stirrup and then stood and patiently waited again. Bran's hands shook a bit as she separated the leather reins from the abundant gold mane, chastising herself for not having done this before she was in the saddle. But Val waited while she got herself together.

She looked to Daga for encouragement. He grinned his approval and nodded once.

A light touch on her flanks from Bran's heels was all the magic her horse needed to prompt her to move off. Bran felt the calm swing of the warm body beneath her and noticed the quiet bob of Val's head. She relaxed in the saddle, getting in time with the horse's steps. Then her heels cued the horse for a faster gait.

Val's trot was a lot smoother than any other horse she had sat to thus far. She squeezed her lightly again wondering if she could gait. Immediately, Val swung into a swaying, ground-eating pace. Bran smiled as she guided the horse around in a circular pattern in the cavern. Val's gait seemed designed for her comfort. She sat tall and proud and felt the wind of their speed comb her hair. Bran touched Val again and sat deep in the saddle as her horse began to do the spine-rocking canter. The horse's mane flew up and stung her face and Bran only laughed. This was wonderful!

She noticed her uncle waving to her and she pulled Val to a halt. He was holding a small bow and a quiver of arrows out to her.

"Let's see if you can ride that magic horse of yours with no hands!" he challenged.

She smiled, understanding at once what he meant. Daga gestured for her to use one of the torches at the far end of the hall for a target. She nodded and guided Val with one hand on the reins to the far side of the hall. Val waited for her to sling on the quiver and ready the bow.

Bran decided to take a few 'dry runs' first just to see how it felt working a bow from a position which moved with great speed. She first cued Val to pass the target at a pacing gait and mimed reaching back for the arrows, notching them and firing. Val performed admirably which was good because Bran fumbled the motions a bit and dropped the bow the first time. Then she took several dry runs at a gallop. She felt a bit more confident of her actions by then.

Finally Bran decided to try the real thing. She cued Val to gallop a straight line across the cavern. Val obediently complied. She managed to grab her first arrow and notch it without too much difficulty but when she fired, the arrow flew wide.

She tried this again. The arrow thudded home at the base of the torch.

She had run out of cavern space, so she had to stop and turn and try this again from the other side.

Again another miss. But her hit struck the center of the fire in the torch, creating a shower of sparks.

She pulled Val to a stop and looked to Daga for approval.

Yaffa stood next to him along with Varg her father.

Yaffa's eyes glittered with pride almost brighter than the gold chains wound through her flaxen hair. Varg held a strange distant look in his eyes.

"Like I said, she's just like her mother," Varg grumbled.

"And this is a bad thing, my love?"

Yaffa chuckled then to Bran. "Come here tomorrow with your wonderful little horse and I will teach you how to use a spear from her back."

Bran stared in surprise and could only nod her response. Yaffa nodded back and turning from the hall, left with a sputtering, weaving Varg in tow.

Daga looked back at Bran and his black eyes shone in the dim light. "You've done very well this day, my dear."

CHAPTER 9

Bran was so eager to show off her new magical horse to Vilmar. But with an effort she concealed it. She decided to show up for their regularly scheduled ride every other day on a different horse. She wondered how long it would take him to figure things out.

The first day she showed up on Val as she had first pictured her pony, a flaxen chestnut. Vilmar's jaw dropped when he saw her come riding up to him on her brand new horse.

"Don't tell me your father actually got you a pony for your birthday!" he said in surprise.

Bran openly beamed at him.

"He didn't," she replied. "This is a present from my uncle, Daga. Her name's Valynt."

Vilmar nodded, impressed.

"He certainly knows how to pick them. That horse is beautiful!"

Bran chuckled in pride and they rode on together.

The next time they rode, Bran mounted a short, fat, shaggy piebald pony.

"Hey!" Vilmar exclaimed. "What happened to the perfect pony?"

"Oh, that one!" Bran said feigning disappointment. "I decided it was too tall for my liking so I got a new one. Her name's Val II."

"Ya should of stuck with Val I if you ask me!" Vilmar muttered just barely loud enough for her to hear. Bran just laughed and Val shook her head making the multicolored mane dance.

The next time they rode, Bran was upon a gigantic, heavy-boned black horse.

"Don't tell me," Vilmar called up to her as she towered above his horse. "This one's named Val III, right?"

"Correct," she replied with a smirk. "I decided I like them BIG!"

Vilmar could only grumble incoherently. Bran tried her best to hide her mirth.

The next time they rode, Bran showed up on a buckskin mare with a roached mane.

"Wait just a minute!" a thoroughly flabbergasted Vilmar spouted. "Something smells fishy here. Am I to assume this one's named Val as well?"

"Of course. What other name is there for a mare?" Bran teased him coyly.

Vilmar spurred his horse and rode a circle around Val, glaring at the animal disapprovingly.

"Aha!" he shouted and pointed at the mare's right flank.

"Aha, what?" asked Bran as she blinked innocently at him.

"All of your 'Val' mares have had this mark!" he fumed accusingly.

"So?" she replied. "What of it?"

Vilmar reached over and laid a hand on the buckskin's glossy neck.

"I knew it!" he exclaimed. "She's magic! They're all magic! They're all the same horse!"

Bran sniffed in scorn.

"It took you long enough to figure that one out!" she replied. "I would have expected better from a young wizard."

She aimed a sly backward glance at him and kicked the buckskin Val into a canter. The sound of her laughter carried by the wind fluttered back to him. With a loud growl, Vilmar gave chase.

Bran's days were very busy now she had come of age. Half were spent learning to speak the different guttural languages of other races she might encounter and learning warfare from horseback under the tutelage of her mother. The rest of the time she spent riding with Vilmar or working her forge. She found herself in a rush to produce as many weapons of any kind as possible for the impending war.

She also pushed herself hard with the languages, although learning goblin, gnoll and ogre was really quite simple. Such species had no use for reading, only communicating to others of their kind. Their speech also lacked any descriptive terms. Affection among these people was mostly geared toward the race and not the family unit or the mate. Such things were viewed as easily replaceable. Warriors, wealth and power were the true measure of an individual in their society. Bran found it depressingly unchallenging work but pushed herself to learn from the knowledge that soon she may need it.

The lack of a deadline worried her immensely. The war might come in three years' time or tomorrow. She simply had no idea how long she would have before she was called upon to make use of these skills.

She enjoyed the times with her mother in the great cavern most. Bran could feel her skill at the craft improving more every day. When she was atop Val's back with a weapon in hand, she truly felt at peace with herself and her lot in life. She belonged there.

One night Bran and Yaffa were sitting by their home's fire enjoying a pipe and a bull's horn of mead. It had been a long, full day and Bran was tired. But she was not yet ready to go to bed.

"Tell me of your horse, Ma," she asked suddenly in the quiet. "What was she like?"

Yaffa chuckled privately to herself.

"He, you mean," she corrected. "I rode a stallion. His name was Mayhem."

"Mayhem!" Bran breathed in wonder. "What was he like? What color was he?"

"He was what I call a paint wannabe. He was all white except for a patch of black over his head. He was short as a pony but built like a blocky draft. He had blue eyes and a shaggy mane and tail and feathered feet. You should have seen the coat he grew in wintertime! He was as fuzzy and soft as a northland's fox cub. He looked cuddly and slow but this fellow could get up and dash or spin like a much lighter horse. Others always teased me about riding a great warhorse instead of something lighter and more nimble, but Mayhem never moved like that.

"There was no horse better at poor weather scouting. In snow or fog he would simply vanish and he could move as silently through a woodland floor scattered with brittle sticks like a field mouse. In a battle charge he was always in front of the line no matter how many missiles they tossed at us. If an arrow struck home it only made him madder and more deadly to deal with. In close quarters we worked like a team. It was too dangerous to get near me because of him clearing the field of warriors around me. The only ones who could do me any harm were archers or wizards. And I was the best archer in my day. They couldn't shoot me if I pulled a bead on them first."

Bran noticed the wistful tone her mother spoke with when she talked of Mayhem.

"How did he die?" she finally whispered hesitantly wanting to know so badly but also not wanting to intrude on her private memories.

Yaffa looked Bran full in the face for a long moment. Then she turned back to stare deeply into the fire's glowing embers.

"It took a wizard to finally part me from my dearest friend's back. I was in the middle of a huge fight and many dead were piling up around me. None could touch us! We were at our finest hour that day. We were each other's shield-wall. It was glorious!"

She paused briefly and gave a deep sigh.

"Then I felt Mayhem scream inside of me. He burst into flame beneath me. I remember shouting his name as I leapt off him and I smelled the stink of burnt skin and hair. Mayhem turned into a living torch under me."

Yaffa's voice faltered into silence. Bran didn't dare look at her mother. She couldn't handle seeing the grief. She wished she hadn't asked at all.

"I wasn't much good at fighting after that. The captain of my company noticed the effect it had on me and removed me from duty. She knew my heart had been broken by the incident. I quickly married your father afterwards and took to spying for the Yazu. I have never ridden another horse again.

"Mayhem will never truly be gone from me. In my heart, he is still my partner in battle and always will be."

Yaffa poked absently at the coals, stirring up the flames again.

"Did you ever find the wizard who did this to you?" Bran asked her mother.

"Nope, lucky for him," Yaffa replied with a voice full of vengeance. "If I did, I'd give him a taste of his own medicine."

She sighed and sat back from the fire as the flames rose and the heat became more intense. Bran mirrored the motion.

"All I ever found out was his name. Savas-Zev, the War Wolf. The goblins call him 'Cherno'."

Bran knew enough of the goblin speech by now to know 'cherno' translated to 'the Black Wolf'.

CHAPTER 10

The days crept slowly toward spring. In the world above, the land was full of change. One day the weather would be clear and slightly warm and one could just feel the ground opening up and stretching after its long winter's sleep. The next day would be cloudy and full of intermittent, scuttling snow showers as winter threatened to never loosen its cold grasp. Some days Bran and Vilmar rode crackling through thin ice, other days their mounts' bellies were splattered thickly with mud and grime.

In Tor Ambroc, the days were much the same as the nights—for the tunnels knew no seasons. The large main furnaces burned day and night and the dwarves endlessly toiled no matter what time it was outside, as dwarves will do.

One day, Bran was hammering ceaselessly on her family's forge when her mother interrupted her.

"Bran, child. You need to come to the eastern trader's gate right now. This is very important," Yaffa said in a flat voice.

Her tone sparked many questions but Bran said nothing. She only obeyed her mother without a word.

The little wooden horse she wore on a leather cord around her neck grew suddenly quite warm, warmer than the forge she had been bending over. Bran wrapped a calloused hand over Val to still her.

As Bran followed her mother, she noticed a strange reaction came over the other dwarves she passed. They were all whispering among themselves. When Bran came into view, they stopped talking and gazed strangely at her as if they were seeing her for the first time. No one spoke to her, they just looked. She supposed from their reaction it was someone other than Vilmar who had come to call.

They stepped through the trader's gates into the free air outside. Bran noticed the dwarf guards were standing rigidly at attention as if some dignitary had arrived.

A dwarf woman sat on a white horse before the gates. Her hair was long and white and separated into four braided locks, two in front and two down the back. Her beard was gray and braided as well. Silver chains were wound through her hair and beard and flashed brightly in the spring sun. She was clad in leather scales and her waist was armored in all manner of weapons. A short bow and quiver were strapped to her back, the handle of a knife stuck out of her boot and she wore a short sword on the opposite hip. She gave the impression if anyone was going to rob her of silver, they would have to deal with her first.

She sat tall, straight and proud on her horse. She seemed at contrast to the old, weather-beaten and knobby looking mare she rode. The horse stood placidly, eyes closed as if asleep, lower lip hanging in relaxation, which gave a most unimpressive and dull looking appearance as her ears flopped like a tired old mule.

"Bran, this is Dra-Oog. My teacher," Yaffa said in a quiet and very respectful tone. "She is the leader of my company. She is to be your teacher as well."

Bran looked Dra-Oog full in the face hoping she didn't appear fearful.

"So this is the fledgling you've told me so much about," Dra-Oog spoke in a commanding voice, which sounded as if none dared oppose her even if she was wrong. She cocked her head to the side and looked Bran over with a critical eye, which was as sharp as an eagle's.

"She certainly has the build of a fighter. And you said she can shoot too, eh?"

Yaffa nodded. Bran said nothing.

"But can she ride?" Dra-Oog said. Her tone was one of a dare.

"Oh yes, I can ride," Bran replied.

"Ah!" exclaimed the other with a laugh. "The whelp has a tongue. I hope it's nothing like her father's!"

She bent low in the saddle and her eagle eyes were fixed on Bran's face.

"So you *think* you can ride, eh?" she challenged. "Fine! Show me."

Without speaking another word, Bran pulled out the little wooden horse.

"Valynt, come!" she spoke.

A small dust devil of sand gathered and Val materialized in front of Bran wearing a light, simple bridle but no saddle. She appeared as a raven-colored mare with a blue-black glossy coat and a double-coated mane. A stardust of swirling white specks colored her right haunch where the knot in the figurine was.

Dra-Oog sniffed briefly.

"So you have a Dahla horse," she said and there was no surprise in her voice whatsoever. "A very good tool. I see Daga's been at it again."

She nodded to Bran to mount up.

Luckily this time, Bran had imagined a horse who would not be too difficult for her to mount. Val was only a little taller than her shoulder and the magic horse helped her by lifting a foreleg for her to use as a stepladder. Bran quickly scrambled aboard the glossy, ebony back and took up the reins.

She glanced quickly at her mother. Yaffa was returning to the gates but cast a backward look toward her daughter. Her face was blank and unreadable. Her expression could have meant anything or nothing at all.

Bran turned back to Dra-Oog who seemed to be waiting for her to make the first move. Bran noticed although the elder dwarf had made no motion, her horse had picked up a change in its rider. The old mare had opened her eyes, which were sparkling in anticipation of an expected cue and had pulled her lazily drooping lip back into place. Her ears flicked nervously and her feet shuffled, waiting.

Val too danced expecting something different this time and Bran sat deep into her back, easily keeping with her motions.

She suddenly hissed and slapped Val's sides with her heels. At once, Val sprang away into a furious gallop, her sharp hooves churning angrily at the soft spring soil. Bran meant to leave this Dra-Oog in her wake the first few strides. But there she was beside her, the old mare easily keeping pace with the smaller black horse. Bran guided Val into a sharp turn, which took them down a steep incline littered with loose stones. She leaned back and clutched desperately with her legs, wishing she had chosen to do this with a saddle. Val slid down the hill, head up, sitting on her haunches to balance and got them both safely to the bottom in a scrambling cascade of stones and small rocks.

And there was Dra-Oog right beside them at the bottom of the hill, her mare easily keeping pace on the dangerous terrain.

There was a small, shallow stream at the bottom and Val splashed happily through it, high stepping and shaking her head. She loved to feel the splatter of water or mud on her belly. She then bunched her hindquarters to scramble up the embankment on the other side and Bran clung like a tick to her bareback.

And there was Dra-Oog right beside them showering them with water and clods of earth as they clambered up the steep but small hill.

At the top of the embankment was an open field of muddy earth and last year's grass. Val shook her head in glee and pulled eagerly on the bit asking for more speed. Slippery though the footing was, Bran decided to give the mare her head and released the tension on the reins. Val gave a happy squeal and a buck and lengthened into an all out gallop. The wind combed their hair and stung their faces. Bran wanted to laugh or shout. There was nothing she liked better than a gallop at this speed. But she kept her mouth shut not wanting to catch any mud flying from Val's madly thrashing feet.

And Dra-Oog was right beside them, her good white mare splattered brown with mud and filth like an old racehorse.

Bran saw a large boulder at the edge of the field just before the tree line. It was at least three feet tall and about seven feet long. It jutted raggedly out of the earth like a knife's blade. She had jumped it before with Vilmar and alone by herself. But she had never tried it at this speed. She cast a sidelong glance at Dra-Oog's mud-splattered face and saw the dwarf staring back at her with a wry smile, catching her thought.

As one they both shouted to their mounts and urged them on with heels and seat. Dra-Oog's mare matched Val's steps stride for stride as they approached. Neither horse showed any sign of slowing or refusing. Then it was too late to turn back or stop.

Both horses, one little and black the other large and white, sailed effortlessly over the boulder and touched down skidding some in the slop on the other side. Their riders cheered them on as they slowed and entered the woods. Dra-Oog immediately swung in front of Val and began to weave in and out of the trees still galloping. Val mimicked her motions to the opposite side.

Then Dra-Oog suddenly disappeared from view. Before Bran had a chance to glance about, she was rammed from the left side. Val stumbled to her knees and Bran clutched desperately with her legs and hands but did not fall off. Val fought her way back to her feet and came up snorting and blowing, ears pinned in anger. Bran felt much the same. She spun to aim a shout at this Dra-Oog only to see the wisp of a tail disappearing in the brambles. Val didn't need prodding, she at once made for the thicket.

But once in the thicket they lost all view of the other horse and rider.

Bran looked about her every which way and saw nothing. Dra-Oog and her mount had simply vanished. She listened carefully and heard nothing. Bran didn't know what to think. She sat there mulling it over in her head for a bit. She finally decided to track them. With all the mud about, their trail should be easy enough to pick up, or so she thought.

She found hoof prints leading out of the thicket to the west and followed them. She topped a small rise in the woods and followed the trail of prints down to the stream at its base. A quick glance told her Dra-Oog had not crossed the stream. This meant she had to have forded the water and either followed its course upstream or downstream. So Bran picked a direction and waded downstream, her eyes scanning either bank. She found no tracks whatsoever after two miles. So she turned about and headed the other way upstream only to come to the same conclusion.

Totally confused and bewildered she wandered about the woods and fields for a couple of hours before finally giving up and heading back to Tor Ambroc.

She dismissed Val and made her way to her family's compound still not sure what to think of it all. Tired, sweaty and splattered with dry mud she opened the door to the family room and stopped in shock.

Dra-Oog sat at the table with the other members of her family looking well fed and well amused, a tankard of ale halfway to her lips.

"Ah! So the wayward soldier has finally found her way home, I see!" Dra-Oog chuckled to the loud mirth of the rest of her family. "It didn't take her long. Pay up, Varg, you old rascal!"

With a snort Varg handed over a small bag of coins.

Bran blinked a few times, started to say a few things and restarted, and finally managed to stammer out, "What do you call it, what you did to me back there?"

The family laughed loudly at her confusion. Even Yaffa joined in.

"That was your scouting test," Dra-Oog chortled merrily. "By the way, you failed."

"Test? That was your form of a test?" Bran objected.

Varg howled drunkenly and slapped his knee.

"Me daughter flunked her first pop quiz!" he guffawed in glee.

"I didn't know I was being tested!" Bran protested indignantly.

"Don't worry, lass." Yaffa reassured with loving motherly humor. "Everyone flunks Dra-Oog's first test. Now you know what they're gonna be like."

"You're right, Yaffa," Dra-Oog replied. "The lass here can ride quite well in fact. Never done the test with any student who rode bareback and stayed on. She stuck like a hound on a rabbit when I rammed her."

Bran grew rather upset when reminded of the incident.

"That was the rudest trick I've ever seen! You never ram another rider! It's dangerous! And very unsportsmanlike of you," she spat back waving her finger at Dra-Oog's smiling face.

"And it happens all the time in battle, my dear," Yaffa said standing up, all the mirth gone from her face. "And that is what Dra-Oog is to prepare you for. Unless you think battle is a quaint little affair where no one gets hurt or a speck of dirt on them."

"C'mon, lassies! What do you think we are? Elves? They don't even stink when they sweat!" Varg nearly shouted.

"Sit down, my girl, and have a pint with us," Yaffa soothed, pulling out a chair and filling a tankard with fine beer. "Tomorrow you leave to join the cavalry of the Yazu and learn how to fight properly. Tonight we celebrate."

"Here's to my youngest returning a hero!" announced Varg in pride and the mugs clashed and clinked.

Bran broke the tankard on her salute. Her father Varg bellowed in laughter and said it was a lucky sign.

Bran suddenly didn't feel very lucky.

CHAPTER 11

Bran watched her parents disappear through the trader's gates after she said goodbye. She fought to keep her face an impenetrable mask although she felt like running in after them and never leaving Tor Ambroc again. Instead she slung her pack over her shoulder and turned about. Dra-Oog was mounting her homely mare, whose ears were once again flopping and lip hanging lazily. Ghost, as the mare was called, was altogether the saddest excuse for a horse Bran had ever seen—in looks anyway.

Bran started to withdraw her Dahla horse but Dra-Oog stopped her.

"I'd rather you save your special friend for those occasions when you need a really trustworthy mount," she counseled sternly. "Best not to waste such a valuable talent on mere travel through safe places."

"What do you suggest then?" Bran asked flatly.

"Well, in the Yazu, it is customary to have a spare mount. Some of us even have more than two," Dra-Oog replied.

"Hmm," muttered Bran. "And how many spare mounts do you have?"

She was expecting a certain answer and was not disappointed with the reply.

"I own a small herd of about ten warhorses. Ghost and Phantom are my two favorites. The rest are mostly used as remounts or training horses for Yazu soldiers," she replied with pride in her voice.

"Are they as beautiful as Ghost here?" Bran asked rubbing the mare's neck in a friendly way as they walked. Ghost butted her with her ungainly head like a herd mate.

Dra-Oog laughed loudly at this.

"Heavens no!" she chuckled. "They're usually even more ugly! Plain or ugly horses don't get stolen. But each one is an excellent warhorse and training mount. They all know their job and are more than happy to do it."

Silence fell between them. Dra-Oog rode and Bran walked.

"I don't have any Dahla horses," she finally confessed.

"Why not?" Bran asked.

"I prefer a real mount," she returned, looking closely at Bran to gauge her reaction to this reply.

"Hmm," Bran muttered again.

"But there are many in the Yazu who do own Dahla horses," she informed. "Let's see, there's Gethin who has two Dahlas, Dusk and Dawn, there's Adya with Snowbear and Firestorm—they're both Dahlas. Let's see, who else? Ah yes! Pall has Stormlance and Whiplash, and Madoc has three Dahlas—Stumpsucker, Glutton, and Say What?"

"Madoc has some odd-named horses!" Bran snorted.

"Their names make more sense when you meet them. Stumpsucker cribs on everything, Say What? always has the dumbest expression on his face when you do anything with him and Glutton, well, that's self-explanatory. Madoc only keeps them around for riding. The three cause too much trouble when they're not under saddle. Madoc likes her horses to have personalities."

"So do I but I prefer trouble-free personalities. Even if my horse 'isn't real'," Bran replied.

They fell quiet again for a spell.

"If I'm going to need a spare horse I know just the place to get one. I'm friends with the farrier in Kopa. He always has a few horses around to buy or trade. We could try there?" she suggested and Dra-Oog readily agreed. Anyway, Ghost needed to have her feet attended to she said.

So it was they found themselves in Kopa town. Dra-Oog talked with Conal while Bran explained what she needed to Vilmar.

"I have just the horse you need if you want reality," he said and led her down to the far end of the barn.

He took her to the small pen where he liked to work his young horses. Standing placidly in the pen, head down, long ears flopped and half asleep, was a black mule.

"Now I know he isn't much to look at but he's all heart and he's just about the best trained thing here. He's a mute so he won't be calling attention to himself. He's also whistle trained. Give him a try if you like," Vilmar told her.

The mule woke up when Bran stepped into the pen. His long ears swiveled up and his large, pale blue eyes opened and gazed curiously at her.

"His name's Echo," Vilmar said. "Whistle and he'll come."

Bran whistled. Echo just looked at her for a long moment. Then he licked his lips and obediently strode up, stopping just in front of her. Bran stepped to his side and began to mount. The just a little too tall mule suddenly stretched out his front end like a dog getting up from a nap. Startled, Bran jumped back.

"It's all right," Vilmar reassured. "He knows you're a little too short and it's going to be kinda hard for you to get up. He's just helping."

Sure enough, the mule had frozen in mid stretch and was staring at her quizzically as if to say, 'Well? What are you waiting for?'

She recovered quickly and scrambled aboard the lean back, which was so different from Val's. Echo stood up and waited.

Bran put him through his paces with Vilmar shouting out suggestions whenever the two of them started speaking a different language to each other. It was mostly just learning what the mule was used to and what he wasn't. Echo was trained to move entirely on leg pressure, which Bran liked. She would need her hands free in the Yazu if she were to learn how to fight properly. Vilmar showed her the special commands he had taught Echo. He even showed her how to get him to lie down on command. But there was one thing Echo couldn't do and this was pace. He was not a gaited mount. His trot was smooth, but it would never be as smooth as Val's flying pace.

Secretly, Bran hoped Val wouldn't become jealous of her 'spare' mount. Bran hadn't wanted another horse. She wanted no one but Valynt. Echo was not the kind of mount she would have considered. She preferred horses and ponies to mules. But Echo definitely had some nice qualities and an agreeable personality.

She finally decided Vilmar was right and she would go with this mule named Echo.

"How much?" she asked.

Vilmar shook his head.

"I'll make you pay for the saddle and bridle to go with him, although you really don't need them, but not the mule. He's my gift to you," he said with a slow smile.

"Gift?" Bran exclaimed. "But what will your Da say?"

Vilmar shrugged. "I don't care," he replied. "I don't know when or if you're coming back and I never got a chance to give you anything for your birthday. When you got Val, I figured you didn't need a horse anymore. I was kinda disappointed. I had been training this guy specifically for you anyway. I really wanted to give you a horse for your birthday. Now I have."

"I don't know what to say," she said in amazement. "Thanks."

Vilmar shuffled uncomfortably. "Just come back to us. Promise?" he said.

"Of course I'll come back," she replied. "Why wouldn't I? This is my home."

Vilmar winced and looked away.

"Wait! What do you know?" Bran asked suddenly suspicious.

"For certain? Nothing," he retorted. "I just think... if we see each other again... we will be different people, that's all. It's just a feeling."

He gave a sigh of frustration and rubbed the back of his neck. Vilmar winced and frowned then continued. "Something big and bad will happen before that. I don't know what it is exactly and it's driving me nuts!"

"Then let's promise here and now to always be friends, whatever happens," Bran said holding out her hand.

"What if..." Vilmar stammered. "What if... when next we see each other... we won't want to be each other's friend? Life has a tendency of doing that, so the old folks say."

"Then we promise," Bran said with a fierce tone of voice. "We promise if my life changes and twists me, you'll come and yank me back to my senses. And I will do the same for you. We won't leave each other."

Vilmar stared hard into her deep green eyes with his ice blue ones. Then he took her hand in a crushing grip. Bran grinned widely back.

"You sure have an impressive grasp for one who is lousy with a forge," she teased.

He returned the grin.

"I guess next time I won't be able to recognize you because your beard will be all grown in," he teased back.

"Isn't it time for you to have some chin hairs? I keep looking. But I don't even see any baby fuzz!"

"Late bloomer, my Da says," Vilmar grumbled crossly.

Bran swung down from Echo and walked him into a stand-in stall while Vilmar went and got a saddle and bridle. He found a simple leather tack with a sheepskin seat and nice, short stirrups for Bran's dwarf legs. They chatted as they worked on adjusting the straps to fit Bran and the mule.

"How's your education with the unicorn going?" Bran asked secretively.

"Slow," Vilmar muttered. "She says I need books. There aren't really a lot of libraries in a unicorn glade."

An idea occurred to Bran.

"I know who can teach you to read and write," she burst out.

"You do? Who?"

"Keld. He's teaching me. I guess class will be ending now. But he has lots of books and can speak ten languages, even dragon," she told him.

"And he's a dwarf?" Vilmar asked hesitantly.

"Only half," she replied. "The other half is human."

"Ah, so he's a muttlith," Vilmar said with a strange quizzical smile. "You know, for someone who is so afraid of being a muttlith, you sure seem to be attracted to them. This can't be good for family relations."

Bran gave a bit too forceful yank on the girth at the comment and Echo tossed his head fitfully.

"Do you want to learn to read or not?" she shot back. She said it like a dare. "How many wizards are illiterate? You going to be the first?"

"I am not illiterate!" he retorted as he slapped down a stirrup. Echo pinned his ears and turned a long suffering, blue eye on him.

"For a farm boy you probably can read quite well. But for a wizard?" she posed.

Vilmar glared at her across the back of the saddle. She had to stand on her tiptoes but she glared right back.

"Fine!" she spat. "Prove me wrong then. Go see Keld and tell him I sent you. Tell him I think you can't do it!"

For a long moment they stared back and forth, neither one budging an inch. The black mule heaved a long sigh, which seemed to lessen the tension. Vilmar slowly smiled.

"You make a very bad liar," he finally said quietly.

"I know," she replied smugly.

She knew he would go and see Keld now.

She led Echo out to where Dra-Oog was waiting with the newly shod Ghost. She noted Dra-Oog's eyes wander critically over the mule. Finally, the older dwarf nodded her approval. Echo would do.

Bran turned to Vilmar as Dra-Oog mounted up.

"I'll come back. I promise," she said earnestly.

He nodded and there was a sad but fond look in his soft blue eyes.

"Remember what I said to you when I first met your Da?" he said quietly.

She smiled and chuckled. "You said something about having the utmost respect for me and wanting no one but me beside you in a tight spot. And then you said I was as a brother to you. My Da was quite tickled!"

Vilmar sniffed in reply. "Well, all jesting aside, it still holds true."

"Oh really?" she smiled back. "Am I still as a brother to you?"

He screwed up his face at the reminder.

"Let's try sister. Would that be better?"

"Yes," she said. "Much."

He knelt down and wrapped her in a bear hug. She found herself clinging desperately to him. Everything familiar and safe to her was being left behind. She felt afraid, terribly afraid of the future. But she knew better than to say anything. Dwarves just did not speak about their fears. She finally separated herself from him and, without looking back, swung up on Echo and rode away following Dra-Oog.

Vilmar stood silently for a long moment staring after them. He wondered if he'd ever see her again. This nagging fear about what was to come was very real inside him. Whenever he thought about the future, he could feel it, like a tight fist in his chest when he was nervous about something. Change was looming on the horizon and it was very near.

Vilmar gave a troubled sigh and breathed a silent prayer to the unicorn to watch over his friend. Then he turned away and went back to the stable full of horses who needed him.

CHAPTER 12

Iyorath Asra strode silently through the camp. He was an imposing figure, the only elf among so many dwarves and he stood out in sharp, graceful contrast to their gruff movements and manner.

Iyorath was a typical elf in most ways. He was tall and lean with long blonde hair and fair skin and features. His sharp eyes were silver gray and his clothes, colored in soft greens and browns, fitted snugly.

On his right shoulder perched an enormous silvery eagle. He had tried to get the eagle to switch shoulders from time to time but the damned bird refused, so his right shoulder was perpetually lower than his left. He was careful to get the shoulders of all his garments padded with thick leather to help protect his fair skin from the finger-sized talons of his eagle who was only obedient sometimes. On his left neck and collarbone was an enormous scar from the bird when they were just getting to know each other. War eagles were handy to have around but could only be relied on part of the time because they were so temperamental. When the relationship was working, having them around was a blessing. But when a war eagle had a bad day, everyone around it had a bad day as well. They were both famous and infamous tools of battle.

Iyorath bent low to enter the extra large tent he shared with Captain Garn-Ithel of the seventh division of the Yazu. Inside, the furnishings were spare on the dwarf side of the tent. Garn-Ithel's bedroll had an oilskin cape underneath and was spread out on the ground. His pack and all its contents were strewn beside it. On the other side of the tent was an easily portable bed set up off the ground for the elf, with a table next to it and a sturdy perch for his eagle when the bird preferred to be inside. At night the bird was posted outside the tent to stand guard. Iyorath insisted on a proper bed off the ground, not because he was better than the dwarves but because it was the only sleeping arrangement which fit him comfortably. He had learned long ago dwarves could make a much better traveling bed than an extra long bedroll to fit an elf.

Iyorath moved over to the perch and allowed the war eagle to step off his tormented shoulder. He then flexed his arm and massaged the shoulder joint a bit to return the blood flow. The war eagle, Rath-Tor was eating far too well lately it seemed. He sighed and sat heavily on his fine bed, rubbing the weariness out of his face.

Garn-Ithel crouched on the ground on his side of the tent, glaring and muttering over a set of dwarf rune stones. Iyorath Asra watched the bent dwarf with growing interest, a smile spreading across his thin lips.

If asked, Garn would insist that divination was merely a hobby he dabbled lightly in, not something to be taken seriously. But Iyorath had been keeping track of these 'dabblings' of late and was startled with the accuracy of Garn's predictions. So now he paid close attention whenever the rune stones were cast, although he said nothing to his friend of the reality of the skill of his hobby. He noticed Rath-Tor, the eagle, was watching closely as well, with his sharp eyes, which could spot a mole in the grass from a cloud's height.

"Well, what is the message?" he asked in a friendly tone.

"Humph!" snorted Garn-Ithel in puzzlement. "A pretty jumble I've cast here! I can't seem to make sense of it at all."

"What was the question?" Iyorath asked again and the dwarf shrugged.

"Just a general request for some illumination on what the future days would bring. I wanted a generic reply. What I got was an epic tale in another language!"

"Well, maybe I can help. Tell me what you think it says. We'll muddle through it together, you and I," Iyorath returned.

Garn snorted loudly as if he didn't think it would be much use.

He spread his hands to the center of the circle of scattered rune stones.

"These five say roughly, *'The wolf will wed the spirit of laughter'*."

"Hmm, a wedding and laughter. That sounds good. The wolf part I'm not sure about. It could be either good or bad," Iyorath thought aloud quietly.

"Just wait. It gets worse! At least I think it gets worse," Garn grumbled. "This says literally, *'Four shall come then the Blood Raven will be born'*."

Garn and Iyorath met each other's gaze. This definitely didn't sound good to either of them.

"A Blood Raven, eh?" Iyorath replied. "What symbology does the raven have to your people?"

"War. I think," Garn-Ithel returned ominously. "It's generally thought of as a bad omen among my people. A Blood Raven means a very bad war or plague."

Iyorath frowned and nodded for him to continue.

"*'The earth shall be plowed with an army of hooves'*," Garn met Iyorath's eyes again.

They didn't need to say it. They were both thinking the same thing. They were sitting in the middle of an army encampment full of horses.

"*'This will cause the mountains to belch forth their most precious gems'*."

"Sounds like a reference to something dwarven or volcanic," Iyorath mentioned and Garn nodded in total agreement.

"*'The Blood Raven's wings will cause the earth to shake down to its core and Darkness will howl'*."

"Another wolf reference. Maybe," Iyorath grunted. "And what does darkness have to howl about?"

Garn-Ithel shrugged in puzzlement and continued.

"*'Metal will drink evil's soul'*."

They were silent a long moment.

Iyorath's brow furrowed in deep lines as he pondered his next words. "Curiouser and curiouser. Sound's like another dwarf reference."

Again Garn nodded and followed it with a confused shrug.

"Maybe. Maybe not. But this is the worst part yet," he pointed to a rune stone which had landed furthest away from the center. It was totally plain and blank of any mark.

"What's it mean?" Iyorath asked innocently.

"*'Unknown'*," Garn muttered grimly.

Iyorath thought deeply, rubbing his ever beard-free chin.

"Maybe it's a good thing. If the outcome is unknown it means the future is still subject to change. Possibly it could be changed for the better?" he suggested in what he hoped was a reassuring tone.

Garn-Ithel nodded not smiling, his face as dark and foreboding as an approaching summer storm. His eyes perused the scattered stones.

"Bah!" he finally burst out and gathered up the runes noisily. "Probably means nothing anyway! I'm no good at this. I'm no cleric. I don't know how to do this right. Just dabbling, I am. That's all!"

Puffing and spouting he stuffed the stones back into their leather pouch and shoved them into his pack. Grumbling and muttering he slapped on his helmet and stood up.

"Guess Dorlan needs me to relieve him on watch, eh?" he asked.

Iyorath nodded distantly and wished him an uneventful turn. The dwarf just muttered, belched and left the tent in a hurry.

Iyorath stretched himself out at full length on his bed and thought hard about what he had just heard. He finally cast his eyes on Rath-Tor his war eagle.

"Well, what do you think of it all?" he said quietly to the large bird of prey.

Rath-Tor's eyes glittered as he gazed sharply back at the elf.

'*He's spot on,*' the eagle's thoughts whispered into Iyorath's mind. '*If the prediction doesn't come true, I'll eat a whole bowl of birdseed!*'

Iyorath smiled at the eagle. "I was afraid you'd say that," and he sighed.

But the smile soon vanished as his thoughts whirled, puzzling over the words of the divination.

It certainly sounded quite ominous.

CHAPTER 13

A week later, Bran and Dra-Oog rode into the Yazu encampment.

Bran's eyes drank in the sights. There must have been about two hundred and fifty white tents scattered about. Each tent had several horses picketed outside. The tents were arranged in a certain order. She noticed they got progressively larger the closer they came to the center. She surmised this was where the great major general slept and conducted business.

Bran observed the dwarves closest to her as they made their way through the camp. She noticed very few male dwarves. The majority were female, which was easily told by the lack of hair on their upper lips. Only dwarf men grew mustaches.

She saw a small knot of dwarf men clustered around a portable forge making horseshoes. They looked up and waved at Dra-Oog peering curiously at Bran.

"Stay clear of the camp farriers, my dear," Dra-Oog cautioned sternly. "They're not as courteous as your human friend."

"Why? We seem to be surrounded in nothing but dwarves. Why do I need to be afraid of my own people?" she asked.

"I never said to be afraid of them. Just be cautious around them," Dra-Oog clarified. "They're flanked by so many good-looking dwarf women they think they've died and gone to heaven!"

"Ah! Flirts, eh?" Bran replied.

"That's putting it rather mildly. Always carry a knife around them and be ready with the insults. They're a little fuzzy on the meaning of the word 'no'!"

Dra-Oog turned slightly in the saddle to lock eyes with her and grinned. Bran nodded comprehending. Her ears caught a snide comment from one of the farriers.

"Hey, Ponz!" came a shout. "Don't you have a thing for redheads?"

Bran growled in distaste and made a mental note to steer clear of this Ponz fellow.

Dra-Oog suddenly saw someone she recognized and gave a shout. Bran was shocked to see an elf and not a dwarf respond to her hail.

He strode up to Dra-Oog and Bran noted he was so tall he stood eye to eye with Dra-Oog as she sat on Ghost. They conversed quietly for a time and Bran had a chance to get a good look at her first elf.

He was everything dwarves were not. While dwarves were short and squarely built, he was tall and lean as a willow whip. Dwarves usually had a very ruddy complexion but his skin was pale as the moonlight. Dwarf hair was normally coarse and had a tendency to be bushy and thick yet his was smooth as yellow glass. There was no beard to speak of on this character and Bran doubted there ever would be from all she had been told about elves.

Dra-Oog suddenly tilted to Bran and said, "I'm needed at the big tent. This is Iyorath Asra, our elven scout. He will show you to your tent and get you acquainted with your bunkmate. See you tomorrow in the practice ring at dawn."

The elf turned and strode up to Bran. She then noticed he had the deepest blue eyes she had ever seen on anyone—human, dwarf or elf.

He held out his arm and she clasped it immediately in typical dwarf greeting. He seemed to be quite familiar with her customs.

Bran dismounted from Echo and the elf offered to lead her mule for her. She decided to allow this.

They were silent a bit as they fell in side by side, the elf automatically shortening his steps to keep pace with her stumpy little legs.

"You're the first elf I've met," she finally said to him.

"Ah," was his reply. "And your first impression is?"

"You look like an ash tree. How long does it take the sap to reach your brain?" she meant it as a joke and he chuckled amiably.

"This lass has a sense of humor. Good. I hate grumpy dwarves," he replied.

"Well, it comes with the breed," she muttered and Iyorath nodded in assent.

"Interesting you think I look like an ash tree. It's what I'm named for," he returned.

"Really?" Bran said.

71

"Now the name Bran," he continued. "What does it mean in dwarf?"

"Raven," she replied. "You'd think with that name I'd have black hair instead of being a redhead."

"One would think," returned the elf considering. "What was your father's name?"

"Varg," Bran said.

"Ah, it means wolf, does it not?"

"Yes, it does," Bran replied.

"And your mother's name?" the elf continued to press.

"Yaffa. And before you ask, it means laughter," she filled in. This elf certainly seemed to be very curious about dwarf names

"Ah, I see. Very interesting indeed. Laughter and Wolf giving birth to the Raven. And how many other siblings do you have?"

"There are five of us in all. I was the lastborn," she replied.

"Ah," the elf mused. "Your mother was Yazu as well, was she not?"

"Yes," Bran was starting to get a little irritated. "You seem very interested in names and my family and such. Does every new soldier get this kind of treatment from you?"

Iyorath Asra smiled gently.

"My apologies, Bran. I did not mean to pry. It is a side effect of being a scout and a spy. I have this urge to know every detail about everyone. You never know what small thing may prove useful. But yes, it was most rude of me. I'm sorry."

Bran grunted. The elf was polite. Too polite she thought. She was getting suspicious.

"Ah, here we are," Iyorath said as they stopped in front of one tent. A dwarf woman with black bushy hair and a muddy-colored beard was busily polishing her saddle. Outside her tent stood a black mule who could have been Echo's twin had it not been for its normal brown eyes.

"This is Delkan, your bunk mate. I hope you two will get along," he bowed politely and handing the reins back to Bran, left them.

Delkan raised her head and Bran noticed her pale gray eyes. She also noticed Delkan wore a Dahla horse on a string of leather around her neck.

"Hey!" she exclaimed with a big smile pointing to her mule. "You've got a black mule for a spare, too. And you have a Dahla horse as well. How strange is that?"

Bran smiled back politely.

"What's your mule's name?" she asked Delkan.

"Pitch. And yours?" she replied.

"Echo," Bran returned. "What's your Dahla's name?"

"Sashay. And yours?"

"Valynt."

Delkan nodded. "Good strong name," she said. "I named mine Sashay 'cause he likes to gait even when standing still."

Bran turned to see if the elf had really left. She suddenly thought of something, which made her chuckle loud enough for Delkan to notice.

"What's wrong?" Delkan asked.

"Just something funny I heard someone say about elves," Bran chuckled.

"Well, spill it then!" returned Delkan not wanting to be left out of the joke.

"Is it true elves don't stink when they sweat?" she asked.

Delkan began to chortle as well. "Nah! Didn't you know they stink like roses? And some smell like daisies," Delkan replied giving a cautious glance to make sure Iyorath was really out of earshot.

"Ah, you and I are gonna have some great fun together! I can't wait to tickle some goblins to death!"

Delkan gave Bran a friendly slap on the back.

CHAPTER 14

Vilmar was ushered silently into the dwarf library. Keld, the scholar, stood with his back to the door, narrowly scanning a scroll.

"You are Vilmar, the farrier's son?" Keld asked without turning around.

Vilmar stood up straight and tall. He tried to quell the nervous energy which had gripped him. He was taking a big risk coming here. The dwarves of Tor Ambroc did not admit just any human to their hallowed halls and he knew he was far from being important enough to normally be allowed inside.

"Yes, I am Vilmar," he replied and his voice cracked.

Keld turned around and removed his glasses.

"Going through the change, are we?" he muttered at the tone of Vilmar's words. He wasn't sure whether it was meant as a jest or not but it was true. Vilmar's voice was changing.

"Aren't we a little old?" Keld continued.

"Late bloomer, my Da says," he muttered.

Keld came slowly up to Vilmar, scrutinizing him all the way.

"Late bloomer, indeed! Not even a respectable beard has sprouted yet. You look more like an elf. You sure you're ready for my teachings?"

Vilmar shrugged. "Doesn't matter," he said. "We all are running out of time. I have to learn to read and write properly now."

"The human race never has enough time," Keld grumbled fitfully. "They're always in a hurry. Do you know how long it takes to learn to read and write in just one language, my boy? Years!"

Vilmar groaned in agony at this admission.

"I haven't got time," he blustered in frustration. "It's gonna happen this year! I have to be ready..."

Too late he bit back his words.

"So that's what you really mean, human," Keld said having figured it all out. "Not too late for a human's lifespan. Too late for what is about to happen."

He sat down and glowered at Vilmar, tapping a long finger in impatience.

"He who controls the dwarves, controls the tide of battle. Isn't that what you told Bran?" Keld growled. "Do you really want to control us?"

"What?" gasped Vilmar in surprise. "No! Of course not! Not me! I just want to be ready to help out when the time comes. You'll need all the help you can get."

He quickly stopped stammering, recognizing how foolish he must sound. Keld was grinning in spite of himself.

"Relax, young human," he laughed waving a long hand about as if it really didn't matter. "Bran has already told me all about you."

"Did she tell you she dared me to do this?" Vilmar grumbled as he sat down.

"Did she? Was any money wagered on it?" Keld asked hungrily.

"No," Vilmar returned shocked.

Keld deflated noticeably. "Pity. The results would have made an interesting bet," a disappointed Keld replied.

He thought briefly, still tapping his fingers and looking Vilmar up and down.

"Very well. I'll teach you what I know. I know a few tricks to help you increase your speed of learning. Once you learn how to read and write in one language the rest will come more easily depending on the differences and similarities."

Keld rose and began to rummage around the shelves, reading the bindings and pulling out random books. Vilmar followed to offer to carry them. Keld muttered broken sentences as he searched and piled more after more books upon Vilmar's awaiting arms, which were only accustomed to hefting hay bales. The stack in Vilmar's grasp kept getting higher and higher. Pretty soon he was having trouble looking over the top, and keeping them balanced was becoming a chore.

"Do I have to know everything in each one of these?" he asked, overwhelmed by the sheer volume of the stack.

"Well, every little bit helps," Keld called out, scrambling to the opposite side of a shelf. "Come along, my boy, keep up. Ah! 'Phrases and Grammar in Five Tongues'! An excellent book! Yes, we'll need this, too. Let's see, what else?"

Vilmar puffed and started to stagger a bit.

"Uh, how fast are you expecting me to learn all this?" Vilmar asked hesitantly.

"Oh, let's just see where you are when the dam breaks, shall we? Come along now. I have some fine books on magical inflection on the other shelf. You would like to learn wizardly things too, right? I figured you might, being as you stink of it."

Vilmar gasped in shock at this remark and suddenly toppled over from the weight of all those books.

"Careful!" Keld scolded. "Some of those are very old and fragile! Not to mention valuable. Pick up the mess and come along now. There's more back here!"

Keld ducked around another bookshelf trying his best not to cackle out loud.

Vilmar sat on the floor and looked about at the scattered piles of books. He really felt like he had bitten off more than he could chew. He wondered if it was too late to back out now. He then thought of Bran's corrosive words claiming he couldn't do it and wouldn't ever be able to. He growled angrily and slowly began to gather up the dusty old books.

He wished he were back in the stable cleaning smelly horse stalls.

"Uh oh!" Garn said suddenly.

"What is it?" replied Dra-Oog.

"I see an angry elf coming our way," he replied.

"I didn't know they could get angry outside of battle," teased Dra-Oog and Garn chortled at her reply.

"This should be fun!" Garn whispered secretively.

"Garn-Ithel!" spouted Iyorath. "Dra-Oog! We have a gremlin in our camp!"

"A real gremlin, or are you speaking figuratively?" Garn asked and Dra-Oog jabbed him a warning poke in his ribs.

The elf just glowered angrily at him.

"Somebody's been in my tent," Iyorath demanded.

"Really? Was anything taken?" Dra-Oog asked.

"No," the elf replied still in an angry tone. "But there were flower petals scattered all over my bed!"

"But I thought elves liked flowers," said Dra-Oog and bit her lip to keep from laughing.

"Maybe you have a dwarf suitor?" Garn mentioned chuckling a bit.

"That's not funny!" Iyorath exclaimed. "And the other day, someone left a potted plant outside my tent."

"Aww!" cooed Dra-Oog sweetly. "You *do* have a suitor!"

"It was skunk cabbage!" he explained in a huff.

"Oh," both dwarves replied at once.

"That was *not* a nice gift," Garn admitted.

"I expect you to get to the bottom of this, Dra-Oog!" Iyorath demanded. "It's upsetting my eagle!"

And with this, Iyorath strode gracefully away.

The two dwarves could barely wait until he was out of earshot before bursting out in raucous laughter.

"Upsetting his eagle, my ass!" Dra-Oog said when she could finally trust her voice again.

"That's an insult to the eagle!" Garn chuckled. "Upsetting *him*, yes, his eagle, no. Rath-Tor is probably just as amused as we are."

Dra-Oog nodded, still smiling and looking fondly after the elf.

"Still," she admitted. "I'm having reports of just such pranks filtering in from all over the camp. Something upset the farriers the other day."

"Do tell," an eager Garn said.

"Well, one of them was engaged in his morning constitution when a bush exploded behind him. He ran all the way back to camp with his pants down and half finished with his business."

"Now that would have been fun to see!" Garn chuckled.

"It was. He was too embarrassed to show his face for days," Dra-Oog replied. "And not too long ago, Ponz was shoeing a rather skittish horse when another explosion went off right behind the portable forge. The horse kicked Ponz and nearly jumped out of its skin in fright!"

"Now that's a bit too much," agreed Garn. "Ponz could have been killed by the horse!"

Drah-Oog nodded in total agreement. "It was a dangerous prank to play."

They both fell silent, thinking.

"Was it a bunny tickler bomb?" he asked. Bunny tickler bombs were small harmless explosives the dwarves sometimes used to cause general distractions upon their enemies. They were quite effective.

Dra-Oog nodded silently.

"Aren't the dwarves of the Fang-Tor province known for inventing the bunny ticklers?" Garn-Ithel said slowly.

"They are indeed," Dra-Oog replied with a smile, seeing where his thoughts were going. "And Delkan is from Fang-Tor. But I also think she had help."

"Ah, Bran helped her?"

She nodded, smiling wide.

"Those two have been rather thick since we decided to bunk them together."

Garn shrugged. "Maybe they should be separated?" he suggested.

Dra-Oog frowned and thought hard.

"No, I think not," she said slowly. "I suspect they'll make an excellent fighting team and if that's the case, it would be worse to break them up. No, I think I'll let Iyorath know of my suspicions as to the identity of his 'gremlins' and then leave him to put them in his junior scouting group. He can teach them and punish them all at the same time."

"Now *that* I'd like to see," Garn-Ithel chuckled, rubbing his hands eagerly together.

CHAPTER 15

Vilmar lay stretched out in the dappled shade of a budding oak. He drank in the warm spring air and listened to the sound of a large animal grazing next to him. His books lay open and scattered on the long grass all about him.

"You should be studying," admonished a voice in his head.

He sighed deeply.

"It's too beautiful a day to study," he complained. "I should be riding through the fields and woods on a day like this."

He was about to continue in this vein but his thoughts stopped him. The other presence caught them immediately.

"You miss Bran, don't you?" the voice, which was still in his head, said.

"Yes," he murmured softly.

He rolled over to gaze at the one who spoke to his mind.

A unicorn doe stood before him cropping the new grass short. Beside her in the grass close to Vilmar, slept her two-year-old fawn, swishing his tufted tail fitfully at a passing fly.

Vilmar looked into the unicorn's eyes and was nearly caught by their spell. They were such a deep, liquid blue. To gaze upon them was to lose oneself in the essence which was unicorn. Moon-like luminescence, which always permeated such a creature, surrounded her. With great effort he resisted being pulled into the glow where he knew he would lose all track of time. He forced himself to see the unicorn outwardly instead of inwardly. She was just a white animal, albeit a magically wonderful mystical beast.

"It's not fair!" he exclaimed slamming the earth with a fist.

"Have a care, Vilmar," the unicorn cautioned sternly. *"Don't you be treating our Mother so selfishly, infant."*

"I'm sorry," he apologized and truly meant it. "But Bran's been taken away for training and I'm stuck here! She's learning to use a sword and how to scout and spy and find out stuff and do all manner of exciting things. And I'm just stuck here pouring over contractions in five different tongues and constantly repeating the elvish word for parlay!"

"Which happens to be...?" schooled the unicorn.

Vilmar sighed heavily and rolled his eyes. But the unicorn wouldn't release him from her penetrating gaze.

"Fronshall," he intoned slowly with mock seriousness.

"The inflection is on the first syllable. Not the last. Now say it again."

He groaned in mental agony.

"Fffrrooonn-ssshhhaaall," he drawled out.

"Better. Say it from the back of your throat and make it deeper next time."

Vilmar clenched his teeth and pouted resentfully at her, refusing to say it at all.

The unicorn fawn sneezed and startled himself awake. He sat up licking and blinking in the morning sun.

"Your grasp of reading and writing in different languages is coming along amazingly well, my young student. Your pronunciation though, leaves much to be desired. Whatever language you speak, you speak it with an appallingly 'human from Kopa town' accent. Work on your pronunciation, my dear."

Vilmar grumbled and pouted but stopped abruptly when the unicorn doe approached him. He expected a stern scolding.

Instead, she lowered her head and licked his forehead in a motherly way.

"I know it is difficult, my dear. You should have learned these languages years ago. It would have been easier for you then. But you are making great strides. You are handling this much better than Keld or I expected you would."

"About that," he interrupted. "Now can I tell him about you?"

He got the distinct impression of laughter in his head.

"Not yet, my eager one. Soon, but not yet," she replied still grooming him.

Her fawn arose and barged rudely into his mother showing his jealousy. The unicorn shoved him away sternly and encouraged him to go pester his sire.

She returned her attention to the human who still lay on the ground. *"I know the preparation is hard and seems to take forever. But it will be over soon, I promise. And when you finally have a chance to use your newly learned skills, you will wish you were still back in school. You probably won't feel confident enough of your grasp of them. Be patient. Keld and I are grooming you to be a most fantastic wizard."*

"Just as long as Bran doesn't get hurt," he muttered sadly.

"When Bran returns, she will be better equipped to handle herself when backed into a corner. She'll probably end up saving you!" the unicorn counseled. *"Now then, the elvish word for parlay is...?"*

He moaned and dropped his head in front of himself down between his shoulders.

"Fronshall!" he relented in utter exasperation.

"Excellent!" reassured the unicorn doe. *"And what is it in goblin?"*

Vilmar growled in frustration like a big cat.

"I don't remember but I know it doesn't sound nice!" he muttered loudly.

CHAPTER 16

My friend Vilmar,

I'm sure you probably think I'm having the most wonderful time in the army but frankly, I couldn't be more bored! It seems all we do is clean saddles, brush horses and sharpen weapons. If we finish too quickly, some higher up, muckity-muck comes 'round and orders us to do it all over again. Once a day, we're ordered to saddle up and ride in formation through the encampment. This only takes us about an hour. And then it's back to cleaning saddles, weapons and horses. The only interesting thing is we never know when we might be called to form up. Yesterday, the call was given for us to form up at midnight!

I keep sneaking over to the work ring to watch the more advanced members practice and I wonder when we will be allowed to do that!

My bunkmate is a dwarf from the Fang-Tor province named Delkan. I've never met anyone quite like her. For one thing, she just will not shut up! She chatters incessantly about all manner of little things. She says it's a side effect of coming from a family of one father, three wives and twenty-five children! I guess she had a hard time getting noticed. I did observe she would stop talking immediately whenever I ask her if she ever sees any of her family anymore. That's how I get her to stop chattering long enough to fall asleep. I really am curious as to what happened to her family but I don't wish to lose my sleep edge. But please don't think me mean. Delkan and I really get along quite well especially when plotting pranks.

But, oh, how I miss our rides, just the two of us! Riding alone is expressly forbidden to any but the scouts so I have very little time alone and it's grating on my nerves.

I'm glad to see Keld took you on! For a muttlith, he's a great teacher. I hope you pick up things fast. I had trouble with the reading and writing part. I'm much better at the conversation. But I know you'll do fine.

Please do take care of yourself.

Your friend always,
Bran
P.S. So how's the beard coming?

Bran finished the letter with a heavy sigh, rolled it up and threaded it into the message tube of the hound from Tor Ambroc. She stroked the lean hound's face lovingly and gave it the command for where to take the message. The dog wagged its whip-like tail, jumped up, licked her once in the face and was off.

Delkan passed the dog as she came into the tent.

"Writing another letter for home?" she asked and Bran nodded.

Delkan nodded in reply, her expression dark. Then she sighed and shook it away from her face but not before Bran had taken note.

"Our gremlin's been at it," she said to change the subject.

"What?" exclaimed Bran. "Not again!"

Delkan smiled ruefully and nodded.

"Look for yourself," she said and held open the tent flap.

They stepped out of their tent in time to see Dra-Oog sitting on the dapple gray Phantom and glowering at them both.

"Delkan and Bran!" she barked. "Clean that crap off your mounts' hooves! It's not regulation! We form up in an hour and their hooves better be clean and shiny!"

She spun her mount and rode away in a huff.

Bran and Delkan flew to the back of the tent where Echo and Pitch were picketed. All the other dwarves were laughing and pointing at their mounts.

Both mules had their hooves painted pink!

This was the fourth time it had happened.

Dra-Oog chuckled to herself and made a mental note to congratulate Iyorath on his timing. The constant rivalry between the two dwarves and the elf was certainly amusing. Dra-Oog also had no intention of letting Bran or Delkan know who their 'gremlin' was.

At least not yet.

Dear Bran,

Imagine my shock when your family asked me to come live in Tor Ambroc with them! Although I think your mother had a lot to do with the decision. They had fashioned a bed of proper length for me and have bought a few human-sized chairs to make me feel more comfortable. But I do feel like a big oaf living in a rabbit hole! Everything is too small and some of your dwarf kin's quarters have very low ceilings.

I see what you mean about your father! I don't think he's said five words to me. Mostly he just grunts in my direction when he's having a good day. It takes some getting used to. Your mother is lovely though. What a charming personality she has. She's so much like you. She has really supported me and made me feel welcome. So I think she approves of me, human or not.

The lessons with Keld are getting more challenging. He's tossing more and more complicated phrases at me in different languages. But the lessons are getting more rewarding now, too. Sometimes he conducts the lesson entirely in another tongue and I have to try to keep up. I don't think either of us has spoken human in the class for quite some time. What's frustrating is when we bump into each other in the tunnels between classes, he'll decide to quiz me and start talking in another language. I get very flustered and red-faced as I struggle to reply in front of strangers. It seems he delights in embarrassing me! Are all dwarf instructors this way or is it the human blood?

I hope things are better with you. Your mother sends her love.

Vilmar
P.S. What beard? (Sigh.)

Bran chuckled and rolled up the letter she had received from Vilmar. She was thoughtful a moment, remembering happy times at home. Then she turned to regard Delkan.

The other dwarf woman was busily filing and polishing the ornately fashioned brass spearhead until it flashed.

"How come you never receive any letters from home, Delkan?" she finally dared to ask. "What's the matter? Is there bad blood between you and your family?"

Delkan nicked herself on the sharp blade in surprise at the sudden intrusion. Her pale gray eyes looked up slowly. As lightly colored as her eyes were, they seemed dark under the shadow of her thick eyebrows.

"No," was all she had to say.

"Well, what then?" Bran pursued.

The normally jovial Delkan fixed her with the gravest stare Bran had ever seen.

"They're gone," she said simply, too simply for Bran to make sense of.

"Gone?" she repeated. "What, all twenty-five plus of them?"

"Yes, all of them are gone," she said flatly, turning back to her work. "I'm the only one left."

Bran was silent for a long moment and a look of pity crossed her face. Delkan turned her back on Bran's expression.

"How long ago?" she asked softly, sympathetically.

"Six months this sevenday," Delkan said.

Delkan sighed heavily and held up the spearhead to admire.

"It's a pretty thing, isn't it?" she said to Bran.

Delkan wasn't trying to change the subject. Bran knew what she meant. She turned her eyes to the spear. It flashed and shone in the dim lantern light inside the tent. Bran could feel the friendly hum, which emanated from the blade and she knew it was magical. She also knew it was dwarf magic which permeated the blade.

It was beautiful, dangerous and deadly. It housed a grace, which demanded respect and knowledge to be fully appreciated. It was a thing any dwarf could easily love.

Bran stilled her heart and felt the emanations from the weapon with her keenly honed dwarf senses.

"Your father made it, didn't he?" Bran finally asked.

Delkan's only reply was to nod her head once. Bran didn't need to ask the question. She knew the spear was meant for more than killing goblins.

It was hungry for someone in particular.

CHAPTER 17

Keld didn't mean to be taking the outside air this day. He just happened to be conversing with the guards at the trader's gates when a particularly bedraggled and weather-beaten cart, pulled by two wormy mules and driven by an old, crippled figure pulled up.

It was just another trader and a dwarf too, so no one should have been alarmed. Dwarves of Tor Ambroc always traded with the dwarves of other kingdoms. And each dwarf province was known for a particular specialty of trade goods. It was just the fact this dwarf and the cart seemed to have come from quite a distance to trade.

Keld quietly observed the guards questioning the little decrepit figure. He hung back so as not to draw attention to himself but stayed close enough to hear every word.

They exchanged brief pleasantries. But to Keld it seemed the little dwarf was trying a bit too hard to be pleasant.

"Nice day for spring, eh?" the little figure said.

"Wind's a bit chilly today," returned the guard warily.

The little, twisted dwarf shrugged vaguely at the comment.

"When you've been on the road as long as I have... well, it's a nice day for me, I meant," he replied.

The little dwarf turned to face the guards and Keld caught a glimpse of his face. It was so wrinkled barely any detail of features could be seen through the folds. He wore a large patch over his left eye. He was so ancient his beard was beginning to fall out and he had given up braiding it. By the way the guards peered up at him and then suddenly jumped back, Keld guessed his body odor must be pretty pungent as well. Dwarves, as a rule, did have a strange sense of hygiene. They believed blood spilled in battle was good for the skin. But most were in the habit of keeping themselves cleaner than this.

Keld wrinkled his nose in distaste.

"And just where did you come from, if I may be so bold to ask, granddad?" inquired one of the guards careful to control his words and keep his distance.

"Oh I'm from way up north, from the Tor Ingal province," he said mouthing toothlessly.

The guards muttered in surprise.

"That is quite a ways!" they replied.

"Yes, well, there were more of us heading here. Five in all. But the journey took most of the younger ones and only left the toughest old bird to deliver the goods, you see." He nodded agreeably at them and Keld saw a few more hairs fall out of his beard.

"What could be so important that one so ancient as yourself would make the dangerous trip through orc-infested lands to trade with us?" Keld finally spoke up and stepped forward.

"Ah well, just the usual, you know. Gold rings and things, sonny boy," he cackled as he turned his one good but bleary eye on Keld.

Keld nodded distantly.

It made some sense. The dwarves of Tor Ingal were known more for their goldsmithing than for their silver. They were especially skilled at forging magic rings.

"Oh, and I have one special thing from the king of my province to your King Garshan."

He eagerly hopped down from the cart and tottered unsteadily around to the back of his wagon where there were three huge liquor casks. Patting them greedily he explained this prize.

"You are familiar with Venko Donar, the famous mead master?" he asked.

The dwarf guards hadn't a clue to this. But the mere mention of mead and their eyes lit up and they licked their lips in anticipation of his next words.

"They're just young pups," Keld apologized. "I remember Venko the great brewmeister."

"Then you are familiar with the story about him?" the wrinkled dwarf posed.

Keld took this as an insult.

"I am the scholar of Tor Ambroc. Of course I know!" he said in frustration. "Venko Donar has for centuries been working on brewing the best mead in all the world, a brew the gods themselves would fight for."

The old dwarf cackled and clapped his gnarled hands in glee.

"His work has finally paid off, my learned friend! This is his brew. He calls it 'Mithral Mead'! It is his finest work yet and he wishes to offer for purchase a small sample of it to the rulers of all the dwarf realms. He says if King Garshan approves of it, he will send more for a much reduced, one-time-only price!"

The gate guards looked quite gleeful at this and were prepared to crack open a cask then and there but Keld stopped them.

Keld glared suspiciously at the casks. He climbed into the cart and scrutinized the barrels. It was highly unlikely one dwarf kingdom would resort to subterfuge. Most of the provinces were on relatively good terms with one another right now. And anyway, tainted brew just wasn't the dwarf way. Still, these were strange times.

Keld checked the barrels thoroughly while the dwarf guards grumbled and told him to make sure the old fool hadn't dipped into the barrels on the way there. The three casks were completely full and marked with the stamp of the Tor Ingal province. They were marked by Venko Donar's personal signature, which Keld knew well even though he hadn't seen it in years. And the barrels definitely smelt of very fine mead.

Finally Keld sighed and nodded his agreement. With jovial comments the dwarves began to unpack the cart. Keld gave them strict instructions to take the three casks to the king's supply room.

"And make sure only the king's retainers taste the brew first! If they survive to the morning without any harm, then and only then should the king drink it!" he lectured sternly.

They grumbled mightily at this and stomped off with their precious load.

Keld turned back to the old dwarf. He was cackling privately to himself and snorting at the very idea of tainted brew.

"Where are our manners, granddad?" he said as politely as he could manage to the crusty fellow. "You have come a long way and you and your team must be road weary. You're welcome to stay with us and partake of our hospitality. Stay as long as you wish. Eat, drink, maybe bathe and recover your strength in the great realm of Tor Ambroc."

Keld said this with a little bow he usually reserved for dignitaries. He thought the gesture worthwhile if he could get the old dwarf near some hot, soapy water!

"Thank you so much, sonny, but I can't stay. I've already made plans to stay in Kopa town tonight as I have friends there. So if you don't mind, I'll just have the lads unload my cart and I'll be on my way."

And this was exactly what the old dwarf did. The minute the cart was unloaded, he nodded to the dwarves still remaining at the gates and climbing into the cart, snapped the reins on the tired old mules' backs and drove away.

Keld stared curiously after him thinking to himself what a strange character the crippled dwarf was.

The dwarf hunched deep inside his cloak and hunkered down on the hard wooden seat of the cart as he left. When the cart was out of sight he cracked the reins harder and sat straight up on the seat. The feebleness fell away from him and his twisted spine straightened. He seemed to grow taller in an instant.

He removed the useless eye patch and aimed a malicious glance behind him at Tor Ambroc receding quickly into the distance. He grinned widely.

How ironic he thought to himself. The dwarves of Tor Ambroc had accepted their own genocide with open arms. His smile widened considerably.

Savas-Zev was quite pleased with how it had all turned out.

"A plague you are, and a plague you will get," he muttered in satisfaction.

CHAPTER 18

Vilmar strode through the tunnels of Tor Ambroc, his arms laden with books and papers on the pronunciation of different languages. He was sure he had forgotten one page and so he was rifling through the stack as he walked, searching for the missing paper. He was barely paying attention to where his footsteps were leading, so engrossed was he in his search. He did not think he needed to pay attention for he had this part of the Tor's passageways memorized, even the tunnels which had low ceilings where he had to duck slightly.

He turned a corner and something, some other animal instinct, tickled his awareness and warned him to look up.

He stopped walking. Something was not right in this hallway. The air was too still and quiet for a busy underground dwarf thoroughfare. It was completely empty of any people of any race.

And yet, he was certain he was not alone. He straightened up to his full human height, his red curls only inches from the low ceiling. He felt completely on alert like a wild stallion the second before it scents a hiding wildcat.

Something was definitely out of sorts here.

He looked about, his eyes scanning the shadows for... what? He did not know. He wished he had the dwarven night vision, which allowed them to see even in the total blackness of the unlit corridors of their home. He saw nothing but guttering torches, casting their golden, flickering light on the carved stone walls. There truly was nothing more.

Vilmar distrusted the obvious.

Then a gust of wind gently smacked his face from far down the corridor's darkened depths. It made the torches hiss and nearly blow out before they straightened again.

He shivered from the top of his head to his toes for the breath was fresher than any dank, stale air, which lived underground—and cold, very cold. No, it wasn't just cold. It was freezing. An icy blast as of the wind from the forever frozen north, a wind which blows unceasingly over icy tundra and rock-hard lakes for days on end.

He shivered again. Vilmar took a deep breath and when he exhaled, he could see it hanging like a thick marsh fog in front of him. And through the icy fog, which was his exhalation, he saw a dark, shadowed movement far ahead of him.

He peered through the mist and darkness, willing his eyes to define the image. His eyes widened in disbelief and he blinked to be sure.

A tall, slender silhouette of human size was slowly approaching. It was definitely no dwarf, for it was not shaped as a dwarf nor did it move as a dwarf. It was tall and shapely, slightly female but thin, oh so incredibly thin. He could see the ends of the long hair as they wafted straight and slivered against the figure's waist. He could not see the hem of the garment she wore for it went all the way to the stone floor where it seemed to become part of the shadows, which rippled and flowed soundlessly behind the figure. She moved with the grace and sinister fluidity of a serpent, flowing effortlessly and seamlessly from one spot to the next. He could not see any sign of her feet.

Vilmar shivered again as he felt a nameless dread seize his heart. He could not explain to himself why he felt the fear but it proceeded before the figure like waves before a deadly undertow. He felt as if an unquiet ghost was approaching him and he could not control or master his fear. He was helpless to react. Terror rooted him to the spot and horror demanded he not look away.

The figure approached him, stopping at the nearest dancing torch and standing still and silent so he might have a good look. It was a human female but one like no woman he had ever seen before.

Her hair was raven colored, long and straight and she was bare of any jewelry or styling. She wore a plain, flat, black dress, which seemed to be made of darkness. Her skin was pale as snow, too pale to belong to any living thing. Her lips were as blue as the sun-touched ice. But it was her eyes which riveted him and demanded he not look away. Her eyes were not human. The pupils were white as if she were blind and surrounded by blackness darker than any he had ever seen before.

The gaze from those unearthly eyes froze the very blood in his heart and turned the marrow in his bones to icy slivers.

As he stood there frozen and helpless, he watched the blue lips part and move as she spoke to him. But no sound issued from her cold lips. And yet, there was her voice ringing icy and cold in his brain as it skipped his hearing ears entirely.

"*Do not be afraid*," spoke her voice in his brain, "*for I have not come for you.*"

A gust of cold air swirled in his very mind as she spoke.

The books and papers slid heedlessly from his arms. As they hit the ground, his feet seemed to suddenly be freed.

Not bothering to watch those dreaded blue lips smile, he spun and fled from her as if all the hounds of hell were nipping at his heels. He ran terrified through the maze of tunnels to his own small private bedchambers. There he stoked the fire with cold and trembling hands until it was roaring angrily to life. He wrapped himself in every blanket in the room for he was chilled to his very marrow and huddled close to the fire, shuddering and trying his best to forget it had even happened.

Finally, swathed in blankets, huddled in front of a raging fire, he fell asleep.

And he forgot anything had happened outside of dreamtime.

CHAPTER 19

Vilmar walked quietly through the forest glade searching for his unicorn matron. It was the day after the odd delivery at the trader's gates. But Vilmar had no knowledge of this. He was just interested in visiting with the unicorn.

He rounded a large oak and saw the half-grown unicorn fawn. He was really starting to look like a proper unicorn only, unlike his mother, he sported a few wisps of hair on his chin, the beginnings of a unicorn stag's beard.

But it was his stance which startled Vilmar. The fawn was staring straight toward him, eyes wide and ears locked in his direction. He was stiff and trembling, like a startled deer the second before it leaps away. All its attention was focused on Vilmar. The young unicorn flared his nostrils wide and snorted once, then twice—loud, explosive, warning snorts of a newly-sighted danger. Then, for the first time, it spoke to Vilmar's mind and his words were strange.

"You! Stay away from me! Don't come any closer!"

The adolescent unicorn hesitated one second more and then fled as if the huntsmen were after him.

Vilmar was confused. He followed after slowly, trying to keep out in the open and attempted to make his movements as non-threatening as he could. He didn't understand the young beast's reaction.

Then the stag appeared in front of him.

He had never seen his patron's mate. But this unicorn's stance also did nothing to reassure him. On the contrary, the body language the stag was sending Vilmar only alarmed him more. The stag had fixed him with a bold, challenging look, the look of a male whose family is threatened, the look of a male about to defend its mate and offspring.

The unicorn stag pawed the ground angrily and shook its proud head, setting its pearlescent mane dancing in the fractured morning sunbeams. The fawn peeked warily out from behind its father at him, feeling safer now a parent was between them.

Vilmar very slowly backed up a few steps. He knew he could never outrun either of them. He just wanted to put enough space between them to lessen the tension of the moment. He stayed facing the stag and the fawn. He made no effort to flee.

"I don't understand," he said slowly. "I mean you both no harm. What is the matter?"

The unicorn doe suddenly appeared behind them. She strode easily past her mate and son and came to within a few feet of Vilmar. He noticed the tension in the other two lessen considerably at her presence.

She sniffed the air inquisitively before Vilmar. Then strode back to the rest of her family and spoke the soundless tongue of animals to them. Their body language relaxed even more. The fawn wandered away and began to graze on the underbrush. The stag, however, did not leave or relax enough to eat. He remained where he was, ever watchful.

"What is going on?" Vilmar asked. "What's wrong? Why are they treating me like a stranger?"

"Relax, child," reassured the unicorn. *"You just smell different."*

"I've been with the dwarves for quite some time," he replied. "Apparently my scent is different than last time?"

"Yes, it is," the doe said.

She came closer still and touched his shoulder lightly with her lance, leaving it there for one long moment. Vilmar felt as though he had just stepped through a wall of warm water. It was a bit disorienting at first but the sensation passed quickly. Still, he found himself staggered from the experience.

"What was that for?" he asked as he got his land legs back under himself.

"I needed to cleanse you," she explained. *"You have been affected by a disease. My little one had never experienced the scent of infection and it confused and frightened him. He did not know how to react. But all is better with you now."*

"Disease?" Vilmar said. "What disease? I feel fine."

"This is what concerns me," the unicorn replied. *"It would not have hurt you. But you could have given it to any other dwarf you encountered. When was the last time you wrote Bran a letter?"*

94

He thought briefly.

"The last time I saw you, about two weeks ago," he replied.

Then something frightening occurred to him. "Is Bran in any danger?" he asked with growing consternation.

"Probably not. You did not smell like this then. Still..."

She did not finish her thought but strode back to her unicorn mate and conversed silently with him for a bit. Then she returned to Vilmar. The unicorn stag quickly ran away, heading back toward Tor Ambroc, the fawn also in tow.

"I have sent them to watch over the gates leading to the tunnels of Tor Ambroc. Every messenger hound going or coming from there must now be cleansed before it comes within contact of one of the dwarf inhabitants. This affliction only affects dwarves. You will be safe. But please do not touch or go near any strange dwarves from any other province."

"You've experienced this before?" he asked.

Silence was her only answer.

"How severe is this illness?" he asked her gravely.

"I'm afraid it is quite fatal, my dear," she replied with a grim gaze from her deep blue eyes. *"They call it the dwarf pox."*

"Then we must do something!" Vilmar exclaimed. "We've got to tell them and get your family to heal everybody in the tunnels..."

"You will do no such thing!" the unicorn replied sternly. *"It would kill all three of us. You would need a herd of about a hundred unicorns."*

"So I'm supposed to just sit back and watch them all die slowly?"

The unicorn raised her head, but her eyes never left his face. *"Yes,"* she replied levelly.

"I'm not sure I can do that," he said eventually after a very long moment.

"Vilmar, you must do nothing in this," she insisted.

He turned away shaking his head in denial. This couldn't be the way. He couldn't let this happen. He thought of Yaffa, Bran's mother. He liked her so much. Vilmar almost considered her his second mother. He was very fond of her. He thought of watching her die and it sickened him.

"I can't do this," he said in a whisper. "They've become my friends, my second family even. I can't just sit back and do nothing!"

"Vilmar, you must," the unicorn's voice sighed in his brain. *"And you must not say a word of this to Bran. This is not her path. Nor is it yours."*

He was silent for a long moment trying to puzzle through the revelation. He tried to find some way in his mind to change it. There had to be something he could do, some cleric, some incredible healer who could help. But he knew of no one.

"Vilmar, this is very important. You must do nothing," the unicorn repeated.

He growled angrily and punched his fist into the nearest tree. He stormed away from the unicorn without a word.

This wasn't right!

It was midnight and the commanders of all the companies had been called to the main tent for some secret reason. Dra-Oog sat with Iyorath and whispered speculatively about why they had been summoned as were all the other commanders. Vahan Isca, the Field Marshal, conversed privately in the center with his two main advisors, seemingly unaware of the many concerned glances which came to rest upon him from those gathered around. Finally he nodded and stood up, striking the hammer to address the crowd. Immediately all grew silent.

"I have called you all here to tell you some grave news which our spies have picked up. I have received word from the province of Tor Ambroc. It seems this Tor has been infected with the dreaded dwarf pox."

There was a loud gasp followed by much grumbling. The name Savas-Zev was tossed about in not too friendly terms.

Vahan raised his hands motioning he was not yet done with his news.

"Yes, we suspect Savas-Zev is at the bottom of this outbreak just like we suspected he was the cause of the massacre of the Fang-Tor kingdom. They certainly seem related."

"How certain are you it is the dwarf pox?" demanded a captain to the right of him.

"Not absolutely," Vahan replied. "But sure enough to take certain measures. I need not stress to all gathered here the degree of how contagious this disease is. I think we've all heard the stories as children.

I want to make absolutely sure this disease is kept out of the ranks of the Yazu. We are the protectors of our people. It certainly would not do if the first line of defense was wiped out."

There were grunts of affirmation and nodding heads from all there.

"Therefore I must insist on a new decree. No one here, or in any of your companies, is to have anything to do with anything from Tor Ambroc. No letters will be sent there, no messenger hounds from there will be allowed into camp—shoot them if you have to. No dead body of a shot messenger hound is to be touched by anyone! They must be burned immediately on dispatch of the animal's life. No personal leave there will be approved, nothing! I want all contact with Tor Ambroc to cease, even among the non-dwarf members of the Yazu."

Here his gaze turned to Iyorath. The elf paused for a long moment then nodded one time only, understanding the gravity of the request.

"The disease can be carried on non-dwarf members, on clothes, supplies and weapons and can still infect any dwarf it comes into contact with. This is why it is paramount all contact cease. Do I make myself clear on this?" he said sternly and his eyes roved the company, meeting each other pair of eyes personally for affirmation.

Not a word was spoken but all heads nodded.

"If anyone here has any members from the colony in their division, then I would advise extreme caution in how you deal with the situation. If told, they very possibly will want to drop everything and run for home to try to save family members. This must not be allowed to happen! No dwarf from Tor Ambroc will be allowed to leave the Yazu at this time. If they do and they return, they must be shot on sight."

His words chilled them to the bone. The idea of killing another dwarf who was not obviously an enemy was abhorrent. And yet, all understood Isca's reasoning for such drastic measures.

Vahan Isca uttered a heavy sigh and sat down. His next words were softer, more personal but no less important to the group.

"I have witnessed far too many promising young warriors killed before they had the chance to prove their true potential in battle. Such a great loss! And at Savas-Zev's murderous hands! I would hate to give him anymore playthings."

He nodded and waved his hand to dismiss them.

They filed out of the tent in a much more subdued mob and made their way silently back to their own tents one by one. Vahan had given them much to think about.

Dra-Oog and Iyorath stopped and looked at each other in consternation.

"What am I going to tell Delkan?" he said to the dwarf. "She just lost her family, her whole nation, a mere six months ago."

"What are we going to tell Bran?" Dra-Oog replied.

Iyorath considered this briefly. Then, raising a high arched eyebrow in speculation, mused quietly at the dwarf, "Should we even tell Bran?"

CHAPTER 20

Varg had died some time ago. Yaffa was still hanging on.

Vilmar sat in the chair next to Yaffa's bed. She had made a valiant attempt to fight off the disease but was spending more and more time abed as of late. Her smooth, golden hair had become like brittle straw and her skin had taken on a decidedly, unhealthy yellow tinge. A nagging cough had begun to trouble her as well. Sometimes violent fits of hacking would erupt and sometimes they brought up blood. Vilmar had now become her nurse.

"You wear the grim face for me?" Yaffa asked him when he thought her asleep.

"I'm sorry," he replied with a sad smile. "I wish I could help."

Yaffa returned his smile and took hold of his hand reassuringly.

"You can," she said in a much huskier voice than usual. "Stay and talk to me."

He took her tired, old hand in his strong ones.

"What about?"

"Well, for starters," she began. "Why don't you tell me who is training you in magic?"

Vilmar winced before he remembered to hide the reaction.

"How do you know?" he asked evasively.

"I saw you practicing the other night when you thought I was asleep," Yaffa explained. "I saw you light the candles and the fire in the brazier with no spark or flint. The flames just jumped out of your hands. And we all wonder where you get the magic stink from. You smell like a damned wizard. Who has been schooling you, child?"

"A unicorn," he replied. He didn't want to discuss her. He hadn't seen the unicorn doe since she had told him about the dwarf pox. He didn't want to see her anymore.

"A unicorn. Ah!" she breathed and paused briefly before saying. "Tell me more."

Vilmar gave a heavy sigh and did as she bid. He told her about the events surrounding his first meeting the unicorn. He told her about the foal's stone. He told her Bran knew about the unicorn. But he did not mention his last meeting with her.

"Ah!" she said finally after he had given her time to digest it all. "I feel much better now I know where your magic is coming from."

"You do?"

"Of course, child. You must be a very special person to attract the attention of a unicorn. They only accept individuals with the purest of hearts. A person with a unicorn for a patron is always very genuine and cannot lie."

"Oh really?" Vilmar said and a rueful tone crept into his words. He continued on, muttering more to himself than to her. "I'm lying to you right now."

"What did you say?" Yaffa asked sitting up. "I may be dying, but I'm not dead yet! What do you mean by that?"

Vilmar groaned and his eyes pleaded with her not to make him tell. But Yaffa was relentless.

"You tell me what you mean, boy, and don't say it's nothing!" she demanded.

He sighed heavily and confessed everything. "So there! I know you will die. I know all of Tor Ambroc will die and there's not a damn thing I can do to stop it, so the unicorn says."

"Oh child," Yaffa said squeezing his hand. "Do not blame yourself. And do not blame the unicorn. She is only doing what she is able to."

"But I don't understand!" he exclaimed in frustration.

Yaffa leaned forward and took both his hands in her withering ones.

"Listen, son. Listen carefully to what I have to say to you. Unicorns are not gods. But they are close to it. They live in a different world from us as far as perspective goes. They know things, things about the future, things it would take an oracle to predict for us—only with them they don't need rhymes and riddles. It's plain as day to them."

A little cough interrupted her words and she paused.

"The future is a many splendored thing. Some things are set in stone. Some things depend on what path the person chooses. Not all the future is subject to change. If your unicorn friend says it is our fate, our destiny, for all the dwarves of Tor Ambroc to die in a plague, then I for one, trust her instincts."

Her voice became steadily huskier and she stopped to clear her throat noisily.

"She will step in or step back as fate permits. She can do no more. A unicorn's powers are not without limitations. So please do not begrudge the beast her job. I am sure she cares deeply about you, and the fact you are so frustrated by this must wound her greatly."

Yaffa leaned back on the pillow and took a deep, raspy breath. "It is no mean thing to have a unicorn care about your life and your safety."

Vilmar grumbled and stared hard at the floor.

"Promise me you will get past this and continue your training with her. Promise me, Vilmar," Yaffa said.

Vilmar muttered some more but finally agreed. He could deny Yaffa nothing if she demanded it of him.

"Bran is not included in this plague, I know," Yaffa said softly. "And for this I am extremely grateful."

Vilmar gaped at her when she said this.

"How did you know that?" he asked flabbergasted.

"On Bran's birthday, Kusa, the oracle, predicted her future. And now I understand a particular line in his prophecy. *'Your people will need you when you think all is already lost.'* Now I know what he meant."

Yaffa turned her eyes to Vilmar and there was a fierce light in them. Yaffa's spirit was still interested in battle.

"After all of us are dead and gone, Bran will return. She will return to carry out her people's vengeance. I really wanted to be the one to end Savas-Zev's cruelty. It is obvious to me now that is not my path. So maybe my daughter will have a hand in eradicating this evil from the earth. You will help her in this."

Vilmar's eyes glittered dangerously and he smiled.

"That's it, boy!" Yaffa chuckled roughly. "If you run into the accursed wizard, you think of me lying here on my deathbed. Let the thought give power to your magic! You make him pay! You both make him pay!"

"It would be my pleasure, my lady," Vilmar said and he squeezed her hand tightly.

Yaffa started to laugh but her laughter melded into a coughing fit. Vilmar quickly braced her thin form as she struggled for breath and held a rag to her mouth. This episode brought blood up again. Finally, the horrible coughing ceased and she lay back, gasping and panting to catch her breath, wiping the blood from her faded yellow beard.

"There's something more, something I want you to have, and something I want Bran to have."

"What is it?"

Yaffa directed him to a small, safe-like portal dug into the wall and disguised by magic to hide it from strange eyes.

"Behind the secret door you will find a little wooden chest. Give it to Bran when you see her. It has a certain magical item and a letter in it for her. Since we are all infected, you had better let your unicorn friend have at it before you give it to her. Just to be on the safe side, you understand."

He nodded.

"And the other thing is the hound. I have no idea what will happen to the rest of the hounds since they seem to be out of work. Take them to the unicorn and let her do her thing, then set them free if you wish. But Snow Crow is the best. And now she's your hound. Take good care of her, she was always my favorite."

Vilmar smiled and thanked her. He had never told Yaffa, but the white hound was his favorite as well.

"You need your rest now," he scolded gently. "I'll be back to check on you later."

Vilmar tucked her in, then kissed her forehead like a doting parent. He blew out the candle and left the room.

Yaffa sat up the minute he was gone.

"You dear, sweet boy," she muttered to the dark. "What would I have done without you these last months?"

Then quietly, her fevered hands found the tiny vial of lethal blue liquid she always wore about her neck.

"Savas-Zev," she muttered angrily into the dark. "You have controlled every aspect of my life. You will not control my death!"

Her hands working quickly, she uncorked the bottle.

CHAPTER 21

One evening, a small patrol of about ten dwarves led by Dra-Oog left the encampment. Bran and Delkan were in this group.

Dra-Oog sat on her gray Phantom and addressed them. "It has been decided this group is doing well enough with their training to earn the right of being 'blooded'. Congratulations!"

There was a surprised pause from the assembled dwarves. Then, as one, they began to hoot and cheer. Finally they were to put their newly learned talents to the test! Finally they would see battle and earn the right of great tales and songs to be written about them.

"A small band of goblins has been sighted wandering rather close to this encampment. None must be allowed to escape. Take no prisoners. Kill any goblin you encounter. Is this clear?"

A great eager shout went up from the dwarves before her and Dra-Oog grinned back at them. She loved when the young soldiers were blooded!

"Very well then," she told them. "Go back to your tents and gather your favorite weapons and mounts and return to this spot in one hour. Iyorath and myself will accompany you to make sure none of you go weak on us. And if any fall this day in battle, I will sing your praises to the great Lord Dragon so you may enter the Warrior's Feast Hall with head held high and no shame on your spirit. Good hunting, warriors of the Yazu!"

The small group practically raced back to their tents for their articles and were all assembled back in less than an hour's time. Bran and Delkan had both chosen to bring out their Dahla horse mounts. Bran had planned Val to appear as a black mare this time and Delkan's Sashay was a flaxen chestnut-colored stallion slightly taller than Val. The horses stirred restlessly sensing the importance of the summoning.

Sashay paced eagerly in place, rocking Delkan gently like a ship at sea. Delkan carried her family's great spear. Bran had her bow and the last sword she had made.

"I suppose since your spear is magical it has a name?" she whispered to Delkan.

Her friend nodded without looking at her.

"It's called *'Goblin Tickler,'*" she replied with a wry smile. "Did you remember your horn of fog?"

"Of course," Bran shot back. "I never go scouting without it!"

Iyorath shushed them all from where he sat on his large, leggy chestnut gelding named Saraneth. He explained they were to split into pairs when they got near their quarry, always keeping the other rider in view, and surround the goblins if possible. The horns of fog would be blown when the attack was imminent to confuse the goblins. Bran and Delkan had also brought along a small assortment of 'bunny tickler' bombs as well for further confusion.

Iyorath gave the command and they moved out with Dra-Oog taking up the rear. They rode along at a silent but quick pace for about eight miles over the rolling countryside. There was no talking and they avoided any land with brush, which was too noisy to move through.

It was about midnight when Iyorath signaled them to halt. Dra-Oog came to his side and the group gathered in an expectant hush around them. Dra-Oog hooted like an owl and three scouts on foot melted out of the underbrush and approached. They resorted to hand signals to keep as quiet as possible.

The foot soldiers informed them as quietly as they could that there was a small encampment of about fifteen goblins in the vale over the next hillside. There was a large fire blazing and only two inattentive sentries posted so they had assumed the goblins were not expecting trouble.

Dra-Oog instructed everyone to split up into pairs and move to surround the goblins. The horns of fog would be blown to confuse their prey. The fog would not hinder the dwarves' eyesight as it only affected the enemy. At the horn blast, all were to charge the goblins *en masse* and take out as many as they could. This agreed, they moved out scattering into pairs.

Delkan and Bran moved in a westward direction praying no horse would neigh and alert the goblins. But as they crested the hill they saw there was little chance of the goblins hearing. They seemed to be in the middle of a great feast and were making a terribly loud drunken ruckus in their celebration. The liquor they raided must have been very good.

Bran guided Val on down the hill with leg pressure alone as she brought out and prepared her bow. A glance to her side showed Delkan was doing the same with her spear. They guessed someone had blown their foghorn for, although there was no sound, great waves of fog began to roll and curl about their ponies' legs, growing thicker with each passing step.

They approached within a couple hundred yards and stopped. It was enough distance to get a good speed up before crashing the camp. They stopped in thick cover with no heavy trees before them, giving them an open space for moving and firing.

Bran glanced toward Delkan. She sat still as if glued to Sashay's perpetually rocking back. Her mount's ears flickered constantly forward and back, awaiting the signal he knew would come. Sashay was tense but in control. Well, this was about as in control as Sashay got! As long as his feet were moving the tiniest bit, he would await the signal. But it did make Bran nervous Delkan's horse might rush the horn.

Bran could feel the expectation in Val beneath her. Valynt was trembling and Bran could feel her hindquarters bunching like tightened springs. She could also feel the great heart between her calves pounding with excitement. She whispered gently to calm her. Both of Bran's hands were busy with the bow, concentrating on her target goblin. She knew she had to trust Val to stay there until the signal was given.

A great loud ringing horn blast sounded. The goblins as one, stopped whatever they were doing and their eyes bulged. They then spun to make a dive for their weapons as the thunder of hooves came from all around them.

One fell dead, an arrow through his throat as his great claw closed around a weapon's hilt. Another twisted, grabbed an axe and spun to the advancing horsemen only to have an explosion go off in his face, blinding him. Val ran straight over top of him bursting into the firelight of the camp at the same time every other horse did.

Val gave a great leap and soared over the fire as Bran got a second shot off to the side, skewering another goblin through his lower arm. He gave a great screech and dropped his weapon. With a spray of gravel, Val and Bran dodged a horse and rider coming the other way and raced out of camp. Bran took the reins in one hand and spun Val around on her haunches. With the other hand she threw down her bow and drew the sword instead. A goblin was turning to face them and she stabbed him through the side of his ribcage. She let the force of her passage spin him about and spill him off her blade. She turned to find another target and assess the general battlefield.

Delkan had spitted a goblin and was backing Sashay expertly away to free her blade. A goblin leapfrogged onto Sashay's back behind her, brandishing a wickedly jagged knife. Bran screamed a warning to her.

But Delkan had the situation well in hand. She aimed a vicious fling of her head backwards and connected with the goblin's nose, caving it into his skull. She clutched his dagger with her free hand just as Sashay pinned his ears and reared straight up. Delkan clung like a tick but the badly maimed goblin had no idea how to stay on a horse through such a move and tumbled off the back.

"No one but me rides Sashay!" she spat and added, "Thanks for the knife."

She clamped her legs and signaled her mount as she saw five goblins make a move to surround her. At once Sashay tucked his nose in and began to pivot in place on his hind legs, his front legs spinning in a tight circle. Delkan held out the spear as they spun and swept the mass away from them.

Bran saw out of the corner of her eyes two goblins bolting for Val's tail. Val must have seen them, too. Up popped her hindquarters and out snapped her hind hooves with the speed of a striking snake. Her hooves connected with the jaws of both goblins, snapping back their heads with a sickening pop.

"Never sneak up on a strange mare, boys!" she laughed aloud.

There was a sudden shout from Delkan and Bran spun toward her.

She had pinned a goblin to a rock by his shoulder with her spear and waved to Bran to finish him off. But when she got to her, Bran was taken aback at what she saw. The goblin was still alive and laughing hysterically. It was laughing so hard it had dropped its sword.

"Go ahead, finish him!" Delkan shouted.

Bran raised her sword but almost immediately lowered it.

"What's the matter with you?" Delkan screamed. "Kill it!"

"But," stammered Bran, "he's laughing at me."

Delkan gave a frustrated growl and jerked her spear free from the goblin. Immediately, it stopped laughing and snatched up its sword again, charging Bran.

"Oh no, you don't!" Bran replied and with an angry slap, knocked it out of its hands. Her backswing opened up his chest and he fell at Val's feet.

"Feel better?" Delkan muttered.

"Much."

She looked at Bran and grinned ear to ear. "So what did you think a magic spearhead named *'Goblin Tickler'* did?"

Far away in a large tent, Savas-Zev watched the scene unfold in his scrying bowl and frowned. He turned his fearsome gaze on Dask who stood by his side.

"You see the one named Delkan, the one with the magic spear?" he said pointing to the bowl. Dask looked into the bowl and swallowing with difficulty, he nodded.

"I want the spear taken from her and I want her incapacitated."

Dask blanched white and trembled as he asked the next question. "Sir? You don't want her killed?"

Savas-Zev stepped back to his plush chair and seated himself. He folded his fingertips together and gave a slow, malicious smile.

"No, I don't want her killed. I want her incapacitated. If she has the audacity to survive the massacre at Fang-Tor then I want everyday hereafter to be an eternal hell. Make it so she will never ride again, if you please," he said with feigned politeness. He gave an exaggerated wave of his long hand and dismissed his servant.

Dask bowed low and raced out of his presence.

Savas-Zev leant forward and caressed the lip of his scrying bowl with the gentle touch of a lover, calculating his next move with sadistic desire, and relishing how the events to come would play themselves out. He would enjoy each little surprise he had planned for them.

But then he frowned to himself, remembering the second dwarf in the scene. His thin brows knitted as he searched his memory for something distant and long ago.

The other dwarf had bushy red hair and a beard just long enough to start braiding. She was obviously a juvenile. She looked so familiar to him somehow but he couldn't quite place the face.

Now just who did the dwarf remind him of?

"It's not right," Delkan nearly shouted at Iyorath. "She deserves to be told!"

It was the morning after the very successful skirmish with the goblins. The newly blooded dwarves had stayed up late celebrating their first victory. Bran had already retired and was dead to the world. Iyorath had chosen this time to reveal the bad news from Tor Ambroc to his friend. He thought since Delkan hadn't slept a wink with all the partying and would be obviously quite tired, he might not get much dissention from her. Plainly he had miscalculated the stamina of most dwarves.

Delkan was livid at the news.

"If you think I'm just going to stand by and say nothing while my dear friend's family is massacred the same way my own was, you're sadly mistaken!" she spouted at him as she paced back and forth.

"Delkan, please listen to me," Iyorath tried vainly to calm her. "It is imperative you say nothing whatsoever to Bran about this. If you do, we may lose her."

"Maybe it's worth taking the chance," Delkan fumed stomping about. "I can't believe what I'm hearing! By the Great Dragon, what kind of cowards do you think we are?"

"I would be wary of calling anyone a coward in this situation," the elf cautioned, trying his best to diffuse her before he himself exploded. "We cannot afford to lose anymore young fighters."

"Oh, I see! You'll save the few while letting the masses be slaughtered?" she replied. "But I guess it's all one could expect of an elf then, eh?"

"Delkan, you don't really mean..."

"Of course I mean it!" Delkan argued now approaching him and glaring up at his face. "You elves are always counseling us to back off when action should be taken. You live so long, you get to thinking you're gods or something!"

"Be careful what you say, Delkan, or..." Iyorath reasoned but the angry dwarf cut him off abruptly, not caring a bit about pushing the elf.

"Or what?" she nearly spat. "You'll do something which will actually make a difference?"

Iyorath suddenly picked Delkan up and slammed her back into a tree at eye level for him. His deep blue orbs were blazing like a boiling sea.

Delkan was startled for the merest of moments. Then she smiled and began to chuckle softly at him.

"It is a bit much to expect, I guess, of an elf. How could you understand what it is to be a Yazu?" she taunted softly.

"I may not be a dwarf or a female but I am as much a part of this army as you are my young, misguided friend," he said in a quiet tone, which held a thinly veiled warning. "You would do well to remember this."

He forced the anger out of his voice and his body and relaxed. He eased Delkan gently to the ground and released her. She shrugged off his grasp as he continued.

"And to remember we have a common enemy who has attacked more than just dwarves. This struggle is personal for so many here including myself. You do not need to be a dwarf to earn Savas-Zev's attention. You just need to be in his way."

Delkan gazed up at the elf with renewed interest. "You?" she asked and he nodded silently. "What did *you* do to make yourself a target to him?"

"I tried to be a wizard."

"Tried?" asked Delkan. "You tried and failed?"

His silence and the gravity of his expression was his answer.

Slowly, quietly, in a voice barely above a whisper, he went on. "It took my family's death to teach me I was never meant to be a wizard," he explained. "You see I come from a long and proud line of elfin magic users. All I ever wanted to be was a wizard. I refused any other path even though it was right for me. I didn't want to shame my family."

He saw he had sparked the young dwarf's curiosity. He motioned to a couple of nearby stumps and they seated themselves for the tale.

"My parents were both wizards. So were my older twin brother and sister. The magic flowed in them and through them. But with me, it made a drastic detour around to avoid me. No matter how I tried or how hard I studied, magic never worked for me. But I kept trying even though it made me the laughingstock of family get-togethers and outings."

"Well, I can't fault your determination," Delkan said and a brief smile whisked across the elf's sad face. The reply was so dwarvish!

"How did you run afoul of Savas-Zev?" she asked.

"My parents had decided to take my twin siblings and eradicate this evil from the world forever. But everyone counseled them to leave me behind. They said I would ruin everything if I was included in this venture and it was too important a mission to screw up."

"But you went anyway," Delkan said and after a time, Iyorath nodded.

"They managed to delay but not stop me," he continued. "I found my parents and twins just as Savas-Zev struck them. Foolishly, I struck back at him thinking, and wrongly so, my magical blood would afford me some protection from his attack. I was so stupid!"

This last sentence was said with such a tone of self-loathing Delkan's heart was pained by it. She said nothing though and allowed him to continue.

"He flung me across the room and into a wall. I found him bending over me and laughing when I awoke. He held a crystal ball in his hands. The crystal had four stars of light spinning around inside. He told me he had taken the souls of my family and trapped them within the crystal. Their bodies still lived but if their souls were not returned to them soon, their physical forms would die. He then disappeared."

Iyorath sighed and rubbed his face wearily.

"You never found the crystal in time, did you?" Delkan said quietly.

"No, I didn't and I never did find out where he had escaped to," Iyorath said in a heavy voice. "I cared for the bodies of my parents and siblings as long as I could, searched for magic ways to extend the brief time which was allowed to them but in the end, all my plans crumbled to dust in my hands. They are truly dead now. And elves should not die."

He sighed again and covered his eyes.

"The worst part of it is I can still hear them in my head. Their souls are trapped and cannot go on. They are restricted from going forward or back. This is the most horrible torment imaginable for a soul. Every night I fall asleep to their wails for help. Every time my mind is still, I hear them. I yearn to help them and I cannot. So, I am in as much torment as they are. We are all trapped in the web which Savas-Zev has spun for us."

After a long silence, he continued.

"I joined up because I thought if I could not stop him personally, then at least I wanted to be part of the organization which did. There is my revenge."

Delkan thought deeply for a bit.

"I am touched by your story, really I am," she said hesitantly not wanting to be rude.

"But?" the elf asked.

"But it still doesn't change things with Bran," she said. "She has a right to know what is going on at home and a right to choose whether to leave and help or stay here. And I am still going to tell her if you don't."

Dra-Oog suddenly stepped out from behind a nearby tent. The look on her face told them she had heard most of the conversation.

"Iyorath and I are your commanding officers," she said sternly. "We can order you to keep your mouth shut to Bran."

Delkan nodded considering, acting not at all concerned Dra-Oog had heard her.

"My answer is still the same," Delkan replied, raising her head proudly. "If you don't tell her, I will. She should know. It's her right."

Dra-Oog nodded quietly, her eyes narrow and angry.

"Very well then," she said and the tone of finality in her voice told them she had reached an important decision.

"Delkan, you are to report at once to Garn-Ithel's company."

Iyorath stood up looking surprised.

"They are heading out on patrol within this very hour. A larger company of goblins and some trolls have been sighted and they are wary. You will go with the company to dispatch them."

"Is Bran coming along?" she asked hesitantly.

Dra-Oog's silence and stormy expression were her only answer.

"You're doing this to punish me, aren't you?" she declared in shock.

"Delkan, a soldier of the Yazu is expected to follow the orders of her commanding officers. She is not expected to approve, like or agree with those orders. She is just expected to obey them. You will go with Garn-Ithel and you will learn to obey his orders today. If you comply well enough, you may live to see Bran again. Is this understood?"

Without waiting for a reply, Dra-Oog stalked away. Delkan turned to face Iyorath but he had shielded his expression from any emotion.

"Be careful, Delkan," he warned. "Be sure to empty any anger from your heart before this fight. Having your mind elsewhere in a skirmish can get you killed. And trolls are some pretty tough customers. Forget this conversation and watch your back."

He left her standing there with whirling emotions. The horn blast for Garn's company to form up jolted her back to her senses. She sprinted to get her weapons and her mule, Pitch.

CHAPTER 22

Bran rolled over and groaned. The liquor from the night before had left her head reeling and her vision blurred. Oh, but what a good time they'd had! At least, what she could remember of it. She moaned and started to stand but fell out of her little cot. She felt like she had been bucked off a very tall horse. The earth felt much harder than the night before. She crawled to her knees and slowly clawed her way to her feet.

She noticed Delkan's cot had not been slept in. This was very strange. She staggered unsteadily out of her tent and shielded her eyes against the sun's light. When her eyes had adjusted and her head decided to spin slower, she roughly estimated the time of day to be around sunset. It seemed she had slept the whole day away.

She rummaged clumsily about her camp searching for something to wash away the furry taste in her mouth. She found the mules' bucket and dunked her head into the icy cold water, gasping in shock as she withdrew it. She shook off the excess like a wet dog and glanced around blinking.

It was then she noticed only her mule, Echo, was picketed next to their tent.

Her head cleared faster at the realization. She ran about their tent, taking quick note of the things which were missing. Pitch was gone along with his saddle and bridle. *Goblin Tickler* was also missing along with its owner.

Maybe they had been called to form up while she was still in her drunken stupor, she supposed. So she ran about the encampment and noticed the rest of their company was still there, minus Delkan of course.

"Gethin!" she called to another dwarf who sat outside her tent polishing her saddle with three other dwarf ladies. "Have you seen Delkan anywhere?"

Gethin exchanged worried looks with the other dwarves.

"Dra-Oog ordered her to go out and deal with another troop of goblins," she replied. "She was to join Garn-Ithel's company."

"What? With no sleep after our first encounter?" she said puzzled. "Why?"

The other dwarves shrugged unable to help her with this.

"Dra-Oog wasn't too happy with her, last I heard," said Gethin. "We think she was sent out to be taught a lesson. At least this is what the camp gossip says."

Bran's face wrinkled in confusion.

"Well, uh, when did they leave?" she asked rubbing the back of her neck totally perplexed by this strange turn of events.

"Mid-morning," the other returned. "They should be returning anytime now if all went well."

Bran muttered her thanks and turned away. She wandered through camp aimlessly, splitting head forgotten, her thoughts in turmoil.

What was Delkan in trouble for? Could it be she got caught in another prank? If this were true, would Bran be the next one to be 'taught a lesson?' Would they be split up over this?

She had no idea. But after a little thought, she supposed it had to be something other than their pranks. This only would have earned them a reprimand, not being sent out on a dangerous patrol. No, there was something else going on here.

She decided to find Iyorath and ask him. Somehow she felt better questioning the elf rather than the stern-faced, dwarf warrioress. Bran had heard tales of Dra-Oog when she became really angry and did not want to discover the truth of this the hard way.

She found the elf on the edge of camp with his eagle. Rath-Tor had just caught a nice, fat rabbit and the elf was having some trouble persuading the bird to release it.

"Iyorath, do you know if Delkan is back yet?" she asked him.

She stopped suddenly at the look on his face. His eyes were glassy, as if from unshed tears. He turned away.

"What is it?" she demanded. "What has happened?"

"Garn-Ithel's troop just returned," he reported without looking at her or turning to face her. "Their ambush was successful. There was only one casualty."

Bran's eyes widened slightly.

"Delkan?" she whispered in horror.

Iyorath nodded once.

The color drained from Bran's face.

"The healers are working on her now. It's too soon to know anything yet," he said but she barely heard him.

Bran spun on her heels and raced through the Yazu encampment to the healers' tent. It stood next to the largest tent in the center. She zigzagged between people and horses, barely hearing their shouts. Her heart was in her mouth, her lungs labored and her feet stung from the abuse but she didn't care.

Delkan had been hurt. She was a casualty. It couldn't be possible.

Bran's mind screamed, refusing to believe it.

'Please, don't let it be too bad!' she pleaded with any deity there was. 'Please let it be minor!'

But a vicious dread was growing within her, a feeling she did not want to face.

She rounded the last tent and saw the entrance to the healer's quarters loom into view. A knot of people was gathered around the entrance and red-robed healers were going back in through the tent flap.

Someone was screaming in sheer agony, over and over and over.

Bran yelled Delkan's name and hurled herself at the entrance.

Dra-Oog and two other dwarves caught her and wrestled her back.

"Who is this?" demanded a very irritated, red-robed elfin healer.

"Her friend," Dra-Oog managed to inform him as she struggled to shove Bran back.

"Well, keep her outside then!" the healer ordered. "She'll only interfere with things. Take her away!"

The three dwarves were trying, with much difficulty, to do so.

Then next thing Bran remembered was Dra-Oog's fist crashing into her face and sending her mind into black oblivion.

She woke up some time later. Her head was still spinning slightly and she felt her left eye swelling shut from the punch to her face.

"Now," Dra-Oog said as she sat down beside her. "Are you going to listen to what I have to say or am I going to have to tip you over again?"

But Bran's frenzy had lessened considerably.

"I'll be good," she mumbled with difficulty through her bruised and swollen cheek. "Delkan?"

"Delkan lives yet," Dra-Oog reported. "But it will be very touch and go for a while and the healers must be free to do their job if they are to save your friend. This may take a while."

"I'll wait," Bran muttered.

"Wait is all any of us can do right now," the elder dwarf consoled.

Dra-Oog left her sitting on an upside-down bucket, wrapped in a sheepskin. Some time later, Garn-Ithel joined her to talk.

"What happened to her?" she asked him. "Is Delkan going to die?"

Garn gave a great sigh.

"Might," he grunted briefly. "She's lost an awful lot of blood."

They sat still and silent for some time, neither one talking, just watching the other soldiers lighting their lanterns one by one as the daylight dimmed.

"This was not supposed to happen," he finally muttered. "I was supposed to teach her a lesson. She was just supposed to get roughed up a bit. She was not supposed to almost die."

"What happened?" Bran asked again.

"The trolls did it," he explained his voice faint and distant from the fog of shock he was still in. "They shot Pitch dead from underneath her. We had to cut a path through to get to her and by then the damage was done."

Garn took a deep breath and held it for a long time before he spoke again. "They cut off her legs, Bran."

Bran looked as though someone had punched her in the gut. She stammered helplessly a bit before she could finally get out the words.

"But... you saved the legs... right?" she asked.

Bran knew if healers had a small touch of magic, they could do wondrous things, even reattach a severed limb. They had several elfin healers in camp who were quite strong in healing magic. Certainly, she thought, they would be able to heal Delkan.

"No, we couldn't," Garn said with a haunted look in his eyes. "As I said, we had to fight our way through to get to her. By this time, those accursed trolls had already eaten her legs and they were starting to gnaw on Pitch's body. There was nothing left to save."

Bran felt sick. The thought of what had happened to her friend revolted her. She squeezed her eyes shut and shook her head to erase the mental image from her mind.

"Damned trolls!" she whispered flatly.

Garn nodded and sighed heavily.

"This is all my fault," he moaned hanging his head. "She had such talent with a weapon. Now it's all over."

Delkan would be crippled for life, unable to stand or walk or run. She would be doomed only to sit and watch the world go by, denied an honorable death in battle.

It was too cruel. It was not right.

Bran wrapped the sheepskin tighter and her mind receded into black thoughts.

They waited for Delkan to come back to them.

Bran left the healers' tent a short time later unable to bear the sounds. She could hear Delkan's screams coming from inside where the healers worked to stabilize her. It sounded like they had given her something to bite down on but she was screaming through it. It took a lot of pain to make any dwarf cry out. The sounds from Delkan went right through Bran like an icy wind in winter. Finally, she couldn't bear it any longer.

Garn-Ithel went with her. He was more a comforting presence than anything else. She knew his misery was akin to hers so she let him stay with her for a while in her tent.

They spoke a little. Mostly they just sat and stared blankly into the coals of the small campfire. She made a hot brew to warm them but it was wasted. The drink's heat could not warm their hearts.

Finally, hours later, an elfin healer approached their tent. Bran and Garn-Ithel stood expectantly, trying to keep the dread from showing on their faces. Dra-Oog and Iyorath came with the healer. Dra-Oog's face was impassive. Iyorath simply looked drained.

"She'll live," the healer said with a long, tired sigh. "We finally got the wounds to stop bleeding just a little while ago. But it's been quite a blow to her. I can do nothing to heal her heart."

"Can I see her?" Bran asked.

"I gave her a sleeping potion to put her out and help her body to start the healing process," the healer informed.

Garn-Ithel shrugged.

"She's been awake for too long fighting this," he muttered. "Throughout the whole ordeal, she never lost consciousness. And she was awake long before we were sent out."

"Yes, since the first fight with me," Bran mused distantly. "I still want to see her."

The tall, thin healer looked narrowly at Bran, considering this option. Finally he nodded.

"Your friend is an extremely tough customer," he admitted with a wry smile. "No sleep, a night of drinking followed by a nearly fatal wound, an arduous trip back to camp leaking blood all the way and she never blacked out or gave in to exhaustion. But then, she's a dwarf. Why am I surprised?"

He nodded again and gripped her shoulder reassuringly.

"If anyone can survive this suffering and turn it around, it will be Delkan. But you too are tired. I will see if we can't have another cot set up alongside hers. I know you don't want to sleep, but sleep you need and sleep you will have if I have to drug you to do it! Now come with me."

He led her back to the healers' tent. Delkan's cot was at the far end behind a blood-splattered privacy screen.

He gently guided Bran to her bedside. Bran shivered and looked at her friend's face. Delkan's expression seemed very tired but at peace. Her bushy black mane and brown beard were matted with troll ichor. Her clothes and face were speckled with dried blood. Her eyes came to rest on the Dahla horse she always wore about her neck just as Bran herself did. Bran sighed heavily.

She then forced herself to look toward the foot of the bed where the sheets went flat far sooner than they should have. She began to shudder without understanding why.

The healer's touch on her shoulders made her jump and chased away the trembling.

"Do not be afraid," he said softly. "She is in no pain now."

The healer sat down across from her and fixed her with his hawk-like gaze.

"Give her a good look over now before she wakes up. This is the way she will be for the rest of her life. You both will have to deal with it now. I hope you are friend enough to stand by her through this."

Bran looked up at him in shock.

"Why wouldn't I stand by her?" she asked in an insulted tone. Bran thought briefly and continued in a softer voice. "This could have been me."

"Maybe, but I doubt it," the healer said.

Bran didn't understand his words.

"This is Delkan's path and hers alone. She must come to grips with it within herself. It will be a lonely road for her to walk. And she will have to walk it alone. But she will need your support."

His words were puzzling. She couldn't make any sense of them. So she shifted her mind to other things.

She looked at Delkan's peacefully sleeping form critically, estimating just where the sheets went flat after her torso.

"Will she ride again?" she asked hopefully.

The elf sniffed and left her saying, "Not likely."

She hated his tone of voice and she hated his words. She decided right then and there she did not like healers very much.

Bran awoke some hours later to find Delkan already awake and sitting up, staring blankly off into the distance.

She sat up and called her name softly. It was then Bran noticed Delkan's wrists were bound and there was a guard posted next to her bed.

Delkan's eyes dropped to her lap and she grunted wryly.

"They've put me on a suicide watch," she explained. "Somehow they think a poor, crippled dwarf is a threat."

Bran glared at the stone-faced guard. Delkan caught the look and smiled.

"Will you do me a favor, Bran?" she asked quietly.

"Anything, as long as it isn't slitting your throat," she replied and her wounded friend smiled.

"Don't worry. It's not that. Not yet at least," she turned and stuck her tongue out at the guard who continued to remain impassive.

"Since they think I obviously can't be trusted with anything sharp... will you do the *ashra* ceremony for me?"

The *ashra* ceremony was a ritual of grieving for the loss of a life or of a way which would no longer be, giving thanks and recognition for the past and accepting the struggle to continue. Bran was greatly flattered and nodded, squeezing her hand and left to get the supplies.

She returned a short while later with a bowl of warm water, a towel, scissors, some sweet smelling oil and a sharp razor.

"Don't worry if you nick me," Delkan reassured. "The brief pain will be nothing like what I've just gone through."

Bran understood it well enough. Taking a deep breath she took the razor and set to work on scraping the thick, black hair from her friend's head. Hesitantly, she started to chant and Delkan joined in to strengthen and reassure her. As the long blue-black locks fell from Delkan's skull, they chanted the ancient words in the old dwarf tongue. They called to the gods and the spirits of those dwarves who had passed before, to notify them one of the living had endured a great tragedy and needed support.

Their voices blended and complimented each other. Soon the dwarf guard joined in, adding his deep intonation to the beautiful ancient words. Another dwarf voice rose from somewhere in the healers' tent and another joined in. Soon every dwarf within earshot had joined in the old chant and the air vibrated with the power of their voices.

The elfin healers came hurrying to see what the ruckus was about and the guard stepped in front of them without ceasing his chant. The message of his body language was clear. They could watch but not interfere with the *ashra* ceremony.

Bran continued to scrape Delkan's mane as if they weren't even there. Delkan's bushy hair gave way to the smooth, shining skin of her scalp. Her voice faded. She now drew strength from the chorus about her. She could feel the vibration of the old ones who had gone before in the air around them. Delkan had bowed her head and shut her eyes, absorbing what she needed from them, consoling her spirit. Bit by bit, Bran shaved Delkan's head until she was completely bald.

Quietly, Delkan whispered to Bran, so as not to disrupt the empowering chant, "Go ahead. Take the beard as well."

But Bran refused and coming around to the front of the bed, looked her friend sternly in the eyes.

"I will cut but not shave the beard. You are a dwarf, not a gnome."

Delkan relented and let her scissor the length of the beard until there was not enough to braid. She then cleaned up the stray hair and massaged sweet smelling oil into her friend's bare scalp.

"It is done," she said just as the dwarf voices faded one by one into silence. Their guard was the last to stop his chant, letting his rich, deep voice linger on the last few notes fondly as they were suspended in the air.

He then strode up to Delkan and in plain sight of the observing elf healers cut her bonds.

"It is done," he repeated to them. "No one who has chanted the *ashra* would commit suicide. It is a spiritual affirmation to continue, not to give up. Those beyond will hold her to the promise she has just made."

He turned back to Delkan and bowed in deep respect to her. He then silently left their presence.

Bran sat down beside her wounded friend. She took Delkan's hands and said nothing to her but touched her friend's forehead with her own. One single tear on each cheek traced its way down Delkan's face. She refused to allow the others to fall. They just stayed there, enjoying each other's company and soaking up the fading energy from the ritual.

They felt deep in their hearts performing the *ashra* ceremony had helped them both immensely.

CHAPTER 23

Bran now became Delkan's nurse. She never left her friend's side for the first two weeks after the attack. Dra-Oog relieved her temporarily from her soldiering duties to see to her friend. It certainly freed up the healers from Delkan's daily care.

She massaged Delkan's back when she became bedsore. She changed her bandages and slathered healing salve on her wounds. She helped her in every way and kept her spirits up as well.

Members from their company stopped by to visit but as time went on, their visits became less frequent and finally ceased altogether. Bran hated them for this. Dra-Oog and Iyorath stopped by as regularly as their duties permitted and kept them appraised of the goings on in camp along with Garn-Ithel. They did not stop coming.

Garn-Ithel's visits actually increased over time. Pretty soon he was checking in on 'his girls' every day. He even decided to help out with Delkan's daily care and Bran was grateful for the break. He also seemed to have a very sympathetic ear whenever Bran or Delkan needed it. Garn-Ithel was turning out to be a great friend.

One time Delkan asked him to bring her a pile of small pebbles and put them by her bedside. Whenever Delkan needed Bran or needed something of anyone, a pebble would smack them. Bran grew to hate those damn pebbles!

"Do me a favor and never make her a slingshot!" she grumbled at Garn.

But Garn only grinned slyly. The next day, a slingshot magically appeared next to Delkan's bed. She quickly became deadly with it and would have people fleeing and cursing from her pebbles.

But Delkan was suffering from frequent bouts of depression between these times.

One day, Bran awoke to find her staring quietly at her Dahla horse and turning it over and over fondly in her hands.

"I will never ride Sashay again," she said quietly to herself.

"Never say never," Bran told her.

But Delkan glared scornfully at her and only repeated, "I will never ride Sashay again."

A few days later she saw Delkan straighten up expectantly as she heard a horn blast. Bran watched the emotions play across her face as she heard someone bellow for a troop to form up. She heard the clink of the bridles, the neigh of horses, the scuff of hooves and the eventual thunder as the troop left the encampment on another scouting expedition.

She sighed in sad longing, wanting so much to be back out there.

She was progressing more and more in her healing every day. Her wounds had closed and the new skin was looking thicker and healthier. She was becoming more and more independent. She was learning to move around with her torso and had even rolled out of bed a few times and been found on her way out of the tent, crawling on her strong arms.

In a way, this both amused and saddened Bran. It was good seeing her friend so determined. But then she wondered, where could she possibly go?

One day, when she and Garn were alone, she asked him this.

"Delkan's almost healed up," she said. "Now what will happen to her? She can't go home. There's nothing left. Maybe I could get my parents to take her in. They took in Vilmar."

"I don't think it's a good idea," stammered Garn suddenly. "You know how your father is."

She nodded in agreement and Garn uttered a secretive sigh of relief to this.

"I'll see what I can work in my clan," he said. "There shouldn't be much of a problem. We have quite a few old campaigners. They're quite good craftsmen."

Bran turned her head so Garn wouldn't see her curl her lip in utter disgust.

Delkan, a craftsman. How degrading! And she was hardly old enough to be considered 'an old campaigner.'

"She's certainly deadly enough with the slingshot you gave her," Bran mused ruefully. "Couldn't we use her here? There's nothing wrong with her arms. She could still shoot or wield an axe…"

Her voice faded into the distance as she saw the 'How ridiculous!' look coming from Garn.

She returned her head to her hands.

"She can still fight," she mumbled quietly.

"The only people she will be fighting now will be obstinate nurses and master healers!" Garn growled back. "Delkan's fighting days are over."

Bran disagreed but kept her thoughts to herself and grunted in return.

The next day Bran and Delkan were sitting outside the healer's tent soaking up the sunshine. It was a glorious day and Bran had found the perfect spot in the dappled shade under a tree, away from the many staring eyes.

Bran saw a messenger hound lope silently through camp. It suddenly occurred to her there had been no letters to her from home for quite some time, several weeks in fact.

Something was wrong. She could feel it in her marrow.

"Bran? What's the matter?" Delkan asked.

"I just realized, I haven't received any letters lately," she told her. "It's not like Vilmar not to write for so long. I need to drop him a note."

"Bran, you can't. It's not allowed," Delkan told her slowly.

Bran gave her a shocked look.

"Not allowed?" she sputtered. "Why not? Who gave such an order?"

Delkan heaved a great sigh and looked warily up at Bran.

"I never told you how my family died, did I?" she asked.

"No," she returned. "And anyway, what does how your family died have to do with me not being allowed to write a simple letter home?"

"Quite a lot actually," Delkan replied. "Now sit down. This tale will take a bit of telling."

Bran remained standing and glared at her. Delkan fixed her with a mean stare and Bran finally relented. Delkan had her full attention now.

"My family died six months ago. The pain is still fresh. But I have to tell you their story. There are certain... similarities between us now.

"Savas-Zev killed them all, my whole big family along with my whole clan and every single dwarf who was dwelling in the Fang-Tor province at the time. I was gone from home when it happened. I was out on a boar-hunting trip with a neighboring elf tribe my people had decided weren't as irritating as most elves. You see, my family is known for their passion in exciting boar hunts and I was no exception. Anyway, I was away from home when it happened.

"Somehow a delivery of tainted dwarf mead made it into Fang-Tor. Whoever drank the mead got the dreaded dwarf pox. Once the disease latched onto a few dwarves, no one needed to drink it to get it. Just being around an infected dwarf was enough to infect all the other dwarves. The local elves we traded with, found out about the dwarf pox and sealed up the gates to Fang-Tor. No dwarf inside was allowed out and if they escaped they were shot on sight.

"I went a little mad when they told me my homeland was off limits. They kept me locked in a cell until every dwarf died and then they went in and collapsed the tunnels. Fang-Tor is now a tomb and no dwarf is allowed to approach within fifty miles of the place. The elves guard it night and day. For my own safety, I was banished from my home.

"I never got to say goodbye to my family. I am homeless and clanless now. All because of Savas-Zev."

Bran was silent for a long time, digesting this news. She then turned her green gaze back to her friend.

"So, why tell me this?" she asked not comprehending.

"Because he's doing the same to Tor Ambroc right now," Delkan replied and the gaze she fixed Bran with was a haunted one.

"No one is allowed to go to Tor Ambroc. If any messenger hounds from there are sighted, they're under orders to shoot them on sight. If any dwarf goes there and returns, they too will be shot on sight. Especially you, Bran."

Bran felt lightheaded and sick all at the same time. She paced around the tree trying to get a grip on her feelings. They only swirled and grew. She took a deep breath to clear her head but her nausea increased. She finally ran to the back of the tree and vomited her guts up.

This could not be happening. Her mother... her father... were they already dead? What about Vilmar? How would this affect him?

"I wasn't supposed to tell you," Delkan continued. Bran heard her only distantly through a fog. "They had decided to keep this from you to protect you. Protect you!"

Delkan snorted in disgust at the comment.

"I don't know whether they were really trying to protect you or they were just afraid you would bring it back and infect all the Yazu. I argued you had a right to know what was happening to your family. When they heard I was going to tell you anyway, they sent me out with Garn-Ithel and I came back like this. The ironic part is, I hadn't told you yet. So I was punished before the crime was committed."

Bran had wandered back to collapse in shock in front of Delkan. She looked shakily up to her face.

"My family... my mother... Daga?" she stammered.

Delkan gave her a look of such pity and shook her head in denial.

"I'm so sorry, Bran," she whispered. "I wasn't supposed to tell you at all. What will you do?"

"I don't know exactly," Bran said as if drugged. "Go and stop it, I guess, somehow."

"Bran, please think about it, will you?" Delkan pleaded. "If you do decide to try and stop it... I won't say you shouldn't. I don't think the Yazu's policy on this is the right thing. But if you do go, think. Think very hard about this. Don't just go charging off without a plan. Please think very carefully about this. Promise?"

Bran nodded vaguely, barely hearing.

Her family might be dead. And there might be nothing she could do.

Bran did think instead of bolting for home. But after Delkan's great revelation, Bran needed space. She went back to her tent and gave the cold shoulder to any who approached. She wished for more privacy for her thoughts than the middle of a war camp.

She did think about it. She thought very hard. She paced in her tent and was at a loss at what to do. Her heart screamed at her to run home now, this very instant. Her head understood the restrictions and the decrees concerning her home. But other more personal questions kept coming to the forefront of her thoughts.

Was Yaffa still alive? What about Varg? And Daga, did he yet live? Where was Vilmar and what was he doing about all this? Could he do anything at all? And the unicorns, could they help? They should help, Bran thought, but she also knew unicorns could be strange beasts in desperate times.

What should she do? She found herself pacing in front of her horse paddock next to her tent. Then she noticed Echo her mule. He had stopped grazing and was staring expectantly at her as she paced, even mirroring her motions as much as he was able. He expected her to do something. He expected the something to include him. His strange blue eyes never left her for one moment and his grass was forgotten.

She strode up to him and stroked his sleek black sides reassuringly.

"Yes, dear one. We are leaving," she whispered secretly to her friend. "But not now, not during the daylight. No one can see us leave, understand?"

He butted her gently with his face and would have nickered if he'd had a voice. Bran smiled and was glad he was mute. It would make their leaving easier.

Maybe the unicorn could help. She could do something at least.

CHAPTER 24

My dear friend Iyorath,

 I know about the dwarf pox in Tor Ambroc. Delkan told me. Now, please don't be cross with her. She felt she was doing the right thing. I have not gone busting off for home. I have considered this carefully. I love the Yazu. But I have to see if I can be of any help at home and I must know if any of my kin yet live. I will do my utmost best to avoid any contagion; you have my word on this. A certain helpful... situation... may present itself and aid Tor Ambroc. I am leaving to see what I can do to push things along this way. I promise nothing. But I must at least try it my way first. If I fail, then you may condemn me with my blessing. But please give me a chance to put my theory to work.

 I hope I will see you all again in better times.

 Your young pest,
Bran
P.S. Look after Delkan for me and protect her from Dra-Oog's fists. I know she will not be pleased!

Iyorath growled and crumpled up the parchment in frustration. This was not good! Everything they were afraid of happening had occurred. He cursed his decision to ever tell Delkan anything about Tor Ambroc.

He made for the healers' tent at a running walk on his long legs, uncrumpling and rereading the note over and over again, trying to find some way out of this mess. This was definitely turning out to be a bad day.

Delkan was talking to Garn-Ithel at her bedside. They both looked up at Iyorath's approach. Garn stood up protectively and Delkan straightened when they saw the look on the tall elf's face.

"She's gone, isn't she?" Delkan asked in a very small voice.

"Yes, she's gone, no thanks to you!" Iyorath said and flung the note at her. "Are you happy now?"

"Good!" Delkan said smugly.

"Who's gone?" asked Dra-Oog as she entered the healers' tent.

Her pale gray eyes took in the situation and the friends, noting the only one missing. She strode angrily up to Delkan's bedside.

"No!" she growled and the healers, as one, scattered. "Delkan, you didn't! Please tell me I'm thinking the wrong thing!"

Iyorath answered for her.

"Bran's gone. She went back to Tor Ambroc."

"Fool!" Dra-Oog screamed.

Quick as a striking snake, her hand flew out and she slapped Delkan hard across the face, knocking her back into the pillows.

"How dare you!" Garn bellowed shielding Delkan from any more attacks. "How dare you strike a wounded soldier!"

"Oh Garn, drop it! Why do you think I didn't use my fist?" she bellowed back.

Delkan was holding her stinging face but her eyes were blazing, gray storm clouds.

"Delkan's not helpless! Not from the lightning I see in her eyes now," Dra-Oog scolded coldly. "And she's no longer a wounded soldier. When the healers clear her, she's out of here! You are no longer a Yazu! You are dead to us!"

Delkan shrieked and hurled herself at Dra-Oog in pure fury but Garn held her back.

The elder dwarf turned away from her as if she were dead already.

"Iyorath, you have the fastest horse in camp. Go after Bran! Bring her back before she can cause any more damage. That is all!"

She turned from the three and stalked out, making healers cringe all about her.

Iyorath turned back to Delkan who slumped helplessly in Garn's arms whimpering. He gave her a frustrated yet sympathetic and helpless look and turned to go.

"Wait, elf," Delkan demanded of him.

Iyorath turned back.

Delkan raised her head slightly, revealing one eye, glittering lightning in angry determination above her arm.

"I'm going with you," she said clearly, defiantly.

"What?" exclaimed Garn in shock. "You can't! You're a..."

"I'm a what? A legless cripple?" she finished for him. She turned her gaze on Garn and he recoiled from her like the healers had just done from Dra-Oog.

"I made this mess and I'm going to clean it up," she returned stubbornly. "I'm going with you."

Garn-Ithel said nothing for a long moment. He just stood there fidgeting and chewing on his lower lip. Finally he nodded.

"If it be the case and you're set on this, then I will help you," he said.

"Garn!" Iyorath protested. "Don't encourage her!"

"It can be done," he insisted. "The dwarves of my province were skilled leather workers and I'm one of the best. I'll fashion a harness or a backpack or something for her to ride in. Don't worry. I know I can do this."

"I'm not worried about that," Iyorath muttered. "Delkan, what are you going to do if we get attacked?"

"I just lost my legs! I still have my arms. Have you forgotten?" she reached under her bed and withdrew her little slingshot. "Now are you going to keep arguing the point or am I going to have to shoot you?"

"All I have to do is move out of range," he muttered.

"True," she nodded and then declared with a huge smile, "But you have to sleep sometime!"

CHAPTER 25

Bran had ridden all day with only two brief stops to rest Echo. When she stopped for the night, Echo immediately lay down to take a deep sleep. Bran shook her head and grinned at the efficiency of the mule. He knew they would be on the road again soon and he was taking advantage of what he knew to be the longest stop they had. She had ridden him more this one day than she had for a long while and she was concerned as to how he'd hold up. They had a lot of miles to cover to get to Tor Ambroc and she wanted to get there as fast as possible. But she wasn't about to run poor Echo into the ground.

She touched the carving of Val, which hung about her neck, thinking she could have used the Dahla horse instead. She was sure Val would make the miles just fly. But there was no way Echo could have possibly kept up with the stamina and speed of the magic horse. And Bran would have needed Val most when she got home, the exact time she would have had to rest her magic horse. What would have been best was if she had two Dahla horses instead of one. Now she understood Dra-Oog's words when they'd first met.

Of course, she could have used Delkan's horse Sashay. She shook the thought out of her head the minute it intruded. Delkan may have convinced herself she would never ride again, but it was not Bran's place to take or even borrow Sashay from her. And what was more she could not have done it to Delkan. It would deprive her friend of the last thing which was truly hers. If Delkan hadn't offered Sashay to her, then she was not going to ask. It just wouldn't be right.

She sighed to herself deep in her own thoughts. Her sigh was mirrored by Echo's snore. She chuckled softly so as not to awaken him. She knew the mule was treating her as the lead horse in the band. He would allow himself a deep, on the ground sleep if she stood guard over him. She would not get into her bedroll until he awoke to take over guarding her. It was a good thing horses needed so much less sleep than a two-leg.

She knew sleep would come slowly to her tonight, in spite of the long ride. Her mind was still spinning with thoughts and possibilities, emotions and doubts. She stood up and wandered aimlessly about her small fire, stretching out the kinks from the day's ride and rubbing her neck in worry. She finally returned to sit across from her snoring mule and added a few more twigs to the coals to make the fire blaze up again, crackling and popping.

Was her mother still alive? Did her father yet live to trouble all he came in contact with? Where was Daga in all this? And poor Vilmar, how had this affected him?

She ran a forge-weathered hand through her bushy red hair and rubbed her face wearily. She just did not know and it was the not knowing which was killing her. Dwarves are not a patient lot. She wanted to take action now. Bran would have felt so much better if she could have lopped off some goblin's head rather than spend her days traveling to get home. At least she would feel she had done something useful.

She rummaged through her pack and brought out the letters Vilmar had written her. She re-read them all now with a new perspective, noticing he said less and less about her family in each one.

In the very last letter he had written, he spoke of his own family and not a bit about hers. He had done nothing but talk about his younger sister Dwyn in the last letter. Bran had met Dwyn before and had always dismissed her. She had found no redeeming qualities in the human child just bordering on becoming a woman. Dwyn was too humanly feminine and pretty, or so her family thought at least, to inspire much affection in Bran.

Vilmar had written that Dwyn, his younger sister, had finally 'blossomed' and the local young men had taken notice of this fact. Conal was beside himself running off her potential suitors who, of course, were not good enough for his daughter. Dwyn, who loved all the extra attention, was not making his job any easier.

But he had also stated in this letter he had gone to visit his family and had ended up staying and not returning to Tor Ambroc and his lessons with Keld. Was it because no one was left? Her heart beat a little faster in apprehension for those she had left behind and she frowned in concern.

She stroked her beard and glared angrily into the coals. She didn't want to hear about Vilmar's useless, human spawn little sister! She wanted to hear something of her own family.

What was happening in Tor Ambroc right now? And why did Vilmar say nothing of it? What was really going on?

CHAPTER 26

Vilmar rubbed his face wearily. He wasn't sleeping well lately, of course, why would he? The majority of Tor Ambroc was dead or dying. He had stopped living in the tunnels. He could no longer stand the stench of the dead and the dying everywhere around him. Lessons with Keld had ended for the half-dwarf had dissolved into a poor wretched, guilt-ridden misfit of a person, unable to die of the pox but unable also to truly live with himself. He blamed himself completely for the plague and refused to leave the dwarf compound, saying it was his punishment to watch his kin die as he had let their doom in the front door. He had devolved into a babbling madman. He was of no use to anyone, especially himself.

The smell of the dwarf pox was rancid in Vilmar's nostrils. He smelled it everywhere he went. He had bathed frequently, thinking it was on his clothes or skin, scrubbing hard until his flesh was raw and irritated. Still he could smell it on him. He smelled it even in his sleep. How was he supposed to live like this?

He rubbed his entire face and felt something scratchy at his jaw line. He rolled over and crawled on his hands and knees to the nearby pool in the moonlit glade. He stared blankly at the reflection, which looked back up at him from the ebony depths. It was the face of a complete stranger.

"I just feel that if we see each other again, we will be different people."

The words he had spoken to Bran at their parting came back to him. Bran would never recognize him now. His long-awaited beard was finally coming in.

But it was coming in snow white like an old man's and the eyes which stared back from the youthful face had seen far too much suffering for one so young. They had a haunted and helpless look to them and his face was all dragged down by sorrow.

He struck out at the reflection, shattering it with his hand.

"What good have I been to anyone lately?" he mumbled in despair.

He was only an adolescent. Why then did he look like a sad, tired middle-aged man?

"What am I, unicorn?" he spoke out loud to the darkness. "Wizard? Druid? Healer? Or just a pathetic wannabe of all those things wrapped into one?"

"Your time is fast approaching, Vilmar," returned the unicorn's voice in his head. *"You now stand on the cliff of your destiny. Your wings are grown. When the right gust of wind comes, you will fly."*

"I could have done something by now!" he growled. "I'm not a babe in the woods when it comes to the healing arts. I could have done... *something!*"

"Smearing salve and bandaging horses' legs will not stop the dwarf pox, my dear," the unicorn counseled. *"You were never meant to be a healer or a druid, my little fawn."*

"Then what am I?" he shot back with some heat. "I was certainly no help to Tor Ambroc!"

"Remember Yaffa's words the night she died, young human. You could do nothing because it was not your destiny. I could not help anyone in Tor Ambroc because it was not my destiny."

He sat up suddenly curious. "You know your own destiny?" he asked.

"Every unicorn is born knowing their own destiny. My son knows his."

Vilmar gave a heavy sigh. "Well, it would certainly help us two-legs if we were born knowing it."

There was unicorn laughter in his head.

But Vilmar could not laugh or even smile in response. The tragedy at Tor Ambroc had chased all humor from him.

"What *is* your destiny?" he boldly asked her.

"I am to assist and nudge into motion certain events that will bring about the downfall of Savas-Zev. You factor into this, my young student."

"Savas-Zev killed all of Tor Ambroc?" he asked.

"Yes."

"Who is he?" Vilmar asked.

The unicorn sighed heavily and stepped into the fractured moonlight. Coming to the side of the pool across from him, she folded her delicate legs and lay down on the ground for a long story.

"Savas-Zev is evil personified. He started out as just a normal human child. But certain events unfolded in his life to encourage a deep resentment of the dwarves and their talents and riches. This resentment eventually metamorphosed into a senseless hatred of all things dwarvish. He has made it his life's work to eradicate all dwarves from existence in this world. This hatred has extended his life far beyond its normal limits. Tor Ambroc wasn't the first dwarf province he has wiped out."

"How many dwarf kingdoms are there?" Vilmar asked.

"Originally, there were eighteen great dwarf kingdoms who sprouted from the genesis of all dwarves, you might say. The mountains themselves gave birth to the four founding tribes of tunneling peoples and all dwarves nowadays can trace their lineage back to these four families.

"At this particular time, there are nine kingdoms left from the original eighteen. Savas-Zev is getting his wish. Soon there will be no dwarves at all."

Vilmar's jaw dropped in shock. This meant nine whole communities of dwarves had already been utterly wiped out by the evil wizard's designs. How many lives had been ruined by Savas-Zev? He was staggered at the scope of this hatred. Vilmar could not imagine ever hating any one race so much. But he also realized if this were to continue, it just might get very easy for him to do so.

"We can't allow this," muttered Vilmar. "If he can do this much damage to one race, threaten its very existence, what's to stop him from eliminating any other race who gets in his way?"

The unicorn's blue eyes glittered darkly at him from across the pool.

"Ah, now the fawn begins to see," but there was no humor in her tone. *"Yes, he must certainly be stopped at all costs. Bran is not the only dwarf who has lost her entire clan to his madness. There are many others like her out there, lonely survivors, the last of their kind and kin. This is one of the reasons the Yazu exist."*

"And how do I figure into all this?" Vilmar asked after a very long pause.

Her eyes glittered even more and she raised her pearly neck proudly.

"*You are my champion,*" she said simply. "*You are the sword I shall strike this menace from the earth with. You will join with other like champions, some looked for, some unexpected. You are my green wizard.*"

He looked up at her in surprise.

"I've never heard the term 'green wizard' before," he said. "What does it mean?"

"*Well, some people like to call them 'greenies' but it's the same thing. Green wizards are a very special kind of magician. You are aware many wizards specialize in their powers. There are some who work with fire, some with storms, on down the line.*"

He nodded and she continued.

"*Well, green wizards don't specialize. They have a unique bond with the world around them. They tap into the five elements which exist and can meld them any way they choose and use them for defense or attack, with the elements' blessing of course. So a green wizard could literally burn down a house one minute, then cause a rainstorm to douse it the next. Do you understand?*"

"I think so," Vilmar said. "How is this 'special bond with the elements' attained?"

He got the distinct impression the unicorn was smiling at him.

"*I'm so glad you asked,*" she chuckled in his head. "*They surrender themselves to the power of the elements. They accept them in all their violence and gentleness, take them into themselves and become one with them and each element will bless the green wizard with its power. Just like you're going to do right now.*"

There was a stunned silence from Vilmar. The unicorn quietly rose to her feet and circled the pool to come to stand next to him.

"I wasn't expecting that," he finally managed to stutter out.

The unicorn was amused and smiled smugly down at him.

"*Life has already thrown many things your way you did not expect,*" she replied kindly. "*Let us see what we can do to get you some skills which will make you feel less helpless when disaster strikes, shall we?*"

Vilmar stood up eagerly at this.

"Great!" he exclaimed. "What do I do?"

"Well for starters, you are to get onto my back," she replied simply.

Vilmar immediately took two backward steps away from her.

"You mean ride you?" he asked in a very small voice.

"Of course."

There was a long uncomfortable silence from the young human.

"I can't," was his eventual answer.

"What do you mean?" she laughed into his brain. *"Of course you can! It's just like riding a horse except you will not be in control of where I take you."*

"But you are no horse!" he stated. He seriously doubted riding a unicorn would be anything like riding a horse but how was she to know this?

"Besides, it's forbidden," he muttered sheepishly.

Now she really did laugh, a high-pitched, ringing, mane-dancing whistling cry of a laugh, which was also nothing whatsoever like a horse's.

"What human nonsense is this?"

Vilmar looked crestfallen and shuffled nervously in the grass. Without looking at her he explained.

"As a child, I was taught if a human rides a unicorn, it will diminish their power. Take away their magic, I mean."

The laughter in his brain sounded again but this time it was kinder.

"As if you could ever, in a million years, diminish me!" she chortled affectionately to him and nuzzled his arm gently.

"That is a silly human superstition born out of immense respect and awe for what we are. Riding a unicorn is only done in the rarest of circumstances. And this situation certainly requires it. Now mount up, fawn."

Vilmar obediently did as he was told and slid quietly onto the silken pearly back and took hold of the magical mane. The world went blurry as she began to move underneath him. He felt she was going very slowly and yet the scenery all around became strange and unfocused.

"Where are you taking me?" he asked through the fog.

"Each magical beast has a special safe place, a place of power which parallels your own world. I am taking you to my special place, my seat of power. This is the only way we can travel there. Do not be afraid. I will protect you."

Her words had barely had time to fade when her legs stopped moving. Vilmar slid down from her back and looked about.

They were standing in a beautiful green meadow scattered with flowers bordered by a forest. There was a huge blue lake before him fed by a misty waterfall out of which a rainbow sprang. Snow-capped mountains rose from far away and met the crystal blue morning sky.

It was the most beautiful place Vilmar had ever seen. The colors in everything were so vibrant, as if an artist had just touched the canvas and the paint had yet to dry. Everything was flowering and the birds were singing their spring songs as loudly as their little voices could muster. He took a deep breath, drinking in the eternal spring which permeated this place with every one of his senses. He could practically taste the beauty in the air.

This was paradise!

The unicorn was smiling at him.

"Happy?"

"Yes," he replied with enthusiasm. "I don't ever want to leave!"

The unicorn's smile broadened.

"Oh you may beg me to leave when we get done here," she chuckled.

"What do you mean?" he asked as he flopped down in the warm, thick, aromatic grass.

"You are not visiting heaven. You are here to be initiated. Every paradise has its teeth."

He looked warily up at her. This certainly sounded ominous.

"At least, you humans would call it an initiation. My kind would think of it as a beautiful, blessed thing—your second birth, you might say. But it may be rather frightening to you. If you do not listen implicitly to my instructions, it may prove deadly."

"So... what do I have to do to be initiated as a green wizard? Slit my wrists or something?" he said as he stood up.

"You must surrender to the elements. This is the key. Surrender. You will experience each of the elements at their most violent and destructive. Do not try to protect yourself from it, do not fight it or flee from it. If you do, you will die. Let it happen. Do nothing and accept it no matter how threatening it may appear. Surrender to it and it won't hurt you. Do you understand, Vilmar?"

As she spoke, he felt himself sinking into the mud, which had suddenly appeared under his feet. He tried to lift his leg out only to find

139

himself sinking faster. He forced himself to relax. Obviously earth was the first test.

He felt the mud pressing in on him as he sank lower and lower. The mire engulfed his waist and crept higher. He withdrew his hands and then let them too sink deeper into the mud.

A thought suddenly occurred to him.

"Wait! How do I breathe?" he exclaimed in fear.

The unicorn laughed.

"You let the earth breathe for you. She has been doing this for centuries. Trust her, Vilmar."

The mud had reached his neck. He took a deep breath. Then, looking at her, he forced all the air from his lungs. The last thing he saw was the unicorn nodding encouragingly at him. The mud completely swallowed him whole.

He had to force himself not to fight. He felt he was being buried alive. He could feel the rich, warm earth and roots and earthworms all about him. He felt the force of all the earth and stones piling upon his head were crushing him. He dared not open his eyes. His heart began to panic. But then, he forced his mind away from himself and directed it outward, observing what was happening. He did as the unicorn said and let the earth breathe for him. And it was only then he could really see and understand what she was trying to tell him.

He felt the heartbeat of the world itself. He felt old, terribly old, and at the same time, young as a spring colt. He could experience all the seasons at once—spring, summer, fall and winter. He had always believed fall and winter were the seasons of dying but now he found it wasn't so. They were only the seasons of sleep and slow renewal. The dead who were put into the earth, nourished and fed her, helping her to feed those above who were yet alive. He swam within the earth and heard whatever passed within and above it. He heard the trees talking their slow, long discussions and heard the grass whisper and gossip among the different blades. He was the mountains, he was the trees, he was the granite and the gems and metals. Everything in the earth, even the rocks themselves, were alive and aware of all which went on in, around and above them. And he realized suddenly, it had always been this way. His time as a human had taught him to think in other ways, erroneous ways. But the earth was there before his consciousness had existed. It would be there to receive him at the end. He was no longer afraid. The earth was nothing to be afraid of. He was forever safe in its warm, motherly grasp.

He took a deep breath and opening his eyes, saw the earth had released him from its gentle hold.

Vilmar found he missed it.

The unicorn was before him, smiling and nodding.

"The Great Mother accepted you graciously," she whispered in a reverent tone. *"I fear it will not be so easy for your second test."*

As she spoke this, she looked behind her and Vilmar found he had been released someplace else.

He and the unicorn stood on the very edge of a volcano's caldera. Poisonous fumes and steam rose from beneath them and rivers of molten fire swept around them. The air was hot and the wind tossed his hair and the unicorn's mane with wild abandon.

"Fire is the second test, eh?" he asked already knowing the answer.

Wordlessly the unicorn nodded.

Vilmar turned and looked into the fiery volcano's swirling depths. An enormous lake of magma churned beneath him.

"Remember, it will only burn you if you fight it. Accept the fire."

Vilmar nodded and took a deep breath, filling his lungs with the noxious and potentially fatal steam. Then he jumped into the vat of lava before him.

This time he really was afraid! He could feel the heat crisping his skin as he fell, he felt the water burned from his eyes, his clothes charred from his body and his skin starting to sizzle. Then the lava engulfed him completely and his world went orange.

He felt the total and utter destruction of fire, of how it burned grasslands and forests indiscriminately, towns and cities, forests and countryside, everything laid to blackened waste in its path. He felt how the two-legs used fire, from warming their homes and hands, to cooking their food and smelting their metals. But always it was a fickle tool, so eager to get away from its masters to wreak destruction wherever it wished. It burned meat for the two-legs to eat and yet it would just as easily burn and consume the peoples of the earth whether they willed it or not. Its hunger was fathomless and ever unappeased. But as it destroyed, it also created, renewing the tired earth and forming new land where there had been none before. It was death and rebirth all at once. And the earth needed the fire as the fire needed the earth. Fire was at the heart of the earth. It was not evil in and of itself. It simply existed because of the need to exist, the need for action taken. Fire was the heart of battle of any kind, mental or physical.

Suddenly he was aware of a presence in the fire, as if the heat itself were a person. It rushed up to him and swirled angrily about him, aware of his intrusion into its hallowed space. It demanded questions of him and before he had a chance to respond, it dove into his very soul and took those answers without awaiting his permission. Every fault or shining quality of his personality was laid bare for the fire to see and scrutinize. The fire swept its fury about him, enveloping and devouring completely what it had discovered. There was a long moment while it blazed and roared about him. Then, suddenly, it laughed and Vilmar was not sure whether the laughter was joyous or in scorn.

He was spat rudely back onto the earth, smoking as if charred but otherwise unharmed. He coughed as the breath came back to his fried lungs and he tumbled downhill until finally coming to rest at the cloven hooves of his unicorn patron.

Gasping, he crawled onto all fours like a dog and looked meekly up at her.

She chuckled softly at him and nuzzled his scorched hair with maternal affection.

"I see she spared you," she murmured softly into his mind. *"That's about as gentle as she gets."*

Vilmar coughed and sputtered as the necessary moisture came back to his form and he stood up.

"She?" he asked, his voice dry and raspy. "The fire's a she?"

"Of course. Couldn't you tell when you were in there? I thought it would be obvious to you."

"Well, it is now," he muttered and rubbed a hand through his crackling, sooty hair. "I don't think the great *she* liked me very much."

"Of course she likes you," the unicorn laughed back at him. *"She let you live!"*

"Well, in that case, she must love me," he chuckled ruefully.

He patted out the smoke still issuing from his clothes, which had been reduced to scorched rags.

"If this keeps up, I'll be naked by the end," he jested.

"Being naked never bothered me too much. But I understand it's much different for you pink-skinned two-legs." she commented as she led him through the dense forest undergrowth to his next challenge.

There was a strange heavy mist in the air and the foliage dripped with moisture.

Vilmar heard a thunderous roar ahead. He brushed the last few branches out of the way and stepped out of the forest.

They stood on a rocky path, which wound its way up alongside the tallest waterfall Vilmar had ever seen. The roar of the hurtling water was deafening. The wildly flying spray drenched him within minutes and he found his body hissing from the contact of the water with his heat-blessed form. A cloud of fog surrounded him. He felt the fire was angry at this test. Fire hated water and a part of him felt he must hate it, too. But fire also understood it must allow this test.

"Your third test, young fawn," the unicorn spoke to his mind. *"Remember the lessons you learned throughout the last challenges and you will pass this one as well. Learn to breathe the water as the fish do. Do not be afraid."*

Part of him was not afraid. He turned to the waterfall and, just for a moment, allowed himself to enjoy the spray bath. But inwardly he felt the fire half of his torn emotions scream and recoil, hissing from the wet touch. With an extreme effort he pushed this new side of his personality to the background of his consciousness. The fire was not happy at this new test. But he told himself it must allow this confrontation. He insisted on it. Vilmar took a deep breath of wet air. Then he leapt off the cliff into the pounding rush in a graceful dive.

Too late he realized he should have been afraid of the water test. The fire had told him so. The turbulent white water tumbled and spun him about until he had no idea which way the surface was. The force of thousands of tons of water beat and pummeled his frame harder than any fist and forced him to release his held breath. He felt he was going to be tossed to death by the water. The incredible pressure made him feel he would soon explode, shattered into a million pieces by the sharp daggers of spray flung toward him from all sides.

He was suddenly plunged into the calm depths at the bottom of the waterfall. Automatically, he paddled and kicked for the surface, needing air for his straining lungs. But the force of the pounding water kept him deep underneath and unable to get to the surface. He was drowning! He could see the sun's light through the fractured barrier above his head but he could not reach it. He kicked harder, his lungs were burning for want of air.

Then the unicorn's words came back to him.

"Learn to breathe as the fish do."

Taking a great leap of faith, he forced the rest of the air from his lungs. He watched helplessly as the bubbles of precious air left him and floated peacefully up to the freedom of the surface he could not reach. He inhaled nothing but liquid and went limp, allowing himself to float. The water could do as it willed with him. He let go of everything.

His mind floated in the watery ether, which surrounded him. He felt the essence which was water and asked for its wisdom. The watery world opened about him. He watched as the salty ocean's waves beat stones on a shoreline to sand over millennia of time. He watched as the sun's heat drank in and evaporated the water, changing it into fresh rain to nourish the thirsty land and streams and lakes. He watched as streams carved canyons over many thousands of years, shaping the land as they fed it. He watched as destructive mudslides swept away all in their path while, at the same time, they redistributed new earth to strange, nutrient-starved places. He watched the hurricanes churn the ocean and the shore's land, etching new terrain and bringing a rich infusion of sea life to the peoples and animals who lived along the coast. He watched thunderstorms blast down the plant life in the land, clearing the way for the young to thrive and grow. He saw undersea earthquakes create great walls of water, which completely ruined the first land it struck. He saw it ruin and renew in the same action, destroy and create.

He saw it grow cold and hard, felt it in his bones as it turned to ice and snow. He watched the cold devour some, and harden others. He watched as creatures and humans adapted their lives around the frigid temperatures. But he also noticed the beauty in the harshest season. He saw the frost paint masterpieces of art on trees and ice-covered lakes. He watched the snow sparkle in the sunlight as if mingled with a million gems. He saw icicles drip, freeze and eventually release into life-giving water again. So beautiful and at the same time so cold and forbidding a force.

And yet, life could not survive without the blessing of water to nourish it. Little life there was which could survive with no moisture of any kind. Water cleansed and nourished, destroyed and rebuilt, raged and flowed throughout the world. It was powerful and gentle, a blessing and a curse and yet, through it all, a definite necessity.

Vilmar's face broke the surface of the water with the gentlest of tinkling sounds. He opened his eyes and remembered to breathe again.

He was floating on the surface of the lake near the shore. The unicorn stood knee-deep in the indigo pool beside him.

"Paradise has its teeth," he said to her and she chuckled.

"You did not expect this one to be difficult, did you?" she replied.

"I was wrong," he answered.

"Yes, I thought I was going to lose you there for a moment. Please don't make me worry again."

"I will not make the same mistake twice," he said and sat up. The water cascaded off him in rivulets, parting gently from his frame. "I hope I do better the next time."

He stood up and found very little of his clothes remained at all. His boots, which had been singed before, had been completely torn off by the force of the waterfall. A scorched and tattered shred of a tunic remained and very little of his breeches had survived past the waistline.

"I wouldn't worry too much about your state of dress, little fawn," the unicorn replied, catching the thought. *"Clothes won't help you too much in the next test anyway. The elements find them quite unnecessary."*

"Yes, but *I* might need them!" Vilmar returned.

"You'll need them later, not here and not now," she informed. *"Now you are to follow me."*

He obediently did as she bade and slogged clumsily out of the lake onto dry land after her. She led him through a small forest to where it gave way to a large, clear plain.

He looked about and saw nothing but plains and sky. He looked at her in confusion. As he did so, he noticed a stiff breeze had kicked up, quickly drying his ragged clothes and skin. The wind tossed his red hair and made the unicorn's white mane stand up like a thunderhead cloud. The air itself felt electric and moist. He could smell the rain the clouds had yet to shed. It made his skin prickle.

"The next test is wind," she told him and nodded her lance to a point on the horizon behind him.

He turned to face it and watched a truly incredible thing happen.

The sky had gone all stormy and dark clouds were gathering. He watched them billow and swirl and lightning crackle. He felt the wind sting his face. And then the clouds condensed into a tail-like, spiraling structure reaching down to the ground. The light in the air changed to an ominous green shade. A blinding sheet of what he thought was rain began to pelt him. But then he realized the rain hurt far too much and stung where it hit him. He shaded his eyes and peered through the storm.

It was hailing.

Vilmar had never seen hail before. He had always wanted to but now he realized hail was better appreciated when there was a roof overhead, not standing outside in a field, naked to the storm's wrath. It stung, bruised and froze his unprotected skin.

He peered ahead from the protected shield of his hand and what he saw made his eyes go wide in shock and his blood go cold.

The tail of cloud had touched the ground and was churning up a great black cloud of destruction at its foot. It was definitely turning black and becoming funnel shaped. He could feel the thunder through the soles of his feet as the sound was conducted through the ground.

It was a tornado and it was making straight for him.

He had heard tales of tornados before but he had never seen one. He found it both fascinating and terribly frightening all at once. He remembered stories the old folks told about tornados ripping up trees, splintering them, and then sending the splinters completely through a solid fence rail. He suddenly felt like the target for an arrow.

He looked behind him to the unicorn.

"Do not run from it. Face it. Let it take you where it may. Do not be afraid."

'Easier said than done!' he thought to himself.

He turned to face the twister bearing down on him with all due speed. He struggled to remember he had just been buried alive, burned and drowned and had still survived. What could this possibly do to harm him?

The thought became harder and harder to believe as the tornado came closer. He could hear the dull roar of its winds grow louder as it approached. He saw trees torn up by the roots spinning wildly inside, small stones too were flying about along with great chunks of earth, now pulverized which gave the twister its color, along with all manner of other debris swept up from within its path. He could smell its violence.

He felt the wind buffet and tug hungrily at him. He thought curiously then it almost seemed like a giant baby who did not know the harm it could do when it got really playful. He stood firm although he knew it would do no good. The tornado was practically on top of him now. The roar of the wind chilled him to the bone with dread. The

146

lightning crackled and struck the ground close to him, singeing his nose hairs from close proximity.

Then suddenly, the wind scooped him up and spun him end over end. He was flying but totally out of control, a mere plaything of the tornado's incredible winds. He saw the earth beneath and above him as he tumbled and immediately felt seasick. He was sucked deeper into the great coil of spiraling wind and his vision went black from the myriad of debris the wind had scooped up and decided to take with it. He was battered and scraped from all the many things the twister had picked up along its path. He felt the air in his lungs forced out from the pressure around him. He thought he would be crushed flat within the depths of the roaring, raging wind.

He accepted the destruction.

Then everything grew peaceful and quiet.

Puzzled, he opened his eyes to find his body had melted into the invisibility of the air itself. Without eyes, without senses, he observed what it was to be the wind. The shape and contours of the land molded and added force to the wind. In the mountains, it blew cold and fierce, driving most life below the blowing snow and howling winds. But he heard the voice of the wind as it howled around the rocky crags and found it beautiful. He heard the wolves as they mimicked the wind's song and was amused. He swept down from the mountains and tickled the treetops just to hear them whisper. He blew down to the flowered plains and made the fields ripple so the plants could pollinate. How could any plant survive without the wind to help blow the pollen or the bees their way?

He flew effortlessly over the ocean and caressed gently its surface until it was almost as smooth as glass. And then he slapped and churned it into a huge boiling cauldron. He joined with water as it rained and he sang with the joy of life as lightning struck. Wind was song and sound and it reveled in any sound it made either by whistling down the cold mountain peaks, or tickling the chimes humans made, or swinging the great heavy bells, which normally resisted its force.

He was the force, which blew the relieving breath of air over parched lands, bringing the rain it so sorely needed. He was the first cold breath of winter and the first warming heat of spring. He was the gentle aid for fishermen and also their bane when the waves were whipped to a violent froth. He was the air, which warmed, and the air which slew. He was the breath fire needed in order to burn, and the force which made puddles disappear into the clouds. He could knock down trees in rage or burn them with lightning. He could shake the nuts and fruits from the branches to reseed or feed all manner of creatures. He was gentle and deadly, soft and harsh. But everything needed to breathe to exist. He sang and he danced, he loved motion and sound. To be the wind was a wonderful, powerful, joyous experience. It was simply great to be alive.

He floated gently on the downdrafts to where the unicorn stood awaiting him. She saw him before he got his physical form back. He landed softly on the earth and watched as his hands slowly reappeared before him. He laughed and then immediately felt like crying for the wind had parted from him. Vilmar took a deep breath.

Suddenly, he collapsed to the earth, convulsing as if in a seizure. He was hot all at once with lightning running along every nerve ending. The next instant, he was freezing cold and wet. His tongue seemed to turn to mud in his mouth. He gasped and coughed, shivering and sweating all at the same time. He could see things differently, see every aura of every living thing and hear as well every whisper of every blade of grass to every shout of every human. It was deafening and overwhelming. It was all going too fast for his brain to keep up. He curled himself into a tight, shuddering ball.

"What's happening to me?" he managed to choke out.

He squeezed his eyes shut. Nothing looked right. Nothing sounded right. It was all too much! What was wrong? He was panicking.

"Oh no! I was afraid this would happen! Quick! Take hold of my lance," the unicorn's voice came to him as through a sea of voices.

"What? Why?" he stammered in confusion.

"Just do it!" came the order.

His body was racked with sensations and thoughts his mind couldn't keep up with. He tried to do as she bid but he could no longer see her as he was used to and his hands flailed blindly in the rainbow of wild colors which was suddenly his vision. The inane babble of sounds soared and echoed louder in his ears and he screamed. He felt he was going mad.

Then his fingers closed on a hard, thin, spiraling object, which somewhere, in the confused depths of his mind, told him was a unicorn's horn. He clutched desperately at the lance as lightning crackled across his eyes and tornados swirled in chaos in his lungs.

There came a sudden jolt and a charge of energy was released within Vilmar. The charge was pleasantly cleansing. Strange things were still happening inside of him, but they were more distant now, easier to deal with.

"What was all that?" he gasped with what he thought was his real voice. It seemed to echo in his head.

"Vilmar, listen carefully to me now," the unicorn slowly explained.

His mind grasped hold of her words like his hands clutching her horn, refusing to let go.

"You've just been blessed by the four elements. As a result, you now have a piece of each of their powers rooted deep within you. Life will never be the same for you. You must learn to control these powers. If you do not, your powers will spill over and burn all others you encounter, not to mention keeping you in a constant state of exhaustion. You must learn to cork the bottle!"

"How... do I... do that?" he stammered out.

Things were starting to look strange again and the constant yammering voices in his head were getting louder. He moaned with dread of the madness, which was to come.

"I will teach you. Now listen carefully, my fawn."

Later, much later, he opened his eyes. He felt as if a century had passed since he had blacked out. He ordered his eyes to focus on what the earth told him were branches waving peacefully above his head. He saw them in his normal vision.

He uttered a deep sigh of relief.

"How do you feel, my fawn?" spoke a familiar voice in his head.

"Better," he replied. "Less scrambled and scattered. I feel whole again."

"That is very good," replied the unicorn.

He thought quietly to himself. "But I don't feel the same as I used to."

A mental chuckle drifted unbidden through his thoughts.

"My child, you will never be the same again," she explained patiently. *"You have taken a huge step forward, toward your eventual destiny. The past will forever be the past. Today your new life begins."*

He turned his head to look at her. The unicorn lay nearby, her delicate white legs curled gracefully beneath her belly. Yet she seemed somewhat dimmed, as if the glowing white color of her hide had been muted slightly. This concerned him and he thought back over what had just happened.

"Did you drain yourself helping me?" he asked.

This time the unicorn's voice sounded sheepish and embarrassed.

"A little. I need to relax and recover my strength. But I am in my place of power and here I have all the time in the world to do so."

"I'm sorry," he apologized. "I never meant to harm you."

She smiled back at him and nuzzled his hair affectionately.

"I am aware of it. It was necessary to get you through the tests of the elements."

"How many others have passed the blessings of the elements?" he asked curiously.

"Vilmar, this is your life, not a competition," she scolded gently.

"I know, I'm just curious. I've never heard of a green wizard before you told me about them. Are there very many of us?"

She looked him sternly in the eye. *"Many say the green wizards are only myth and legend. This is because so few initiates actually survive the tests. Usually one of the elements ends up consuming them because it is too difficult to let go. Or, if they do make it to the end, they are consumed by the madness."*

Vilmar thought hard about this fact. "The others didn't have a unicorn patron like you to help them through it," he said.

"This is correct."

He thought hard again. "You didn't cheat to get me to be a green wizard, did you? Didn't break some all-important rule by helping me, right?" he asked in honest concern.

This question provoked a loud verbal laugh from the unicorn.

"A unicorn cheat? Heavens no! The thought is absurd," she whinnied musically. *"But I'm glad to see your moral code is still intact."*

She tossed her milky white mane and peered narrowly at him.

"How do you feel deep inside?" she asked pointedly.

He sighed and thought carefully before answering. "I definitely feel different. I feel like there's all this power churning inside me just below the surface and if I get mad or out of control of my own emotions, it will explode. So I guess I better be real careful about letting others push me too far."

The unicorn nodded slowly.

"That would be a safe assumption. Be careful how you live your life now. You may feel like you have the power of a god, but you do not. Be careful how, when and where you unleash this power. I cannot stress this enough."

He nodded in return. "I will do my best," he replied honestly.

"And how do you feel about the elements which surround us all now?" she asked.

He closed his eyes and thought about the horror and beauty of all the tests he had just experienced. "There's so much more to this world than I had ever dreamed before. The power of the elements... it goes so deep. It's hard to describe. Each element is a whole world unto itself. And yet it's all connected. No one element survives alone. At the heart of the earth is fire. And earth makes what fire consumes. And fire cannot exist without the wind. And hurricanes are not wind alone but water as well. And earth cannot sustain life without water, on and on and on. They all need each other. It's amazing... staggering... and incredibly beautiful."

His voice trailed off as he remembered.

"Hey, wait a minute!" he exclaimed. "I just remembered something! I've only experienced four elements. You said there were five!"

She smiled gently.

"I was wondering when you'd figure it out."

"So I'm not done yet! There's still the fifth element to go through."

The unicorn's deep blue eyes glittered mysteriously.

"That is spirit. You must pass this test on your own with no help from me. You will be experiencing the blessing of spirit throughout your entire life. There is time yet, my young fawn."

Vilmar let his head sink back to the grassy pillow in defeat. The first thing he thought about was how he had almost gone mad like the other poor initiates who hadn't made it to the end. If this was what happened to them after only four elements what would the blessing of spirit do to him when he received it?

Would it tear him apart?

CHAPTER 27

The war eagle Rath-Tor sat in the branches of a tall oak and quietly listened to the conversation below as he devoured the fat rabbit he had caught earlier. Garn-Ithel and Delkan were talking quietly as Iyorath scrutinized Bran's letter over and over again for clues.

Delkan had held up amazingly well during the journey. She complained much, which only told Iyorath she was feeling fine. Garn had fashioned a backpack-like leather pouch for her and Iyorath had tried carrying her on his back as they rode. He soon found out even a legless dwarf was much too heavy for his thin frame to support, so they had switched her to Garn's back. This seemed to work out better. When his sturdy back tired, they strapped her to the side of his speckled horse like a saddlebag and switched his baggage to the other side to counterbalance her blocky weight. When they stopped for the night she insisted on taking the first watch since, in her words, she had done nothing all day and was still fresh. They had traveled like this for a week. Delkan had routinely shot a rabbit or a squirrel each night during watch and if she could rouse one of them before Rath-Tor got to it, they had fresh meat. So she was definitely pulling her share. Although both Garn-Ithel and Iyorath were getting tired of being pelted with pebbles from a well-aimed slingshot as their wake up call!

A pebble whisked between the elf's hands, ripping the letter out of them. Iyorath gave a frustrated growl and glared up at Delkan, her arm frozen in a shot pose with a crooked grin on her face.

"What is it?" he spat at her.

"Every night you've been reading that letter!" Delkan said. "What are you looking for? What didn't you see the first thousand times you read it?"

Garn snorted and tore off another hunk of bread passing the other half to Delkan.

"Haven't you memorized it yet?" he muttered.

Iyorath sighed and rubbed a long, delicately fingered hand through his silky, blond locks.

"I'm trying to figure out what she meant by 'a certain helpful situation may present itself.' Obviously, she thought she could do something to stop the dwarf pox and I'm just trying to figure out what. Did you two have any secrets or did you tell each other everything?" he explained.

Delkan shook her head.

"Bran and I were very close, but not that close," she replied. "I never told her about what happened to my family until I found out it was happening to hers. And she knew I was holding something back from her. So if I was keeping a secret from Bran, I see no reason why she would have to tell me everything about herself."

Iyorath frowned and rubbed his smooth, hairless jaw. "That's not very helpful, I'm afraid."

"I know," Delkan replied flatly. "I do know she had a young human friend who she said smelled like magic."

Iyorath thought hard about this comment. He had heard about the dwarves' uncanny sense of smell when it came to non-dwarf magic.

"Did she say he was a wizard?" he asked.

"The feeling I got from her was even he didn't know what he was yet," she said.

Iyorath's frown was more pronounced this time, his high-arched brows knit in concern.

"Give it up, lad," Garn-Ithel put in. "She didn't say because she didn't want us to know. And we won't know until we have her in front of us to ask."

"I just wish she had confided in someone what her plan of attack was in this situation," the elf said crumpling up the letter and stowing it away in his bags.

"Maybe she had no plan," Delkan suggested. "Not until she gets there and sees the lay of things at least."

Iyorath somehow had to agree with this reasoning.

Rath-Tor looked up from the ravaged hide of the rabbit and cast his sharp eyes further on down the way they needed to go. They were only a few days' ride from Tor Ambroc. But the eagle could make it in one day's flight.

Maybe he would fly ahead tomorrow and see 'how things lay.'

Complete chaos ruled Kopa town. Most of the buildings had been set ablaze and the few inhabitants who were left were either in hiding or fleeing, screaming in terror. But to the goblins and trolls who had ransacked the town, it was all one big party.

They had been quite thorough, as their master had ordered. The peaceful townspeople had been killed and all comely women taken hostage for 'play' later. Any treasures to be found had been looted and livestock gathered for the obligatory after-raid feast. Most of the goblins had already started the feasting immediately after they emptied the tavern of every cask of liquor which had been stashed inside. It didn't take much to encourage the trolls at least. Trolls always had voracious appetites and normally started snacking on their prey before it was even dead, whether it be horse or human.

Through all the bedlam, Dask strode purposefully, scrutinizing each group of hostages. Finally, he found what he was looking for.

He came upon a small circle of rough looking, half-drunk goblins. They had captured a poor, teenaged girl and were roughly tossing her from goblin to goblin, laughing in great glee as she wailed in terror.

Dask grabbed the girl and roughly wiped the bedraggled strawberry blond curls from her face to peer briefly into her eyes. The goblins grumbled and muttered at this, afraid their play would be stopped.

But Dask only shoved her back into the circle and motioned to the leader of the small group to step aside with him. The large, leering goblin obeyed grudgingly.

"What Boss's head man want with pretty?" he snarled.

Dask nearly gagged on the goblin's foul breath but with an effort, he controlled himself.

"Play all you want with her," Dask told him. "But when you're done, let her go. Don't kill her."

The ugly goblin screwed his face up in confusion at this unexpected order.

"No kill?" it spewed, spitting froth from its blackened mouth. "No kill, no fun! Play and kill is! Why no kill?"

"Boss man said so," Dask shot back.

"Boys not be happy!" the goblin growled back as if the order tasted bad. "Boys want to play and kill!"

"Haven't they got plenty of other hostages to play with? Let them take out their frustration on the others. Just don't kill this one. Boss said so. You don't like it, go ask Boss man why!" Dask replied.

The goblin grumbled but shivered at the suggestion he visit the master. The goblin started to turn away.

"One other thing," Dask said and the goblin half turned back, scowling. "The Boss man says to bring any dwarf you find to him alive."

"Dwarves?" the goblin leader grumbled back. "Is no dwarves. All dwarves dead. All dwarves here at least."

"Boss man say there may be a few scattered dwarves come back to check out their home. These dwarves are very important to him. Boss man wants to play with these dwarves in particular. Understand?" Dask returned.

A savage grin crossed the goblin's face showing all of his rickety, yellow teeth.

"Boys watch Boss man play with these dwarves?" the goblin asked lecherously. "That be real good fun!"

"Perhaps," Dask replied knowing the eagerness such a reply would fire in the goblins' hearts.

The goblin chuckled ominously and went back to his wench tossing with more glee than before.

Dask made his way to the center of town to the large log cabin where the ill-fated mayor had once lived. The huge, oaken, double doors had been blasted off their hinges and replaced by a large sheet for some sort of privacy.

Dask stepped through the doorway into the parlor beyond. Several of the more trusted servants were unpacking huge boxes of things, moving the wizard's personal articles into his new headquarters. Dask continued onward into the next room where the wizard himself was unpacking his more precious magical items.

"It is done, Lord," Dask told him.

"Good," Savas-Zev replied. He was unpacking a huge box of crystal balls, all carefully bedded in thick straw so as not to break. A large, specially made shelf with little alcoves had been nailed to the far wall and he carefully transferred each globe into a separate compartment.

"Have you told the troops to keep on the lookout for any dwarves?"

"This too has been done," Dask replied.

"Excellent!" Savas-Zev said. "Do inform me if any dwarf named Bran is apprehended. I am most eager to discuss things with her."

"Of course, sir," Dask said then added, "Sir? You were right. This raid has been most beneficial to the troops' morale."

Savas-Zev did not smile at him and Dask knew better than to expect it. Dask only bowed low and left the wizard's chamber.

CHAPTER 28

Bran loped Echo along at an easy but fast gait. They had now entered familiar country. They were only a few miles out of Kopa town and she was keeping her eyes peeled for any hint of trouble. So far she had seen nothing but this had only made her more suspicious. Everything was quiet, too quiet. The back of her neck prickled. She felt she was being watched.

They broke out of the small woodland trail onto a long grassy field. She pulled Echo to a stop and looked about warily, using all her senses. She still saw nothing. She decided to err on the side of caution and made Echo skirt the woods instead of head down the open trail where it would be easy for any spying eyes to pick her out.

Echo suddenly halted, long ears trained forward on some object his animal senses knew was there. He snorted explosively, a warning snort and shuffled nervously.

Bran peered narrowly ahead. Something blue crawled along the ground, whimpering pathetically. Bran shaded her eyes from the sun and looked closer.

She couldn't be sure, but it seemed to be a human figure. She urged Echo to approach at a quick-stepping trot. The mule did as he was bid but stopped, snorting and blowing about fifty feet away. By then Bran could see clearly it was a human woman badly wounded and splashed all about with blood. Echo shook his head fitfully and pawed, not liking the smell.

Bran swung down and walked cautiously over to the huddled, shivering figure. She carefully touched the person's shoulder.

At once the figure came to life, springing away and scrambling on all fours like an animal to the nearest bushes, wailing piteously as if she had been assaulted.

Bran tried to console the person but dwarves are not known for being gentle.

"Shh. I won't hurt you," she said hoping to sound reassuring. "What happened?"

A face framed in strawberry blonds curls, slowly peered timidly out from the bushes. Bran found to her shock she recognized the face.

"Dwyn!" she gasped.

The figure recoiled back into the bushes. Her clothing was shredded and her feet were bare. One arm seemed to have been broken and she cradled it tenderly, like a babe, to her wounded chest. Her eyes were wild and her face was black and blue with bruises. Bran could only see one of her eyes. The other was swollen shut. Bran could guess what had been done to Dwyn from the state of her clothing. No one needed to tell her what horror Vilmar's little sister had just endured.

Bran felt an intense rage start to burn hot in her, warming her cheeks and forcing her hands to clench into fists.

"Dwyn, listen to me. I'm Bran. You remember me, don't you? I'm Vilmar's friend. You remember your brother Vilmar, don't you? Please don't be afraid of me."

Her voice shook as she spoke. She was trying desperately to keep the anger out of her words. She sensed Dwyn had already experienced too much anger.

She held her calloused hand out to the frightened human girl.

"Please don't be afraid of me," she said.

"Vilmar?" Dwyn finally said in a slow, shuddering voice.

"Do you remember him?" she asked the girl.

Dwyn whimpered a little, tugging at her hair and chewing nervously on her split lip.

"Vilmar... is... my brother," she bleated like a frightened lamb about to be slaughtered.

Bran wanted desperately to find out what had happened to her. But she decided reminding her of the incident might be too much right now.

"And who is Conal?" Bran asked.

"Conal?" she bleated in confusion.

"Yes, Dwyn. Tell me who Conal is," she pressed.

"Conal... is... my Da," she managed to get out. A small smile at this little victory flickered briefly across her wounded face.

"Conal is my Da," she repeated with slightly more confidence.

"That's right. Very good," Bran encouraged, feeling somewhat foolish. "And where is Conal right now?"

Her face screwed up in confusion.

"Where... Da?" she repeated slowly.

"Yes. Where is Conal, your Da?" Bran pursued doggedly.

Dwyn chewed her lip and tugged at her hair again. She began to rock and moan quietly.

"Please, Dwyn," Bran begged. "This is very important. Where is your dad?"

"Burning," she whispered, her one eye wide and unfocused.

"What did you say?" Bran asked.

Dwyn began to shake her head back and forth wildly.

"Burning! I said burning! Da's burning and Ma's burning, they're all burning! All but me. Me they not burn. Oh, I wish they had burnt me as well!" she shrieked suddenly and then got quiet and hunched down as if someone had heard her.

Bran's heart leapt to her mouth. She shuddered with dread.

"Is... Vilmar... is he burning as well?" she asked afraid to hear the answer.

"Yes!" she said at first, then, "No."

She whimpered and moaned a bit. Her one eye was dull and unfocused. She clutched desperately at herself and began to shudder. Then the words came streaming out in a terrified, babbling torrent.

"Oh, I don't know! I don't like this game anymore! Take me home. Oh, please take me home and then go away. No! Can't do that. Home burning, remember? Everything's burning except for the nasty, ugly, mean, goblins. They never burn. They just make me do things. Horrible things! Oh, go away! I don't want to remember anything anymore. Everything's bad!"

She crawled deeper into the bushes and began to sob quietly to herself.

Bran's thoughts whirled in chaos. Kopa was burning. Goblins had raided the town. Conal and his family were dead and maybe Vilmar, too.

Her heart pounded wildly. Was Dwyn telling the truth? Or had she already been through so much she could no longer tell fact from fiction?

Bran hurriedly went back to Echo and rummaged about in her packs. Returning to Dwyn, she pushed a blanket and water skin and some hard bread close enough to the wretched figure for her to reach it.

She knew Dwyn would probably not take the offered aid from her hands but if she left them within reach while she was alone, she just might.

"Dwyn, I'm going to find out what happened," Bran told her as the girl cowered beneath the bushes. "You stay here and wait for me. I'll be back soon. Stay hidden and stay quiet."

Without waiting to see if she would respond, Bran returned to Echo and swung aboard the mule. She trotted past the huddled figure and when she was far enough away, spurred it to a full gallop. As they ran, she loosened the long-handled axe strapped to her saddle rings. A fierce, grim light was in her eyes.

Goblins had come in force to Kopa town.

She growled in barely pent up rage. She hardly knew what to believe about Dwyn's fragmented story but she knew one thing. Most women who had been raped by humans would not say they had been raped by goblins. Bran believed the goblin part of Dwyn's story. She set her jaw at a hard angle and urged Echo on faster. The well-trained mule dutifully obeyed the cues from her legs and voice.

They had barely traveled a mile when she felt Echo check his speed. Immediately, Bran snatched up her axe from where it hung on the saddle. At the same moment, she felt something thud into Echo and he gave a violent shudder. She felt his spirit leave in an instant and then they were both falling to earth. Her battle-honed senses were the only thing which saved her from getting crushed under Echo's body hurtling earthward.

Half relying on the emergency dismount Vilmar had taught her, half on her training, she kicked her feet free of the stirrups and somersaulted off the saddle, landing in a tumbling roll a safe distance away from Echo's crashing body. She rolled end over end a short distance and came up in a lunge, her axe brandished in front of her. A quick glance at Echo's huge, black bulk lying motionless a few feet away told her the mule would not be galloping ever again. Another glance at her surroundings told her she was completely hemmed in by goblins, twenty at least.

She turned her rage at Echo's death into battle fury and uttering a great roar, charged the nearest goblin. His hand and his head left his body in quick, satisfying succession. Keeping up the momentum, she spun on the goblin she heard advancing to her rear and gutted him with one deft sweep. A strike to her right and she lopped the end off another's spear.

She knew she was outnumbered. So, she also knew she had to keep her speed up and kill or maim as many as possible, as quickly as possible if she was to make it out alive. She thought about her mother who was probably dead and thrust the pointed butt of the axe handle in another goblin's face, blinding him with a horrible yell. She batted one off balance with the flat of her axe and jumped on his crotch when he fell, making him shriek in surprise and pain. She danced on him with her hobnailed boots while rearranging the faces of others. She felt the blood gush on her own face and reveled in the destruction she had caused.

At least she did until that blasted net descended over her head, fouling her axe and weighing her down. She bellowed and shouted and fought as they piled on top of her to knock her down. Once she shook them off but more piled on and bore her to the ground. An especially fat goblin stepped on her wrists and she had to let go of the axe, howling in pain and fury. The axe was worked out of the net and tossed out of reach of her short stubby arms. She fought to get out her dagger but the fat goblin stood on her other wrist ending this prospect. It took five large goblins to pin her down and another two to worm their fingers through the net and deprive her of the other weapons. They then wound the net securely enough about her to restrict any attempts to escape or even fight. This done, they gathered in a satisfied knot about her, panting and laughing at her attempts to get loose.

Then, as one, they all began kicking her with their large, pointy-toed boots. She rolled herself into a ball and covered her head with her arms. As they kicked, one big fellow kept shouting orders at her.

"Dwarf say name!" he demanded. "Dwarf say name, we stop. No say name, we no stop!"

She growled and shouted at them they should all go to hell. They just laughed.

"Us or you?" the big fellow guffawed rudely. "You be there before me. Now say name!"

The blows continued to rain down upon her. Try as she might, a few well-aimed kicks did connect with her head. Finally she relented.

"Bran!" she gasped and the kicking immediately stopped.

"Bran, is it?" the head goblin grunted in satisfaction. "Bull's-eye!"

He gave a truly evil sounding laugh. His comrades echoed his mirth. He turned to the others and barked an order in goblin, which Bran understood only too well.

"Tell Big Boss Man we catched him a special present. Tell him we bring it to him well tenderized."

The last thing Bran saw was Echo's strange blue eyes open wide but sightless. Then her world dissolved into the blackness, which was his hide.

CHAPTER 29

"Keep your eyes peeled behind, Delkan," Garn-Ithel said to her as they rode along. "We're very close to the human town Bran was always tellin' us about."

Delkan yawned and flexed her arms. They had been riding along for hours with no rest. No rest for the riders and horses at least. Delkan had done nothing but snore away. She was getting very tired of waking up with a stiff neck from these saddlebag snoozes. Her shoulders were sore from the constant rubbing of the horse's hip as it flexed with each step and she was sure the horse didn't much care for having a live saddlebag wiggling and flailing back there.

She stretched as much as she was able and wondered if they were attacked what would she do? The angle was all wrong for archery—she would end up bumping the horse with her pull elbow any way she shot unless she shot directly forward or back, and if the horse was running, well, there went that idea! She couldn't work her slingshot effectively either. To do this, she would take a chance in snapping the horse on the flank with the recoil strap and she knew all too well what affect that would have.

She scratched the stubble on her head which was growing back in and thought hard. She finally loosened her dagger on her side, deciding this would be the only way she could go if they were attacked.

"I wonder what's happened to Rath-Tor? I haven't seen him in a while," Garn muttered.

"He's been gone since the night before last," replied Iyorath.

"What?" exclaimed Garn-Ithel in surprise. "What happened? You two have a fight or something?"

Iyorath's glare chased the mirth from Garn's face.

"He never said anything to me about it," the elf grumbled in a low voice. "I have no idea where he went or when or if he'll be back."

Garn shook his head and grunted disapprovingly.

"You need to have better control over the war eagle of your'n," he said critically.

Iyorath spun his big chestnut horse on Garn and the little speckled pony.

"Let's get one thing straight! No one controls Rath-Tor! No one ever controls any war eagle! They do as they please," he fumed at the dwarf before turning his back on him again.

Delkan whistled softly to herself and said privately to Garn, "By the Great Dragon, he's getting grumpy! What, did he sleep on a stone last night or something?"

"Misses his great big cushy feather bed off of the ground I guess," Garn muttered back to her. "Still, you have to admit, the eagle picked a strange time to leave us. Just when we need him the most."

Delkan grunted in admission and glared angrily about at the undergrowth where anything could be hiding.

"It certainly would be nice to have some eyes above to scout around right now," she said.

She kept her own eyes focused behind them and scrutinized every bush or thicket. But try as she might she saw nothing. Her dwarf eyes were better suited for the darkness of the tunnels, not the patches of light and shadow in a woodland setting. She growled uncomfortably to herself. There was just too much here to hide behind. A small regiment could be out there and she'd never know it. Her fingers clenched automatically on her dagger.

Another two hours passed as they wound their way forward slowly through the scattered forests and fields. The narrow trail gradually widened and became a more obviously well used path as they went along. They could feel they were getting close.

Iyorath suddenly pulled his horse to a stop and peered closely at the ground next to his horse's feet.

"What is it, elf?" Garn asked. "What do you see?"

"Footprints," the elf replied simply, then looked at him with a grim expression. "Goblin and troll tracks."

Garn muttered a curse under his breath and Delkan hissed in dread, sliding the dagger free from its sheath.

A small, fist-sized rock flew out from the underbrush suddenly and skipped across both horses on their rumps. The chestnut reared straight up with Iyorath clinging expertly to its neck. The small speckled pony uttered an insulted bellow and bolted, taking Garn and Delkan along with it. The echo of harsh cries and derisive remarks in goblin voices sounded behind them.

Garn had his weapon halfway drawn when the pony bolted. Now he was trying to regain his seat and stirrups and not drop his axe all at the same time. He bounced clumsily about which only further upset the beast, causing it to buck wildly while galloping along. Garn managed to stay aboard for only three hops, then the pony sent him sailing into the underbrush, axe still in hand and cursing all the way down.

This left Delkan strapped helplessly to the side of an out of control pony, rocketing through the thickets with wild abandon. She couldn't reach the reins and the metal stirrups were banging crazily about her face. She felt the saddle slip. She realized if she didn't do something quickly, she would soon be riding the pony's belly and well within range of the wildly thrashing hooves. She swiveled her torso in the leather harness Garn had made for her and clutched the two straps which buckled her onto the saddle. She quickly began to saw at the one strap with her dagger. It popped free and she felt the pony's stifle began to kick her on the side of her ribs. Desperately she grabbed the other strap and again began sawing away. She felt the saddle slip some more and pulled herself up out of range of the pony's hind leg while grasping with her free hand to the off-side of the saddle's seat. Branches and leaves were whipping and scraping her face but she ignored them all. The only thing which existed was her savagely sawing dagger on the leather strap.

It sprang free, and she felt herself slip. The only thing holding her now was her left hand on the off-side of the saddle's seat. Then the pony's hoof connected with her chest and hurled her far away and free of the mad creature. The breath left her in a whoosh and she had the sensation of flying through a blurry, green landscape. Delkan hit the ground hard on a steep slope and tumbled down the incline. She threw out her hands wide to slow her descent. She felt the dagger, which she still clutched in her right hand, as its blade snapped in half. The hill was apparently very high but at last she came to a crazily bumping, thrashing end of it and her body pitched up against a large rock. Her wild momentum stopped.

She took a deep breath and her chest burned like a furnace's fire from the pony's kick. She thought dismally if her chest hurt now, how much more it would hurt the next morning. Then the world went blurry and she lost all consciousness.

CHAPTER 30

It was midnight when Delkan finally regained her senses. She cracked her eyelids open and looked about warily. She lay at the bottom of the hill where she had tumbled. The forest all around her was making normal, peaceful forest sounds. The night was clear and lit by a large, full moon so bright it cast shadows.

She made as if to move and immediately wished she hadn't. Every nerve ending lit up with fire. She felt as if she had been tossed in a gemstone tumbler. Everything hurt. She could feel clearly every bruise and jab from every rock, stone and broken twig she had rolled over in the descent downhill. Her face was scraped and bloody from her mad dash through the thickets and her nails were torn and crusted with earth from her downward trip. Her fingers were nicked from her attempts to cut the leather straps with the dagger and every breath hurt. She felt as if a heavy stone was pressing all the wind out of her and her lungs screamed in agony when she tried to expand them. And what's more, she smelled of adrenaline sweat, blood, chewed-up earth and crushed plant juice.

She knew the pain was only temporary and it meant she was alive. But right now the life of an invalid didn't seem quite so bad. At least she wouldn't have to worry about getting kicked by crazy ponies.

But then she remembered Bran. She remembered her friend could be in serious trouble because of the words she had said to her. If Bran had walked straight into a goblin trap and died, it would be all her fault. She had to do something to make it right.

Grinding her teeth against the pain, she sat up on the meager stumps of legs she was left with. Her head swam at the effort and agony roared throughout her body as she made the blood flow to her limbs. She inclined her head backwards and just concentrated on breathing for a bit. The crisp summer night air cleared her head somewhat. Then she painfully unstrapped and wriggled her way out of the harness, which had nearly killed her. She took another break to breathe and clear her head from this small effort.

Something flashed in the moonlight next to her, catching her eyes. It was her broken dagger now half the length it used to be. She did not know what good it would do her, but she picked it up in a blood-smeared, earth-caked hand.

Somewhere she heard the gentle babble of a brook. She remembered she was thirsty. Hand over hand, inch by painful inch, she crawled down to the stream which tinkled nearby. It wasn't too far away. She dunked her head in the water and gasped at how icy it was. She surmised it must be snowmelt from the nearby mountains. She drank in deep the icy flow and then attacked the grime and blood, which caked her little, square frame hissing at the stinging contact with the cold water on her wounds.

She then crouched there, dripping dirty, bloody water and tried to think. What was she going to do now? Where was she and how could she ever hope to find Garn and Iyorath? She decided crawling aimlessly about in the woods calling for help wasn't a very good idea with goblins so close about. She wondered if Garn and Iyorath were still alive. If they weren't, she guessed that would be her fault, too. What good had she done to anyone so far? If Garn and Iyorath were dead they had probably at least taken a few wretched goblins with them. What good had she done lately? Just shot a few rabbits for dinner and been a talking nuisance of a saddlebag. How was she going to fix this? Did she even have a chance?

A rustle in the bushes suddenly caught her attention and brought her back to the present. Her gray eyes glanced about and she tensed. More rustling sounded from more feet. She could see nothing but she knew there were many things all about her. She clutched up her broken dagger and scrambled quickly for the underbrush nearby. She missed her legs so much right now! She made it to a bush just as she heard feet dancing lightly across the wet pebbles of the streambed. She curled herself under the bush with her back to the little stump and spun about to face the sound, half a dagger held at the ready. She felt totally helpless. Here she was, a legless dwarf huddled underneath a thorn bush, brandishing a broken dagger at the enemy. Oh yes, it would be worth a fine song of glory to sing to the Great Dragon at her death!

But she stopped in shock at what approached, stepping into the slivered moonlight of the streambed.

A great, white messenger hound stood in front of her, its leather harness bearing the runes of Tor Ambroc still buckled around its chest. She crawled out of the bush and put down her broken dagger.

She recognized the dog. It was the one who had always carried letters for Bran, the one called Snow Crow.

The bushes behind the dog rustled and more hounds stepped forward into the clear moonlight. They all wore messenger harnesses, all stamped with the insignia of Tor Ambroc. Delkan remembered the decree of the Yazu, no dwarf was to touch or have any dealings with the hounds of Tor Ambroc because they might be infected with the dwarf pox and every hound from there was to be shot on sight. She hoped they wouldn't come any closer.

And they didn't. Snow Crow sniffed the air between them cautiously, then turned and left as if she had important business elsewhere. The other hounds watched her leave, and tightened their semi-circle about her while, at the same time, keeping their distance. Some even yawned and lay down near her.

Delkan nodded, understanding their body language. Snow Crow had gone to get someone and she was to wait. By the reaction of some of the hounds, it might be awhile. But they would guard her until then.

It wasn't as long as any of them thought. Soon there were footsteps behind her.

She snatched up her dagger and spun about, just to be on the safe side.

She found herself staring at glowing white, horse-like legs, which ended in the cloven and tufted hooves of a goat.

"Oh my goodness! Whatever happened to your legs?" said a voice inside her head.

The surprise of this rocked her backward and before she knew what she was doing, she was crab-walking in reverse away from... a unicorn!

"You—you can talk!—In my head!" she finally managed to stammer out.

"Well of course I can, silly. All unicorns talk like this," it replied with some heat, pursuing her. *"And you still haven't answered my question. What... happened... to... your... legs?"*

'Persistent for a unicorn!' Delkan thought to herself. Aloud she said, "Trolls took them. Trolls ate them."

"Trolls ate them?" repeated the voice in her head in absolute shock. *"How horrible! You poor thing!"*

Inwardly Delkan winced at the 'poor thing' remark.

There was a long pause from the unicorn while it thought about this.

Then it asked innocently, *"What's a troll?"*

Delkan growled inwardly again. Obviously, this was a very immature unicorn!

"Trolls are very ugly, bad creatures with big appetites," she explained with an impatient sigh. "Let's hope you never encounter them!"

"Oh. Okay," was its wide-eyed reply.

There was another long, uncomfortable silence.

"You should meet my mother. I bet she could fix you," the unicorn finally said in her brain.

"Fix me?" Delkan said in confusion. "You mean she could help me grow my legs back?"

"Of course!" replied the unicorn confidently. *"At least... well... I think so. She can do everything!"*

"Uh hunh," muttered Delkan. "Tell you what. Why don't you go get your mother and I'll ask her myself if she can fix me, okay?"

"Okay," the juvenile unicorn said and eagerly sprang away. *"I'll be right back! Don't go anywhere!"*

Delkan just shook her head in exasperation. "I just think I'll take a little stroll through the woods while you're gone," she muttered sarcastically.

CHAPTER 31

Bran's consciousness floated aimlessly through the ether of her mind. She didn't remember what had just happened nor did she think she wanted to. She just wanted to float here, out of time and out of space, disconnected from her body. Just drift in the timeless sanctuary of this dream state, lost and safe from all who could hurt her.

But she was a dwarf and this did not sit well. Dwarves do not run or avoid their problems, they attack them with a dogged determination. Her true dwarf nature forced her to realize this was wrong, things were happening while she floated uselessly here, important things which would affect her life. She had no time for this.

Against her will, her heart forced her to remember.

Echo was dead.

She remembered with a jolt his strange, pale blue eyes looking through her because they no longer belonged to his spirit. Echo's soul had fled his body. This faithful, mute companion, this beast of burden who had been trained so well and had so obediently, and reliably followed her every command without question, had died because of a decision she had made. Echo was dead and it was all her fault. If she had thought for just a moment before she reacted, if she had paused the briefest of instants to take a deep breath and clear her head, maybe, just maybe, she would not have urged him to dash at a mad gallop into a territory she knew was dangerous. What would Vilmar have to say? Bran felt as if she herself had shot the bow which killed her dear Echo.

In her mind and body, she moaned in grief.

Then her dwarf sensibilities shook her again. She had no time for grief. Remember? Goblins had taken her captive. In a rushed instant, she relived the flashes of memory from the most recent past. Unaware her body obeyed, she strained against her bonds. The unconscious state she existed in was beginning to dissolve.

She became aware of a smell, which permeated her dreams. No, it wasn't a scent, it was a stifling, choking reek of an odor. It resembled vaguely the stench of a dead body succumbing to the natural effects of a humid climate, festering and bloated. It was the stink of magic, non-dwarf magic, and evil magic—wizard magic. She had never encountered the smell before but this is what her mind told her. Vilmar had never smelled like this.

She gasped abruptly and came back to herself with a jerk.

"Ah, so nice of you to join us, my dear," a sinister voice said calmly.

Everything seemed so fuzzy and unclear at first. Her head was swollen and throbbing dully from blows of the goblin boots. Her fingers tingled and her arms ached from where they were secured, stretched out wide from her body where they supported the rest of her hanging frame. Her shoulder blades were warm and hot in a painful way and her neck sore from sleeping with her head hanging forward onto her chest. Now she was aware of it, she found it difficult and painful to expand her lungs in this position, dangling like a boulder from her wrists.

Slowly, as her vision cleared, she looked about to get her bearings of the prison in which she was trapped. She was strapped high up on the wall of a large, log-cabin styled room. It was lavishly furnished in the sort of soft, cushy items a human might enjoy. But it was also decorated with different, strange, mystical things a powerful magician might find useful. A strange looking frame of shelves was nailed onto the wall and within each little alcove sat a glass ball with stars whirling crazily inside. There were hundreds of these little glass, fist-sized balls.

The wall across from her had been blasted out, leaving a huge charred hole wherein four horses abreast could have easily walked. The open space was now blocked by a swirling mass of dark clouds, which churned in upon itself like a miniature hurricane.

But midway between her and the hole in the wall stood a person, a wizard.

"Savas-Zev, I presume," Bran growled in hatred.

"Ah, so you have heard of me," the wizard said smiling slowly. "I'm glad to see I'm so famous among your kind."

Savas-Zev approached her, smiling all the while. He was tall and thin and in his robes swirled a myriad of dark colors, which contrasted sharply with his pale eyes. His face seemed chiseled from the bark of a rough tree, all stretched out and extremely narrow.

His odd-looking eyes were glittering brightly now in anticipation of what was to come.

"Infamous is the word I'd use," Bran put in for him. "What do you want?"

"What I want from every dwarf. To make you cower in fear of me," he replied hungrily licking his lips.

Bran actually gave a wry smile at this remark.

"Not gonna happen," she chuckled. "Sorry to spoil your play."

"That's what they all say," Savas taunted. "Some hold out longer than others. But eventually, they all give in."

Bran raised her chin resolutely and her eyes sparkled a challenge back to him.

"I don't believe you," she said.

Savas-Zev smiled widely, seeming not at all bothered by her resistance.

"And so it begins," Savas chuckled. "I do so love this part. Especially when I have a Yazu to play with."

Bran's eyes narrowed, remembering the curse of the name. Savas-Zev caught the look and the thought.

"So you think it will hurt me now I've said it and you'll be vindicated." He chuckled loudly in scorn. "My girl, I've spent a lifetime deciphering how to unravel your dwarf charms and spells. I am now an expert at it. Your little word curse has no effect on me. Sorry to spoil *your* play."

He turned from her and walked over to the shelf with the globes. He tenderly caressed a few, considering his next move.

"You came here seeking answers. You had heard Tor Ambroc had suffered some kind of disaster, correct?"

Bran said nothing. Unaffected by her silence he continued.

"You have family members here and wanted to see if they yet lived. Maybe you hoped they had somehow escaped. Maybe you thought you could help?"

Again Bran's only answer was silence.

"My plague was quite thorough, my dear. Although I did save a few lives to toy with."

He picked out a particular globe and made sure she saw him do it. He wandered slowly back to her corner of the room.

"Maybe you wonder how it was I knew your name?" he said as he polished the stone with his sleeve. His demented eyes met hers. "Yes?"

She again refused to answer.

"Your family has always given me particular trouble. So, I make it a point to give them particular trouble. Your mother held out quite long," he said this while locking eyes with her. So he saw the slight spark in them when he mentioned her mother.

"Ah, so that's it," he whispered in a voice she was sure to hear. "You don't know whether she's alive or dead and you're looking for her. You want your mommy back. How sweet!"

Savas-Zev held up the globe to examine it better. He turned it slowly in his hands and the star inside spun and darted about, as if attempting to escape his touch.

"Well, I guess you could say she's still alive. After a fashion," he told her.

He began to chortle in glee when he saw the light of acknowledgment fire in her eyes. All the color drained from her face. She swallowed with difficulty, her pains gone in an instant.

Yaffa's spirit, her very soul, was trapped inside the crystal?

Bran blinked and looked hard at the globe, then the chuckling wizard, then to the wall of shelves each holding a separate crystal ball.

There were hundreds of them.

"They're called soul cages, my dear. They are my most prized possession, my souvenirs of each glorious conquest. I have a collection this large from each dwarf community my army has razed. Some are from other places but most of these are from Tor Ambroc."

He held out the globe to her, tempting her.

"Here is your dear mommy, Yaffa," he told her. "She put up quite a brave fight. But she quailed at the end like they all do. Would you like to hear how I did it? Would you like to know what I told her that made her scream and grovel at my feet?"

Tears were flowing, streaming down Bran's face like rain.

"I... don't... believe you," she stammered uselessly.

He smiled the most hateful smile she had ever seen on anyone's face.

"You keep telling yourself that and one day you might actually believe it. If you live long enough."

Savas-Zev's eyes narrowed and he laughed softly. Coming closer, he slowly and tenderly wiped the tears away from her cheeks.

"Ah, dwarf tears," he whispered in feigned sympathy. "I should save these for another spell. I'm sure they will eventually prove useful."

He waved his wet hand and the tears turned to crystal. He strode over to what looked like an alchemist's worktable and picked up a glass bottle. He then made a fist and Bran's crystal tears shattered like threads of frost. He poured them into the bottle and corked it.

"Yes, very useful indeed," he mused almost to himself. "The tears of a soon to be dwarf martyr. Now what could I do with these, I wonder?"

Bran bristled in revulsion. She wanted to spit in his face or bite his nose but she was afraid he'd taste like his magic smelled. She wanted to do something, anything to hurt this monster. She could only shiver and hate him.

"Oh, I think you *do* believe me," he said to her. "And what good have you done for them, your family, your whole community? What good could you possibly do them hanging up there on the wall?"

Still smiling that maddening smile of his, he retreated a step.

"What did the Yazu think they were doing, sending a half grown, girl-child like you to do the work of a seasoned warrior? You are far too easy to break, my dear. But I have one more treat for you, Bran."

Savas-Zev replaced Yaffa's soul cage to its alcove in the shelves and returned to her. Bran tried to memorize which shelf he put it on but her eyes were watering so bad everything was blurry. She couldn't see.

"You must really hate me now, my dear, after I killed your kin and trapped your mother's soul and all," he said to her but she barely heard him. "What would you do, I wonder, if you were free? Relieve my shoulders of a swollen head? Jump on your magic horse and trample me?"

He backed off slightly, considering the prospect briefly.

"Yes, I believe you would and happily," he muttered. "It's a shame you no longer have your magic horse."

It was then Bran noticed Val was no longer on the cord about her neck where the little Dahla horse belonged. She looked up in shock.

Savas-Zev was holding Valynt in his right hand.

"Now, let's see if I remember this correctly," he said as he paced in front of her. "Your mother had one of these horses too, didn't she? I killed that one, burned it to a crisp in a pillar of fire which was just glorious to behold."

He came up to whisper in her ear.

"Then I found out I had made a mistake. I should have never destroyed her Dahla horse. I should have taken it from her and her horse could have then become my great war steed."

He drew back his hateful presence a bit and grinned sadistically at her.

"No matter, because now I have you. I can take your horse. And you won't be able to do a thing about it, my dear," he chuckled softly.

Bran's heart was pounding loudly in her ears. Her blood was boiling as she quietly tested the bonds which held her arms. But they were secure and held her fast. She thought of a million different unpleasant things she would do to Savas-Zev if she were free.

He held her little Dahla horse in front of her, just out of reach, ever teasing and taunting her.

"You don't know how to use it," she replied obstinately.

"I don't need to," Savas purred in deceptive sweetness. "Because you're going to tell me, aren't you?"

Bran growled, twisting her wrists and jerking violently at the cuffs, oblivious to the pain shooting down her arms. Her numbed hands were clenched in white-knuckled fists.

"Never!" she slowly snarled in a low voice.

"Oh, I think you will," Savas-Zev replied. He came quite close, putting his face inches away from hers so she could smell his breath. He tantalized her by stroking the little Dahla horse gently, tracing light patterns with Val's tiny, wooden hooves across the skin of her face. She could feel the familiar warmth of life in the little wooden horse.

"You see, I have a spell which will make anyone, even a dwarf, tell me anything I want to know no matter how well guarded the secret. Rest assured, you will tell me how your little Dahla horse is used, whether you will it or no."

Bran wished she had a vial of poison, like her mother once had, to drink and wished her hands were free to drink it. She also wished she could get in just one good stab at this hated wizard before she died. It was a futile wish.

Savas-Zev stepped back and held out Valynt's Dahla horse to her. The tiny wooden horse stood proudly upon his open palm just out of reach. Bran could see clearly every small detail, every cut of the carver's knife, every tiny shading of the wood grain and the little twisted knot on the figurine's hindquarter.

"Now tell me," he ordered.

His voice lacked the previously simpering tone and was now cold and hard.

Bran shut her mouth and set her jaw. Silence was her answer. Savas-Zev ordered again. She glared daggers at him and shook her head in denial. He ordered one more time in a softer tone. She raised her head and stared him defiantly in the eye without uttering a single peep.

The wizard was silent one moment more, smiling as he thought. Then he raised his left hand and his long, spidery fingers wound themselves in a certain intricate pattern. He spoke no word. Bran could see the glittering, smoky tendrils of magic weave from his fingernails as he etched the pattern in the air through the spectrum she normally used in the darkened tunnels of her home. The air in the room grew hot and heavy.

Bran stiffened as the tendrils of magic knotted themselves into a mass between her and the wizard. Then they blazed to life and the spell hurtled like a flaming arrow into her face. She struggled, resisting with every obstinate power of her dwarf core. She felt as if someone else's spirit was in her body, making her do things she never wanted to do, things which were against her will. She fought them, growling in restrained fury at the demand forced upon her. She began to tremble and sweat violently.

One corner of Savas-Zev's mouth tipped upward in a wry smile. His eyes narrowed as he waited patiently. He held up his hand again, turned it so the back of it faced Bran and bent his fingers twice toward himself, summoning the power back to him. At once the intruding presence within Bran left with a huge leap, dragging some of her spirit along with it. She sagged forward on the cuffs and moaned from the strain the action put on her tormented wrists. She immediately felt exhausted, as if a part of her soul had left with the wizard's magic.

The moan was a sound and that sound released the floodgates of her tongue. Before she could recall or stop it, the words were flowing forth, words of explanation as to how to use the Dahla horse. Everything she didn't want him to know came spilling forth from her traitorous mouth she was no longer in control of. And all the while, he stood there smiling broadly, his bright teeth flashing in mockery of her dwarf resistance.

Savas-Zev had won. Valynt was truly his now.

She screamed in rage before she realized this was exactly what he wanted her to do. She stretched and strained against the cuffs, making the blood flow from her wrists. She hurled curses at him as he turned his back on her.

The wizard totally ignored her.

He stepped up to the blasted hole in the wall housing the magical storm. He held the Dahla horse and called Valynt's name. Immediately, a sandstorm gathered in front of him, spinning and coalescing into a solid, dark shape. The shadowy shape became clearer and more distinct, more obviously horse in appearance.

A large, black horse stood in front of him with elaborate red trappings. Its mane and tail were long and luxurious. Its shining black eyes were Valynt's eyes.

The great warhorse looked with concern to Bran and in even more surprise at the wizard who stood before it.

"Magnificent!" Savas-Zev mused as his eyes hungrily devoured his new pet. "Better than I had ever hoped."

"Val," Bran groaned in a voice barely above a whisper and she sagged helplessly in her bonds.

Valynt raised her head and nickered softly at Bran and was promptly smacked on the nose for it by the wizard. The great black horse rocked back on her haunches in surprise and fear from the action.

"You are mine now!" the wizard growled in warning to the horse. "She no longer exists!"

But Bran saw the blow and came roaring to life on the chains.

"Don't you ever hit my horse again!" she snarled as she leapt angrily against her restraints, ignoring the complaints of her body. She braced her dangling feet against the wall and shoved off to the full extent she could manage.

"I daresay you won't be needing a horse anymore, magic or otherwise," the wizard informed her. "Dwarves should never be allowed to use magic. Look at this! You've taken a perfectly wonderful tool and ruined it by giving it emotions! Fool!"

Savas-Zev grabbed the reins harshly and mounted the great, black horse in one graceful swing. Valynt bobbed and shook her head, not liking the stern hold on her mouth from the wizard.

"One ride should be sufficient to wrest control away from your influence. When we return, your dear Valynt will do what I want without question. She will not even notice you anymore. Think well on this, my dear."

With that, he swung Valynt roughly about and leapt through the swirling storm of chaos, which filled the charred hole in the wall.

Bran sagged limply on her bonds. A sob developed deep in her chest, which she never released. The pain of her imprisonment returned with a vengeance and she receded back into black dreams. It was so hard to breathe now. Her lungs burned from the effort.

"Val," she whispered dismally. "I want my horse back."

Iyorath and Garn sat on the ground and recovered their strength. Both were breathing hard. Their clothes were slashed and ripped and their faces splattered with blood. About them lay a score of dead, hacked goblins. Both elf and dwarf still clutched their weapons warily, in case any survivors jumped through the bushes.

"Where *is* she?" Iyorath gasped, nearly out of breath.

He sat with his back to a tree, elbows on his knees and head inclined forward, worn out with exertion. He panted wearily and his fingers, which still gripped his sword, shook slightly.

"This young dwarf lass has proven to be a great deal of trouble," the elf muttered in irritation, gazing up with one sharp blue eye, through the disheveled blond locks at his partner.

Garn only grunted in total agreement.

"Maybe she would have been more obedient if she had been an only child instead of one of several litters!" Garn sniffed. "Still, the lass has gumption."

Iyorath sighed and stood up, stretching his limbs experimentally.

"Well, her 'gumption' is going to get someone killed!" he muttered again. "If she's not dead already."

Garn thought for a moment. Then he put down his mighty axe and rummaged about his person finally pulling out a small leather bag. He upended the contents into his hands, shook them briefly then cast the rune stones on the blood-soaked ground.

Iyorath stood guard while he did this although he really wanted to peer closely at the pattern of fall for the stones.

"What do they say?" he asked the crouching dwarf.

Garn considered the stones, stroking his mussed beard absently.

"They say we should do nothing about Delkan. She is safe," he grunted.

"What?" exclaimed Iyorath and came over to scrutinize the fall although he could make even less sense of the stones than Garn. "We're surrounded by scattered hoards of goblins. How could she possibly be safe?"

"I'm just tellin' ya that's what the stones say," explained Garn, waving a hand at the ground in front of him. "They say unmistakably Delkan is safe."

"Safer than you're about to be," rasped a harsh voice from above their heads.

Garn sprang to his feet, stones forgotten and axe held at the ready. Iyorath spun about brandishing his sword and looked up to the trees.

Rath-Tor sat on a lower branch, his sharp eyes glittering dangerously at them both.

"Nice time for you to show up! We could have used some help back there, ya moldy ol' crow. Where have ya been?" sputtered Garn in exasperation.

Rath-Tor shook his head in a very eagle-like way and spoke again.

"Silly two-legs! No time! No time! A band of goblins is just over the next rise and heading this way! If you don't follow me right now, you'll be shredded rabbit by the next hour. Now follow me," and it flew away.

Grumbling mightily, Garn scooped up his stones still muttering non-stop.

"If I ever catch that speckled brat of a pony who dumped me and ran off with Delkan, I'll lop its head off!" he sputtered.

Iyorath only grinned and shook his head.

Chapter 32

The young unicorn stood with his father and waited. The unicorn stag was grazing calmly but his two-year-old offspring could only pace fitfully. Scattered messenger hounds walked or lounged nearby, seemingly unaware of the youth's nervousness.

Finally the mother unicorn reappeared, stepping silently through the brush. The stag raised his head and the young one danced happily up to her.

"I have spoken to your dwarf friend and she has told me, quite honestly, how she lost her legs," she told them.

"We can help her, right?" said the youth eagerly.

The mother turned her eyes on her fawn and a stern light flashed in them, which made him back up unexpectedly.

"I will do nothing of the sort!" she told him.

"What?" exclaimed the little one. *"Why not?"*

"Because I do not think it is right to reward disobedience. She countermanded a direct order from her commanding officer. She was wrong. I will not reward the offence by healing her. Nor do I think it's entirely possible to do so."

"But... but... we're unicorns!" he stammered, not understanding. *"We're supposed to heal. It's what we do!"*

"We also are supposed to advise," she told her son. *"I will not heal this dwarf."*

The young unicorn fidgeted and stomped in agitation.

"She needs healing," he stubbornly put in. *"If you don't heal her then..."*

The mother considered her fawn briefly.

"Do what you will," she told him in a gentler tone. "But I will not condone or assist you in any way. This is not my destiny. Good day, my son."

She strode past him while he stood there, pouting and pawing. The young unicorn went back to pacing fitfully.

"It's not right! She needs healing," he muttered when she had left.

"That may be, my son," replied the father. "But maybe she should come to the healing on her own. Maybe it will mean more to her spirit's journey."

The youngling glared in frustration at his dad. Then he shook his head, shaking his short, curly, snowy mane about and continued to pace angrily, wearing a track into the grass. Finally he stopped and faced his father defiantly.

"Then I will do it!" he said resolutely. "I'll do it all by myself if I have to."

The stag stepped quickly in front of him.

"You were advised to do nothing," he sternly reminded him.

"I was advised, not ordered," he returned. "If no one will help her, then I will do it."

The stag sighed deeply.

"Your mother is not even sure it is possible," the father pointed out. "You may drain or kill yourself doing this and still accomplish nothing."

"The attempt is never nothing. It is at least something, some action taken. I mean to do this, Father, with or without you," he replied.

The stag thought for a long moment. Finally, he gave a deep sigh and nodded.

"If this is the case then I will help you," the stag told his son. "Your mother would never forgive me if you died trying. You will need the guidance of an older and dare I say, MUCH WISER individual if you are to help at all."

"Thank you, Dad," he said.

The older unicorn shook his head knowingly and glared at his son. To himself he thought, 'Ah, the birth of wisdom. I hope he doesn't break his young heart over this. And yet, maybe it will all be for the good.'

The stag sensed he might have to say farewell to his son's innocence.

It would be regrettable but necessary.

He gave another heavy sigh.

Bran had no idea how long the wizard had been gone. All she knew was she could no longer escape to the blessed fog of unconsciousness anymore. It was getting increasingly difficult to draw breath. She could no longer feel her extremities and the last time she had looked at her fingers, she found they were blue. She doubted she would ever have use of them again.

She heard the sound of the wizard's return. Almost against her will, she looked up. She wanted to see if Val had returned alone, or at least still had the spark of fight left in her.

It was a horrible sight.

Val returned, head low and eyes lifeless. The glorious black mane hung damp and limp upon the once proud neck. The horse was soaked everywhere with sweat and foamed up about all the trappings. Blood ran from her mouth and her lips were torn from the constant sawing motion of heavy hands on the reins. Steam rose from the great black horse and her legs shook with exhaustion.

Bran's heart ached for her old friend. She looked desperately for some sign of recognition from the horse, some glance or plea for help, to let her know there was still some sort of concerned relationship there between them. The horse met her eyes and Bran immediately wished she hadn't. The look was accusing. She had betrayed her by letting Savas-Zev take Val away from her. How could she have let this happen?

The lifeless eyes turned away and resumed staring hopelessly off into space, hoping the new cruel master was now done with her.

Savas-Zev was looking at Bran intently, observing every emotion and grief-stricken wrinkle which passed over her face. He smiled in supreme satisfaction.

"So," he mused sadistically. "By breaking the horse I have broken the rider. How appropriate! How does the pain feel, my dear? Crushing? Brutal? Overwhelming? The end of all your hope?"

"Go to hell, you bastard!" Bran muttered and the wizard just laughed.

She sagged her head dejectedly. She ignored her laboring lungs and succumbed willingly to the blackness of her inner mind.

The wizard wondered if he had just one more empty soul cage left.

CHAPTER 33

Vilmar lay pillowed in the long, thick summer grass, his mind drifting pleasantly. He was starting to really enjoy this new turn his life had taken. Sure, bad things had happened just recently and he knew he couldn't change the past. But he felt well equipped now to handle any problem which might happen next. He felt young and strong and very much alive.

He was constantly amazed by the sort of things he could do now. Just by touching a tree and concentrating the tiniest bit, he could feel the sap flow and the leaves whisper. If the wind blew, he could scent like a hound, picking out and identifying the many faint smells it carried from nearby or faraway. He could recognize people by their own personal, individual smell. He could feel the fire smile at him, he could even put his hand within the flames and watch it caress him fondly without harming him. The water spoke to him and carried him messages just like a dwarf hound as it nourished him. And the earth constantly spoke to him. At the slightest effort, he could open himself to all the hidden signs the elements always carried with them. He could read the elements like a book printed in large letters. It was an incredible, intoxicating experience.

There were still things he needed to perfect. It was difficult for him to completely shut down the elements, to revert to as he had been before. It was difficult and what was more, he didn't like it. This new feeling was like he had discovered a novel sensation which had previously been hidden. He felt like a blind man who could suddenly see. He knew he didn't need to see; he could get along without it quite well. But there were so many facets to this new way and he so wanted to totally explore and investigate, whether they were bad or good. The experience was enriching and fascinating to him right now.

He remembered his previous discussion with the unicorn as he held and stroked Snow Crow's pearly, white head.

"Can I talk to the animals now?" he asked and the unicorn laughed gently.

"My dear, you could always talk to animals! You were born with the talent. Your ability to do so now has just been stepped up a notch. But it will not be as easy as you think."

"What do you mean?" he asked.

"Well, talking to animals, non-magical animals like our dear friend Snow Crow here, will be a bit tricky for you. It will be a little like reading in a different language but having never spoken it so your pronunciation is all off. Talking to animals is nothing like the way you and I converse."

Vilmar turned to the unicorn and his expression begged her to continue.

"Animals who are not magical have a very different way of communicating, than say, unicorns. In their minds, they live in the moment. You will have to exist in their moment to talk to them. The past is a vague thing for them to grasp, the future is even more difficult. A horse knows if it approaches within the other mare's personal space, it is going to get kicked. But it cannot grasp the notion, if this human does this thing, there will be war in the future. Understand?"

Vilmar screwed up his face in concern.

"I think so," he replied. "So if I tell them there is a bad man who wants to destroy the entire world..."

"Too much," broke in the unicorn. *"Just shorten it to bad man. Keep it brief. And cut the flowers out of your words. It must be short and direct."*

Vilmar nodded understanding.

"Keep it in the moment," he said and the unicorn nodded in agreement. "I guess I won't be having any meaningful conversations with ants anytime soon!"

The unicorn laughed.

"I would certainly advise against it," she replied.

"It sounds very tricky indeed," he sighed.

"You have your entire life to perfect it," she told him. *"You have plenty of time. Don't be so impatient, my little fawn."*

He sighed in his remembering and snuggled down deeper in the long, fragrant grass stems. He wrapped the heavy green cloak about him as a chill breeze blew briefly. The cloak was a gift from the earth and with it, he could vanish into any surrounding, as well camouflaged as a chameleon. Its fibers were strange, yet smooth to the touch and it always smelled of the earth in spring.

He sighed in contentment. He was starting to feel comfortable in his own skin.

He dozed lightly, drifting within his mind's inner secret places. Pleasant dreams flitted in and out, like bees hovering over a field of flowers. But slowly other dreams crept into his consciousness, dreams which ventured unbidden from a source other than his own mind.

It started slowly at first, with just brief flashes of light, which lasted no longer than a blink of his eyes. But they interrupted his dreams in a curious way, pulling his attention more to them than to the peaceful, vague images of sleep. Still sleeping but only lightly now, he focused his inner eye on the flashes.

The first thing his mind grabbed hold of with any certainty was fire, a great, huge conflagration of hungrily crackling flames. What were the flames consuming? He forced the images to slow enough to recognize and identify them.

A town was burning, a great town, a familiar town. He knew the town.

Kopa was burning.

With a sudden gasp, he awoke with a jolt and sat up.

He looked about in alarm. Nothing seemed out of place. He paused to catch his breath and calm his racing heart. Was it then only a dream?

He paused, sensing his surroundings. Something was clearly not right. The normal woodland sounds seemed distant and far away. He felt strangely separate from his surroundings as if he were still caught in the dream.

It had seemed so real, so tangible. He had never dreamed so vividly before. Something was definitely not right.

He took a deep breath and sank his consciousness deep into the warm, friendly earth. He could feel his fingers becoming the roots of all the plants who encircled him. The earth welcomed his thoughts happily, joyous to be acknowledged by him. He asked the earth what had happened, whether the dream was true or not. Immediately she replied.

His mind was swept away with a speed which left him dizzy, to the ground outside his father's farrier shop. With the earth's eyes, he looked.

His home was burning. He could see the flames, smell the smoke and charred flesh and he could feel the blood seeping into the ground. Every building was burning, and there was too much blood for the earth to digest all at once. Around the town of Kopa, the earth was imbalanced. The earth had not caused this, nor had any other element.

He was snapped back with a jolt to his body. The acrid scent of burning flesh still thick in his nostrils.

Vilmar bolted to his feet and began running for home. He did not see the obstacles in his path. He jumped logs before him, barely glancing at them long enough to gauge the leap. He shot through brambles and vines, uncaring if they should snag him. His feet pounded the earth and his lungs labored for air. He thought nothing of himself. He only wanted to get to Kopa as soon as possible. Maybe it hadn't happened yet. Maybe it was just a premonition. If this was true, he might still be able to stop it somehow. His heart in his throat, he ran onward, fearing the worst.

He was almost there when a scent he knew as familiar, intruded through the smoky smell, which clung to his nostrils. He slowed and looked about using more than just his eyes to seek out the source of the odor.

He spied a patch of blue huddled whimpering underneath a clump of bushes. The blue spot smelled like home, like his home, like his family. He slowed still more and crept quietly and slowly toward the color which did not belong to the forest. On his hands and knees, senses wide awake and alert he crept around the front of the bushes.

Dwyn was curled there in a dejected, ragged little ball. In shock Vilmar reached for her and then stopped. He had smelled something more.

He could smell goblins on her. And he smelled something else. He recoiled from this other smell and began to shudder violently. Dwyn wailed quietly in despair as she looked up at him. She knew she had no need to tell her brother what had happened to her. He already knew. He could smell it.

Vilmar's hands clenched in fists and he felt his face flush in an anger he had never before experienced. Dwyn's innocence had been ripped from her. And where had he been? He had not stopped it from happening. He could have stopped it. He felt certain now he could have prevented it. But he had not been there when she needed him most and this unspeakable thing had happened to her. He ground his teeth without knowing it. He had not been there and he hated himself for it.

He turned away from Dwyn, too consumed with anger to say a word. He began to walk to Kopa town. His footprints smoked with every step he took. His blood was boiling. He had no thought other than to kill as many goblins as he could. At this very moment, he wanted to rid the world of every last goblin. Time stood still for him. Every emotion inside of him was bubbling and seething in intense fury. He did not see the forest around him. He did not see anything but the path which lay winding before him, the path to his destroyed home.

And then there was a blurry white shape in front of him, standing steadfast like a pillar of pure white snow against the raging bonfire, which was just below the surface inside of him.

"You're not going to stop me this time, unicorn," he growled in a voice which sounded very strange to himself.

"I probably should but I won't," came the answer. *"I only want you to listen to one thing I have to say and then you can blast every goblin to beyond for all I care!"*

"Which is?" he did not have the patience for talking right now. He also had no intention of being wisely counseled out of this.

"Look at the body at your feet. Don't you recognize it?" she said.

Vilmar cast his seething gaze downward. He was so angry he had not noticed he was about to trip over a great dark shape. A dead mule laid there, a black mule. He knelt to examine the animal more closely.

"Echo!" he finally said in shock.

The unicorn nodded pointedly.

"Bran has come home. She was taken prisoner. She is the wizard's special toy now," the unicorn informed him in a flat tone.

Vilmar's fists clenched tighter, making the knuckles go white. He began to tremble dangerously.

The unicorn shivered a bit and retreated a step. She had to pick her words cautiously now for he was furious enough and powerful enough to hurt her. Carefully she continued, keeping her words brief and concise.

"She yet lives but I'm not sure for how much longer. When you march into town, boiling with the lust for revenge, please be sure not

to parboil the other prisoners or Bran. Do something good with your anger. Rescue Bran."

The unicorn backed out of his way and made no move to stop him.

"Now, do as you will, green wizard," she said softly and bowed deeply to him, foreleg bent and spiraling lance touching the earth.

He barely glanced her way and did not acknowledge the gesture. He just marched straight past her. The prints his boots left sizzled and smoked the grass beneath them.

"No one can stop you now, Vilmar," the unicorn said more to herself than to him.

Vilmar was on his own. The unicorn shivered again, afraid of him and for him. Right now the young green wizard was a force worth being afraid of.

Thoughts came with great difficulty to Vilmar. He wanted to destroy something, anything completely right now. He felt hot all over. He felt as strong as an angry god. The sky above him billowed with dark storm clouds and the earth rumbled ominously beneath his feet. He felt strong, incredibly strong and powerful.

The elements responded to his rage. The earth heaved slightly about him but not under him. He continued to walk forward and the surrounding trees shuddered and leaned away from him, bushes and thickets parted for him. No plant or thing impeded his passage.

He left the shelter of the forest and stepped upon the main road going through Kopa town. He could see the charred remains of his stable and home buildings. Automatically, he turned toward them. He wanted to see his family.

He found the body of his father easily. Conal lay face down in the ashen earth, hand still clutching a pitchfork as a weapon. Carefully, Vilmar turned his father's body over and his face twisted at revulsion at what he saw.

Conal was half body, half burned skeleton. Some of his face remained frozen in a perpetual grimace of pain and horror.

Vilmar turned his face away and let the body slide back down to the ground. His hands were covered in ash, blood and gore from his father's remains. He stared blankly at his hands and the muck registered dimly in some distant part of his brain.

Vilmar said nothing but looked about his home. He could smell and see the charred remains of horses, which had once been stabled safely within these walls. In his mind's eye, he could hear their screams as they were burned alive. The stench of the burned was so strong he could taste it.

He slowly stood up. He bowed his head and backed away from the first home he had ever known. As he did so, what was left roared suddenly into flames, burning all before him. He looked deeply into the raging, crackling flames. The wind from the fire whipped his red-tinged locks and warmed his already hot face.

Silently, he turned from the bonfire, which had been his home and continued onward down Kopa's city streets. A harsh wind spun about him as he went, setting his hair to dancing and his green cloak to billow wildly about him.

A goblin saw him and fearlessly came charging up brandishing a spear and laughing gleefully. Vilmar locked eyes with the goblin and its cries were suddenly choked off. Its eyes bulged, and dropping the spear, it clawed frantically at its throat. Gasping and struggling for breath, it sank to its knees in front of Vilmar. The young wizard continued to glare impassively as the final gasp left the goblin and it fell over dead. Vilmar stepped over the body and continued on. He still said nothing.

A goblin watching from a charred wall to the side, readied its bow and took careful aim, shooting an arrow at the lone figure.

Vilmar never looked but stopped and caught the arrow in an outstretched arm. The arrow blazed into flames in his hand and was ash in a matter of seconds. He then turned his face and locked gazes with the archer. The goblin only had time to drop his bow and turn before, with a shrill shriek, he became a pillar of cracking flames.

Vilmar continued his silent walk, smelling for Bran.

Another cheering goblin came charging up to Vilmar, waving a sword threateningly about its head. A bolt of lightning struck him dead in an instant before it could even screech in surprise.

From the relative safety of a burned-out building, Dask watched him advance. He turned quickly to a band of goblins beside him and ordered them to rush the young wizard in a mob. Shouting with confidence, they obeyed, each one brandishing a different wicked looking weapon.

They never made it there. There was a rumble and a groan and the earth opened in a great fissure around Vilmar. Screaming and shrieking they tumbled downwards as the earth fell in about their heads.

Vilmar continued onward unopposed. The charred remains of buildings suddenly exploded into flames about him, roaring, hissing and twisting in power.

Dask silently retreated, commanding every soldier he passed to go and stop the strange figure in a dark green cloak who was slowly and stealthily advancing through the town. He saw two enormous ogres with heavy clubs come stomping by, looking for the cause of all the commotion. Dask only pointed and growled, "Get him!" They were more than happy to comply.

Chuckling maliciously, they approached, not expecting any trouble from this lone human figure in green. A great bolt of ball lightning hurtled abruptly past Vilmar, blowing his sandy red hair about in its wake, incinerating them in an instant.

Vilmar barely slowed in his march as still smoldering chunks of ogre fell like smelly hail around him in sickening plops. His eyes were forward, his attention on something other than his attackers.

But still the enemies came on in ever-increasing numbers. Vilmar barely noticed them or what became of them.

Four huge trolls rushed him, seeking to attack from four sides all at once. The earth reached up and grabbed the legs of two, holding them fast as they struggled in confusion to wrest free their legs. Their confusion changed to alarm, then panic as the earth beneath them changed into deep mud and slowly began to swallow them.

The other two made it up to Vilmar and took hold of him roughly by the arms. Cheering in victory they hauled him off of the ground. This broke his concentration for just a bit. Quietly, Vilmar looked each one in the eye in turn and smiled, not at all concerned they had apprehended him. This one small gesture from him killed the mirth in their faces and they tightened their grip in wary suspicion.

"Easy, boys," Vilmar whispered to them in an ominous tone of voice. "You're hurting me."

Their eyes bulged as they rethought the wisdom of their decision to touch him. They glanced earthward quickly as the ground beneath their feet grew blazingly hot. Before they could hop away, the earth turned into bubbling lava. They bellowed in pain and immediately dropped Vilmar onto the burning, orange lava bed where he stood calmly, completely unaffected by the molten rock. He watched emotionlessly as they were devoured, steaming and sizzling by the liquid rock beneath them. He felt nothing for their pain and agony, nothing at all.

Still calm and quiet, he made his way down the bubbling mass of quickly cooling lava, leaving footprints in the molten rock as he left. His leather boots were completely untouched by the heat. He continued on his way.

He barely noticed a huge crowd of about fifteen archers as they blocked him with arrows already notched in their bowstrings. He continued to march stony faced ahead. A command was barked by a goblin voice and as one, all bowstrings twanged. And as one, all the arrows flew straight up into the air, ignoring the direction they had been fired, and then came straight down to impale each of their respective bowmen.

Vilmar stopped his silent advance and closed his eyes. Clenching his fists and setting his jaw, he reached out with his mind. He fished about mentally for any life force which seemed to be goblin. Finding many, he called on fire.

Throughout the small town, goblins burst shrieking and screaming into flames, consumed to mere ash in brief moments.

He opened his eyes and the green wizard continued onward in his silent march.

Vilmar shoved the dying goblins in front of him roughly out of his way and continued. Above him, black storm clouds swirled and thunder rumbled, shaking the earth. The roar from the firestorms around him grew deafening. He could hear the war cry of the fire he had summoned. The voice of the flames spoke to him, laughing, singing, hissing and growling in intense joy at its own destructive vitality. He smiled at its powerful joyous dance, completely unafraid.

Dask watched him and began to fear for his own safety. This one lone figure, this strangely cloaked boy had totally decimated the ranks of their army all by himself. None opposed him. None could stop him. No one but Savas-Zev and he was gone right now. Dask thought about this briefly. He decided it would be a very good thing if he did not attract this young and obviously very powerful human's attention. Silently, Dask melted into the shadows and disappeared.

Vilmar smelled a familiar scent coming from the building in front of him. It was not human, or goblin or ogre or troll. He could smell the sickening faint traces of a wizard who was nowhere around. But this scent was different. It smelled like molten metal and forge fire and horse. It smelled like a Yazu warrior.

He stood before the huge blasted and hastily replaced doors of the mayor's opulent cabin. All his senses told him Bran was somewhere inside this building. He pulled back the powers of the elements and stopped them from destroying this house. He took hold of the ornate doorknobs and with amazing strength, ripped them completely off their weakened hinges and cast the doors far behind him like they had been fashioned from paper. Without hesitating he strode into the great house.

The minute he stepped inside, he heard voices in his head... strange, insistent voices.

"Wizard! Green wizard! Help us!"

The words were spoken by four different voices simultaneously.

He looked about with his heightened senses.

"Free us, green wizard!"

"Where are you?" he spoke aloud.

"In the little bag on the table to your right. Free us!"

He found the table to his right. The surface was littered with all sorts of strange and curious things, but what attracted his eyes immediately was the little, leather drawstring pouch, hardly bigger than his fist.

He picked up this plain, unassuming bag.

"You need to save your friend first. Then you can free us," spoke the voices in his head.

"Where is she?" he asked.

"In the next room chained to the wall. Hurry! She has very little time left!"

He tied the talking bag to his belt and at once strode into the next room. A quick glance about and he found Bran. Swiftly, he rushed over to her and looked up at where she hung from the wall like a grisly portrait.

His heart ached in pain when he saw her condition.

"No!" he whispered in agony.

She was in pretty bad shape. Her clothes were ragged and bloodied along with her face. Her short, powerfully built arms and hands were blue from lack of circulation. Her head hung forward on her chest and if he hadn't known it was Bran he would have thought she was a male dwarf. When last he had seen her, her beard wasn't completely grown in like it was now. It looked pretty shabby, too.

"How dare they!" Vilmar muttered angrily.

He swallowed with difficulty and tried to calm himself. His hands shook as he reached out and touched her skin. She felt cold, terribly cold to the touch and did not react. He held his wrist up to her mouth, testing for breath. The faintest little breeze from her blue lips tickled the hairs on the back of his freckled wrist.

He gestured briefly and the cuffs sprang open with a snap, dropping their contents. Vilmar caught her as gently as he could and turned her over in his arms. He cradled her tenderly like a helpless babe as he knelt there on the floor and tried to rouse her. He patted her face and rubbed her arms, trying to get the circulation back into her limbs. She stayed cold. Vilmar took a deep breath and called on fire to be passive. He took hold of one cold arm and felt the flush of warmth leave him and go to her. He placed his hand over her chest and called on wind. A little dust devil spun about them and her chest began to rise and fall more deeply.

She gave a tiny moan and stirred weakly in his arms. The sound brought tears of relief to Vilmar's eyes.

"Come on now, Bran, open your eyes and talk to me," he whispered gently. "Call me a fool, bare-faced human or something. Just let me know you'll make it a little longer. Please, Bran, wake up."

Bran's eyes cracked open a slit.

"Vilmar?" she managed to rasp out.

"Yes, I'm here," he replied, trying not to shout in joy.

"You're hot," she mumbled softly. "So very hot. Dwyn was right. You are burning."

Her eyes closed and her voice faded into silence.

"I'm not burning," he reassured her. "I'm alive and you're alive and we're both safe. Do you hear me? You're safe, Bran."

She moaned again as if in refusal. She muttered something Vilmar could not quite make out.

"What?" he asked. "Bran, say it again. What did you say?"

"Val," she mumbled and her tone was one of complete despair. "Val is gone. He took Val away from me. He's got her now."

Vilmar growled deep in his chest and his eyes, which had quieted, blazed with an inner cold fire once more.

"We'll get Valynt back. I promise you we will. We will get her back."

He clasped Bran tightly to his chest and rose to his feet. Bran slipped back into dark dreams and he let her. Vilmar wrapped the green cloak tightly around them both. He pulled the fire back inside him and left the wizard's lair.

He stepped outside and looked about him. Everything was ablaze and in chaos. He looked up to the sky with its seething, boiling, black clouds. He drew his hood down to shadow his face fully. As he did so, there was a crash of lightning and a rolling boom of thunder. It began to rain furiously, a freezing, sleeting pounding rain, which sliced through everyone who sought to avoid it. The ground quickly turned to an icy mush beneath the feet of everyone but Vilmar.

He left the town of Kopa. His footsteps now housed a thick cold, sheet of ice within them. It began to hail and snow in his wake even though it was midsummer.

No one stopped him. No one dared to even try.

He disappeared like a dream into the steadily increasing mist.

Bran's mind drifted absently. She wasn't sure if she slept or was unconscious. Images flitted in and out as if she were delirious. She saw Vilmar speaking to her. At least she thought it was Vilmar. His eyes were fireballs and he was rimmed all about in flames. His voice was the voice she knew and recognized. But she wasn't sure if it was really Vilmar or some trick of Savas-Zev. Maybe the wizard could read her mind now. Maybe he could invade her thoughts and torment her here in the one private place which was left to her. She wasn't sure what to believe anymore.

A quiet voice intruded into her drifting thoughts. It called her name gently.

"Bran. Bran, dear one. Can you hear me?"

The voice was soft and motherly. She resisted, trying to flee deeper into the darkness of her mind.

"Bran, please don't run from me. You are safe now, child."

'Who are you?' she asked fearfully.

"I am the unicorn Vilmar has told you so much about. Remember his unicorn patron?"

She said nothing in reply.

"Bran, you have gone through an incredible ordeal and suffered greatly. But this is now over. You are safe. Vilmar is here too and he is also safe. You are both under my protection."

'And... Savas-Zev?' she muttered in a quivering voice full of dread.

"*You just concentrate on resting, relaxing and healing. Just sleep, dear child. I will talk to him. It is time for Savas-Zev to realize he has made some very powerful enemies. He has much to answer for.*"

Bran smiled in her dream state. The unicorn would deal with the wizard. It was more than just. She let herself relax and float. She felt a pure presence settle beside her with the intention of healing. She relaxed more and accepted its presence. It felt warm and motherly and she immediately trusted it without question. She truly felt safe.

Bran slept deeply.

CHAPTER 34

Delkan felt as if she had opened her eyes before she was truly awake. She blinked several times to clear her vision. Slowly she focused on the branches and cool leaves waving peacefully above her head.

Something big and important had happened. She felt decidedly different as if magic had brushed across her and left with her some of its essence. And it definitely wasn't dwarf magic! It felt very strange.

She tingled all over. Every pore in her body was lit with magical power. She felt like she was sparkling, like an elf at a night wedding, as if the full moon had come down and taken up residence within her short squat form. It was very odd to her earthy, dwarf senses.

She wondered if her newly grown beard had fallen out. Maybe the unicorn had turned her into an elf! How horrible that would be!

This sudden thought made her sit bolt upright in horror and her hands automatically went to her face. With great relief she discovered her beard was still there. She looked at her hands. They were still the stubby fingered, calloused and forge-hardened hands of a dwarf. She heaved one huge sigh of relief.

She then looked to her left at the figure who lay beside her. The unicorn fawn lay next to her, legs tucked neatly beneath him, barely bearded chin resting heavily on the earth. But he too seemed different, diminished somewhat. He had glowed before, like she imagined all unicorns to do. But now his bright glowing whiteness was gone, as if his magical sense had faded. He seemed like an ordinary white horse with a horn where a horse never should have a horn.

Something was wrong with him. He almost seemed depressed.

Delkan wondered if it was possible for a unicorn to get depressed. It certainly couldn't be healthy for a creature meant to heal to be struck with despair.

Delkan reached out with fingers which still buzzed in a frustrating way and laid her hand on the chalky hide.

"Unicorn?" she whispered carefully. "Are you all right, smiley face?"

"Smiley face." Delkan's mother used to call her this when she became serious. She hadn't thought about what she was going to say, it had just popped out. It brought back painful memories. With an effort she swallowed them.

"I have failed," the fawn's voice sighed dismally in her mind. *"I have failed you and I have failed myself."*

Delkan remembered what he was talking about. The unicorn was supposed to have gotten his mother to heal her. Just like Delkan suspected, the mare was not able to even attempt it. Delkan knew better than to question an elder unicorn. So she had been shocked when the fawn stepped forward to try. But not shocked enough to stop him.

Maybe she should have.

This is why she felt so tingly and strange! The unicorn fawn had tried to help grow her legs back.

Had he really failed?

Delkan was afraid to look. But she felt something was different about her lower extremities. She took a deep breath and closed her eyes. Slowly she counted to ten. Then she opened her eyes and forced herself to look down.

She did not have legs. She had no lower legs, no calves, no ankles, no feet, and no toes to wriggle.

What she did have were two stumps. The right one stretched away from her and ended in a smooth, rounded end to right above where the knee joint would have been. The other ended somewhat further with a small little hook, which looked to be a shrunken facsimile of some sort of joint.

Delkan frowned critically. She reached out and touched the leg stumps. They felt real enough, warm and alive as skin and flesh should be. She scratched the stumps lightly, leaving red marks on the white skin and was pleased to discover she could feel the claw of her nails on the new flesh. Experimentally, she moved the stumps by rolling onto her back and pedaling madly. They responded as she expected them to, even the little hook on her left stump flexed and moved at her mental command.

She nodded. This seemed quite promising. No, she did not have her legs back. No, she could not walk.

But maybe she could still ride!

The thought sent a charge of excitement racing through her veins.

She touched the little Dahla horse she still wore around her throat. Maybe Sashay was not lost to her. The very thought brought tears brimming to her eyes and a big lump to her throat. With another great effort she swallowed them. She spoke aloud to the unicorn fawn. "I do not consider this to be a failure."

The fawn's shamed expression turned to an incredulous one. He lifted his head and opened his eyes, not comprehending.

"But... you cannot walk. Not now. Not ever," he said in confusion.

"I am not concerned with walking," Delkan replied. "I want to fly! You may have made this possible."

The unicorn looked utterly perplexed. He turned in shock from Delkan's face to his sire who had come up to stand next to him and back to Delkan again.

"I don't understand," he stammered.

"I do," spoke the unicorn stag and his eyes twinkled at Delkan. *"Come, son. I will take you to our safe place to recover from your ordeal. Delkan must have some time to herself to properly test her theory."*

Delkan smiled widely back at the elder unicorn.

"I don't want to see him again without his smile!" she scolded. "Understand?"

The unicorn stag's eyes sparkled merrily and he nodded. The youth just blinked dumbly at them both, still not comprehending anything at all.

Delkan stared at her new stumps for a very long time after the two had left. So many possibilities whirled through her mind and not all of them were good. She would be taking a big chance with her heart right now. If this didn't work...

She shook her head, not allowing herself to finish the thought. She had to think ahead right now. She had to stay positive. Now how was she going to do this?

She thought backwards over the things she had experienced in her short life. She remembered a time, which seemed centuries ago, a time when her whole large family was still alive. She remembered going to a human festival. The humans were always having festivals of some kind or another. She normally found them to be tedious, overly ornate affairs with lots of disingenuous bragging and posturing for some silly reason or another. But one memory about a certain summer festival leapt out at her as she thought of it. She remembered the tilting competition. It was a strange human custom. Delkan had thought it a waste of good soldiers for the sake of entertainment, watching two competitors injure themselves in peacetime for the play of the crowd, all of which were probably too cowardly to attempt the act when it was really needed.

But the armor was fascinating. Of course, any armor was fascinating to a dwarf. She remembered sneaking her way into the stable yard where the competitors were arming up, just to get a closer look at the horses' and riders' armor. At the time she was sure she could have designed and fashioned much more sensible weaponry without all the frills and pageantry the humans obviously thought was so necessary.

She remembered a strange yet ingenious design attached to the sides of the horse's saddle. It was half of a metal tube fixed firmly to the saddle skirts meant to protect the front of the upper legs of the riders from the lances. It was metal in front and nothing in back.

Maybe she could imagine Sashay with a modified version of this contraption to help her ride. She thought about it briefly and nodded. It just might work.

Her hand trembled as she touched her little wooden Dahla horse and her heart pounded nervously in her throat. She took a deep breath and forced down her apprehension.

"Sashay!" she called.

There was a slight quiver in her voice as she tried to keep her tone confident. How long had it been since she had seen her magical friend? Months? He must be wondering what had happened.

A small breeze rippled the grass at her side and Delkan watched as the gust of wind condensed itself into a spinning, miniature tornado of dust and color. Slowly, a dark shape took form within the dust devil. It darkened even more and became a definite horse form. The wind abruptly vanished leaving a flaxen chestnut stallion with a wildly dancing white mane and tail standing before her.

Sashay turned and sniffed at the strange saddle with the metal tubes fixed to the skirts. He then turned to face Delkan and gave one wary, explosive snort.

Delkan blushed in sudden understanding. Her horse was used to seeing her standing, not reclining helplessly on the ground, not crawling like a stalking lion.

Cautiously, Delkan cleared her throat and Sashay jumped at the suddenness of the sound. She remembered she had first designed Sashay with the ability to understand her words. She prayed now the gift really was true.

"Sashay," she spoke the name softly. "Remember me? I'm Delkan."

Her magic horse sniffed the air between them cautiously, snorting with every breath.

"I got injured a few months back. I lost my legs. I'll never walk again. For a long while I thought I'd never ride either. But some things have changed. I'll need your help more than I ever did in the past. Mounting you will be... difficult."

As she spoke, Sashay approached and bumped her side with his muzzle. The touch seemed to relax and reassure the horse immensely. Quietly, he investigated Delkan's prone body lying on the ground before him. He gently touched her all over and finally came to the stumps, which were her legs. Sashay spent a lot of time there, just sniffing and touching her stumps. At last he raised his long neck and pointing his head straight up into the air, curled his lip and snorted one last time.

Without being told, Sashay curled his front legs and deposited his great bulk onto the ground beside her with a loud grunt. He turned his neck about and nuzzled Delkan with a paternal whicker.

Delkan's tears nearly spilled over. She took a deep breath. Her fingers wound into the beautiful white mane, which covered dark flame-colored hide. Delkan bit her lip and swung what was left of her right leg over Sashay's wide back. The stallion waited while she got herself settled. Delkan slipped her stumps behind the metal sleeves. She then took the leather straps which were behind them and buckled her legs securely to the metal sleeves. This done, she took another deep breath.

"Okay, boy," she said as her voice shook and cracked. "I'm in."

The head in front of her nodded as Sashay uncurled his front legs and lurched powerfully to his feet. Delkan clung to the mane desperately, afraid to use her legs. Her heart was pounding in her chest. For several long moments she just sat there crouching on his back, looking at the ground so far below her.

She was on Sashay again, sitting as a rider is supposed to sit. She licked her lips and blinked several times trying not to panic.

Sashay was standing quieter, longer than he had ever done in the past, just waiting for her command. She felt her horse's ribs heave as he sighed and then, quite suddenly, he began to rock in place, like he always did.

Delkan clutched desperately, fearfully with both her hands and her legs, expecting to hit the dirt any second.

But she didn't. She stayed in the saddle safe and secure. Sashay rocked away, pacing in place and never once did Delkan slip.

Slowly, the fear subsided from Delkan and she gave a little nervous laugh. Sashay nodded his head and flicked his ears. Her stallion stepped out beneath her and Delkan tried sitting a little straighter, a little taller. She remained securely in the saddle.

Delkan laughed again and tried cueing her horse with her inner thigh, to speed up a bit. Sashay immediately swung into a fast pace. Delkan still remained on his back, rocking in time with the horse's agile steps. A wide smile began to grow on her face. She cued Sashay faster and the stallion happily slipped into a canter. Delkan sat straight and tall and didn't even wiggle.

Delkan laughed out loud and arched her face up to meet the sun. She let the wind comb her sprouting hair and her beard. She leaned forward in the saddle and felt Sashay increase his speed. She felt the power of the surging body beneath her and shouted in joy. Once again, she felt her stallion's mane whip and sting her face and she reveled in the feeling. She drank in the wind of their speed in relieved elation. She was where she belonged. Everything seemed possible.

She could ride again!

Savas-Zev could smell the smoke before he got to Kopa town and he knew something was wrong. The charred wood and burnt flesh smell was too new.

He kicked Valynt in the ribs with his spurs. The horse beneath him groaned and fought the bit, tossing its head about, flinging bloody froth from side to side. The wizard ground his teeth and spurred his mount again. For a magical steed this one was increasingly obstinate. Just when he thought he had its spirit mastered, Valynt would dredge up more resistance.

Resentfully, the Dahla horse gave in, teeth gnashing hatefully on the harsh bit. Valynt was already weary and dripping with sweat and she knew she would get no kind words or gentle consideration from this new master.

They clattered through the icy slop into Kopa's main street. Valynt shivered at the sudden change in temperature. Savas-Zev looked about dumbfounded at what he discovered. Patches of snow and slush pocked the ground with a cold mix of icy mud. The remains of buildings were burning again in raging firestorms, which hissed and roared as if the fuel was more volatile than it actually was. Scattered about were skeletons of goblins still licked hungrily by flames. The couple hundred contingents of his troops who had taken up residence in Kopa seemed to have been decimated by some great force.

Savas-Zev could smell magic everywhere, wild untamed magic. Its lingering reek laughed at him, surrounding him like a furtive demon, amused at his attempts to discover its source.

He hailed a panicky goblin as it ran by.

"You there! What happened here?" he demanded in an angry tone.

The goblin shrieked in terror and fell screaming to the ground. It kept wailing one name over and over. "*Skrahgg*," it was saying.

Savas-Zev rode on barely comprehending. It was a name he distantly remembered. He had to dust the cobwebs off the basic goblin mythology he had learned many, many years ago without really caring about it at the time.

Skrahgg was a goblin legend. It was a fireside ghost story told to very young goblins to teach them to obey without question or the *Skrahgg* would get them. *Skrahgg* was a human wizard with a personal vendetta against all goblins. The *Skrahgg* had sworn to pursue their kind until none were left.

But Savas-Zev knew this was all fiction. The *creature* had never really existed, it was just a fairy story.

But something had happened this night to make all the goblins believe it was true.

He rode onward to his cabin headquarters. He found it still to be standing, minus its great double doors, which had been ripped off their hinges as if by a giant. Silently he dismounted and dismissed his magical steed. He saw Dask coming to meet him.

"Ah, maybe I will get a less cryptic answer from a human instead of foolish goblin superstitions," he muttered with great irritation. "Did you see what went on here?"

"Yes," replied Dask. He wore a blank expression.

"And? Were we attacked by dwarves or an army of humans?"

"No, sir," answered Dask flatly. "A young man did all this."

"A great and powerful wizard!" whined a passing goblin who fell to the ground and groveled in the mud in front of Savas-Zev.

The wizard's eyes blazed at the suggestion anything could hurt him and seeing this, the goblin cowered lower, whimpering pathetically.

The wizard's eyes turned back to Dask for confirmation and he nodded once.

"What kind of wizard?" Savas-Zev asked Dask and he shrugged.

"I'm not really sure. He seemed just a boy."

"An acolyte? An apprentice did all this?"

Dask stepped as close as he dared to his master so the groveling goblin wouldn't hear their words.

"Look about you, Lord. Does this seem to be the work of an apprentice?" he muttered as angrily as he dared. "I sent every force we had assembled here against him and he tossed them aside like rag-dolls. Nothing stopped him."

Savas-Zev glared at him with demonic eyes. With a mere wave and a shrug, the wizard extinguished the raging fires. Dask got the message. Whoever this young upstart was, the wizard felt confident he could snuff him out as easily as he had just done to the surrounding fires. Dask cast his eyes downward and backed up a step.

"I was not here," he whispered and his tone held a barely veiled threat. "If I had been here, I would have crushed him like the bug he is."

"He... stole your prisoner... Lord," the goblin managed to squeak.

"What?" Savas-Zev burst out.

He turned and rushed into the cabin. A quick glance about showed him the empty cuffs. He growled and ground his teeth in frustration. He glanced further around the room, looking to see if anything else was missing.

He noticed the little leather bag was gone.

At this revelation, his eyes grew wide and he uttered a deep wail of despair.

"It's gone!" he shouted. "He stole the grimoire!"

With an infuriated snarl, he swept everything off the table and overturned it. The cowering goblin fled into the night screeching without a backward glance. Savas-Zev just stood there bristling with rage, while Dask slowly began to back away from his master's growing temper.

A thought occurred to the wizard just then.

He turned his head slowly and impaled Dask with his gaze.

"You took it!" he hissed in a venomous tone. "You must have taken it!"

Dask suddenly found himself unable to turn or move in any way. His throat was instantly dry and the blood pounded in his ears.

"Master, no!" he pleaded.

But Savas-Zev was in no mood to hear his reasons.

"You think I haven't noticed you staring at my spell book, watching where I hid it, which spell I used? You've always dreamed about replacing me. You never could have done it on your own, but with the book to aid you... At least you thought you could."

Dask licked his lips in a frantic sort of way and his eyes glanced hastily about for some sort of escape.

The infuriated wizard crept closer, claw-like hands clenching and unclenching.

"Idiot! Do you really think you have the wit to comprehend what's in the book? Ignorant fool!" he accused creeping closer.

Dask squirmed within the confines of the spell, trying his best to break free. He had seen the wizard get mad like this before, had observed the ominous swelling of power within him and noticed the robe turn to brilliant, angry red like it was doing now. He had never wanted the master's fury aimed his way. But now he was a target in Savas-Zev's sights and there was no way he could escape being held against his will.

"I swear to you it wasn't me, Lord!" he begged.

"Liar! Thief! You should have run away when you stole it. Did you really think I wouldn't suspect you, my right hand slave?"

Dask gave up the fight. He wished he could just will himself to faint away. But this had never been a skill he was particularly good with.

"Tell me where you hid the book and I may spare your life, you miserable little rat!"

Dask wailed hopelessly. "As I said before, I did not steal your grimoire."

Dask hoped the end would be quick.
But he knew the wizard better.

CHAPTER 35

The smell of burned flesh was now heavy inside the cabin as well as outside. Impassively, Savas-Zev turned his back on the crisped and barely surviving shell, which had once been the human called Dask. He cared not what became of it. Dask no longer existed to the wizard's mind.

He turned and made his way into the inner chamber where he had once held Bran captive. He stalked about the room deep in thought.

He knew in his heart Dask had not stolen his leather bag. But his fury had been so great, it needed some sort of outlet and Dask was conveniently available at the time. But he still desired to get back his spell book. He paced back and forth, brooding about his stolen tome.

Finally, he relented and went to his scrying bowl. He grasped the sides tightly to calm himself and peered into the ever-dark depths of the magical liquid.

"Show me the thief!" he commanded angrily in a low voice.

The reflective depths of the bowl swirled and changed shape, shattering the image of a glowering wizard, and became cloudy like a sky before a storm. The black water swirled and steamed threateningly, then began to bubble and boil. The liquid suddenly rose out of the bowl like a dancing fountain and Savas-Zev sprang backward in surprise.

It had never behaved this way before.

Cautiously, he approached the scrying bowl and peered carefully over the edge. The water had gone calm and flat in an instant. No images did the surface show, not even one of his own face.

The wizard was perplexed.

"Show me the thief!" he demanded again in a sterner, louder tone.

The liquid abruptly went white as milk and the still water hissed loudly back to him.

"I will not!" came the answer.

Savas-Zev jumped back a step or two.

The bowl had never spoken to him before. The wizard's mind raced.

Then it had contacted someone else, someone who could spy on him as he had done to the rest of the world, someone magical.

"Who are you?" he asked warily, his thoughts spinning with possibilities.

There was a long pregnant pause followed by laughter. "I am the herald of your doom," came the answer.

The wizard tried to laugh in scorn but the laughter died on his lips and he did not know why. A tiny shiver of apprehension ran up his spine, like a child who knows he will soon have to answer for a recent transgression.

"Who are you?" he asked again in the softest of whispers.

Again the laughter came echoing from the depths of the bowl.

"Savas-Zev," was its reply. "For centuries I have watched you. I have watched you maim and kill, torture and destroy, wipe out families and whole communities and could do nothing because it was not time. No more! Now is the time for you to answer for your many sins against the dwarf race. Now is the time for those you have wronged to rise up and deal the final blow. Now is the time for you to know fear."

Savas-Zev circled the bowl warily. He was speechless. He did not know how to respond.

The strange voice chuckled at his discomfort and continued. "You were paid a visit today, Savas-Zev, by my champion. He knocked on your great doors but you were not home to greet him. How rude of you! Did you think you were the only wizard of power left in the world?"

Savas-Zev continued to stare incredulously at the bowl. He began to shiver in earnest. What was it about the voice, which went through him and shook him to the core like a parent's cutting remark?

The bowl chuckled musically at him again.

"Poor Savas-Zev! Even now he refuses to believe in his own mortality! How long have you cheated death and extended your life beyond all mortal grasp? What price did you pay to live the life of an elf? Oh, that's right! You never paid any price! Well, Savas-Zev, the day of reckoning is at hand!"

The liquid bubbled once and began to steam and hiss like a basket of angry snakes.

"I have groomed my champion to meet you, wizard. He is your equal, a foe well worth your dread. He is my sword, and his blade is sharp and his bite deep. The Blood Raven shall spread her great wings over all you have warped and twisted. The earth will swallow your evil but reject your body. You will be trampled under by the thunder of a thousand hooves and caged by magic of your own making. Those from the mountains' roots have already begun the song of your death chant. Do you hear them now, wizard? Where shall you run from the justice of so many souls you have wronged? Poor Savas-Zev!"

The bowl began to hum and whistle all at once and he covered his ears against the deafening pitch. The sound reverberated off everything in the room and he could feel its thunderous vibration invade his body and through the measured beating of his heart. He ground his teeth and fought the sound as it rose to a decibel he did not believe existed. Just when he thought he could stand no more, there was a blinding flash and a shattering sound. Instinctively, the wizard ducked down and covered his head with his arms.

Silence returned and it too was deafening in a final sort of way.

Warily he looked up and about. Nothing had been harmed but the bowl. It lay in shattered and steaming pieces scattered about on the floor. Of the liquid, which had once resided within there was no sign.

The scrying bowl had destroyed itself.

Or something else had destroyed it.

The unicorn strode delicately through the woods seeking something. She wound her way soundlessly past whispering leaves and slivered sunlight. A gentle breeze animated her mane and set it to tickling her pearly neck as she peered around tree trunks and past bushes. Finally she came to a stop and looked from side to side. She closed her eyes and sighed one time.

"What are you doing up there, my little fledgling?" she asked simply. She inclined her head sideways to gaze up into the branches overhead.

Vilmar looked down and smiled, not at all surprised she had found him. "Thinking," was his terse reply.

"Really? Just thinking?" she repeated.

Her mind's voice lapsed into silence. Her silence pulled Vilmar's attention back down to the ground. She stood there gazing up at him with her deep blue eyes, swishing her tufted tail.

"Well, what else would I be doing?" he retorted. He really wasn't in the mood for conversation, especially the type he suspected the unicorn to pull out of him.

"Are you really thinking or are you running from yourself?"

Vilmar gave a frustrated sigh and buried his head in his arms. She knew him too well. "I have a lot to think about."

He felt rather than saw the unicorn smile at him.

"I daresay you do!" she chuckled back at him softly.

Vilmar shifted in his perch in the tree. "Why didn't you stop me?" he asked in a whisper and the mildly jesting tone was gone. It was replaced by a look of such naked fear and dread, raw as an open wound. The unicorn audibly tsked in reply. His ice blue eyes were wet and large like those of a very scared child thrown into an adult situation.

"I could not have stopped you. You would have hurt me," she whispered in the most sympathetic tone she could muster.

"Me? Hurt you? Is it even possible? You're so ancient," he asked as the tears shivered on his lids.

"This is how I have schooled you. To take on the things you will be called to do, you must be extremely powerful. Powerful enough to injure a unicorn."

"But I wouldn't have..." he bit back the words, understanding now just how unsure he was of the answer. He buried his face in his arm as the tears flowed down his freckled cheeks.

"I'm not sure I want this," he mumbled into his sleeve, afraid to look at her anymore.

"I know, my dear fawn, I know," she whispered back. *"The training has forced you to grow up so fast. Your emotions now have to play catch up with what you did. This is so much to ask of anyone."*

"But I killed!" he murmured guiltily. "And I know it was only goblins but still, I ended a lot of lives in a fit of rage. Was it right? No! Why am I even asking? No killing is right!"

"Is killing a chicken for food right?" she asked.

"Well, that's different! It's for food. Especially if it's in winter," he hastily put in.

"And if a person threatened those you love and you had to kill to stop them?" she posed.

"That's different, too. It's self defense or defense of your family!" he added quickly.

The unicorn's deep eyes narrowed. *"And if a pack of goblins raped your sister?"*

Vilmar snapped his mouth shut, his excuses suddenly dried up. He was quiet for a long time.

"And if a certain wizard condoned the act or even ordered it?" the unicorn suggested.

Vilmar met her gaze. His sky blue eyes were smoldering and the tears were gone.

"I did not stop you from marching into the dragon's den for two reasons. First: I could not stop you. You would have seriously injured or killed me. Second: Savas-Zev needs to know his opposition has some very big teeth. He needs to feel fear. Long he has been afraid of nothing and rightly so. Savas-Zev needs to be reminded he is mortal. He can be killed. You reminded him of the fact yesterday."

"How much damage did I do?" Vilmar asked in a very small voice. "It seems so faint and vague right now."

The unicorn looked at him closely. *"Are you sure you want to know this part?"* she asked.

Vilmar met her gaze again and for a long moment said nothing. Then he swallowed and nodded once.

The unicorn sighed heavily and nodded in reply. *"You incinerated eighty-two goblins and thirteen trolls."*

Vilmar's jaw dropped at this and he stared incredulously at her. He clutched the tree because the world seemed to spin and whirl. But he grabbed in the wrong direction and felt himself falling out of the tree, clutching at air. The earth rushed to meet him and he braced himself for the impact.

Hitting the ground was not as painful as he expected it. The earth seemed to grow suddenly soft beneath the tree and he bounced as if landing on powdered snow. He rolled over and shook his head, still feeling somewhat nauseated by his reaction to what he had done.

"And... I can do this... again?" he asked in a very small voice.

The unicorn nodded. *"You will have to. Savas-Zev cannot be rehabilitated. He must be removed permanently."*

Vilmar suddenly felt very small and insignificant.

"Am I to strike the killing blow?" he squeaked softly.

The unicorn sighed once.

"I'm not sure. Part of the future is not yet set in stone. You may just play an important role in getting it to happen. You will contribute in the days ahead. But I'm not sure it will actually be you to kill him."

Vilmar gave a long, relieved sigh.

"I certainly hope not," he replied. "Because the way I'm feeling right now, I don't even want to slaughter a berry to eat!"

The unicorn chuckled softly in his mind. *"The feeling will pass. You just need some time to come to grips with things. Don't worry, my dear. I will be very close to you in the days to come, should you need me."*

She stepped closely and licked his face maternally. *"By the way, I didn't know being a green wizard also included being a thief."* She looked pointedly at him.

"What?" he blurted out.

"You took something from the wizard."

Vilmar reached down to his belt and untied the leather bag, showing it to her. "I've been afraid to open it," he said.

"Wise boy!" she replied. *"It might be trapped."*

She stepped forward and touched it lightly with the tip of her horn. The bag leaped and danced in his palm from the contact and then lay quite still.

"It is now safe to do so," she informed him. *"I think you will find the little bag to be much larger on the inside than the outside. I will also not be surprised if you pull out a different item every time you reach in your hand. Even if you were certain it was empty."*

Vilmar slowly loosened the drawstrings and cautiously reached inside. Even though the bag was barely larger than his fist, he found he could reach his entire arm inside up to his shoulder. His fingers brushed something cold, hard and round. He made a blind grab and the thing went neatly into his palm. Carefully, he drew it out.

It looked to be a simple crystal ball with four points of light spinning crazily about inside.

The unicorn gasped and stepped back quickly.

"What? Is it dangerous?" Vilmar asked suddenly almost dropping the globe.

"Only to those trapped inside," replied the unicorn in a whisper. *"It is a soul cage."*

"Then we should destroy it!" he asked.

The unicorn nodded. *"It can be easily destroyed by smashing it into a hard object. It is only a little tougher than glass. But I would not destroy THAT particular soul cage just yet."*

"Why not?"

"Because there are elf souls in it and it is only right an elf should destroy it. My advice to you is to keep it until you run across an elf, whoever it may be, and then give it to them to destroy."

Vilmar nodded in total agreement. He wound the crystal ball in soft leaves and grass and a bit of sheepskin and put it carefully in his pack.

He then decided to reach again into the wondrous little bag. His hand brushed across something large and square. Carefully, he introduced his other arm into the bag and wrestled out of the mouth, with some difficulty, a huge, leather-bound book with metal clasps. It was very heavy and he lay it on the ground with a thud and a grunt.

The unicorn lunged ferociously at the book, suddenly shoving Vilmar roughly aside. He fell backwards onto the ground with a surprised exclamation.

It was then Vilmar saw the book's cover had a huge eye bulging out of the leather and that eye was beginning to open!

The unicorn bellowed in rage and thrust her lance deep into the opening eye. There was a deafening shriek and lightning stabbed upwards and outwards from the book's cover. The unicorn held her lance in the wounded eye and braced herself on powerful legs, which now failed to appear quite so delicate. High-pitched screams and deep roars rumbled from inside the book and it began to shudder and smoke. The tome bucked and struggled underneath the unicorn lance but she would not release it. She held it firmly pinned to the ground until the smoke dissipated and the horrible, demonic sounds turned to dying wails. Then, slowly she withdrew her lance and backed away. Black ichor dripped steaming and hissing from her spiraling horn.

"Don't tell me," Vilmar gasped when he dared. "What the eye sees, the wizard sees?"

"Exactly!" she replied.

"Then feel free to knock me aside anytime you want!" he said as he dusted himself off and sat up.

The unicorn shuddered and stomped one delicate leg angrily.

"But the contact with the book told me more about it than I wanted to know. It's covered in dwarf skin and written in dwarf blood."

The unicorn gave a violent shake of her body, trying to rid herself of the book's energy. *"Ick! I need a bath in holy water!"*

"Then maybe we should destroy this, too?" Vilmar asked.

"Hmmph! I'd like to but I think we better keep it," she answered shaking her snowy mane and stamping her foot again with distaste. *"This is Savas-Zev's personal spell book. It could prove most useful."*

"It could also prove most dangerous to anyone else who chose to use it," Vilmar grumbled. "I'd rather not touch it ever again! Dwarf skin!" He shuddered in utter disgust and revulsion.

"We may have to find a way to deal with that," the unicorn said.

Vilmar kept his complaints to himself. He didn't like the book and didn't want to go anywhere near it, let alone have to touch or use it. It reeked of death and rotting bodies.

It smelled evil to him.

CHAPTER 36

Bran slowly opened her eyes. Her vision fell on the jagged roof of a cave's ceiling. Her body screamed to her in a million places from her wounds. She still felt very stiff and sore. Her chest hurt if she took a deep breath. The skin on her arms and hands was returning to a more natural color but was still quite pale. At least her skin was no longer blue, and feeling—although not pleasant—was returning to her extremities.

She stirred a bit, ignoring the pain to find herself on a straw mattress heaped with skins. Her bed was a bit too comfortable for a dwarf's taste. It would have been just right for a sensitive-skinned human.

"Welcome back to the land of the living," said a voice to her right and she carefully swiveled her head to the side. "It is not yet time for you to meet the Great Dragon, Bran, my friend."

"Vilmar!" she exclaimed. "Am I dreaming?"

Vilmar grinned widely. "If you are, do you really want to wake up?" he asked.

He was right. If this was a dream she certainly didn't want to wake. Her eyes drank in his face and every detail that had changed since they had last seen each other. He still had his shocking red hair and crystal blue eyes and wildly freckled skin. But now he sported a small beard which wrapped his chin warmly. Bran noticed his beard had come in white. She supposed something bad had happened to him and shocked the color out of it before it had even started to grow. Apparently hers was not the only story to tell here.

"You have lived too many waking nightmares as of late, Bran," he told her and she silently nodded in agreement.

She peered closer at his eyes. He was only a teenager, his skin still smooth and unwrinkled. But his eyes seemed old—so old, tired and sad now.

Bran stiffly sat up, and reaching out with only half-frozen fingers, took hold of his hands. They too seemed alive and real, she found to her immense relief. But they seemed a bit warmer than a normal human's hands should have been, like a dwarf bent too long over a forge's fire. Her cold, white hands enjoyed the heat from them.

"Then that was you and not a dream," she said. "You did come to rescue me."

"Yes, what a surprise!" he chuckled. "I always thought you would be the one to rescue me."

She gave him a teasing look. "Just wait!" she replied. "There's time yet for that."

She leaned back and snuggled happily into the furs. She fixed him with another teasing look.

"Vilmar?"

"Eh?" he responded.

"When you freed me from that damned wizard..."

"Yes, what of it?" he answered not guessing where this could lead.

"There were tears in your eyes," she said quietly but with a wide grin.

"No, there wasn't!" he retorted somewhat flustered.

"Yes, I saw them," she insisted.

"You saw nothing!" he spouted and turned his red face away.

"Liar!" she teased.

"Don't you call me a liar!" he fumed. "Now stop that! Remember what happened last time you called me a liar!"

She grinned even wider. "I left," Bran said simply.

"Yes, and all hell broke loose afterward!" he scolded.

"It was the same for me where I was," Bran said.

That shut him up for a time. They just stared at each other for a long while.

"Well," muttered Vilmar, giving in at last. "I'm glad to see that I did a good job removing the despair spell that was on you. You're back to your exasperating old self again!"

"Would you have me any other way?" she asked gently.

Vilmar was quiet for a long uncomfortable moment. "No," he said at last. "No, of course not."

Bran nodded. "I'm glad to see that your beard has finally started to sprout."

She winced at the effort, and reaching out, took his chin in her stubby-fingered, calloused hand and turned his face from one side to another, scrutinizing it critically. She finally nodded and grunted in approval. "It suits you quite well. You're starting to look very mature. Let me braid it for you in warrior locks when it gets longer and you'll be quite handsome."

Vilmar blushed all the way to his roots. "Stop that!" he said embarrassed.

"Stop what?" she said.

"Stop making me blush!" he growled. "Women do that! Not men!"

Bran barked in laughter even though it stabbed her chest with lightning-like sensations.

"Hah!" she retorted in scorn. "I'm a dwarf lass. Remember? Those rules don't apply!"

He got up to leave, muttering something about her still needing her rest. And she did for she found that this little conversation had tired her out immensely. But she couldn't let him go that easily.

"Oh, Vilmar?" she called and he resentfully turned to stare her in the eye. "I'm glad I was worth the tears," she said simply.

For a moment he just stood there fidgeting uncomfortably. Then he nodded. "I missed you too, Bran," he said.

She smiled a true dwarf smile. "Likewise, 'brother'," she teased.

But the look was genuine and grateful.

CHAPTER 37

Iyorath picked his way soundlessly through the forest followed by the crashing, stomping, sputtering Garn.

"Damned sharp-beaked pigeon is leading us in circles!" he spouted as he disentangled himself from the vines and briers that Iyorath had somehow completely avoided.

The elf turned to look at him and stifled a chuckle. Garn-Ithel's face was red as a barn. Dead leaves, thorns and vines crowned his bushy hair. He was definitely not suited to hiking about in the woods.

Iyorath looked up into the high branches overhead where Rath-Tor sat comfortably, worrying a squirrel carcass.

"I think most war eagles would take offense at being called a sharp-beaked pigeon!" he replied quietly.

Garn harrumphed grumpily at this and sitting down on a nearby log, began to pick twigs and earth out of his hairy ears. The elf could see quite clearly his companion didn't really care what he called Rath-Tor at this particular moment. He obviously had no use for either the elf or the eagle.

"That lice-ridden bird hasn't brought us any closer to Delkan or Bran and just barely kept us from being discovered by goblins the past few days!" Garn snapped. "I can't make any rhyme or reason out of where he's leading us other than we're climbing. But I tell you one thing for certain, elf. The first tunnel I chance upon, I'm jumping down it and ne'er lookin' back again. You can take your chances by yourself. At least the bird will keep you fed!"

Garn was in a foul mood. Still grumbling and cussing, he wrestled off his leather boot and shook out the pebbles and earth that had somehow found its way inside during their hike. Iyorath picked up the word 'useless elf' in all his muttering.

Iyorath looked back up at Rath-Tor and shrugged apologetically. The eagle's eyes glittered at the elf but the bird said nothing.

"We seem to be lost," Iyorath mumbled quietly to himself.

But Garn-Ithel heard him.

The dwarf threw up his big hands in exasperation and scoffed. "Ha! Ya think?"

He wagged his beard and turned his attention to his other boot, which seemed to be glued onto his leg. He puffed and pulled in exertion to extricate the shoe from his foot and his red face began to turn purple.

Iyorath considered not helping at first. Then he thought better of it and wordlessly assisted. The boot came off with a pop, which tumbled both elf and dwarf head over heels in opposite directions. They sat there covered in leaves and brambles and regarded each other.

Garn suddenly began to chortle uncontrollably. Against his wishes, Iyorath joined in for seeing a dwarf laughing was infectious.

"What?" giggled the elf.

"Well, I do declare!" laughed Garn. "Elves don't smell like daisies when they sweat. They stink just as bad as the rest of us!"

Iyorath felt his face turn red.

"I thought you said this was going to be a good day for us when we woke up this morning!" Garn said as the elf strode over to him.

"That was just because of the dream I had last night," he grumbled as he held out his hand and helped the dwarf back to his feet.

"Eh? And what did you dream about last night?" Garn asked as he took back his other boot and wrestled it back onto his squat leg.

"Unicorns. Three to be exact," he whispered sadly.

Garn looked him suddenly in the eye and was quiet for a long time.

"Nice dream," he muttered in return. "But I daresay no unicorn in their right, pure mind would want to be anywhere near Savas-Zev right now."

Iyorath nodded silently, sadly.

"It was a very nice dream though," Garn added gently as an afterthought. "Unicorns are always nice to dream about."

They said no more to each other and continued on their slow, painstaking way through the woods.

The sun climbed higher and the day grew warmer. They found some berries to eat and munched on them as they walked. But they both were growing increasingly hungry. Their food stores had been strapped behind the saddles and so were gone with the horses.

"What I wouldn't give for a good bit of stew or venison," Garn muttered as they stopped for a break. "Any sort of meat would stick to my ribs better than berries and last year's half-sprouted nuts."

Iyorath nodded. "If you promise to stump along a little quieter, I'll see if I can catch us a rabbit or a squirrel or something," the elf suggested.

"Why should you catch it?" Garn said. "Just get your bird to catch it for us."

The dwarf waved his hand to the leafy canopy above them, then stopped abruptly.

Rath-Tor was nowhere to be found.

"Blast it!" fumed Garn. "Dratted bird's left us again!"

Iyorath craned his neck about, searching above. "I told you, you never should have called him a sharp-beaked pigeon!" the elf complained. "There goes our huntsman!"

They both spent several minutes looking about for the eagle.

Then Garn suddenly noticed that Iyorath had frozen rigidly in position.

"What is it?" he whispered coming up to peer alongside him. "What did you see?"

There was a strange look on Iyorath's face. His eyes were wide and his mouth tight. "I thought I saw a unicorn," he murmured quietly.

"You did," spoke a strange voice in both their heads.

Slowly, as one, they turned around.

A tall, white unicorn stag stood behind them, regarding them quietly. It was a shaft of moonlight during midday, a patch of sparkling cold and white snow in summer's heat. And it just stood there looking deeply into their faces all smudged and grubby from crawling around in the woods for days. Its eyes were fathomless, like the deep ocean and its mane floated gracefully about its neck and shoulders in the slightest breeze. It swished its tufted tail and tossed its head, flouncing its long white beard as if making a comment.

"You are seeking a wizard," it spoke to them.

Iyorath knew that wasn't quite what they were looking for but he felt wrong about correcting a unicorn, so he just nodded wordlessly.

"Which wizard do you seek?" the stag asked.

They gaped at the creature, not understanding. "There are two?" Garn stammered in surprise.

The unicorn stag nodded as if the whole world knew that. *"Of course,"* the stag retorted. *"Now, which wizard do you seek?"*

Iyorath swallowed with difficulty. "Whichever one the unicorn is allied with," he replied quickly without completely thinking his answer through.

He sensed humor from the magical creature before him. Its deep blue eyes twinkled merrily at him.

"Indeed. Whichever one the unicorn is allied with," the unicorn repeated. *"How quaintly you put it."*

The creature turned as if to spring away back into the dream it had come from but it paused briefly. *"Then you must follow me,"* it replied.

It trotted gracefully away into the underbrush then stopped, awaiting them. They followed as best they could. The unicorn led them for quite a long time and always seemed just about to lose them altogether. Then a patch of pristine white would appear at the edge of their sight and a pair of deep blue eyes would beckon them to keep following.

"It seems your dream wasn't so far off after all, elf," Garn puffed as he struggled to keep up with the elf and the magical creature.

"Hmmm. It would seem," Iyorath agreed quietly.

"But what is a blessed creature like that doing here so close to hoards of goblins and Savas-Zev?" Garn questioned.

"I haven't the foggiest idea," Iyorath replied. "But at least now I understand Bran's letter a little better."

"Eh?" rumbled Garn as he clambered over a log the elf had easily crossed. "How d'ya figure that?"

"If Bran knew about the unicorn, then that explains why she thought she had a chance of changing the situation. It explains her mysterious 'theory' she had to try out."

Garn grunted and scrambled up the steep slope after Iyorath. "About your dream last night," he puffed and Iyorath came back to lend a hand.

"Thanks," muttered the dwarf and continued. "You dreamed of three unicorns. Think there's more than this one here?"

Iyorath looked ahead of them. The unicorn stag was perched on a rocky outcropping, standing in a brilliant shaft of sunlight that made his white coat glow in iridescence.

"I don't know. But it's certainly possible," he said.

"Well, the more unicorns to help us the better!" grunted the dwarf. "Hell! I hope there's a whole army of them out there!"

"I think an army of unicorns would leave more tracks," Iyorath returned confidently.

"Really?" said Garn grinning widely as he stopped to catch his breath. "Do you now? Then why haven't we seen any tracks from this one even though we've been following him two hours now?"

This stopped Iyorath cold. The dwarf was right. They hadn't seen any tracks from the stag even though they had been crossing the same ground.

Garn was chuckling to himself. "Some master tracker you are, elf!" he teased. "Can't even find a unicorn's footprint!"

"Well, how many unicorns have you ever run across?" Iyorath fumed and sped up purposely trying to lose him.

"This one's me first," Garn informed.

"Mine too!" the elf shot back hotly.

"What? I thought unicorns were especially attracted to the fair folk! They certainly aren't attracted to dwarves!"

"And how many unicorns would you run across living in your dark tunnels?" growled Iyorath. "They require moonlight and waterfalls to exist happily."

"Humph!" grunted the dwarf. "I thought that the dumbest elf would be an expert on unicorns since your people hold them in such high esteem."

"Yes, but we don't keep them as pets, if that's what you mean," Iyorath fumed back.

He stopped to catch his breath and think. "Unicorns are blessed animals created by the earth's need for a master healer. They are guardians of purity and enemies of darkness. But they have always been rare. If they became a common sight, then their magic would fade and disappear forever. They would become ordinary just like..."

"Just like a horse?" Garn finished for them. "Is that why it's forbidden to ride one? Because it will make them ordinary?"

"Partially," Iyorath explained. "Riding is a form of dominance. And why should anyone dominate something so pure and good?"

"Riding can also be a partnership," suggested Garn. "A pairing of equals, a bonding of kindred spirits with neither master nor leader."

Iyorath nodded silently, agreeing.

"And when a unicorn is ridden, that is the kind of bond it is. A pairing of equals to accomplish a great goal through the blending of the talents of both."

The elves had a word for this rare bond. Garn-Ithel knew that word. "*I'Olana*," he breathed in reverence.

Iyorath nodded. They continued to follow the unicorn in silence.

And then the unicorn really did disappear.

They came to a stop in a woodland clearing near a shivering pool fed by a small waterfall tumbling over a jumble of large boulders. It was a pristine and pure feeling place, a place where any unicorn would feel safe and at home.

Rath-Tor sat quietly in a nearby tree branch, preening his feathers in the spray of the waterfall.

"Are we to wait?" Iyorath asked above the sound of the crashing water.

The war eagle paused to regard them silently but did not answer.

"See?" accused the elf. "You've insulted him! He'll probably never speak to us again!"

Garn-Ithel harrumphed as if that wouldn't be such a bad deal and ignoring them both, stripped off his clothes and jumped in the pool. The elf resisted for a time. He felt that having a grimy little naked dwarf paddling around in a pool that a unicorn had guided them to was somehow blasphemous. Then the wind changed direction and he caught a whiff of his own aromatic body and decided it wasn't such a bad idea after all.

They scrubbed the trail dust from their bodies and let the pounding waters of the fall bring the blood back to their skin. Then they dunked and wrung out their filthy clothes and hung them on the bushes nearby to dry while they basked on the rocks in the patchy summer sun. They knew the unicorn was nearby and would guard them.

They awoke some time later and redressed in their cleaner, only slightly damp clothes. They were just wondering what to do next when Iyorath noticed the eagle gazing sharply into the underbrush.

The elf followed the bird's gaze and shot suddenly to his feet.

They were being watched by a figure in a dark green cloak with a deep hood pulled over its head so that none of its face could be seen. They had no idea how long the figure had been standing there.

Seeing that they had noticed him, the figure stepped into the sunshine and removed the hood from its face. They found they were staring at a youth still in his teens. He was only slightly shorter than the elf but Iyorath surmised that one day, the way adolescents grew, the youth would outstrip his own height. His features were definitely human. He had a shock of wild red hair about his head and a profusion of freckles across his face. His young beard had just started to grow but it was coming in white. The youth's eyes were a bright clear blue—as blue as the summer sky on a clear day.

"This whippersnapper can't be the wizard the unicorn was talking about," Garn hissed to him. "He's far too young to be a wizard of any kind!"

But Iyorath wasn't so sure. He stepped closer to the figure, circling the pool that was between them. He stopped suddenly when he saw the clear image of a beardless unicorn doe standing behind the green-robed figure, deep in the woodland's shadows. The unicorn tossed her head wildly, warning him with her body language not to approach. The elf reached out with his mind, feeling with the only magic he possessed, the aura of the strange young man before them.

Garn heard the swift intake of the elf's breath.

"What is it?" he whispered urgently.

"This is no ordinary wizard, Garn, my friend," the elf whispered back to him. "He is a green wizard!"

The dwarf did not understand.

"What's th' difference?" he muttered in confusion.

"Quite a lot, I'm afraid," he informed. "For one thing, the regular wizardly rules don't apply to green wizards."

The dwarf puzzled this over briefly. "So, is he friend or foe?" he questioned abruptly.

"He has impressed the unicorns," Iyorath breathed with reverence and then cast a backward glance at his diminutive friend. "What do you think he is?"

"The unicorn said you were seeking a wizard but he is wrong," spoke the youth suddenly to them.

"Yes," replied Iyorath warily.

"You are really seeking a dwarf, a young female dwarf to be exact," the human continued.

Iyorath started to reply "Perhaps..." but Garn-Ithel butted in rudely.

"Actually we're seeking two females," he supplied.

Iyorath stepped sharply on the toe of the dwarf's thick boot but Garn didn't feel it.

The young human's eyes switched to Garn's face and he smiled. "Of course you are," the human said. "Delkan and Bran."

Iyorath rocked back on his heels in surprise.

"You know them?" he stuttered in shock.

"Well, I know Bran quite well," the youth went on. "We were great friends before she went away to join... the army. This Delkan I've never met. I only remember Bran's accounts of her she wrote me in her letters. Delkan is the dwarf that never shuts up, am I right?"

Iyorath's wall of caution crumbled and he laughed. Garn joined in the laughter with his own harsh, deep voice.

"That sounds about right," Garn replied with a wide grin.

"Well, Bran I stole away from Savas-Zev just a few days ago," the freckled youth informed them.

In an instant both the dwarf and elf's smiles disappeared.

"He had Bran?" Garn growled threateningly.

"Indeed he did. She wouldn't have lasted much longer if I hadn't found her. But she's recovering now, quickly I might add. She feels good enough to bitch at me on a regular basis because I still won't let her leave her sickbed."

Iyorath rolled his eyes sympathetically and groaned something along the lines of 'stubborn dwarves'. This pulled a chuckle from the human.

"Now Delkan I still haven't met but the unicorns tell me she's fine and will be meeting up with us later."

"I suppose the pranks will start up again with those two reunited," Iyorath grumbled miserably.

The human gave him a perplexed look.

"We'll explain later, boy," Garn replied. "But right now we'd like to know who you are."

The youth's eyes flew wide and he flushed with embarrassment to the roots of his red hair.

"Of course!" he muttered apologetically. "How rude of me! I am Vilmar."

They likewise introduced themselves to Vilmar.

"Ah, the blacksmith's son," Iyorath exclaimed in sudden understanding.

Vilmar winced in pain and his youthful eyes became suddenly dark and shadowed. "I'm afraid the blacksmith is dead along with the rest of my family," his voice suddenly became very soft and flat of any emotion.

The elf and dwarf's faces reflected sympathy for his loss.

With a resolute effort Vilmar changed the subject. He turned his attention to Iyorath.

"You're an elf, correct?" he asked peering closely at the features that separated him from the other races.

Iyorath nodded.

"Then I have something for you," Vilmar said. Producing a pack, he began to rummage about inside.

"The unicorn said it's a bad thing and needs to be disposed of, but she wouldn't let me do it. She said it would be better if an elf did the honors and since you are the first elf I've ever run across..."

He let the sentence dangle. Garn suddenly became wary and his big hand went secretly to his hunting dagger. But the human called Vilmar totally ignored him. Finding what he wanted, he held up a small bundle carefully wrapped in sheepskins and dead grass. Slowly, with great care, he unwound the bundle and held out the prize to Iyorath.

All color drained from the elf's long face. His blue eyes grew big and round, and his mouth became a harsh slash on his white face.

A small, fist-sized globe of clear crystal sat peacefully in the youth's freckled hand. Its surface was totally smooth and transparent. Four stars of light spun wildly inside, hammering against the inner surface as if trying to escape.

Garn-Ithel's knuckles tightened on the handle of his dagger.

"What is that, lad?" he asked the elf.

"It's a soul cage," answered Vilmar for him.

"No," whispered Iyorath in a shuddering voice. "It's *the* soul cage. The one that holds my family's souls, the one I've been searching for, for so very long."

"I found it in Savas-Zev's house. Take it. Free them," Vilmar said and placed the globe in Iyorath's cold, shaking hands.

For a long moment, Iyorath could do nothing but stare at the crystal ball in his hands. The stars inside whirled and hummed, trailing stardust behind them. The globe was glowing brighter than Vilmar had ever seen it do before.

"Why do you hesitate?" Garn murmured. "Destroy the thing!"

226

"It's just..." Iyorath stammered, trying to make sense of the myriad of feelings which swirled within him that very moment, mirroring the frenzied motion of the stars within. "For so long they've been in my head, crying to be freed, wailing in spiritual torment against their imprisonment. Now they're actually here with me."

His voice stuck in his throat and it was only with great difficulty that he was able to continue.

"They're closer to me now than they have been in centuries. We're all together again."

The elf's wide blue eyes became quite glassy and wet.

Vilmar stepped close and put a consoling hand on his shoulder.

"Yes, they're here and you're here. And they're still in torment. They're still caged. They spoke to me as well and I also have heard their torment. I know that's not what you want for your family," he murmured softly into Iyorath's pointed ear.

"If you free them, they will be with you always, son. The dead are never really gone from us. It's just their bodies that leave us," Garn-Ithel spoke up.

"And their bodies died long ago," Iyorath said softly. "I know. I watched them die. And I buried them myself. So very long ago. I remember."

"You will always remember your family," Vilmar said. "Just as I will."

"Just as we all will," added Garn gruffly, his gray eyes dark and shadowed.

"Yes," agreed Iyorath slowly. "Yes, I will."

Vilmar stepped back away from him. Garn mimicked his motion.

"Free them, son," Garn told him. "Let them go so they can come back. Let them go."

Iyorath suddenly braced himself like he was holding a spear. His eyes found an especially jagged boulder jutting out of the waterfall, away from the cascading torrent and he aimed his swing for it. He launched the globe for that rock with an incredible cry of emotion. The soul cage flew like a white, flaming arrow to the boulder and shattered into a million glittering pieces of sparkling glass. A bright, white light issued forth from the fractured glass. It rose like a comet in the midnight sky and then separated into four parts. Slowly, the four stars came back to earth and surrounded the elf. As one they began to hum and glow until Iyorath was totally obscured by the shield of light created by the four stars. Then abruptly the lights blinked out as if they had never existed.

Iyorath lay motionless on the ground. Garn ran up and crouched next to him. Carefully he turned him over to find the elf awake and conscious. Iyorath's beautiful face was streaked with tears of loss and relief.

"They're free as they should be," he whispered softly.

Garn nodded. "Ya done good, lad," he said to him. "That's been a long time coming, hasn't it?"

"Too long, I'm afraid," he replied in relief and sat up. The world spun crazily so he lay back down.

"Just take a breather there now, Iyorath," Vilmar told him. "We're in no hurry and we're safe here. You just went through a bit of an ordeal so just relax a bit."

Iyorath nodded, quietly agreeing.

Vilmar turned away and a cloud crossed his face. Garn's sharp eyes caught it.

"What is it, boy?" he asked.

Vilmar shrugged to him to step out of earshot and the dwarf obeyed.

"These soul cages," he explained in a soft voice so Iyorath hopefully wouldn't hear. "There are more of them. Savas-Zev has lots of soul cages."

They turned about suddenly at the sound behind them.

Iyorath had heard. He was sitting up shakily, bracing himself on his arms. His clear, blue elfin eyes blazed hotly.

"There are *more*?" he snarled like a cat about to spring.

Vilmar gave a deep sigh and relented, nodding sadly.

"Iyorath, there are hundreds of them!" he told him quietly.

CHAPTER 38

Bran hobbled gingerly through the forest, leaning heavily on the cane Vilmar had made for her. She puffed with exertion at every step as she strained to retrain her legs to pump and propel her up the small incline. Vilmar had completely taken over her healing and this was part of it. Her limbs had been starved of blood for so long, hanging on the wall as Savas-Zev's prisoner, that the blood had to be retrained to flow to her extremities. Vilmar had ordered her to take daily walks to aid her healing and had forbidden her to ride anyone's horse. Bran was ready to strangle her young friend as she struggled her way up the small incline. He was lucky he wasn't with her, she thought sullenly.

Well, she wasn't completely alone, she corrected herself as she stopped at the top of the rise to gasp for breath. She knew the unicorns were out there, unseen but not unaware. They would protect her. She tottered feebly over to a fallen tree and slowly seated herself for a rest.

She shook her head in frustration. She was too young to need a cane, too young for a small hill to be any sort of obstacle to her tough form. Yet, here she was leaning on a stick just to help herself walk. She puffed and gasped, her lungs burning. She had to get better soon. She had things to do, a wizard to stop, by the Great Dragon! She was too young to start acting old.

She leaned back against the rough bark of the tree behind her and felt a pointed knob jab her in her back. She remembered what she had stuffed in her pack before she had left to begin her Vilmar-prescribed "therapy."

She straightened up and unslung the pack. Slowly, she withdrew the box and carefully looked it over.

Vilmar had given it to her that morning. He said it had come from her mother, Yaffa. She had given it to the young wizard for safekeeping until he saw Bran. Vilmar had said Bran should probably open it when she was alone. The cave she was recuperating in had become steadily noisier with the addition of Garn, Iyorath and now the ever-joking Delkan with her new stumps. It was rarely quiet there now.

Bran gazed at the simple latch but did not touch it, knowing that it was probably guarded with a spell to keep prying hands from tampering with the contents. She softly spoke the traditional family charm all dwarves have for special items. The clasp fell free and its lid swung open.

Inside was a letter rolled up in a scroll and sealed with Yaffa's personal insignia. The seal was unbroken. Next to it was a small felt bag bulging with something inside.

Bran removed the scroll and ran her fingers lovingly over the parchment. These were the last words her mother would ever say to her, she thought sadly. She held onto the feelings for only a moment and then broke the wax seal and began to read.

> *Dearest Daughter,*
>
> *If you are reading this, then what I feared and dreaded for so long has come to pass and I am now dead, along with probably every dwarf in Tor Ambroc. Hopefully, I will have taken control of my own passing, rather than succumb to what the wizard has in store for us all. I had hoped to stop this somehow. I have failed for the last time. I write this to you hoping that you will succeed where I could not.*
>
> *By this time you will have probably heard about a wizard called Savas-Zev who has made it his mission in life to eradicate all dwarves from this world. He just might succeed. So many dwarf provinces have already fallen to his plots and schemes. But I also listened to Kusa's prediction on your birthday and I believe I understood more than most dwarves who heard it. I believe that you—or something you do—will end his hated reign of terror over our people. Do you not remember Kusa's words, "Your people will need you most when you think all is already lost"? Do not forget them, dear child. This battle is not yet decided. Not by a long shot.*
>
> *I do not know what help or wisdom or clue you will have most use of in this struggle. I have lived my entire life with one goal: to stop Savas-Zev. That apparently is not to be my fate. I hope my*

last-born child will have a hand in it though. It would give my rest much peace.

Stick close to your young friend Vilmar. He too will have a hand in this unless I miss my guess. He may be a human and a wizard, but he is the finest dwarf friend I have ever seen and a wizard all dwarves should accept whole-heartedly. He will not abandon you to the dark.

Do you remember when you asked about my own Dahla horse, Mayhem? Well, I'm sorry to say I lied to you when I told you about him. I'm not sure if he is... dead. I believe I dismissed him to his own plane before he was burned too seriously. But his scream of pain before I did went through me like an icy knife and I was too afraid to ever recall him to see if he yet lived. Yes, your mother, a dwarf warrior, was too afraid to check and see. I include this Dahla as a gift to you. I would have given him to you at my death anyway. I just did not plan on it being this soon. Maybe, because you do not yet love him the way I do.... did, maybe you will be brave enough to see if Mayhem survived the ordeal. I hope he made it. Mayhem was more than a magical mount. He was my dear friend and partner. I do so hope he made it.

And, in closing, I want you to know that I love you and I've always been proud of you. I wish I could have seen you grow into adulthood properly. I resent that our last meeting must be this way. I trust that you will make it right. May you shoot straight and your arrows never miss. Please sing the song of my life to the Great Dragon if there is a chance for it.

Fondly but in haste,
Your mother, Yaffa

Bran crumpled the letter in her lap. She was still and glassy eyed for a long, long time.

Time seemed to stop for her right then. Her reactions were distant and only vaguely connected with the present.

This letter only confirmed what Vilmar had told her earlier, that her mother had taken her own life by poison. Savas-Zev did not have her spirit trapped in a soul cage. He had never come into contact with Yaffa and, therefore, could not have possibly entrapped her spirit. Savas-Zev had lied to her yet again.

She had to swallow several times before the large lump in her throat left. With a supreme effort, she shoved her feelings aside and picked up the small bag lying in the box. She withdrew her mother's Dahla horse. It was threaded on a silver chain and was carved as plainly as hers had been. Like Val it felt warm and alive in her hands like living flesh. But Yaffa's Dahla horse figure was scorched and singed and smelled strongly of acrid smoke still after all these years.

She should have put the letter and the Dahla horse aside. She should have dealt with her own emotions. But instead, she called Mayhem's name in a clear, strong voice.

For a long, breathless moment, nothing happened. She wrinkled her brows in confusion and frowned.

Suddenly there was a deafening crack like thunder and an explosion seemed to go off right in the air in front of her. She threw up her arms over her face and tumbled backwards over the log. Cautiously she peered over it, ready to dive back down in case anything more dangerous happened.

A black storm cloud hovered in the open space in the forest right in front of the downed tree she crouched behind. It swirled and growled ominously. It reminded her of the door of storms that Savas-Zev had used to ride her Val through and for a moment she wondered if this was one of his many tricks.

Then there was a brilliant flash of lightning and a white horse with a black head leaped through the storm clouds and landed on the forest floor before her.

A strange voice spoke in her head. *"Finally! It's been too long. What kept you?"*

Bran stared at the strange animal, wide-eyed and open-mouthed. He was a large, blocky, white stallion with a finely shaped head. His mane and tail were thick and long and his feet were feathered like a draft horse's but he was nowhere near that big. He was the size of a large pony. His eyes were pale blue and shone strangely out of his dark face. He was ringed all about in white flames that burned but did not seem to harm him.

"You are not Yaffa!" the voice in her head said in shock.

The creature pinned his ears and stamped a large, hairy foot angrily, tossing his wild mane. But then he stopped and sniffed the air in front of him. The white flames crackled about him and yet did not burn the surrounding vegetation.

"Ah! I see," spoke the voice again in sudden realization. *"Yaffa's filly!"*

"How is it that you can talk to my mind?" she asked in a trembling voice.

The blue-eyed stallion regarded her curiously.

"It was the way Yaffa designed me to be. Didn't you know you could do that?"

Bran gulped and shook her head dumbly. "I had no idea!" she stammered.

They regarded each other silently for a bit.

"Wait a minute! I know of you!" the horse said. *"You're Valynt's bond dwarf!"*

Bran's eyebrows went skyward.

"You know Val, too?" she said eagerly, standing up.

The stallion stamped angrily again and snaked his head threateningly toward her.

"Valynt said you gave her away!" he demanded. *"She said the man you gave her to isn't very nice. She even said he's cruel and heartless! Why would you do that?"*

The stallion mock charged her, stopping only just in time. Bran stepped back and stumbled over some underbrush. Sitting on her backside she looked up at the angry stallion towering over her.

"WHY?" he demanded again.

"I never gave her away," she growled back into his face. "He took her by force. He stole her and made me tell him the magic words to command her."

"He was a wizard?" questioned the stallion, backing off slightly.

"Yes! The worst kind of wizard! A wizard that hates dwarves."

The stallion retreated more, thinking for a moment. *"My apologies then. It WOULD take a wizard to do that."*

"I want Val back!" Bran said venomously. "I want her back now!"

The stallion bobbed his head in affirmation.

"And I'm sure she will want that too once she understands the situation. But this will take some doing." He pawed the ground fitfully and snorted.

"I'm aware of that," Bran resentfully agreed.

They were silent for another long, uncomfortable moment.

"I still would like to know where Yaffa is," he spoke to her at last. *"I am her bond horse, not yours."*

Bran was silent for a long moment. She finally gave a heavy sigh and said in a soft voice, "She's dead."

The horse called Mayhem threw up his black head, blazing with white fire and stared at her in shock. He uttered a deep sound from his gut that appeared to be a groan of pain.

"I'm sorry," he said abruptly. *"I must go back to my own plane. I need to grieve my bond mate properly."*

He turned his back to her but paused briefly before he left. *"I suggest that you do the same."* Then Mayhem was gone with a flash like before.

The forest around her seemed very quiet and still. The reality of her situation crashed in upon Bran. She stared blankly at the ground before her feet without really seeing it at all.

Yaffa, her mother, was truly dead.

A ball of emotion welled up inside her. She bowed her head as a great sob was torn out of her chest.

All alone in the woods, surrounded by trees and vegetation, protected by unicorns, she poured out her grief in tears and great body-shaking sobs. The silence of the forest folded in about her like the gentle comfort of a mother's arms.

CHAPTER 39

Delkan and Bran sat laughing and joking at the entrance to the cave. A large bonfire had been kindled and they sat along with Vilmar, Garn and Iyorath, enjoying the first roasted meat they'd had in quite some time. The unicorns were nowhere to be seen but the friends knew they were protected and shielded from evil eyes. Rath-Tor sat on a low branch and eagerly caught any rare strips of venison that Iyorath tossed to him.

"So is the unicorn fawn your patron now?" asked Bran of Delkan.

"He seems to think so," replied Delkan with a grin as she carved off a large hunk of meat from the deer roast that was crackling and sputtering over the fire. She divided the generous hunk and passed half to Bran.

"Isn't that kinda unusual for a unicorn to adopt a dwarf to teach?" Bran asked through a juicy mouthful.

"Extremely unusual," answered Delkan as she settled herself more comfortably on the ground next to the stump Bran sat on. "His mother seems to think he broke some cardinal rule by doing that but he's insistent on claiming me."

"Probably 'cause it's kinda hard for a unicorn to protect someone who is underground most of the time," Bran supposed.

Delkan nodded in agreement.

"Probably," she said. "But I don't care. I have no intention of ever going into the tunnels again. Enemies expect a dwarf to be underground. So I better stay above ground. Less likely to be cornered that way."

Bran nodded thinking and then smiled as a thought suddenly came to her. "I guess the fawn likes you 'cause you're just as stubborn as he is."

Delkan laughed but nodded in total agreement. "A young, naive unicorn fawn and a dwarf. Can't get much more stubborn than that," she laughed. "He's completely clueless about life and has no idea how evil, evil really is. But I kinda like him hanging around. He's like an admiring kid brother."

Bran laughed. "You'll probably have to save him instead of the other way around!"

They had a good laugh over that and then fell into a comfortable silence as they turned their attention to the meat before them. Garn joined them with a flask of beer the unicorns had found and deemed safe for consumption.

As she ate, Bran looked across the fire to Vilmar. He sat at the edge of the fire's dancing light, talking privately with Iyorath.

"Now that's something I never thought would happen," she muttered almost to herself.

When the two other dwarves looked up, she nodded her beard at Vilmar.

"I never would have pegged those two to get real buddy-buddy so quick. They've been chatting all hush like that every night now," she said.

"Jealous you might be losing a friend?" suggested Garn slyly.

"Not at all!" Bran replied quickly, a little too quickly. "I can share my friends. I'm glad all you guys get along. I just never thought Vilmar and Iyorath would get so close so fast. I mean he's a human and Iyorath's an elf. Vilmar and me are just young pups! And Iyorath, he is... how old?"

Delkan shrugged uselessly.

"I don't know for certain. But he's old! Garn, do you know his age? You two used to be bunk mates," Delkan asked.

Garn scoffed derisively.

"He's older than any dwarf has a right to be and he's still considered a teenager by elf standards," he muttered.

"That's right," Bran put in. "So what could they possibly have to talk about?"

"Plenty," Delkan said in a quiet but respectful tone of voice.

Garn and Bran stared at her in confusion. Their looks forced her to explain.

"Well, think about it," she said. "Vilmar is a green wizard and from all accounts a mighty powerful one at that. But he's all alone in being a wizard. He probably feels more comfortable in training horses than using magic. And he's had some pretty spotty schooling from what you tell me. Yet he's got all this power threatening to bust outta him.

"Now Iyorath may not be a wizard but he was raised by wizards. It seems his whole family is into that kinda thing. He's got so much experience with magical sorts of things even without being any kind of magic user. He can explain things to Vilmar, especially about the way he's supposed to handle all this stuff in his head and heart. I'm not sure the unicorn, having been a unicorn all its blessed life, can quite relate to that."

The other two nodded, agreeing with this assessment.

They watched the two talk in silence and then saw Vilmar bring out a great, heavy book with a blasted cover.

Garn hissed and began to mutter angrily under his breath. "I wish he'd destroy that damned thing," he grumbled getting up and stalking about, kicking sticks and stones like a petulant child.

"Vilmar needs to learn spells and things," Delkan said in support of the young wizard.

"I know. But does he have to learn them outta a book made from our skin and written in our people's blood?" Garn sputtered in a louder voice.

"If those spells can help us defeat Savas-Zev then the poor dwarves who were sacrificed to make that book will be vindicated," Bran said softly.

Delkan chimed in nodding, "Think about it, Garn. He'll be brought down by something made from our own flesh and blood. Won't that be worth it?"

Garn only harrumphed grumpily while his eyes shot daggers at the book Vilmar held in his carefully gloved hands.

Bran noted the gloves and added, "Anyway, it's not like he enjoys touching that vile book. You can plainly see he hates it."

Garn grunted sullenly in reply to this statement.

The war eagle bounced and pattered awkwardly on the ground toward them.

"Someone approaches," Rath-Tor rasped abruptly.

Bran and Garn jumped to their feet and grabbed for their weapons. Delkan snatched a small stone and readied her deadly slingshot. Seeing their reactions, Iyorath jumped to his feet while Vilmar stashed the book clumsily in his pack.

The war eagle shook his feathers and squawked obstinately at all their reactions.

"I did not say it was an enemy," he screeched and flew up into the trees.

They lowered their weapons somewhat but did not put them away. Cautiously, they peered into the darkness in front of the cave. Iyorath, with his sharp elven eyes, was the first to spy the person.

"There," he gestured into the darkness to their right.

A small, square-shaped figure, hooded and cloaked in dark brown was taking the steepest way up the grade to their cave.

"Have you no welcome for an old friend?" it puffed as it stepped spryly into the campfire's light.

The small group backed warily away, their hands still on their weapons, guard still up. They glanced uncertainly at each other and back to the small person before them. Vilmar melted into the shadows just outside the fire's light.

"Who are you?" asked Bran in a commanding voice that shook a little at the end.

"One who is well known to all but the elf," the figure replied and removed the hood.

A dwarf stood before them with raven hair and a long, braided black beard tucked into his belt and dark eyes that glittered like hematite stones.

The dwarves started in shock and as one they all exclaimed the same name.

"Daga!"

Then they started again and stared in confusion at each other. The same question was on all three's lips.

"How do you know Daga?" they again all asked at the same time.

"Well, he's my brother," stated Garn.

"But, that impossible," Delkan insisted. "He's my uncle and I'm nowhere near related to you!"

"Uh, excuse me. He's my uncle, too," Bran interrupted. "And I don't believe I'm related to either of you."

Delkan's face screwed up in utter confusion.

"How is that possible?" she said.

Daga's eyes flew from one to another. He said nothing but he was grinning widely and his black eyes sparkled as if he had heard a really good joke.

"Is this one of Savas-Zev's tricks?" glowered Iyorath and he took a threatening step toward the new dwarf, his hand on the hilt of his short sword.

"You don't want to be attacking me, elf," Daga warned shortly, still smiling but there was a cautionary tone to his words. "I'm more than a match for you. And I've lived far longer than you or any of your kin will ever know."

Daga calmly made his way to a nearby stump and seated himself, totally unconcerned by their suspicious demeanor.

"Besides, you don't want to be killing the best friend you may ever have. I can be quite helpful against this wizard that worries you so much," he informed them. "And no, fair elf, I am not in league with Savas-Zev. Quite the contrary."

"But you can't be related to all of us," Garn-Ithel said still reluctant to put away his weapon. "So who the hell are you really?"

The thing they thought was Daga chuckled and shook his head, blue-black beard wagging from side to side. Then he looked up at the elder dwarf and his face grew suddenly quite grave.

"Know this, Garn-Ithel of Drock Tor: I am your brother," he said earnestly.

Daga then turned to Bran. "And Bran, I am your dear, beloved uncle who stood by you and encouraged you to learn to ride, the uncle who gave you Valynt as your first Dahla horse," he said with a fond smile.

He then turned to Delkan still smiling affectionately. "And Delkan, I am your uncle as well, the one who actually heard you above the babble of all your many siblings, then who encouraged you to go on the boar hunt that would eventually save your life from the Fang-Tor pox."

"But how is this all possible?" asked Bran in a breathless whisper. "Who... or maybe the question should be... *what* are you really?"

"I think we all would appreciate the truth this time," Iyorath said in a warning tone.

Daga's eyebrows went skyward and his teeth flashed as he smiled.

"The truth?" he sniffed. "Laddie, that's what I have been tellin' you all this time—the truth."

He shook his head again and waved a hand at them. "Sit down!" he urged. "And please put away your pointy sticks. They will be rusty by the time I'm done my tale. Sit and relax, please."

Slowly, grudgingly, they obeyed.

"That's better," Daga said and pulled out a long ornately carved pipe with a very worn mouthpiece. Impatiently, they waited while he filled and lit it, seeming to take his sweet time doing so. Finally, with a long sigh, he began.

"My mother's name was Shafta, the First wife..." he started.

Garn who bolted abruptly to his feet, interrupted him. "Liar! That's not possible!" he sputtered.

"Uh, excuse me," Iyorath said. "That name obviously means something to you, but some of us are in the dark about dwarf genealogy."

"Shafta, the First Wife was the first dwarf woman ever," Bran informed.

In the silence that followed, Daga fixed Garn with a hard stare.

"I'd caution you not to call me that again," warned Daga sternly. "I may be many things but a liar is certainly not one of them. And I beg you to remember who was always eating dust when we wrestled as boys, my dear 'brother'."

"Please continue then, 'uncle'," Bran said, her voice dripping with mock sweetness.

Daga fired her a strict glare but continued with his story. "As I was saying, Shafta the First Wife was my mother and Druga the Bold was my father. I was born in the dawn of dwarf time, firstborn of those that were first spat out from the rocks. Although my parents died eons ago, it was foretold that I would linger on until the major threat against the dwarves was finally eradicated. Until then I am ageless and timeless, a true dwarf and yet something not quite dwarf. I foresaw the coming of Savas-Zev and yet I was forbidden against doing anything to prevent him from being or from growing into the monster that he is today. All I could do was watch the ruin he caused to my people and prepare for the day when the dwarves could free themselves from his misery. I was given a certain bit of magical power to aid in this eventual end, gods be praised. I brooded for many years on how to help my people. Finally, I decided that to best save the dwarf race, they had to leave their tunnels to fight. Those that fought had to have special talents. They had to move swiftly and cover great distances. They had to get over their inborn stubborness and deal with other races well enough to strike up alliances they could call on in times of need. For I knew only too well what need they would have of such alliances someday. The survival of their race would depend on how strong such bonds of friendship with other races would prove to be.

"Now talents: I petitioned to the dwarf gods for them to approve of my idea for an inborn ability in certain dwarf families. They blessed my request and I made sure certain bloodlines of dwarves would carry the urge to explore the above world, to make friends with other races and mainly to have a natural-born fascination for horses."

"And the Yazu came from this?" Delkan interrupted.

"Came from it? My dear, I created the Yazu in the first place," he laughed, and pulling the pipe out of his mouth, pointed at her and Delkan. "My dears, you two are the product of my blessing—or curse, depending on your point of view—that I put on this race so many centuries ago. Do you realize that within every generation, usually every family has had a troublesome daughter who wanted to ride horses and carry a sword and race the wind above and far away from the tunnels of her people? I designed the Yazu to be the greatest cavalry warriors this world has ever seen. They had to be. Because they would become the protectors of their race."

He went silent for a moment staring proudly at the both of them.

"I think I did a fine job," he said grinning widely into the flickering firelight between them.

"Then... I guess you also came up with the idea of the Dahla horses too, eh?" Garn said.

Daga turned to him. "Well, now that was an interesting turn of events. In my long life I have had many adventures. In one of them I had to jump through a mirror to escape being caught by a much younger master Zev. It transported me to another plane full of animals and beasts much like we have here. Somehow a horse from that world ended up on our plane and died. It was Savas-Zev's fault of course, the result of dabbling with magic he was not yet ready for. Well, the horses on the other plane are very intelligent, brave creatures and are insanely protective of their own kind. They were furious that one of their own had died far from home and not even her body could be returned. So I struck up a deal with them. That's where the Dahla horse comes from. They were more than happy to assist me in this endeavor and they don't care how long it takes just as long as they get their revenge on him. The bond between me and the Dahla horse spirits has been a mutually beneficial one."

"Until now," moaned Bran miserably.

Vilmar stepped out of the shadows from behind Bran and reassuringly clasped her shoulders.

"I told you, Bran. We'll do everything in our power to get Val back," he said with a gentle squeeze.

Daga sat bolt upright at Vilmar's sudden appearance.

"Ah!" he said. "The boy is now a green wizard."

Vilmar winced and hesitantly stepped closer into the firelight. "Not quite, sir," he muttered sheepishly. "The unicorn says I still have one more test to undergo... that of spirit."

Daga's eyes took on a strange light and his smile increased in girth. "Ah yes, the spirit test," said Daga quietly, standing up. He rubbed his hands together and stepped a little closer to Vilmar. "Well, let's see if we can remedy that, shall we?"

And with no more warning, he walked up to Vilmar, growing larger and more transparent as he did so. Before he had a chance to do anything, Daga walked into his body!

There was a screeching, wailing sound and a rushing wind followed Daga's form. In the wind were screaming ghostlike faces, hundreds and thousands of faces. They rushed suddenly at Vilmar and impaled themselves in his chest shrieking like a hoard of banshees.

Vilmar shuddered as the force of the spectral host smote him hard. He had no time to put up his shields, no time at all to react until it was too late. And then all he could do was shudder as wave upon wave of disembodied spirits were sucked against his will into his body and into his very soul. He experienced every one of their lifelong memories in an instant and still more kept coming, flowing into and not out of him, filling his mind with their incessant babble. He fought because it was the first thing that occurred to him to do, fought to push their thoughts away. But more just poured streaming into him, filling the already crowded room that was his psyche. He collapsed in a shaking, convulsing mass to the ground, thrashing as if in a seizure.

Bran, with a cry, immediately rushed to his side and reached out for him. But before she could get to him, Iyorath snatched her back.

"Don't touch him!" he warned. "This is the final test. Leave him be."

"But he certainly don't look too good," Delkan observed doubtfully.

"That's cause he's fighting it. If he fights it too much, they'll kill him," the elf told them.

"But can't you help him, lad?" Garn asked.

The elf shook his head.

"The only one who can help him is Daga. And he's in there," replied Iyorath biting his lip in worry.

Vilmar arched his back and was making frightening, choking sounds. His eyes rolled wildly back in his head.

"I've got to do something," Bran shoved her way past the elf and grabbed a flailing arm. She clasped his right hand in both of hers and fastened a crushing grip on his hand.

"Relax, bud," she muttered to him, not sure if he was able to hear her or not. "It'll all be over soon." She glared angrily up at the elf and added. "One way or another." Against his better judgment, Iyorath took the other hand in both of his. "Let go, Vilmar. Just let it happen," he murmured to Vilmar's twitching form.

Deep in the tormented recesses of Vilmar's mind he heard one voice above the rest, a voice he recognized.

"Hold it down, will ya! Can't you see you're scaring the boy!" it bellowed above the din.

It was Daga. "Now lad, what did the unicorn tell you to do through all the other tests? Just relax and accept it? Why don't you try doing that and I'll try telling the masses not to overwhelm you too much. It'll take longer but we're in no rush. They just get a little eager, that's all. They never meant to scare you. Just relax, that's it. You're allowed to breathe while this happens."

Bran didn't know if Vilmar could actually hear her but his form suddenly stilled and ceased to thrash about. His breathing was still rapid and his eyes stared blankly ahead.

"This will be a long test," Iyorath informed with a worried sigh. "But it seems he's doing better. Get a blanket and watch him closely until he comes around."

"Are his eyes supposed to be doing that?" Delkan asked.

"Yes, that's normal," Iyorath replied with barely a glance.

The elf left to stir up the fire. Bran exchanged a doubtful glance with Delkan and turned back to Vilmar.

Her friend's eyes were changing. They weren't just changing color, it seemed the entire eyeball, both of them, were turning a smoky, black shade.

She held Vilmar's hand and glared angrily at Iyorath's back.

'If anything goes wrong with my friend...'

She didn't finish the thought.

Bran and Vilmar made their way quietly through the forest. Bran still needed assistance from the cane so Vilmar had to stop and wait for her every now and then. They chatted comfortably while they walked through the deepening afternoon.

"You sure you can see alright?" Bran asked him.

Vilmar's fit had passed but it left him with strangely colored, dark eyes. At times the cloudy blackness seemed to swirl and change like the myriad of colors in a glass marble.

And the eyes were still completely dark from lid to lid suggesting that the eye's entire surface was that shade. Bran found it incredibly unnerving.

"I can see just fine," replied Vilmar. "Although I wish I had a mirror in order to see what you're describing."

"No, you don't!" Bran sniffed disapproving. "It's creepy looking!"

Vilmar laughed and shook his head.

"I'm still the same person," he said to reassure her.

Bran sat down on a large rock in the middle of a small clearing, her back to the long shadows of approaching evening.

"No, you're not," Bran said dismally. "None of us are the same. Not anymore."

She lapsed into a sullen, brooding silence. Vilmar noiselessly seated himself next to her, hoping his presence would console her.

"I miss your blue eyes, crystal clear like aquamarine," she said softly.

Vilmar sighed deeply. "Well, they certainly seem to work just the same. And yet there is some difference."

Bran's eyebrows arched somewhat. "Like what?" she asked, curious in spite of herself.

Vilmar frowned and thought hard for a moment. "Well, there's this shimmering faint aura on everything, especially people. If I don't think too much about it, it's little more than a small nuisance, like seeing double vision. But if I focus on it..." His voice drifted off as he looked at Bran's form differently. "There. The auras become large and bright. They shift and change colors, on people especially."

She shuddered at the focus of such strange eyes. "Maybe in reference to their emotions?" Bran suggested and he nodded.

"Probably," he agreed. "Except I'm not really sure what colors equal what emotions just yet."

"Better learn fast. It could prove helpful," Bran replied.

He nodded in total agreement. "I'll ask the unicorns. They will probably know. They probably see like that all the time," he said.

He bowed his head and rubbed his eyes with a grunt. Focusing his aura sight like that for any short length of time made his eyes sore and tired, not to mention leaving him slightly disoriented. He would definitely have to practice more to get over it.

He sighed again heavily. "Know what I miss?" he asked keeping his eyes shut.

Bran grunted in reply.

"My privacy," Vilmar said.

Bran's face screwed up in confusion. "You saying you want me to leave?" she asked trying not to sound insulted.

"No. Not you. Not out there. In here," he tapped his brain. "Ever since the final test I constantly feel like I'm in a room full of people talking loudly. I'm alone and at the same time never alone. I'm never alone the way I'd like to be. There are all these people in here with me. And they never shut up!"

He sighed and craned his neck backwards wearily, stretching. "At any time one of the many spirits inside will want to talk through me or use my body to do something. I keep having to remind them to ask permission first, they can't just take over like that. I'm telling you this to warn you in case I do or say something that's totally unlike me."

Bran was slightly alarmed. "Should I be worried about these... others?" she asked in concern.

"I don't think so. Leastways, I hope not," he said.

He was silent for a brief moment.

"You know your parents are in here," he whispered softly.

Bran fixed him with a hard stare.

"When they and you are ready, they'll talk. Right now, they understand that their host has a lot on his plate to deal with. I'm still... adjusting... to all this," he stated quite frankly.

Bran thought briefly about this and finally nodded her acceptance.

She took a deep breath and changed the subject abruptly. "What do you think of Daga?" she asked.

Vilmar smiled widely and said without missing a beat. "I think the real question is what do *you* think of him? I already know what I think," he said.

The question took her by surprise. She thought hard and made a few false starts before really speaking. "I'm not sure what to think," she said in frustration, running a forge-baked hand through her bushy red locks. "I feel like he's betrayed me, like he's engineered my whole life before I was even born and like nothing I do or say is my own plan but his. I am impressed by his drive to protect our people. I just wish I wasn't a focal point of it. I want to end the reign of Savas-Zev to be sure, but I don't want all the responsibility of it to lie on my shoulders because I have absolutely no idea how I am going to accomplish any of it. And I feel doubly betrayed because I am convinced now that Daga is not really my uncle. I don't even know who or what he is!"

She perched her fuzzy beard on her fists and glowered off into the shadows.

Vilmar sighed deeply and was silent for a long, long time. "Daga is an entity unto himself. He is a firstborn of a firstborn. He is totally and completely a dwarf—an ancient dwarf—one of the old people your ancestors sprang from with some god-given extra talents to help him accomplish his mission. He desperately desires for the dwarf race to survive. His hatred of Savas-Zev is nearly as old as the wizard himself. But more than that, Bran, he loves you and dearly wants you to survive this struggle to come."

Bran was glaring angrily at Vilmar's face by the time he finished. She hated those strange, dark eyes he now had. "If that's what he feels and everybody's inside of you, why didn't he tell me that himself?" she growled.

Vilmar rocked back in surprise at her reply. "He did not speak through me because he is no longer inside of me. He held open the door for the spirits to enter me but he is free to come and go as he wishes," he said and then added ruefully, "I wish the others were!"

Bran frowned angrily. "Well that's bloody convenient for him!" she snarled, and picking up a stone threw it at a nearby tree.

"Bran, you did not get into this predicament all by yourself and you will not get out of it all alone either. You do have friends. Friends that will fight and die for you."

"I don't want my friends to fight or die for me!" she exclaimed and picking up a dry branch, she stalked angrily about, swatting at the underbrush in frustration. "I just want to take out my beef with that dratted wizard and be done with it without the whole world watching. This is personal."

"Yes, it is," Vilmar reasoned. "And it's also intensely personal for Delkan, and for Garn and Iyorath and for countless other lives affected by this monster of a wizard. And it is also a very personal struggle for me as well."

Bran looked up in surprise at this remark. Vilmar gave her a determined look from his strange, dark, new eyes and explained.

"No one, but *no one,* hangs a dear friend of mine on a wall, tortures her, steals her horse and gets away with it!" he vowed passionately. Then he grinned.

Bran stood there in shock and awe, and then she too grinned.

"What you have gone through has affected others as well. What do you think your friends' reactions were when I told them Savas-Zev had captured and tortured you? They all wanted to tear him apart with their bare hands. They still do! They care about you, Bran. Enough to protect you from ever having that happen again. And yet they also understand that this is your fight and you have to deal with it in some way. At least, that's what they're expecting."

"I'm sorry. I guess I was being selfish," she said and came back to sit beside Vilmar. "I guess I never realized what good friends I have."

She squeezed his hand briefly and went to let go. But Vilmar wouldn't release it.

She turned to face him and their gaze met and locked. There was something different there in his eyes, an emotion she had never seen before. In spite of his newly changed vision, she could still recognize emotions as they played across his face. She had never seen him look at her this way before. It made her feel funny inside, not threatened or scared but attracted in an almost painful fashion.

Vilmar dropped his eyes and swallowed with difficulty, breaking the moment. "Whenever you think you're alone, you come to me," he said. "Or Delkan or Garn or Iyorath. But I'd be flattered if you came to me first. Just don't go through this by yourself."

"You and Delkan are the first on my list," she said with a grin. "Now let go of my hand! Yours is soft as butter, no callouses or anything. That's just not right."

He smiled and slowly, almost reluctantly, released her fingers from his grasp. "I guess you need soft hands to throw lightning bolts at goblins," he jested lightly.

There was an uncomfortable, wordless pause between them. Neither looked the other in the eye.

Vilmar rubbed the back of his neck and muttered, "So now what do we do?"

Bran gave him a look laced with resolute determination. "Now we stop a wizard from wiping out my whole race," she growled venomously.

She grew suddenly quiet and her look softened. "Got any bright ideas on how to do that?" she asked.

"Why are you asking me?" Vilmar shot back in surprise.

It was her turn to look befuddled. "Well…" she started hesitantly. "Because you're the wizard!"

"That doesn't automatically give me all the answers," Vilmar replied with some heat.

"Because you're a green wizard?" Bran suggested, even less helpfully than before.

Vilmar sniffed in sarcasm. "The shoes of a green wizard still feel quite strange on my feet," he grumbled. "I've always had the idea wizards knew exactly where they're going, never confused about anything. But me? I have no blessed idea what to do next."

Bran grunted and frowned, stroking her beard which had grown quite thick by now.

"If it were me," she puzzled aloud, "I would make a magical weapon which was enchanted to kill a particular wizard."

Vilmar sniffed quietly into the deepening shadows. "What a perfectly dwarvish answer!" he replied smirking.

Bran stood up straight and jutted out her beard, taking the reply as an insult.

"And what would you do, farrier's son? Deck him with a well thrown horseshoe?" she scoffed.

"If it was just that simple," Vilmar muttered, shaking his head dismally. His frown deepened. "I think we need the advice of the unicorn and one very old dwarf," he finally said.

The lengthening shadows suddenly dissolved in a blinding white flash of light from a bolt of lightning. The shock of it knocked them both backwards, arms flung outward to shield their eyes. As one, they tumbled along the forest floor as thunder rumbled and rolled.

Bran was the first to spring to her feet, brandishing her cane as if it was a stout dwarvish axe. Still blinded, Vilmar groveled beside her, wincing and blinking, trying to look upward toward the flashing light.

The flaming white horse with the black head had reappeared of its own choosing.

"Mayhem!" Bran breathed in relief and lowered the cane.

Pawing and nickering in friendly tones, Mayhem strode up to her.

"I'm better now," he spoke to her mind, his thoughts tickling her brain. *"I am ready to continue..."*

Mayhem never finished his sentence for just then Vilmar stood up, shaking leafy forest loam from his clothes. Both of them, human and horse, started in total surprise at the sight of one another.

The flames on Mayhem roared and crackled in sudden recognition. The stallion's complete attention was focused on this strange human before him.

Bran gazed in confusion from the magical stallion to Vilmar and gasped. Her human friend's appearance had changed subtly.

Vilmar was wreathed all about in white tendrils of condensation, like fog rising from a secluded lake. His eyes had locked on the stallion's. They had changed color.

Vilmar's eyes were blue once more. But they were not the crystal-clear aquamarine blue they had been in the past. They were now a lighter, ice blue shade. Bran knew those eyes all too well. They were Yaffa's, and they were rimmed with unshed tears.

"You did survive, Dearheart," spoke a female dwarf's voice from Vilmar's lips. "I was too afraid to find out. Please forgive me, dear friend. I should have trusted in your strength."

Mayhem went to Vilmar with steps which seemed pillowed on clouds. He bent his great flaming head, crowned with dark and light tresses and lovingly touched his forehead to Vilmar's breast, allowing himself to be cradled by this stranger's arms. The tears which did not belong to Vilmar, tears Yaffa had restrained all the long years, flowed down the young man's cheeks and were immediately licked tenderly away by Mayhem's large tongue.

"I am so sorry I did not believe in you. I am so sorry," her mother's voice came from the frame of her young friend.

Bran felt the moment too private for her to be sharing. She quietly began to back away, to leave these two strange creatures she loved so well to their emotions.

"Please don't leave, Bran," came her mother's voice again. "This moment would have never happened without you. Please stay, child."

And so Bran stayed. She walked up to Vilmar's side. It was his body to be sure but the eyes and the feeling from him was clearly Yaffa. It felt strange to Bran to be looking so far up to her mother's eyes.

She felt so odd. Part of her wanted to leap into Yaffa's arms, strange though they were, and bawl like a baby. The other part of her insisted this magic was strange, too strange for her dwarf sensibilities to handle and she should get as far away from it as possible. She had no idea what she should feel emotionally. Her chest was tight and her eyes burned and felt wet. She looked down at the ground. It was easier to deal with her mother's spirit being there if she didn't have to look at Vilmar's face and frame housing it. With her eyes closed or directed away, it felt just like Yaffa was really there in body and mind. She could feel the details of her spirit which made Yaffa her mother. She could almost smell the acrid hot metal scent which had always clung to her even though most dwarves smelled this way. She knew, without her eyes, it was her mother.

She didn't quite know what to say. "Mama," she whispered helplessly. "I never got to say goodbye."

She heard her mother sniff at the irony of the situation. Bran's spirit clung to the familiar sound. She squeezed her eyelids shut and two tears escaped and spilled slowly down her cheeks.

"Don't," her mother's voice scoffed gently. "For am I really gone?"

Bran looked up in surprise. Her mother's eyes in Vilmar's face, it was just too weird to deal with. So she shut her eyes again.

"Your... body... is," Bran said in a very small child-like voice. Her words seemed so useless.

"Yes, well it sort of comes with the territory. But does the spirit die with the body?" she reasoned.

"You tell me. You're the one on the other side," the comment popped suddenly out of her mouth before she had a chance to think her words through. Had she been aware, she would have never said them aloud.

Yaffa's husky voice laughed at the brashness of her words.

"Your reply is so completely dwarvish. How could your father ever have doubted you?" she smiled.

Again Bran clung to the sound from home and two more tears trailed down her furry cheeks.

"Bran, child, I am here. I will always be here. You have only to think of me and my spirit is there. Always," her tone was soft and reassuring.

Vilmar's large, freckled hand stroked Mayhem's pearly side, tracing circles in the short hairs, moving in such a way as Yaffa and not Vilmar had ever moved. Bran felt the vice-like hold on her chest tighten and she gasped quietly to relieve the pressure.

"But..." stammered Bran in confusion. "Aren't you trapped in Vilmar's body?"

"Trapped? No. Never," she replied confidently. "I am inside along with several thousand others. But we are not trapped. Vilmar is just... packing us along, you might say. He is a door which is shut but not locked. When the most appropriate moment comes, we shall all open the door. But we shall not disappear or go away completely. I will certainly never abandon my daughter. What kind of parent would I be?"

Bran chewed her lip, considering this. Mayhem turned his head to face her and blew softly in Bran's face. Automatically, Bran's small, stubby, forge-browned hand joined Vilmar's stroking the stallion's white flank.

"But Vilmar said... well, of all the spirits inside... they weren't allowed to just take over like that. They had to ask permission first. You appeared a little suddenly. I take it you didn't ask his permission," she finally managed to stutter out.

"Yes, well, you're right. I didn't. I saw Mayhem and well... I acted without thinking. You will apologize to him for me right, dear Bran?"

Bran sniffed derisively. She wasn't sure she liked any spirit, even her mother's using her friend's body.

"Despite what you think, Bran, your friend Vilmar may have to get used to spirits taking over his body from time to time. I am glad he warned you about it. At the final end, we will take over a bit more and add to his already awesome power he keeps hidden inside. He will need the aid of all of us to accomplish the task which is ahead of him. And it will be very scary for him to do so. But the lesson he has to learn is sometimes one must release all semblance of control and let go to truly be successful in one's endeavors. He must learn to trust others completely. This will be terrifying to him."

Mayhem shook his pearly neck, setting his mane to dancing and snorted peacefully. Bran sat down on a log and thought hard about what Yaffa had said. She finally grunted in affirmation. "That would scare me a bit too," she admitted.

"Vilmar will need your help and your friendship through this. You need to be there for him, Bran. He is as important to this equation as you are. Please don't forget this."

Bran started to look at Yaffa and then remembered and turned away. She instead focused on Mayhem's strangely colored, light eyes in the dark background of his head.

"I will do what I can from the inside," Yaffa told her. "There are many strong-willed spirits in here and some are rather resentful of being held back. But I will do my best to guard him from their heavy-handed ways. They won't get through me if he doesn't want them to. Understand?"

Bran nodded. "Thank you for looking out for him," she said and squeezed Vilmar's hand without looking.

"Always, Bran," Yaffa said. "I have grown rather fond of your friend. I certainly wouldn't like to see him get hurt in any of this."

There was a long, uncomfortable silence between them. Mayhem stamped and swished his tail at some troublesome flies.

"Is... Da... in there too?" Bran finally said into the air between them.

"Yes," replied Yaffa slowly. "Would you like to speak with him?"

Bran was silent for a long, long time considering. The last time she had seen Varg, her father, was just before she had left to join the Yazu. They had smoothed over some of the hard feelings from before but their relationship had still been rather strained. It was clear Varg no longer thought of his daughter as a muttlith. But he also did not approve of her associating with any of the other races. And although he adored his Yazu wife, it was plain he had wanted better for his daughter.

Bran chewed her lip and fiddled absently with a small beard braid as she thought. Mayhem nudged her quietly.

"No," she said finally. "Not yet, at least."

She sensed rather than saw Yaffa nod quietly.

"He is quite eager to speak with you. But when you are ready, he will come through," she murmured to her daughter.

Vilmar's hand touched her shoulder and she felt a loving squeeze.

"I must give Vilmar's body back to his spirit now, Bran," her mother said gently.

Bran forgot and looked Vilmar full in the face. She saw the smoky tendrils of magic starting to recede back into his body.

"But we will speak again soon, dearest daughter of mine," she assured. "Until then stay safe, my child."

Yaffa gave a deep sigh and Bran felt the sensation which was her mother's spirit fade quickly, retreating backwards into Vilmar's form. He closed his eyes and bowed his head as Yaffa's soul withdrew to someplace deep within him. He then, quite unexpectedly, collapsed in a heap to the forest floor.

Mayhem threw up his head and nickered in surprise. The great horse put down his head and sniffed Vilmar's form. He nickered again and the horse's tone changed to one of great concern, as of a mare whose foal is hurt. Mayhem gave an explosive snort and backed away in confusion.

Bran stroked his white shoulder and tried to calm him but the great horse was agitated and avoided her touch. So she went to Vilmar's side and touched his shoulder.

He moaned and stirred.

Bran breathed a sigh of relief. The sound he made was in a masculine tone, Vilmar's own voice once again. He opened his eyes and they were dark marble swirls once more.

"What happened?" he said holding his head.

"Yaffa had some things to say," Bran told him.

"Yaffa?" he repeated. "Damn! I told her to warn me before she did that!"

"Yes, well she said for me to tell you she was awfully sorry," Bran related to him.

Vilmar grunted briefly. He still seemed disoriented and drained.

"Can you stand?" she asked and reached out to steady him.

Vilmar made three starts before he could finally stand up and he needed Bran to lean on because he was so shaky.

"*Who is THIS?*" Mayhem demanded in anger, stomping a great hairy foot.

Bran and Vilmar looked up at the fiery white horse in surprise.

"Who?" stammered Bran not comprehending. "But you were just lovin' all over him!"

Vilmar now stared at Bran in shock.

"He was?" Vilmar gurgled out, now even more confused. He glanced from Bran to the strange white horse, rimmed in fire, not knowing what to think.

"I know Yaffa, my bond dwarf. I do not know HIM!" Mayhem replied in ever increasing anger. *"He smells like a wizard!"*

Mayhem turned his black head to Vilmar and pinned his ears flat against his head, tossing it furiously. One blue eye peered out from behind a mop of long black foretop.

"We... I... don't like wizards!" his mind-voice nearly growled in their heads.

Bran stepped protectively in front of her friend and held out a hand in warning.

"Whoa there, big fella!" she said in a much more commanding tone. "Good wizard! Wizard our friend. We don't hurt *this* wizard!"

Mayhem pawed the ground savagely, churning up the topsoil and tossed his head angrily so his wild mane splashed all about, hiding his blue eyes.

"Hmph!" came the reply from the stallion. *"Don't like wizards at all! Wizard stole our queen and killed her! She died on this plane, far from home. Wizards are always an evil black-hearted lot! Want to kill wizards!"*

Vilmar stepped in front of Bran and began talking quietly to the angry stallion.

"What about green wizards? What about wizards with unicorn teachers?" he said as he quietly approached the stallion.

Mayhem gave another explosive snort and backed away a few steps. Then he squealed loudly and half reared into the air.

Vilmar did not run. He stood there and faced the stallion's fury with his voice as his only weapon.

"You hate wizards because the only wizard you have ever known was evil and hurt you," he murmured gently. "I know of *that* wizard. He tortured Bran. And Yaffa killed herself to escape him."

When Vilmar spoke of Yaffa, Mayhem plunged suddenly forward, bellowing in anger. The mad stallion stood only a few feet from Vilmar. He bellowed deep in his gut again and rose high in the air on his hind feet. His hard, hairy forehooves pawed a wild staccato in the air, each only inches from Vilmar's face.

Vilmar never moved a muscle. His eyes remained locked on the stallion's. He knew it was all bluff and bluster. He did not need to be a wizard to read this horse's body language.

"I'd like to stop the wizard who hurt my friends. Would you like to help me?" he boldly asked.

Mayhem stood there weaving slightly before Vilmar, acting very unsure.

"Is Yaffa's filly coming, too?" Mayhem replied hesitantly.

"Oh yes," Vilmar assured with a smile.

"You bet I'm coming!" Bran chimed in eagerly.

"Bran is coming, along with quite a few other dwarves this wizard has wronged. We're all uniting in a great herd against him. We'd appreciate the assistance of one so noble as yourself," Vilmar told him slowly.

Mayhem wove, quietly dancing side to side from one foreleg to another in his indecision. His dual-toned mane floated and swept about with his movements.

"Maybe. Probably. I don't know," Mayhem replied hesitantly. *"I must talk to the others of my kind."*

Bran and Vilmar looked at each other.

"Good idea," Vilmar said. "We should probably do the same."

"A tribal council?" suggested Bran.

Vilmar nodded seriously. "We all need to decide what we are going to do about Savas-Zev," he replied.

"And maybe many will want to chip in," suggested Bran. "He's made a lot of enemies."

"On my plane, too," added Mayhem. *"My kin will also want to know what is to be done about him. I should probably represent them at the council."*

"I'm sure it could be arranged, being as the unicorns will also want to be there," Vilmar thought aloud.

Mayhem bobbed his head up and down in equine agreement.

"Very well then," he replied. *"I will go and discuss it with them."*

The stallion turned to go but Bran's call stopped him. "Wait!" she said suddenly.

He turned back to her, an inquiring expression on his face.

Bran looked uncomfortably from the stallion to Vilmar and back again. She started to step away as if to speak privately with the magic horse and then remembered, Vilmar already knew.

"Have you spoken with Valynt yet?" she asked softly but Vilmar still heard her.

Mayhem returned to her side and placed his soft muzzle in her hands. He was silent for a long moment.

"Yes, I have," he replied at last. *"The wizard cannot keep her forever on this plane, although I'm sure he'd like to."*

"How is she?" Bran asked slowly, breathlessly. She was afraid of the answer.

Mayhem heaved a deep sigh. *"Not well, I'm afraid,"* he said. *"Every second she spends on this plane with that wizard is sheer torment for her. He is not a gentle taskmaster and demands utter obedience from his men and steeds. She fights his every command but her spirit is weakening."*

Bran's face grew dark and angry and her fists clenched in frustration. Mayhem nuzzled her beard reassuringly.

"But do not worry, Yaffa's foal," he spoke lovingly. *"I told her of you and your desires to get her back, and she cheered up remarkably. She now has the strength to fight more. She now lives in hope."*

Bran relaxed somewhat. "What... what did you tell her?" she stammered in a whisper.

Mayhem stepped closer and wrapped his neck about her in an equine hug of surprising affection. *"I told Valynt her bond dwarf was a brave and strong-willed filly just like her mother. I told her that you would not leave her locked in the stall of darkness forever. I told her that you would soon come to rescue her. She felt much better after that. I saw the life return to her eyes again."*

Bran was silent for a long moment.

"I wish I had seen the fire in her eyes," she whispered simply.

Vilmar came up behind her and kneeling, embraced her. "You will, Bran," he murmured quietly. "I promise you."

She turned into his embrace and hugged him back, burying her face in his shoulder. Her eyes were dry but smoldering with an inner rage.

She would get Valynt back somehow or die trying, she vowed silently to herself.

Savas-Zev was in a horrid mood. For an entire week he had stormed and raged at anyone who spoke to him. The first courier who approached with a message was immediately incinerated for the sin of simply entering his presence. Now his captains were too fearful to risk crossing the threshold of his great house. Dask may have been spineless but he'd had his uses and normally survived every encounter with the temperamental wizard. Now he was gone and no one dared enter his presence without groveling on the ground like a worm.

His fury had abated slowly and now had been replaced by a brooding, thoughtful silence, which his troops only feared more. It meant the wizard was plotting something truly diabolical to inflict upon someone. Many prayed they would not be the woeful target.

Savas-Zev sat at his great table, bearded chin propped on his left arm curled up in front of him. The fingers of his right hand drilled the tabletop in a slow, sequential drone of taps. He glared narrowly at his tapping fingers, scheming silently to himself. He was not at all happy.

He had lost his great tome of spells and his scrying bowl had been destroyed. He felt keenly the loss of both. One or the other he could have easily dealt with although he would still not have been happy about it. But the loss of both artifacts crippled him. If he still had the scrying bowl, he could have easily found the book's thief. If he still had the book, he could have fashioned a new scrying device in short time. Being bereft of both sorely sapped his powers.

He felt the loss of the scrying bowl more poignantly. He did not like being blind to the goings on of the area. It was plain to him there was another magician to contend with—and by all accounts, one powerful enough for him to give true worry. He also knew this other magician was being helped and guided by an even more powerful presence and this bothered him mightily. He had to deal with both threats thoroughly, preferably as soon as possible. But his eyes were now blind. He had no idea from which direction the threat would come or what shape it would take. His only hope was to stay safe within his army, at the center of this world he had created, and hope when they struck, he would have a clear enough warning to gather his magical defenses for a supreme effort to blast away any threat. This was his hope at least.

He frowned and growled low in his throat like an irritated big cat who has been poked one too many times. He did not like feeling cornered. He had to do something soon to get himself out of the situation he had been backed into, something sly and secretive. He needed information. He needed it quickly.

A hint of an idea occurred to him, and a devious smile tugged one corner of his mouth upwards. He rose smoothly and strode gracefully, like a confident dancer into the next room. He went immediately to his rack of soul cages. His eyes lingered fondly over all the glass globes with their twinkling little lights all hopelessly trapped inside. He strode down the shelves, his long fingers tracing lightly across the globes, watching in amusement as the stars within shivered and fled to the far side of their cage, away from his hated touch. Seeing this reaction, he cackled maliciously to himself.

Finally, he found just the crystal ball he sought. He deftly picked it up and observed the star inside as it zipped from one smooth surface to another, racing to avoid him. He laughed softly and tossing it into the air, uttered a single magical word of command. The soul cage immediately dissolved into harmless glitter, which evaporated into the air before him.

The soul was free!

It hesitated one moment only as if hardly daring to believe its luck. Then, it shot like a miniature comet for the nearest door.

"Wait a moment," Savas-Zev cried out in a commanding voice laced with magic.

The escaping soul stopped its wild momentum, frozen against its will in space.

"Did you really think I would actually let you go?" Savas-Zev said. "Oh no, my little once-furry friend! I have a chore for you to perform. You will go and carry out my wishes and then you will return to your safe little cage for all eternity. Or until I have another chore for you to do."

The star before him began to tremble and quake, its light flashing and blazing bright in quick succession.

"Now relax, my friend," Savas-Zev taunted in a pleasant tone as he slowly seated himself in a plushy padded chair. "Your language is unbecoming for one even of your bold, little breed. You are in no position to protest anything. So hush!"

The star shivered and its little light grew brighter in fury as it was magically forced to obey.

"That's better," the wizard said as he luxuriously interlinked his long fingers. "Now then. You shall leave me and discover what sort of threat exists in this valley. There is a great magician somewhere out there and his even more powerful teacher. Find out as much about them as possible and report this back to me. Do this before the waxing of the moon in three days and nights hence, or your soul will be trapped forever in oblivion, unable to continue on its journey. Now go! I'm done with you!"

He waved a long hand, releasing the frozen spirit. The star blazed bright and large and hurtled out the door, away from his presence, trailing sparks behind as it went.

Savas-Zev chuckled quietly to himself, pleased with how things had turned out.

"Who needs Dask?" he thought privately.

Dwyn staggered blindly downhill, her heart and lungs crying for want of air. Propelled by momentum, she was unable to stop as she pitched forward and rolled the last few feet. She came to rest with a plop and a splash in the icy coldness of a mountain stream.

In spite of the cold she lay there gasping and panting as the icy water splashed all about the rocks and her shivering form. Her mind was numb. She no longer remembered anything normal. Her thoughts only clung to what had just happened and the horror of it drove her endlessly to run. She had fled until her lungs pained her and her bare feet were torn and bloody along with the remains of her blue linen shift.

She did not know there were no goblins pursuing her. They existed only in her mind. And yet she felt if she ran hard and far enough, she could escape the horrible memories, which plagued her brain.

It was useless. They were still there. They hovered and laughed and poked her forever in her brain. They wouldn't leave her alone. They were everywhere. The world was nothing but ugly, leering goblin faces.

Somewhere, her ears latched onto a new sound, a sound of someone approaching her from outside her mind.

She heard footsteps splashing through the stream coming toward her.

She wailed hopelessly and crawled away from the sound, bleating like a panicky lamb who knows it is about to be slaughtered. She knew there was nowhere to escape. She huddled in a muddy, dejected ball on the pebble-strewn banks of the stream, whimpering pathetically.

The footsteps did not slow or quicken. They approached with confidence. They knew she had nowhere to go. She listened helplessly to the evenly-measured tread and despaired. Her last hope left her.

The footsteps stopped right behind her and were silent for a long, long time. Despairing as she was, her curiosity finally got the better of her and she peeped out at this new threat from behind a tangle of disheveled curls which had once been beautiful.

A tall figure stood before her, cloaked in layer upon layer of ragged, dark green fabric. Its face was hooded but she could just see the hint of a roughly hewn mask of some kind of dark wood shielding the stranger from prying eyes.

She dropped her eyes to the shining, wet pebbles about her and stared blankly at the heavy, black boots framed by the forest green tatters of material.

The figure groaned with the effort of movement as he squatted before her to better see Dwyn. She shivered at the sound and curled herself into a tighter ball.

The creature spoke. His voice was deep and muffled by the mask but Dwyn heard each word clearly.

"So here we are," it said in a flat tone of voice. "The both of us thrown out in the trash as useless, discarded by all we once knew and loved."

Dwyn said nothing. She only breathed and shivered with cold.

"Let us see what grows from the ashes left over. Come with me," the strange voice said.

The voluminous fabric rustled softly and a hand reached out of the folds, palm up toward her.

Dwyn gasped at the sight and crouched further away, trembling violently.

The offered hand was laced all around with barely healed, severely burned flesh. It still smelled strongly of burnt skin and infection.

The hand did not withdraw or even flinch at her reaction. It remained frozen in midair, still offering to her... what? Safety? Protection?

Her tattered mind could not yet grasp such notions.

The hand remained where it was and the figure seemed perfectly willing to remain there all day if he had to, to get her to react.

"Come," the figure intoned again. "What I offer could not possibly be worse than what you have already endured."

The prospect certainly seemed true to her twisted thoughts. But could she be sure? Could she ever be sure about anything anymore?

She hesitated one long moment.

Then she watched in a dim, detached sort of way, as her own hand, streaked with long-dried blood, nails torn and caked with forest loam, fit neatly into the proffered burnt claw.

She sensed rather than saw the hulking, masked figure before her smile.

Both her mind and heart became blank. She no longer cared what happened to her.

It no longer mattered.

CHAPTER 40

The companions sat or lounged about the fire in front of the cave. No one spoke. Garn stabbed purposefully at the coals, kicking the fire higher and added more fuel. Iyorath walked about the circle with a kettle of freshly made venison stew, doling out ladlefuls to each person's wooden bowl. Vilmar likewise followed him with a wineskin of beer. Bran and Delkan sat next to each other. But they did not talk or look at one another.

There was a loud flapping of wings and their eyes were pulled upward to the treetops, which were painted orange by the setting sun. Rath-Tor landed on a lower tree branch and ruffled his feathers as if commenting on the situation.

"They know," he rasped briefly. "They're coming. They'll be here soon."

The small group exchanged looks. Some nodded, others like Garn only grunted their acceptance of the news. Iyorath and Vilmar sat themselves down and, as if a signal had been given, they all turned their attention to the food.

The messenger hounds were the first to arrive. They melted out of the shadows of the woods and in a smooth flowing tide, swept silently about the fire, positioning themselves next to people. Snow Crow huddled affectionately up to Vilmar. He smiled and tossed her a bit of stewed meat. Seeing this the other hounds each chose a person to cuddle up to, hoping for a bit of meat as well. Two dogs were quickly shooed away from Garn's plate and they withdrew but with ever hopeful gazes on their faces. They watched every mouthful with eager anticipation from the grumpy dwarf.

Then the three unicorns arrived. Each one seemed to materialize from the gathering mist and each came from a separate direction.

Silently they positioned themselves about the campfire, the mare next to Vilmar, the stag next to Iyorath and the fawn between Bran and Delkan.

The unicorn doe raised her head and let loose a sharp, high-pitched whistle. It hung crystal clear on the darkening crisp air, haunting and compelling in its timbre.

They heard the stumping of another figure and they all turned to see Daga come lumbering up the small hill to their fire.

"I didn't think you would be here," muttered Garn in a low voice.

Daga sat down and shook himself like a wet dog. "You're having a council aren't you?" he shot back. "Why wouldn't I be here?"

The air to Daga's right suddenly seemed to open up and with a loud roll of thunder and a flash. Mayhem leapt out.

"Aren't you only supposed to come when called?" Daga grumped at the magic horse.

Mayhem snorted at him and went to stand beside Bran. The unicorn fawn stared in amazement at the white flames which surrounded the magical creature from another plane, and Delkan sensed a flood of questions flitting through his young mind. She motioned to the unicorn fawn now was not the time.

"*I would come whenever Yaffa called,*" Mayhem explained with some heat.

"Humph!" grunted Daga. "You're taking a great chance just showing up whenever you wish. You'll drain your power!"

"That flash and boom's a bit much too," groused Garn. "What if we were sneaking up on something when we summoned you?"

"*I would know the difference!*" Mayhem insisted stomping a hairy foot.

"Would you?" replied Daga. "Hmmm. I hope so for all our sakes. Things are getting a bit serious to chance always making a dramatic appearance."

"*Enough!*" scolded the unicorn doe. "*We have more important things to discuss than to waste time with this dwarvish bickering!*"

She shook her iridescent head and swatted her tail to punctuate the point.

She stepped forward and cast her gaze about the circle of friends.

"*What is to be done about Savas-Zev?*" she asked those gathered.

Garn slapped the ground next to the fire as if he was stomping out a stray spark. "Kill 'im, of course!"

263

Vilmar snorted wryly at the action. "Would it were so simple!" he muttered.

"Wizards are never easy to dispatch," grumbled Daga.

"Oh really?" commented Garn. "Meaning you've tried it?"

Daga shot him a warning look. "Yes," he said slowly in a low voice, tinged with regret. "A very long, long time ago. It didn't work."

"Obviously it was not your fate to do so," replied the unicorn doe.

Daga was silent for a moment. "Or the time to do so," he muttered softly.

"And now is?" asked Bran.

The unicorn sighed heavily. *"Now is the time to choose what course of action we shall take concerning this wizard,"* she spoke to the group. *"And how and when we are to take this course of action."*

Garn sniffed and slapped his thigh to accentuate his words. "Squash him like a bug, and the sooner the better!" he growled.

"And just how do you propose to do that?" Iyorath challenged.

"A magical weapon should do the job nicely," Delkan put in.

"You dwarves and your magical weapons," Iyorath snorted derisively. "That's your cure for everything!"

"You saying my idea's no good?" Delkan retorted defensively.

"He's saying it's been tried before," muttered Daga dismally, hating to play devil's advocate in this argument. "Nothing would make me happier than to take him out with a dwarf-made weapon, enchanted to kill just him. But it's been tried before."

There was a long silence as the friends mulled over this bit of information in their heads.

"Maybe all the times before it failed because you were trying to do just that, *kill* him," Vilmar put in suddenly.

Bran's brow furrowed and she frowned at her friend. "What are you saying, Vilmar?" she asked, not comprehending. "We shouldn't kill him but reform him? I thought of all people gathered here, you would be the last to say that!"

Garn snorted explosively at the comment. "I don't think anyone here *wants* him to be reformed," growled Garn with some venom.

"That's definitely *not* what I'm saying," replied Vilmar. He heaved a big sigh and explained further.

"What I am saying is Savas-Zev knows he's accumulated a lot of enemies who want to kill him. He's fully aware and ready for it. Let's do something he's not prepared for."

"Such as?" growled Garn.

"Maybe all the other weapons didn't work because they were created to kill him."

He leaned forward and made sure he had everyone's complete attention before continuing. "Maybe we need a weapon which won't kill him but rather *ensnare*."

"You want to trap him like a soul cage, right?" Garn said.

"Exactly!"

"How perfect would that be?" Iyorath chuckled ironically with an eager smile.

"But if he's trapped, he could always be freed," Delkan added, always trying to find a loophole an enemy might exploit.

"But if the body is dead, the soul will have nothing to return to," Iyorath returned.

They all knew how well Iyorath had learned this painful lesson.

"If you do this, I want the body," Mayhem jumped in with a snort and a wild head toss.

"Later, proud one," the unicorn stag reassured softly. *"Don't jinx the only chance we might have."*

Daga began to chuckle. "Now this plot just might work," he muttered, quite pleased with himself. "The whelp and I can put such a spell on this weapon which will take Savas-Zev many centuries to figure out. Your great-great-grandkids might have to deal with his spirit's eventual escape but not you."

"Are you talking dwarf lifespan or elvish?" Delkan quipped in good humor.

"Never mind that! Our race will have a chance to recover from all the damage he's done to it," Garn added.

"Quite correct," the unicorn doe nodded. *"Right now, if Savas-Zev is allowed to continue on his path, in a few generations there will be no more dwarves."*

"Or the survivors will be terribly inbred," Bran muttered with a shiver of intense distaste.

"If only one dwarf family takes care to remember its history, they will be able to deal with the wizard's evil soul when his spirit rises again," the unicorn stag said quietly.

"There will be more than one dwarf family who remembers," Garn assured. "For whenever one of us dies, our relatives must sing the song of his or her life's heroic acts to the Great Dragon or our soul will not

265

pass into the feast hall of the great kings of old. We must know our history."

"So that's why you're always swearing by the Great Dragon," murmured Vilmar in sudden realization almost to himself.

"Does this plan sound good to you, Ancient One?" Iyorath asked the unicorn doe respectfully.

She sighed deeply and was silent for a long while, considering. Finally she nodded. *"Yes, it does,"* she replied at long last. *"I think Vilmar has really hit upon something with this idea to trap him instead of kill him. I think this is also the mistake everyone has been making when it comes to eradicating Savas-Zev. We've been so involved with the intent of killing him, we never thought of other options."*

"It seems to me, sitting right here and now, that *is* the only option," replied Daga.

Garn nodded, fingering his braided gray beard thoughtfully. "Nothing would make me happier than to kill him and I think everyone here would agree with me. Savas-Zev has made it so personal to so many of us. But I would be happy with trapping him."

"I'm more satisfied with the trapping solution," Iyorath spoke up. "I want him to suffer... not just die. And if he's trapped in such a way so he is aware of the passage of time, it would be even better in my eyes. Let him learn what a soul cage is all about!"

His gentle blue eyes were smoldering in a long-nursed fire of pain from his own experience.

"Fine!" Bran said in a decisive tone of voice. "Then who will make the weapon?"

"I will," Daga offered right away. "I can shape the magic into it as it's forming. And Vilmar will help me."

"What? Why me?" Vilmar asked in obvious surprise.

"Because no weapon thus far that has ever gone up against Zev, has been touched by a green wizard. Ah, the power you and I could put into it! Just think of it!" Daga's eyes were glinting in firelight, he was so eager to get started.

"And before he makes the weapon, you must consult the elements," the unicorn added.

"I don't understand," Vilmar said.

"Remember what you did and how you felt when you went to rescue Bran?" she asked gently.

His strange eyes darkened and he nodded.

"*You must consult the elements to gain their blessing on what you are about to do. If you do not do this, one day you may call upon their powers in an hour of great need and they will abandon you. There is a quick and a slow way to do this. I will teach you both.*"

"But he apparently had their blessings when he rescued me," Bran told her.

"That was luck, pure and simple," Vilmar quickly put in and the unicorn nodded.

"*You were very lucky that day and also very new to the powers,*" she told him. "*They understood you were angry at a force of magic which had total disregard for the forces of nature and had caused quite a lot of imbalance. Nature understands you will be working to repair these rifts. But never make the assumption their blessing is always assured. They still appreciate being consulted.*"

"Maybe the elements will help with the supplies for the weapon?" asked Garn tentatively.

The unicorn doe turned to look at him and he felt rather than saw her smile.

"*Anything is possible,*" was all she would say.

"So when do we march on this adventure?" Delkan said with child-like eagerness.

"As soon as this weapon is made," Garn replied with likewise eagerness.

"*NO!*" said all the unicorns together.

Startled by this reaction, everyone stared at them.

The unicorns exchanged knowing looks. "*The opportunity will present itself,*" the mare said softly.

"*If you give Savas-Zev enough rope, eventually he will hang himself,*" the stag replied.

"*Just watch and wait,*" the fawn said quietly.

"Hmm," muttered Vilmar. "So timing is everything?"

And here all the unicorns nodded together.

"*Of course!*" replied the unicorn fawn. "*When the time is perfect, you will know.*"

Delkan growled audibly in frustration. "Not now?" she whined petulantly. "You wise ones have to spoil all our fun!"

"*Patience, little one,*" reassured the unicorn stag.

"Yes," agreed Iyorath. "Patience will make the revenge all the more sweet."

The dwarves sat in grumpy silence around the campfire. Vilmar and Daga were off "collaborating" on the weapon.

They had been engaged in peaceful conversation along with the elf only an hour ago. And then the conversation had gotten heated.

It had started easily enough. Bran had asked Daga earlier about what sort of weapon he and Iyorath were going to fashion to ensnare Savas-Zev. Daga and Vilmar had exchanged knowing looks and he had replied, "Let's just let the magic decide what form it wants."

Vilmar had seemed quietly pleased with the answer. But Bran was perplexed. She had returned to the group and voiced her puzzlement.

"Well, of course it will be an axe to slice him through and through," commented Garn.

"I disagree," interrupted Delkan. "I think a war hammer would be much more appropriate. It would satisfy the dwarf desire to squash him flat."

"And why wouldn't a spear be appropriate?" Bran put in. "It would kill him without anyone having to touch him, but be close enough for it to be satisfying."

"A sword is still the right thing to trap a soul in and is the proper weapon for a hero," said Iyorath, interjecting.

As one, all three dwarves turned to him with a disapproving scowl on their bearded faces, and as one all three said, "Not dwarvish enough!"

Iyorath, who had been insulted by the fervor of their disapproval, began to stomp around the campfire grumbling mightily in a very un-elvish sort of way. He finally snatched up his hunting gear and spat something about going rabbit hunting. Three messenger hounds followed eagerly, tails wagging, lean mouths gaping in large smiles of anticipation. That had been two hours ago.

Vilmar appeared about this time looking winded. Bran remembered what the unicorn had said about consulting the elements.

"Did... did everything... go well?" she asked hesitatingly.

Vilmar uttered a heavy sigh and nodded with a broad smile. "Of course," he said in a very quiet voice.

"Did the elements give you something to make a weapon out of?" Garn asked too eagerly.

Vilmar smiled again and nodded. His smile deepened as he saw the expectant looks on all their faces.

He shook his head at their insistence and dug a large dark object out of his pack.

Their eyes lit up in wonder.

He held a large, roughly-shaped chunk of what looked to be black glass.

"Is that... obsidian?" breathed Delkan in a whisper, impressed by its beauty.

Vilmar nodded once.

She reached out a trembling hand to touch it and quickly snatched it back. It seemed as hot as a forge.

"A gift from fire," he murmured in a reverent tone. "She is quite eager to help."

Garn chewed his lip in dissatisfaction. "I can't smelt that. It'll break! You chip obsidian, you don't hammer it like steel."

"You'll be able to work it any way you like after we cast a spell on it. And when you're done, nothing will break it. Fire is eager to hold Savas-Zev's soul in safekeeping for us."

He replaced the chunk in his sack and turned to go.

"Make yourselves comfortable. I have no idea how long this will take. Maybe a single day and night, maybe a week. Magic is hard to predict with stuff like this."

"Shouldn't you take a break?" Bran spoke up. "You look a bit tired. And you are... only a human."

He turned to look fondly at her. "I'll be fine but thanks for your concern. I want to get moving on this while the power is still..." he hesitated, searching for the right words, "humming through me. Don't worry. The elements will look out for me."

He disappeared into the darkness of the cave behind him. As he left the light and stepped into its dark recesses, all the dwarves saw a shimmer of brilliance surrounding his form. It seemed to their cave-sharpened senses, to stand out from his body for several feet. Then he was gone from their sight, taking the auric shimmer of freshly expended power with him.

They turned back to each other and wagged their beards, slightly chilled by the sight.

It was a very long time. Iyorath came back directly with his promised rabbits and three, very spent hounds. There was little talking as they butchered the rabbits and prepared the meat. Their stomachs began to growl almost immediately.

It seemed hours later the meat was finally ready and they had a fine feast. They saved some for Vilmar and Daga should they appear. They didn't. The group stayed up as long as they dared and finally gave up on them and went to bed, rolling themselves snugly into their bedrolls around the fire. They awoke at first light and still no Daga or Vilmar. They reheated the leftovers and ate rabbit stew for breakfast. Still no Vilmar or Daga. They spent the day making repairs to their gear or sharpening weapons. They had a cold midday meal and still no Daga or Vilmar. Iyorath went hunting again and brought back several pheasants and a few fish from the stream not too far away. They cleaned and roasted these over the fire and again made extra just in case. Garn grumbled something about it being like waiting for a babe to be born. They all laughed at the comparison.

At dusk, all three unicorns showed up unexpectedly. When the group saw them, they immediately turned to the cave mouth.

Vilmar staggered slowly out wrapped in his green cloak as if he was freezing cold. He cradled something close to his chest.

Bran and Garn rushed to his side to support him.

"It is done," he said in a tired, cracked voice. Then his marbled eyes rolled to the back of his head and he collapsed heavily like a sack of grain.

Garn and Bran caught him and eased him gently to the ground just as Daga came stumping up from behind, looking none the worse for wear.

"Aw, he's fine!" he said waving off the prone Vilmar as if it was nothing. "He just don't have a dwarf constitution that's all. But be ready to give him a good swig of the strongest brew ya got when he wakes up. Keep him good and warm till then."

He helped them drag the motionless Vilmar closer to the fire. Bran cradled his head in her lap and wrapped a large blanket around the both of them. Delkan gave her a shocked look at this. Bran warned her not to say anything with a return glare.

Delkan stabbed at the coals and threw more wood onto the fire.

Daga stretched himself stiffly and they heard a few joints snap and pop. He sniffed hungrily like a wolf who had just scented its prey.

"Is that meat I smell?" he asked. "Hand it over! I'm famished!"

They passed him the last pheasant on its spit and he hungrily sank his teeth into the bird, ignoring all manners.

"Is it made?" Delkan asked hesitantly as she hitched herself closer to Vilmar.

Daga nodded through a mouthful and wiped the grease on a tattered sleeve. He gestured with a bob of his head to the sleeping Vilmar.

"He's got the baby wizard masher in his arms. Of course the unicorns will have to bless it as well with their magic," he told them as he slurped and licked the pheasant juice from his fingers.

"We intend to," said the stag as the three unicorns quietly surrounded Vilmar's prone body.

"Go ahead. Look! I know the suspense is killing ya!" Daga chuckled.

Bran leaned forward over her friend's chest. She barely noticed the unicorns beginning to glow brightly. Garn, Delkan and Iyorath crowded around eagerly.

Iyorath reached forward with his long arms and began to unwind the cloth from around a stick-like object hugged tight to Vilmar's chest. The last fold was lightly thrown aside and they all gasped in child-like wonder.

"Hah!" grunted Garn. "We shoulda taken bets!"

"Bran would have won!" replied Delkan with a proud grin.

Valynt materialized as a rearing, dark horse with wild, blazing fiery eyes. Savas-Zev made a snatch for the flailing reins and got struck by a hoof in the shoulder in the process. He jerked savagely on the reins to punish the horse. Valynt retreated swiftly, her mouth bared, fighting the cruel pressure and giving a small buck in frustration. The wizard cursed in similar exasperation. Neither one liked the other very much but the wizard refused to stop trying to tame this magic horse. Valynt had resisted him at every turn, only giving in after a furious struggle.

Goblins were rushing madly about carting boxes and packing up camp. The wizard barked a warning at three goblins struggling to drag or push a large wooden chest, which dwarfed them. He glared angrily at their work until it was safely loaded into a large wagon drawn by four mules. The chest held his precious glass globes, his soul cages.

A goblin scout scrambled up to the wizard and knelt meekly before his lord and master.

"Report!" Savas-Zev barked at the shivering wretch. "Have you found the Yazu encampment?"

"Yes, Lord," the goblin quickly said. "We are quite certain of it. It lies two weeks to the north of us."

"Excellent!" the wizard replied. "Take your swiftest scout and have him report to my stronghold. Tell them to muster the full strength of my army and meet us there in two weeks time. Enough of this dawdling! We shall wipe any trace of dwarves off the face of the earth!"

The goblin scout seemed quite gleeful at this news and didn't waste any time in leaving to carry out his orders.

Savas-Zev turned to the three goblins who had packed the wagon and were taking a break to pant and catch their breath. They cowered instantly the minute his insane eyes turned to them.

"You there! I want this entire camp packed up and ready to leave by dawn. Strip the village and leave nothing of value behind. We shall need all the stores of food and drink you can loot. Get to it!"

The three scattered to do his bidding.

Savas-Zev turned to the angrily pawing mare he just barely held. She caught his eyes and with it his thoughts. She began to trot circles about him as he tried, with much difficultly, to find a stirrup with a toe. He finally did so and had to vault into the saddle as she sprang away without waiting for the rider to settle himself. The wizard cursed and yanked Valynt to a spinning halt. He knew this was as still as she would stand for him and he fished awkwardly with his other foot for the other slapping stirrup. With another curse, he finally found it. Completely furious now with his mount's antics, he boxed her ears with one hand and took a death grip on the reins with the other. Valynt arched her neck and gaped her mouth wide until her chin was pressed into her chest. She shook her head wildly, still fighting him and felt the strain pulling on the muscles at the top of her neck.

A glimpse of something white caught Valynt's eye from the forest's edge. She crow-hopped her body into an angle to help her see better.

Mayhem stood there, plain to her eyes for an instant. Then he was gone.

Valynt reached out. She did not need to see him to communicate. She knew he was there, that was all that was necessary.

"*Patience, dear one,*" Mayhem's thoughts reached her. "*Fate is speeding up. It will not be long now.*"

"*Hurry!*" she replied. "*I'm not sure how much more of this I can take.*"

She tasted blood in her mouth from the harsh spade bit worked by an ungentle hand.

"*Your suffering will end soon. I promise. Just hang in there a bit longer,*" Mayhem told her.

"*Just make it soon,*" she begged.

And then the rowel-edged spurs were sunk into her scarred and gashed ribs. She bellowed in fury and sprang away at a gallop, trying to outrun the pain her rider seemed to enjoy inflicting on her.

"*PLEASE make it soon,*" she pleaded to the night sky.

The companions were making ready to depart. They were discussing how best to carry out their plan of executing the evil wizard while they sharpened their weapons. So far all they had accomplished had been to get in a squabble about the details. Iyorath felt they should assassinate him secretly but his plot had problems. Garn wanted to take the whole party in openly and attack Savas-Zev as a group, feeling Vilmar could keep the goblins at bay. Of course Vilmar had problems with this scenario and so on.

The unicorns were exchanging similar looks of disbelief and frustration but had wisely chosen to stay out of the conversation. They just sighed from time to time and shook their pearly heads. The fawn had fallen asleep by Delkan's side.

In the middle of all this, Rath-Tor arrived. He gently alighted on the ground in the middle of the conversation and curled his wings, cocking an interested eye to the group. All promptly ignored him. Finally Rath-Tor screeched a cry the eagle normally reserved for challenge. This did get noticed.

The companions went silent and turned their impatient eyes on him.

"Change of plans, I'm afraid," the eagle rasped curtly. "Savas-Zev is moving."

There was a stunned silence.

"What?" exploded Garn. "We get things fixed just right and he turns tail and flees?"

"He can't leave," Bran nearly shouted. "He's not supposed to do that!"

"When have wizards ever done anything they're supposed to?" grumbled Vilmar wryly.

"What's he up to this time, I wonder?" Delkan muttered suspiciously.

The war eagle rustled his feathers and shook his head pointedly.

"Are you illustrious people by any chance curious as to what direction he's going in?" Rath-Tor cackled derisively at them.

Again he got silence and their full attention.

"He's heading north," the eagle informed and began to calmly preen his feathers.

Delkan coughed suddenly and would have jumped up if she was able to. "He's going after the Yazu! He's going to attack them openly!" she exclaimed.

Rath-Tor nodded in a bird-like way. "I seemed to overhear something of that nature," the eagle said.

"We've got to warn them!" said Garn.

"Warn? No, we've got to stop him before he gets there," Bran said.

"What brought this on?" Iyorath wondered aloud. "Why now?"

"Because we have crippled him and he's running scared. Now is when he will slip up and we have to be ready for it," Daga told them coming out of the shadow of the trees behind them.

The companions stirred uncomfortably at his appearance.

"But how did we cripple him?" Iyorath finally asked. "I don't remember doing anything which would be that threatening to him except saving Bran. Surely he's had other dwarves escape him."

"Maybe from his dwarf pox but not from an ongoing torture session," Bran replied giving him a direct look.

They all turned their eyes back to Daga, begging wordlessly for an explanation.

"I believe the unicorns dealt him a mighty blow by destroying a magical device which was precious to him," Daga told them all.

All eyes went to the unicorn trio and the mare bowed her head.

"I took his all-seeing eye away. He is now blind to our moves," she said.

"You also gloated a bit if I'm right. Terribly un-unicorn thing to do, if you ask me. Isn't your kind supposed to be above that?" Daga said to her.

"I'm a sacred being but I am not a god," she said. *"I couldn't help myself. It's been a long time coming."*

Daga smiled kindly at her and shook his head in a forgiving sort of way. Bran suddenly was struck by how similar these two completely different beings were. They both had seen countless years of the world's turning. She wondered what would be the by-product of so many centuries of watching evil things happen and never being able to change them. The thought made her shiver.

"In any case, you gave him a lot to think about. Which I'm sure he has done. It is what conclusion he has come to which worries me."

Daga then turned to Vilmar. "And you, little, green wizard, you stole his spell book. That was a mighty blow against him as well," he said.

Vilmar shuddered. "I wish I hadn't. I don't care what useful information might be inside, I can't stand to touch it! Written on pages of dwarf skin with dwarf blood! Ugh! Disgusting!" he shivered some more.

"Well, we can't have that, can we? Give me the book, son, if you will," Daga said holding out his hands.

Wordlessly Vilmar dug it out of his satchel and handed the heavy tome to Daga.

The old dwarf took it in his big brown, forge-hardened hands. His eyes grew darker and shadowed as he concentrated briefly. His hands on the book suddenly steamed and smoked. Still he held the book, seemingly untouched by the heat which was issuing from under his hands. The tome seemed to ripple in resentment of his touch. But then it gave a long hiss and fell silent.

Finally, with a deep sigh, he handed the book back to Vilmar.

"There you go," he said. "Just regular ol' parchment paper with red ink writing and goatskin leather for a cover. That better?"

Vilmar touched the book with his bare hands and this time the volume did not make his soul cringe and wriggle in distaste. He sighed in relief and nodded.

"The book is going to be very important to us in the days ahead. We need you to study it night and day. Commit as many of the spells to memory as you can. Who knows what little minor spell might make a big difference when the wizard's time comes?" he told Vilmar.

Daga rubbed his hands and turned back to the party. "Now! With Savas-Zev's scrying bowl and his spell book gone, he is truly crippled. He feels he has to act now, to make some decisive strike to stop or distract us from going after him. So he is choosing to attack. Now we have to step up our assault."

"Great!" said Garn springing to his feet and drawing his battle axe. "I was hoping you'd say that! Let's go get him!"

"Sit down, little brother!" Daga reassured. "I did not mean this very second!"

Garn scowled darkly and with a grumble, plopped heavily down on the log next to Delkan.

"Yes, we should warn the Yazu that Savas-Zev is coming for them. We should also try to gather as many dwarves as are left in the world to help us. There are many more dwarves wandering above ground."

"You're talking about amassing a dwarf army, right?" Bran asked.

"My dear niece, this is exactly what I'm talking about!" Daga replied slapping her reassuringly on the knee.

"This sounds like an all out war!" said Delkan eagerly.

Garn growled like a large, angry wolf. "That sounds like it's gonna take a while!" he grumbled.

"And remember some of us are on foot. It's going to take a long, long while with no horses!" Iyorath pointed out.

Daga chuckled and stroked his blue-black beard fondly.

"Oh, it won't take near as long as you think it might," he chuckled secretively.

Garn frowned darkly.

"So, dear uncle, what have you got up your sleeve this time?" Delkan asked.

"Just you come with me. I've got a rather big surprise for all of you," he chuckled and stumped off into the woods.

They all hesitated, glancing uncertainly at each other. Rath-Tor followed immediately in his odd, half hopping, half stepping bird gait. The unicorns seemed disinclined to come along.

"We have no need of this 'surprise'. But you all need to go with him," the doe said quietly.

The stag sighed and shook his head. *"After all this time you still don't trust Daga when he is the one most worthy of your blind faith. Now go!"*

Shamed by his words, they arose and followed. Vilmar picked up Delkan and strapped her firmly into Iyorath's backpack. Then they all silently trailed after the stumping figure of the dwarf elder.

He led them directly to the pool with the little waterfall where Garn and Iyorath had first met Vilmar. Without stopping, he waded into the pool and stopped before the showering spray. They halted just behind him and waited as the thundering water misted them all with clinging fog. He uttered a few words in ancient dwarvish and waved his hand as if shooing away a bothersome bug. At his words the waterfall's curtain thinned to a slow-dripping trickle. The ground shook beneath them and the boulder beneath the waterfall rolled aside with a crack and a groan revealing a low, wide cave. At once, Daga entered the darkness beyond. The companions again hesitated and then followed him one at a time... first Bran, then Garn and then Vilmar having to bend over to do so, and lastly Iyorath who almost had to bend himself double to enter without banging Delkan's head on the roof of the entrance. Once inside, their feet followed the passage of a small flight of descending steps. When they reached the bottom, even the tall elf could stand comfortably for the roof arched high above their heads. Torches set in sconces along the wall of the room suddenly blazed into light making Vilmar and Iyorath blink. The change from dark to sudden light did not seem to bother the dwarves at all.

Daga stood in a large puddle at the bottom before them, waiting.

"You have now entered my home and workshop," he told them as he turned away.

Daga shook himself like a dog, scattering droplets all about and then proceeded to stride confidently away. The small group scrambled to keep up, their wet shoes leaving squelching puddle bootprints behind them. In the quickly shrinking distance, they heard the pounding of the waterfall resume as the boulder slid back into place, shutting the door behind them and cutting them off from the world outside.

Bran noticed as they followed Daga, there were many closed doors on either side of them.

"Where do these doors lead, Uncle?" she ventured to ask.

"My home," was all Daga would say but the tone of his voice seemed to suggest great pride.

The hallway ended at a huge, wooden door ornately carved and decorated with great clasps of iron and a single doorknob set right into its center.

He turned to face them and though he was not smiling, his black eyes glittered with immense satisfaction at what might be held beyond the great door.

"My workshop," he said simply.

Daga reached forward and touched the doorknob. He did not take hold of it or turn it or speak any sort of command word. He simply brushed his fingers lovingly across the brass knob's surface and the great door silently opened on its own. It swung inward, away from them, revealing a room much brighter than the torchlit hallway.

They blinked, and shielding their eyes as if from the noonday sun, stepped inside the cavernous room beyond.

It took a moment or two for their eyes to adjust to the bright light, which seemed to issue from the ceiling but had no visible source.

Delkan saw it first and gasped loudly. "By the Great Dragon's scales!" she whispered in wide-eyed surprise.

The room was large and empty and hewn into a round shape with no corners, but into every wall was chiseled tiny alcoves from floor to ceiling. Every inch of wall was pocked with these alcoves. Not the tiniest space was left untouched.

And in each and every one of the thousands of alcoves was a tiny, perfectly carved, plain wooden Dahla horse. It was a lifetime's work of one who was ancient, on display for all of them to see.

"I will create a cavalry such as the world has never seen," Daga murmured his vow softly. "They will wash over any enemy like a great storm tide and not one of their foes will be left untouched by the fury of their wrath. So I told myself as I carved each one of these little horses."

He turned about, sweeping his arms toward the figurines.

"They are for you. Take as many as you can carry and give them to as many dwarves as you will run across in the days to come. You will need a vast herd of great, magical steeds to carry our heroes to this final battle against Savas-Zev. Take them. You are welcome to them. They are yours. They are my gift to our future."

CHAPTER 41

Bran sat quietly on her log as the others bustled about making preparations. In her hands she held one of the many little Dahla horses they had all crammed into their bags. She turned the little figurine thoughtfully over in her hands, admiring the simplicity with which it had been carved. Her thoughts were a million miles away.

Vilmar came and sat beside her. She did not acknowledge his presence but kept up her scrutiny of the tiny wooden horse, uninterrupted.

"Is this your new bond horse?" he asked her eventually.

Bran sniffed almost derisively. "I guess it could be if I wanted it to," she said in a flat voice.

"But you don't want it to be," Vilmar finished for her.

She gave a wry smile and shrugged once, meeting his gaze. "I know you wish it was Valynt," Vilmar said with a reassuring pat on her knee.

She shrugged sadly and put the horse away with a heavy sigh. "I wish I still had Echo," she said suddenly.

Then her eyes met Vilmar's marbled gaze. "I'm sorry he died," she told him. "I didn't mean..." She let the sentence dangle in midair and hung her head.

Vilmar's face wrinkled as he guessed her meaning. "You think I blame you for his death?" he questioned.

Uncertainly, she met his gaze. "You mean... you don't?"

He scoffed and shook his head. "Never would I think of such a thing!" he said. "You didn't kill him. The goblins did."

Bran frowned and scratched her beard. "But it was my bad decision which caused his death. If I had thought before I went charging off..."

Vilmar didn't allow her to finish. "Coulda, woulda, shoulda!" he scoffed at her. "Second guessing doesn't make it any better."

"But..." she stammered. "You trained him specifically for me. He was to be my birthday present. I got mad and went charging headlong into the lion's den and he got killed."

"Bran, listen to me," Vilmar explained patiently as he took her hands in his own. "I trained Echo for you to use. I didn't give you a fine lady's horse for you to parade around with and put away the minute he breaks a sweat. Echo was to be your good 'doing' mount. He did that and more. He was true and obedient to his training. Now don't shame his memory by blaming his death on yourself or the decisions you made. He deserves better from you right now. He did what he was told. He was a good mule. What more could any rider expect from his mount?"

Bran turned her face away, pulled her hands out of his grasp and propped her head on her knees.

"Will you take a new Dahla mount now?" he pressed, thinking to change the subject.

She shook her head in a firm denial. "Mayhem and I talked about it," she said with another wry smile. "He has deigned to be my mount for the time being until this situation is resolved. As long I remember always who his *true* bond rider is."

"Yaffa?" Vilmar said and she nodded.

"That's fine by me," she replied. "He'll do for now. But I can tell we're no match. Mayhem makes his own decisions most of the time."

Vilmar nodded and shook his head sympathetically.

"We need to get your Valynt back and soon," he replied.

Bran smiled wistfully. "The sooner the better."

Iyorath crumpled up the sheet of paper he was reading and tossed it back to Garn. It bounced comically off his slightly balding head.

"Rewrite it," he commanded sternly.

"What?" spluttered Garn in frustration.

"You cannot call King Zeki of Tor-Gat a fat dolt!" he explained. "Rewrite it!"

"But it's true," shot back Garn. "You want me to lie?"

"You called King Zeki a fat dolt?" asked Delkan overhearing their conversation. She chuckled and rolled her eyes in mirth. "You really want to meet a horrible end, don't you?" she laughed.

Garn growled loudly like an angry pit dog. "I'm a warrior not a scribe!" he declared forcefully.

"Well, for right now we're all scribes. Now do as you're told and rewrite the letter. And please, please be polite about it," Bran begged as she bent back to her task of busy scribbling.

"Insulting him would have brought his lazy ass's forces even faster and just itching for a fight! I thought it was what we wanted," Garn shot back.

"Yes, but we want to be fighting with them, not *against* them," explained the elf impatiently.

"I suppose you want me to use flowery words with him too, being as he's a king and all?" Garn griped.

He was in a foul mood this day! He had hardly thought writing letters would be part of the preparations for war with Savas-Zev, or that Iyorath would make them address missives to all the dwarf enclaves left in the world. Writing was not one of the skills Garn was known for.

"Heavens no! Perish the thought," Iyorath fired back. "Flowery words are for my people. I sense you dwarves tend to be more direct with your feelings and words. I don't care if it's a lie or not, let's just not start any squabbles between the different Tors. We're supposed to unify here."

"Don't worry. There will be enough fighting for all once we get our kin together. Keep thinking of that, Garn, my old friend," Delkan reassured.

Sounding like a sputtering teakettle, boiling over with complaints, Garn reluctantly complied.

They had been busily writing letters all morning. Every time one was finished, it went to Iyorath for proofreading and when approved, was packed into a message tube which was either given to a messenger hound or a hawk with a magical command of where to take it. Rath-Tor had already left for the Yazu encampment but on the way, had enlisted the aid of more war eagles and they kept turning up in ever increasing numbers. The friends quickly saw they would have more hounds and hawks than messages to carry. So Iyorath told the surplus war eagles who could speak to fly about and contact any traveling dwarf whether alone or in a party and fill them in on the details. Garn had hastily made more leather harnesses for the Tor Ambroc messenger hounds and stamped them all with the Yazu insignia so no one would shoot them. The Yazu did not have a pack of personal messenger hounds. They had just commonly used other provinces' hounds when they came in. But in this way, the other dwarf nations wouldn't shoot them on sight for being from Tor Ambroc before they knew there was no longer any threat of contagion.

Doing these chores took them all day. They spent a fitful night of brief sleep interrupted many times by their own haste to be on their way, and awoke the next morning to call their new bond horses and saddle up.

Bran was mounted on Mayhem and Delkan on the dancing chestnut Sashay. Iyorath had called a tall, leggy black horse who just matched his frame and looked built for speed. The elf named him Ranger. Garn called a grulla-colored, stout pony and named it Blueberry.

Vilmar was nowhere to be seen. Bran told them this was as he wished it. He was to ride ahead and scout the land before them. Daga was nowhere to be seen either. From time to time they caught a brief glimpse of a splash of white disappearing into the dappled undergrowth of the forest so they knew the unicorns were with them even if they were not seen.

Around midday Vilmar made an unexpected appearance. He just suddenly materialized on the trail ahead of them. All their horses startled to a stop and their riders stared. He was mounted on a mare who towered above all of theirs, even Iyorath's lean Ranger. She was a blagdon-marked animal, colored the shade of a gold coin. Her markings looked as if she had jumped into white paint. Her white stockings had a splashed look high above her knees and hocks and there was white splattered all along her belly. She had a wide blaze on her forehead which widened the further it went down her face, encompassing pale blue eyes until her entire muzzle and jaw were white. She had a cream-colored, roached mane and a thick, ground sweeping tail which grew darker the closer it got to the earth.

Vilmar was grinning broadly at their reaction as the enormous mare strode casually up to them.

"Hmmm. I see you also like them big," muttered Bran at last and he chuckled at the private reference.

"Hullo, gang," he said still chuckling. "This is Blink. Say hello, Blinky, my lass."

The mare curled her upper lip at them showing her bright white teeth.

"Humph!" snorted Garn critically. "Bet the mare could do some damage on shield wall!"

"We could use her for a battering ram," breathed Iyorath. "That thing's a monster!"

Delkan moved Sashay closer for a better look. "She's okay, I guess," sniffed Delkan. "Except for those eyes."

The mare pinned her ears and pawed. "Careful now," Vilmar warned. "She's a sensitive lady." He turned his next words to the great mare and cooed gently to her while stroking her golden neck lovingly. "Shhh, dearie. I'm sure they didn't mean it."

Garn brought Blueberry up closer to Vilmar and the giant mare stared down at the diminutive little, blocky pony.

"You plan on making a cart horse or a pet outta that thing?" he said in a warning tone. "She's certainly not built for speed!"

"My Blink lady has some talents which would put any racehorse to shame," he said defending his steed. "Sure, she may not be able to outrun a racehorse. But she's able to wink in and out and she can appear across the finish line without even lifting her legs to gallop."

"And disappear before the arrow hits its mark," Iyorath said figuring out his words.

Vilmar nodded with a wide grin.

"Handy. Very useful."

"That's how I designed my lady, Blink," Vilmar said proudly. "Anyway, I didn't come here to chat. I came here to tell you there's a party of five dwarves on the road up ahead. The unicorns tell me they haven't been contacted yet about the dwarf muster. Should we introduce ourselves?"

"Don't you dare!" spouted Garn suddenly. "You show up on that thing and you'll either scare them off or they'll try to defend themselves from who knows what!"

"It should be a dwarf who meets them and tells them," Bran said. "Delkan. Go to it."

"Why me?" she asked.

"Because you have the gift of gab, my dear," Iyorath said with a quiet bow to her talent of unending conversation.

"That's not funny," she retorted but trotted off at once, chin held high in wounded pride.

She returned shortly with the small group of dwarves. One of them was leading a sad-faced, brown pack mule.

They stopped short when they saw the group ahead of them and they stared suspiciously at Vilmar and Iyorath and the strange but beautiful horses they all rode.

"It's all right," reassured Delkan. "They're friends, even the elf and human."

The one dwarf holding the mule coughed, spat rudely then said, "I smell a dirty little wizard."

"That would be me. And I'm a green wizard to be exact," Vilmar said coaxing the huge mare forward a step or two.

The one who first spoke sniffed critically while the others scowled darkly.

"We ain't overly fond of whippersnappers posing as wizards," spoke one of the other dwarves.

"Of course not," retorted Vilmar. "Savas-Zev is enough to make anyone hate wizards."

At the mere mention of the name all the dwarves frowned and grew grim faced. There was a long uncomfortable silence.

"Savas-Zev killed my entire clan, destroyed my home and all the people of my home. Of all of Tor-Vlen, I am the only one left," he said in a voice laced in hatred. "Savas-Zev!"

He said the name with revulsion and spat again.

Vilmar strode his mare closer. The dwarf holding the mule stiffened and looked ready to attack. They all did.

When he had approached close enough to be heard by all, Vilmar stopped the mare, leaned forward onto the cantle of the saddle and said in a soft, grim voice.

"Savas-Zev killed my family too, burned my town," Vilmar's voice dropped to a vengeful hush, "and his goblins brutalized my sister."

Vilmar sat up and motioned to those behind him.

"He killed Iyorath, the elf's family and trapped their souls. Delkan is from Fang-Tor province, which is no more thanks to him. Garn's home of Drock-Tor no longer exists thanks to Savas-Zev and Bran was just made an orphan thanks to the dwarf pox at Tor Ambroc. Now who here do you think you should be suspicious of?" His voice was low and deadly serious.

"That wizard's evil has touched everyone," Delkan interjected quietly. "You hate Savas-Zev? Join the crowd."

"We ride to join up with the Yazu army to put a stop to him here and now. We seek more dwarves to join us. This has gone on too long.

It must end and end now. You are welcome to join us if you wish," Bran told them.

The dwarves exchanged resolute looks but said nothing for a long while.

Finally the dwarf with the mule stepped forward and extended a hand to Vilmar.

"Count us in then. I am Aldoin from Tor-Vlen. But, ah, you already knew the province. This is Caled from Tor-Ehft and Dervlan from the late Tor-Udo and Torin from Tor-Qui and Gwal from Drock-Tor."

"Gwal is known to me," Garn said. "Though it was a long time ago and he probably does not remember it. I knew your mother when you were just a pup on the floor. What brings your group way out here?"

"Ah well, we are soldiers of fortune seeking adventure along the way," Gwal replied.

"And a war with Savas-Zev seems to be the best kind of adventure thus far," Caled eagerly put in.

"And one brimming with honor," said Torin. "But how are we to keep up with you if you're mounted and we are on foot? Banquet surely can't carry us all."

"Who?" asked Iyorath dumbly.

"Banquet," Aldoin repeated and jabbed a thumb at the mule. "We named her that because the idea was, we run into a monster too fierce, we shove Banquet in front and beat a hasty retreat. But she has turned out to be rather lucky."

"Or bad tasting!" laughed Caled.

They all guffawed and the mood lightened considerably.

"Well, on the transportation issue, this might help," Delkan rummaged about in her bulging pack and then tossed a little Dahla horse at each dwarf in turn. They caught them before they even knew what they were catching. They looked at the little wooden horses, exchanged glances among themselves and then as one turned to stare up at the riders with wide eyes and mouths open in amazement.

"The Blood Raven has come forth," whispered Torin in a reverent tone and their eyes all fastened on Bran.

"It's about damn time, too!" Aldoin said with fervor. "I prayed that I'd live long enough to see this day. The gods have blessed me."

"Then they have a twisted sense of humor," jested Caled. "For you smell like you died a while ago!"

Aldoin went to cuff Caled who seemed much younger than himself and he missed.

But Torin was still in an awestruck mood. "Before I left home, there was a great buzz among Tor-Qui's clerics," he told them as he stepped closer to Bran. "They were having visions and seeing omens and telling us the time was near to a confrontation with Savas-Zev. And they kept babbling some nonsense about a Blood Raven appearing. I only thought it was magical people's mumbo jumbo, nothing which made sense to me. But now..."

His voice trailed off. Hesitantly, he touched her sleeve with a trembling hand. "Bran. Bran means raven," he whispered. "And your hair is red as blood. The Blood Raven has come forth."

"Is it possible? Is it now time?" Gwal muttered doubtfully.

The group of friends could plainly see that his reaction was upsetting Bran.

Delkan urged Sashay to step between Torin and Bran.

"Whether she is the Blood Raven or not is yet to be seen," she interrupted his musings. "A lot has to happen between here and when Savas-Zev is killed. We need to concentrate our efforts toward reaching the goal. Until that happens, we can take stock in no prophecy."

"Yes, it would be foolish to do so," agreed Vilmar. "Come. Call your mounts and let's be on our way. We have a long road ahead."

The group of friends made sure Bran was at its head and Torin was in the back.

Bran had fallen suddenly quiet during this exchange. Vilmar urged his large mare to fall in beside Mayhem. He said nothing but offered his presence as consolation.

"Vilmar, what am I going to do if every dwarf who joins us, somehow thinks I am their savior? I don't want any part of that," she said in consternation.

"I understand," he murmured back. "But it may help the cause if you put on the hat—however uncomfortable it may feel."

"But what if it's not true?" she asked desperately.

"Shhh, Bran," he reassured. "Maybe it won't come to that. Don't borrow more trouble. Just wait and see."

His words did little to comfort her.

Things began to happen very fast in the next few days. It seemed every time they went to sleep they awoke with more dwarves having joined their little group in the middle of the night. Some looked well fed and well bred, others were dressed in simple traveling rags. But all had their own personal stories of horror about Savas-Zev. The mention of unifying to bring about his end brought a bright, fierce light to their deep eyes.

Caled had conjured a little speckled pony to match him, being as he was the smallest of Aldoin's group and after naming the pony Flea, had ridden off at once at a speedy pace. Torin informed them he had a human friend who was a king in the neighboring valley. King Vlek had a deep-seated hatred of Savas-Zev which stretched far back into his childhood. Caled felt certain if the king knew the dwarves were mustering in force against the wizard, he would want to join in. There were a great many weapon-smiths in Vlek's kingdom who would be a valuable asset in the war against Savas-Zev. Barely twenty-four hours after Caled returned, humans began to show up in force to join their swelling ranks. The humans told Bran the very swiftest of messenger riders had been sent all over Vlek's kingdom to recruit any able-bodied farmer or person who could bear arms. People all over the kingdom, even some women were joining up in droves. At his words, Bran glanced at the pack animals the humans had brought with them. The mules were laden with spare swords, spears and shields, some of them small enough for dwarf hands although not as heavy as a dwarf would have liked. Two of the pack mules carried extra food and cooking utensils. She welcomed them into the fold.

Four days into the journey, war eagles and messenger hounds began to return with answers to the letters they had sent out. It took several people to read all the replies.

"Tor-Ingal's king sends his regards and his troops," Gwal told them.

Applause went up from the humans and dwarves gathered.

"Tor-Gat is coming, too," said Iyorath. "Thank heavens you didn't send the first letter, Garn!"

More applause, some cheers and tankards raised in celebration.

Garn-Ithel's eyes held a sly look the elf missed.

"Tor-Zul is making with all due haste from the Ice Peaks to the north," reported Bran. "They're also sending the Golden Warriors along."

At this there was more cheering and stamping in proper dwarven glee. The Golden Warriors had a fine reputation, which preceded them wherever they went. They were led by a troop riding Dahla horses all of a fine, golden color, crowned above and behind with snowy manes and tails. They rarely appeared in all their traditional finery or together in force but this was a very good excuse to do so. The Golden Warriors were the best of the best of any dwarf province. Having them fighting beside the kin of the other dwarf provinces would be an incredible boost of morale for the troops.

"Tor-Gry wants to join the party, too," said a laughing Torin and barked for someone to refill his drinking horn so he could toast them.

"Tor-Ixa wants to jump on the wagon with us," Gwal said with a broad smile.

"So does Myr-Tor and Nls-Tor," replied Delkan with a laugh

"This one is from Dra-Oog," Bran said eagerly and looked up. "The Yazu are coming."

A truly deafening cheer went up and the dwarves began to sing and stamp in glee. The humans brought out another beer cask to celebrate.

Bran noticed Delkan had separated herself from the partying dwarves. She had hitched herself over to the shadows, away from the fire and was leaning against a tree. Delkan had a troubled look on her face.

Bran went to her at once. "Something wrong?" she asked.

There was worry in Delkan's gray eyes. "Dra-Oog is coming," she said quietly.

"Yes. What of it?" replied Bran not understanding.

"Well, we didn't exactly leave on the best of terms, Dra-Oog and I. She sorta kicked me out of the Yazu for telling you what happened to Tor Ambroc."

Bran put a hand reassuringly on her right stump. "Delkan, there are a lot of dwarves joining us who have nothing to do with the Yazu. There are some here who don't even have a province or a family to call home. They will still be allowed to join us. And I'm not going into this war without you, my friend."

"Thanks," Delkan said in a tiny little voice. "But I will still have to face her."

"Yes, you will," replied Bran. "And I will be there beside you when you do."

As their ranks swelled more each day, they had to find more spacious ways of traveling. A large troop of mounted warriors can leave quite a wake. Vilmar continued to scout ahead or behind with his mare Blink. He was in constant contact with the war eagles who flew about and scouted the surrounding land with their sharp eyes for spies or incoming troops.

Early one morning before dawn, a call went out. The Yazu had been sighted heading their way. Bran, Iyorath and Garn mounted up and hastened out to meet them with Delkan trailing reluctantly behind.

Dra-Oog was easily spotted riding her gray Ghost. She melted out of the dark with an enormous herd of mounted warriors following in her wake. Their armor flashed and clinked dimly in the dark and their horses pawed and squealed, smelling other strange horses.

"I see the pox didn't get you after all," Dra-Oog said when she saw Bran and the faintest hint of a smile flickered briefly across her face.

"Nope," Bran replied grinning widely. "I skipped it altogether."

"And now you wear the mantle of hero, I hear," she went on.

Bran blushed a deep red. "Vilmar's the hero," she said waving to her friend who had just ridden up. "I sorta needed rescuing."

"Indeed," muttered Dra-Oog turning to him. "So odd for a human to have to rescue a dwarf. But then you've changed much since last I saw you and it's not just the beard."

She peered narrowly at Vilmar until he began to squirm uncomfortably, pinned under her sharp eyes.

"Yes, many things have changed since then," she mused quietly.

Dra-Oog's eyes next fell on Delkan. Her eyes narrowed and sparkled dangerously. For a long moment they simply stared at one another. The tension in the air between them could be cut with a knife. "Didn't I discharge you from the Yazu?" she finally said sternly.

Delkan swallowed with difficulty. There was a long silence as she hunted for the proper reply.

"As you yourself just said, many things have changed," Bran quietly replied.

Dra-Oog's eyes traveled up and down Delkan critically. She noted she was riding again. She noted the stumps. And she noted the yearling unicorn who seemed to coalesce out of the forest mist and strode up to stand protectively by her side, pawing and tossing his head in a mock show of ferocity.

"You have impressed a unicorn." It was a statement not a question.

"Yes, I have," Delkan replied and raised her chin a bit.

"Interesting," Dra-Oog replied. "A dwarf has never been known to impress a unicorn ever before." She stared at her for a bit more. "I suppose that's how you got your legs back?" she asked and Delkan nodded wordlessly. Dra-Oog nodded in reply. "All the more interesting. You are an independent now in this I suppose," she said.

Delkan nodded once again. This action was followed by another uncomfortable silence.

"Look around you, Dra-Oog," Delkan finally had the courage to say. "There are many 'independents' gathered here who want to fight."

Bran urged Mayhem to step forward. "And we shall need them all, Dra-Oog," Bran said trying to lessen the tension a bit.

Bran dropped the tone of her voice, along with her eyes, and quietly so only Dra-Oog could hear said, "You should have told me about my family."

Dra-Oog also chose not to meet her gaze and her voice became pure ice. "I couldn't afford to take the risk of losing another promising young soldier. Delkan was expendable. You are not. She should have followed my orders."

Bran hissed at her words but with an effort, controlled her reactions. Her words of reply left Dra-Oog with no question where her loyalties lay. "I'm not going to war without my right hand," Bran insisted and in her eyes glittered a warning light.

Dra-Oog turned her piercing stare onto Bran. For a long moment they locked gazes. Then, although no word was yet spoken, the tension from Dra-Oog seemed to dissipate as suddenly as it had come.

"It may be the 'independents', those unexpected additions who change the course of our future. It would be worse not to have them. But I will be very interested to see how this plays out," Dra-Oog finally said.

She turned her steely eyes back onto Delkan. But her gaze had softened the merest bit. "Very interested indeed," she said.

Everyone breathed a huge sigh of relief.

A sudden horn call went up from the encampment behind them. Caled came racing up to them on Flea. He had mounted so quickly he only had time to call Flea with a bridle and nothing else. Bran admired the way he clung bareback to his mount's speckled hide.

"They're here! They're here!" he was shouting to everyone. "The Golden Warriors are coming!" And on he fled to alert the rest of those camped.

Bran turned with the others and rode back the way they had come, the way Caled had been pointing.

Dawn was breaking over the hills. As the sunrise topped the clear plains not so far behind them, they saw a second flash and not from the sun. A large dust cloud was rising high into the air.

A great host of mounted warriors was riding straight for them. They were all dwarven, this much was obvious even from a distance. Their bodies were short and square and they were heavily bearded. Their armor was made from polished damask steel and flashed in the rising sun. The sun's rays glinted brightly upon rows and rows of razor sharp spearheads also made of polished bronze. Their horses were shaped as they were, short and square with round feet and thick legs. They traveled with their noses held high into the air and dark eyes sparkling. Their thick, snowy manes floated like thunderheads on their proud, golden necks. The thunder from their hooves preceded them and followed after like the aftershocks of an earthquake.

A small troop of their leaders swept into camp while their members encircled. Bran and the others watched as row after row after row of golden mounted, gilded riders lined up around their camp and continued to line up as the sun rose higher into the sky and turned their ranks into pale flame.

A single warrior with a gleaming white horsetail flowing proudly from his helmet—which shone like sunlight on snow about his broad shoulders—rode forward and bowed his head respectfully to Bran and Dra-Oog. His eyes were blue and his beard as golden as the horse he rode. Another dwarf rider accompanied him and one swift glance told everyone they were twins, for they both had the same features all except for their eyes. His brother had one gray eye. The other was covered by a tawny leather patch, which bisected a horrible, deep scar, running from his forehead to his chin.

"Dakar of the Golden Warriors at your service," he spoke and waved briefly to his silent companion with the patch. "My brother Rakad. I heard tell the cat had a very important rat to play with. My band and I didn't feel like being left out of the fun. I hope you will have use of us in this campaign."

"I'm sure we will find some sort of job for your troop worthy of glory in a song or two. There will be many heroes made in the days to come," Dra-Oog replied. "You are all most welcome here."

Dra-Oog made some quick introductions. But when she said Bran's name, more than a few of the Golden Warriors turned to stare at her closely.

The grim faced Rakad turned his one eye onto her and speared her underneath its severe gaze. Bran was dimly aware of the others staring at her but they all disappeared in relation to Rakad. His one eye looked her up and down silently and then fastened on her face like a trap. She could smell the magic permeating his form and issuing out from him in thick waves. It made her uncomfortable.

He noted her discomfort immediately and somehow lessened it. He bowed in deep respect to her and, still saying nothing, rode away with his brother.

No words were needed. Bran knew a long discussion with this mysterious Rakad would soon be forthcoming.

Bran fidgeted in her chair as all the generals, commanders and other leaders of the assembled companies filed into the large tent. Delkan sat on one side of her, Vilmar on the other. They were seated right up front along with the most important of the leaders and it made her increasingly uncomfortable. She felt unfit to be included in their company.

"Quit squirming!" Delkan scolded in a private hiss. "You're twitching like a dog with fleas! What's the matter?"

"We don't need to be here," Bran hissed in return. "I know my job. Get Savas-Zev with the spear. Why are we here with all the high up, muckity-mucks?"

Vilmar snorted in return.

"I agree," he whispered in return, squirming in his too small chair. "I feel like a fish out of water. This looks like a dwarf-only party."

"Take it easy. There are a few humans here," Delkan said with a nod to a human who had just ducked double to fit through the dwarf-sized door in the tent. He straightened and shrugged his fine robes back into place and then replaced his golden crown back onto his brow. Three other humans in fine clothes followed him.

"That's King Vlek of Kyran," Bran said. "The human king Caled knows."

"Humph!" snorted Vilmar critically. "They may be human but I believe they come from finer breeding than a farrier's son."

"Oh picky, picky poo!" scoffed Delkan. "We need to be here so all the commanders understand how to let Bran do her job. So, just get over it!"

Just then Iyorath showed up with an elf-sized stool tucked under one arm. Garn was trotting along in tow behind him. Iyorath sat next to Vilmar and Garn sat behind Delkan.

They next saw Dra-Oog weaving among the throng of dwarves. She positioned herself next to the elf.

Bran cast a sidelong glance at Delkan who had suddenly gone silent. Yes, she had seen Dra-Oog. Her eyes were dark and she grumbled to herself and hunkered lower in her chair to seem smaller.

"Who's uncomfortable now?" Bran teased in an even softer whisper.

Delkan just glowered at her.

They all turned as their eyes caught a metallic flash from the tent's entrance. The twin commanders of the Golden Warriors, Dakar and Rakad, strode solemnly into the tent. They made their way to the front of the tent and stood off to the side near Bran. Rakad's one eye flashed at Bran and he inclined his head in a slight but respectful bow toward her. She was compelled to nod in return.

The sounds of murmuring and shifting dwarves hushed quickly as Vahan Isca of the Yazu entered followed by another commander who was obviously one of the Golden Warriors.

They strode purposefully to the fore to stand in front of the friends. His companion was quickly introduced as Vosgi, Field Marshal of the Golden Warriors.

"My dwarven brethren and assorted allies, we have gathered you together to discuss strategies for annihilating Savas-Zev from this world. I know certain prophecies which have been circulating have given most of us hope our deliverance from this monster wizard is at hand. But I would council you to put such hopes aside and to deal with the task at hand. We have been given a chance for hope. It is not certain.

But we must grab at that chance and be sure of our moves if it is to prove true."

Isca then turned to Bran.

"Do you have the weapon with you?" he asked.

She nodded and swallowed hard.

"Then I ask you to please take it out and show it to all gathered here," he said.

Bran swallowed hard again and rummaging in her satchel, brought out the spearhead wrapped in linen. Slowly she unwrapped it from its cloth until it lay naked in her hands. The shiny obsidian flashed reassuringly at her and she felt all apprehension die away. She gave a small private smile and took the spear by its leather-wrapped wooden handle and held it aloft.

There was an appreciative gasp of awe at the beauty of the weapon. Its polished head flashed and sparkled as if it had a life of its own, as if the very heart of obsidian was beating, warm and strong as any dwarf's heart.

"This weapon must make it to Savas-Zev. If any killing blow is to be struck on him this weapon and no other must do it. It was made solely for this purpose."

"It?" asked Dakar from the side. "You call the great weapon all our hopes hang on an 'it'? Did you not enchant it at its creation?"

Bran turned to Vilmar. "I did not make it," she stuttered, suddenly feeling quite foolish in front of all these great people of her race.

Vilmar stood up to rescue her. "It was enchanted at its creation," he assured. "I saw to it myself."

A disapproving growl circulated about the room. "The weapon which will save us was enchanted by a human and not a dwarf?" another voice spoke up from an unseen commander. "Please don't tell me it was made by him as well?"

"I made the spear!" said an infuriated Daga from the back of the tent.

He shoved all others aside, striding angrily to the front and hopped up onto Vahan's table. There was an echoing gasp as the various dwarves recognized him.

"It was made by dwarf hands in the finest traditional dwarf ways, ways which many of you have long forgotten. It is one of the finest things I have ever made and I'll lop the head off any who say it isn't, be they kin or not!"

A single dwarf commander was brave enough to step forward. "But still you let a human wizard enchant it?" he scowled angrily.

Daga spun on him with such fire the daring commander took a step backwards in spite of his accusing words.

"I blessed the spear in ancient chants which have long been forgotten by the children of today. Who here still speaks the ancient dwarf tongue? I do! I have never forgotten the old words and spells from long ago!"

There was muttering from the gathered assembly as they considered this. Daga stalked back and forth on the tabletop, his eyes daring them to have a problem with anything.

"But the creation of this spearhead was a collaboration of sorts," he turned his bold gaze onto Vilmar.

"This young human pup you see here is not as he seems to be. Magick runs through his young veins, stronger than any I have seen in many long centuries of his kind's short life. He is a green wizard, the first of his kind to survive the blessing of the five elements in three centuries and the youngest green wizard ever initiated. He also enchanted this weapon."

There was more muttering as all eyes in the room turned to regard Vilmar and his strangely swirling, marbled eyes.

"And yet, we had further magical help with this spear," Vilmar spoke to the crowd.

The murmuring increased from the dwarven company. King Vlek, the human, standing at the back of the tent, finally asked the question which was on all their minds.

"Who else helped you, son?" he spoke from the crowd.

Vilmar took a deep breath before he spoke. "My teacher, the unicorn."

All conversation ceased abruptly. Vilmar stifled a laugh. He had never seen so many obviously shocked dwarves before in all his life. Some of them actually dropped their jaws and bulged their eyes in surprise.

The commander who had first spoken, finally cleared his throat noisily and with a cough said, "But you did not name the blade?"

"Nah!" said Daga with mock humor. "I thought I'd leave it to you guys. It's your future." He hopped off the table and left the tent leaving everyone gathered to stare after him in stunned silence.

Vilmar nodded considering certain possibilities. "Yes, it should be named. Possibly in a public naming ceremony where all can add their own blessing onto it?" he suggested.

There was a pause among the dwarven congregation. Then they all began to murmur to each other and nod their approval.

Bran winked and flashed Vilmar a wide grin. Her young human friend had made a suggestion, which rang dear to the hearts of her people. They would not soon forget his contribution.

"You may be a young human sprout but you think like a dwarf," Dakar said with a wide grin. "Very well. We'll name the blade three days hence from now. That will give us more time for the stragglers of our kind to get to camp."

"That is if Savas-Zev doesn't attack us before then," Dra-Oog muttered grimly.

That night, after the great meeting, Bran was making her way back to her tent when Aldoin stopped her.

"I wonder if I might have a private word with you, lass," he said in a hushed tone.

"Of course," Bran replied, not having the foggiest idea about what he wanted to say.

She stepped off the trail from between the tents and they went to stand beside a lonely torch at the edge of the woods.

"What's up?" she said.

The older dwarf seemed uncomfortable and fidgeted a bit. "It's like this, lass. I know how shameful it is to refuse a gift. Please don't take this the wrong way." He handed her back the Dahla horse she had given him when they first met. "I don't really have a use for this," he said with a slightly embarrassed tone.

Bran looked from the little wooden horse carving in her hand to him and back, trying to puzzle through what he meant. Finally, she thought she understood.

"Ah!" she said suddenly. "You have Banquet to use."

At this suggestion, Aldoin uttered an explosive guffaw.

"The mule? Heavens no, child!" he retorted. "Throwing a leg over her back is a sure way to take a dirt nap and no mistake! She's a pack and driving beast and nothing else."

Bran's face crinkled in confusion.

"But... I don't understand," she said.

"Look, lass. It's a great thing you're doing here. And it's been a long time coming. But not every dwarf has the need of a Dahla horse. And it's no mean thing to be a foot soldier in a war. They do have some advantages, which riders don't have. Look at all who have shown up already. Not all of our kin are mounted, nor do they need to be. Just being a part of this is enough. Now do you understand?"

Bran did understand all too well. She felt her face flush in embarrassment. "Then I shouldn't have been giving a Dahla horse to every strange dwarf I see."

"No, no! I didn't mean that, lass!" Aldoin assured her. "It was part of Daga's plan to have the finest dwarf cavalry this world has ever seen. But... maybe... if someone refuses a Dahla... you should just let it be, eh? Don't take it too hard. You've managed to gather together the greatest force of dwarf kind which was ever seen at any time. And it will be enough."

Bran nodded seeing the wisdom in his words. She thought about it and smiled.

"Thank you, Aldoin," she replied.

The elder dwarf patted her reassuringly on the cheek.

"For you, Trinket, anytime. I'll be here," he said.

Then, without another word, he disappeared into the shadows of the camp leaving Bran to ponder the wisdom of what he had said.

"Absolutely NOT! It's too dangerous!" said the unicorn.

Her tone startled Vilmar. He had never heard his teacher speak so angrily. And yet he persisted. "Please? I have to do this. I have to know what I'm up against. I need to meet Savas-Zev," he coaxed gently.

"You impertinent child!" retorted the unicorn shaking her head and stomping a delicate leg in fury. *"Do you want to ruin everything we've done up to this point?"*

"No, of course I don't," he replied. "And I do understand what you're saying. But Savas-Zev is an aged, experienced wizard and I'm quite a juvenile in everything. I have to size him up in some way, find out what his weaknesses are so I know how best to exploit them when the time comes. Please?"

The unicorn snaked her elegant head at him and waved her horn threateningly in his direction with her ears pinned.

"You'll ruin everything!" she insisted.

The stag and fawn had been watching this exchange from the safety of the underbrush. The fawn crept slowly back into the underbrush, shivering at the force of his mother's words. The stag simply observed in silence.

"There IS a way to do this," he finally spoke up.

His mate spun on him furiously. The stag held his ground calmly.

"There is a way," the stag spoke again. *"It is not without its dangers but I do believe it is less hazardous than an actual meeting face to face, in person."*

"How?" Vilmar asked eagerly.

"Don't encourage the boy!" the unicorn's tone was a mental hiss of displeasure.

The stag faced his angry mate and strode resolutely forward.

"You face him," said the stag, *"in Dreamtime."*

The doe was still angry but thoughtful and quiet for a moment.

"It has many risks," she said, swishing her tail fitfully, already sensing she was fighting a losing battle. *"You could still be killed."*

"Yes," replied the stag. *"But only if he touches you. You must not let him touch you in Dreamtime."*

"If he does, you will never waken," she added, helpfully. *"You will die because he will have separated your soul from your body."*

"So I will die in my sleep," Vilmar said with a wry smile. "How ironic! Doesn't everyone want to die in their sleep?"

"This is no laughing matter!" the unicorn doe said stomping her other foreleg this time to properly punctuate her words. *"Death in Dreamtime is still a real death. It's too dangerous!"*

"We can do this," Vilmar insisted. "Won't you please help me?"

There was a long silence. The doe glared angrily at her mate and he faced her anger stoically.

"Please?" Vilmar pleaded. "I want... I *need* your help in this. Please?"

Somehow Vilmar ended up at Bran's tent around sunset. He looked about the dwarf encampment, lit with the flickering light from countless fires and torches. Every campfire had a small knot of quietly talking dwarves about it.

Every fire but Bran's. She was probably the most famous dwarf here and yet she sat by herself. She looked up when she noticed his boots.

Vilmar smiled uncomfortably at her. She flicked the same sort of smile back.

"Do you want to be alone?" he asked softly.

She thought a moment and then snickered softly and gave a slight twist of her neck. "Not from you," she said. "Pull up a stump."

He quietly did as she bid.

For a long moment they just sat there, watching the sun slowly dip below the horizon, framed in red and yellow splashes of color. The smell of smoke and cooking was thick in the air but neither of them were hungry.

"I wonder how many more of these we will see, sunsets that is," Bran murmured.

"Hmmm," Vilmar mumbled back.

Silence again reigned.

"Do you really think you're going to die in this war?" Vilmar asked.

Bran shrugged as if it didn't matter, a typical, taciturn dwarf reaction. "War is war, Vilmar," she said plainly with wisdom beyond her years. "Anything could happen."

Vilmar nodded considering her words. "I guess only a fool would not expect his number to come up," he said.

Bran nodded as if she had already come to terms with the eventual possibility.

"I just wish..." she let her voice trail off.

Vilmar looked over at her. "What?"

He found she was fingering the small Dahla horse of her mother's, turning it over lovingly in her hands. Yaffa had painted it white with a black head, just like Mayhem.

He knew she missed her mother. There was no need to say the words. They all missed their families right now.

"I wish I could ride Valynt into this battle," she said so softly. "Mayhem is not really mine. He's not bonded to me like he was to my mother."

She closed her fist about the Dahla horse and looked off into the deepening darkness of night.

"He's so much different than Valynt. When I'm on Mayhem, there's always this wall between us, like he's shouting at me from far away. With Val, our thoughts are one, like we're twins."

Vilmar nodded understanding completely. "That's how it should be when the horse is perfectly matched to the rider," he said.

Bran sighed heavily.

"You know, if I could ride Valynt into this battle, well... I would believe the gods themselves were on our side," she said.

"That would add a bit of confidence to your sword arm," Vilmar replied with a chuckle and she replied in kind.

Vilmar suddenly became quiet and serious again. "I wish I was still a blacksmith's son," he told her. "Do you know what I would give to never do another spell and just train horses for the rest of my life?"

Bran sniffed a bit louder. "C'mon now, where's the glory in that?" she laughed.

Vilmar smiled in return into the dark. A grim thought intruded into his mind. He hoped he'd see her again after tonight.

Vilmar knelt quietly in the dark woods. The only light was from the three unicorns who surrounded him, glowing like pale ghosts in the night.

His heart was pounding wildly in his chest with nervousness. He didn't know how he was supposed to sleep he was so wound up. All he had to do was wait for the signal from the unicorns before he could proceed.

So, heart fluttering like a fragile, terror-stricken bird, he waited.

Suddenly the fawn opened his eyes.

"Evil sleeps," he heard the littlest unicorn say. Being the most innocent, the fawn was more easily sensitive to the fluctuations of energy.

The doe opened her eyes. *"It is time,"* she said gravely.

"Then let us begin," replied the stag.

Vilmar took a very deep breath, closed his eyes and bowed his head as they approached him, brandishing their spiraling horns like weapons before them.

"Remember," whispered the unicorn doe gravely. *"If he touches you in Dreamtime, you die. I cannot save you if you make any*

mistakes. *Neither can Daga or the many spirits who swirl inside you. You will be completely alone.*"

"Yes, thank you," Vilmar replied solemnly. "I will remember."

"*See you do,*" returned the stag. "*We risk much allowing this. You could jeopardize all our futures.*"

Vilmar opened his eyes and looked the stag evenly in the face.

"I won't screw up," he said and then gazed at the shivering fawn's deep blue orbs.

He felt a lump grow in his throat as the gravity of what they were saying struck him. With a supreme effort, he swallowed.

"I promise," he assured fervently.

Then three unicorn spiraled lances, humming with power, touched him from three different directions at the same time. He convulsed violently as if in a seizure. His marbled eyes rolled back into his head and he collapsed onto the soft green mosses of the forest floor.

The unicorns stepped back. The doe uttered a heavy sigh.

"*Now what?*" her son asked innocently.

"*Now we wait for him to come back,*" the father stag said simply.

"Or not," added the doe.

She folded her delicately formed legs and lay down beside Vilmar, close enough to cradle him with her belly and legs like a foal. She gently laid her beardless muzzle alongside his forehead maternally and inwardly prayed the young human would come back to them.

She had a very bad feeling about this course of action.

Vilmar fell spinning through a thick gray fog in Dreamtime. He felt dizzy enough to vomit until he remembered he'd left his body behind. The realization seemed to steady his descent and calm his emotions.

He found he could halt his momentum with a thought. He felt relieved not to have the clamor from a million dwarf voices raging in his head. But he quickly pushed aside his relief. He was here to do a job, a very dangerous job. If he allowed himself to enjoy his momentary privacy too much, he might fall victim to the one he sought.

Vilmar looked about with his spirit eyes. He still seemed to have form, the familiar shape he was used to. He raised his hands before him and saw a shadowy, transparent facsimile of how he appeared in the real world. His arms were very pale and spattered with freckles. He still seemed to be wearing the same clothes he had on when he left the unicorns. Everything just seemed misty and ghost-like here.

He turned his attention away from himself and reached out with his mind searching for another presence. He tried to ready himself for anything. There was no guarantee Savas-Zev would appear as ethereal as he did. For all he knew, the evil wizard could be the smoke which surrounded him.

Vilmar found it incredibly easy to locate the spirit he sought. He simply concentrated on the nearest evil essence. He could sense it, then even smell the presence. It smelled like rotting meat, just like Bran had said.

Warily, he willed his spirit in this direction.

"Are you the sorcerer's apprentice who has caused me so much trouble?" spoke a voice confidently, as if it had nothing to fear.

Vilmar stopped and checked his surroundings to make sure he wouldn't accidentally float straight into his foe.

He saw nothing. But his senses told him Savas-Zev was directly ahead.

"No sorcerer has taught me," he replied cautiously.

There was a derisive cackle from right in front of him.

"Obviously! Your magical aura has a very unskilled feeling to it. Are you sure you're ready to face me?" replied the voice in a slightly mocking way.

Vilmar chose to say nothing.

"Who taught you?" the voice suddenly demanded.

The words were spell-wound and Vilmar felt compelled to reply. He bucked the spell easily and refused to answer.

"I see your tutor has taught you the value of silence," replied the voice in a more thoughtful tone.

Each of them considered their next words carefully before proceeding.

"I find it very rude of you to banter words with me without a proper introduction," Vilmar fired back. "I will not treat with a voice in the mist. Show yourself!"

"The hatchling has a sense of propriety, I see," replied the voice. "Very well. I will play your little game as long as it proves interesting to me."

The mist coalesced in front of Vilmar and took shape. Before him stood a tall, thin man, much taller than Vilmar. He was dressed in wizard robes which seemed to shimmer and shift in color but always seemed to be some odd shade of velveteen black. His beard was sparse and pointed, his face narrow and his pale gray eyes riveting. They fastened on Vilmar like a spider on a drowsy fly and refused to release him from their grasp.

"I am Savas-Zev, Annihilator of the dwarf race," he announced proudly.

Vilmar managed a determined smile, amused at the wizard's boldness.

"Not yet. Not if I can help it," shot back Vilmar.

This was met with peals of laughter from the thin wizard before him. "At least you have a sense of humor about the issue," he chuckled. "I may not kill you after all but keep you by my side to teach you the error of your ways."

"You've already taught me enough," Vilmar replied. "Your spell book was most illuminating."

The laughter died instantly on the wizard's lips. His inhuman eyes went wide with shock and his hand shuddered as he pointed a long-nailed finger at him.

"*You!* It was you who stole my spell book!" he spouted.

Vilmar shrugged casually. "Hey, I thought it was a fairy tale but I found it much more interesting," he allowed himself the jab at humor and hoped he wouldn't soon regret it.

"And my scrying bowl!" Savas-Zev fumed, clenching his clawed spirit hands into fists.

"You had a scrying bowl, too?" Vilmar said innocently. "Well, that certainly explains a lot but I only took your book. I have no idea who peed in your scrying bowl."

At this Savas-Zev uttered an inhuman shriek and launched himself at Vilmar's apparition with clawed hands.

Vilmar gave a surprised yelp and automatically moved his legs to jump back. Except here, thoughts worked faster than actions, so his motions were rather slow.

So many crucial things happened in the next few seconds.

His eyes went wide as he realized the wizard was actually trying to grasp him, not with spells or incantations but with only his long, spidery fingers. Obviously, the wizard knew all he needed to do to trap him by touch. Spells here were unnecessary.

At the same time he noticed a small bulge beneath the neckline of the wizard's robe.

Bran's words suddenly flashed into his thoughts. *"I wish I could ride Valynt into this battle."*

Could it be possible that not only were Savas-Zev's robes duplicated in Dreamtime, but also any talisman regularly worn? Dahla horses were creatures not of this world but another. How would it work in Dreamtime?

The unicorn's warning also came back to him in a split second.

"If he touches you in Dreamtime, you die."

Making a grab for the Dahla horse would take him within reach of the wizard's greedily grasping arms, increasing the risk of being touched.

Was it worth it? He bit his lip, debating the action for a split second.

He then took a deep breath and decided to risk it. He thought of his arms snapping out and clutching the mysterious bulge beneath the wizard's robes. He prayed desperately it wasn't a useless trinket or an item magical enough to sear his hands off.

He watched his spirit arms shoot out and swipe desperately at the robe's hem, bringing himself within the infuriated embrace of the enraged wizard.

Vilmar's right hand closed about something small and hard but warm as skin. He recognized the shape to be of an animal of some kind.

He heard horses neighing in triumph in his brain.

At the exact same time, Vilmar's left hand landed palm first solidly on Savas-Zev's chest mirrored by the wizard's right hand landing squarely on his breastbone.

The unicorn doe reared her head back and shrieked a cry of such pain and devastation the surrounding woods shuddered down to their roots.

"We are lost!" she wailed to the world. *"We are lost!"*

CHAPTER 42

Bran's sleep had been troubled all night. She had been having bad dream after bad dream and awaking after each only to have no memory of what had disturbed her subconscious mind so much.

But the last dream was the worst. Her whole world was red, like she was staring at things through a shard of red-stained glass. Suddenly a raven appeared, hovering in midair right in front of her face. But it too appeared red. It cried and scolded her, flapping its great red wings in front of her face. Its feathers were wet. Every time it beat its wings, red droplets sprayed her face like blood.

And then she heard Vilmar's scream of agony ringing and echoing over and over with intense pain through her head.

Bran gave a shuddering gasp and woke suddenly, sitting bolt upright on her cot. The abrupt sensation of imminent danger had woken her with the speed of a cold slap across the face.

"Vilmar!" she shouted and vaulted off her cot, sprinting out the door of her tent.

She had no idea where she was going but chose to trust her instincts. Propelled by a force she did not quite understand she fled into the misty darkness of the woods, heedless of anyone she passed. Cold fear wrapped icy fingers around her heart and attempted to squeeze the madly pounding organ to permanent stillness. She fought it off and concentrated on pumping her short legs like the pistons of some little machine. She had no idea what she would discover. She only knew she had to get to Vilmar before...

Before what?

She had no idea. And she was afraid to think very far ahead.

Vilmar felt pain sear his chest with the touch of Savas-Zev. His head reared backwards and a yell of agony was wrenched forcefully from his lips. Through eyelids barely cracked open, he could see the gleeful grimace of success fold the wizard's face into a death's head smile of hellish joy.

'I have failed the unicorns and all of us,' was Vilmar's first thought.

He still clutched the little Dahla horse with a grip death could not have pried apart.

Herds of mystical horses thundered through his brain, winding themselves among the pain he now was experiencing.

He felt the wizard's other hand, his left hand, scrape and clutch, landing like a fist. The consequence of this action was a line of pain jerked across the back of his neck, biting into his cervical spine with the keenness of a hot knife. This new pain created confusion in his mind as to its source and then he remembered.

He too wore a talisman. He wore it every day of his life since he had gotten it, day and night, whether he bathed or not. It had become so common he had forgotten it was there most of the time.

Savas-Zev had grabbed the unicorn fawn's hippomane.

Why it did not simply snap off he did not know, it was only secured to his neck with a simple leather string. It should have broken easily.

But it did not break off. It stayed safe and secure around his neck.

Savas-Zev had no idea what he was holding for Vilmar's tunic hid it from view. The wizard had grabbed the hippomane through the fabric. He only thought he had discovered the source of the boy's miniscule power and could easily surpass the spell on this little trinket.

He couldn't have been more wrong.

Vilmar called on the power in the hippomane, a power which was, as yet, untried. He had no idea what would happen.

The unicorn fawn squealed and bucked in the moonless night. His spine twisted as he threw himself, like a free horse which has just been saddled for the first time into the air.

"No!" he shouted in his mind. *"We fight together!"*

The fawn began to glow brightly. He reared upwards, throwing back his head and his just budding lance speared the image of the full moon in the night sky above. A humming sound began to radiate strongly from the juvenile unicorn.

Again the trees shuddered in fear and awe.

A blazing light suddenly shot outwards from the hippomane making the flesh of the hand holding it glow and the bones show darkly against the pink membrane.

Savas-Zev jerked his free hand back to cover his eyes and found he could not remove his left hand from whatever object he held. The white light continued to blaze outward from the stone. His one hand over his eyes wasn't enough. He could still feel the intense pain as the bright light grew brighter still, until it seemed he held a tiny sun in his hand. His left hand was beginning to sear and char, acrid smoke issuing up from the source.

Vilmar was untouched. The light seemed bright to him but not painfully so. His agony was gone and he could see the effect the hippomane was having on the wizard.

"Release me and I will release you," Vilmar ordered in a commanding tone.

Savas-Zev growled and writhed in pain as the stone increased its attack on the wizard.

"Release me from Dreamtime!" he ordered again.

The wizard moaned in frustration as he comprehended Vilmar's words. His free hand waved a weak command and Vilmar felt things around him starting to change. Savas-Zev began to fade swiftly from view.

Vilmar quickly snapped off the Dahla horse from the cord around the wizard's neck and commanded the hippomane to release Savas-Zev. It did so abruptly.

Vilmar seized his opportunity and fled Dreamtime.

"This is not over, hatchling!" the wizard bellowed after him. "You will face me again!"

He awoke with a shuddering jolt. His eyes popped open and were marbled once more. And once again the multitude of voices were in his head, all questioning why.

"You inept FOOL!" the unicorn stag screamed into his head. *"You could have been killed!"*

The stag pawed the ground viciously, churning up the forest loam and then mock charged as if to spear him with his lance. The enraged unicorn stopped short and tossed his head wildly, setting his frothy mane and long beard dancing.

"What on earth made you ignore our warnings?" he demanded.

Vilmar felt shaky and weak. He was bathed in sweat and the night was cold so he began to shiver violently. He could barely manage to crawl to his hands and feet but he had to.

He had to see if the unicorn fawn was all right. He looked to his right and saw the unicorn doe standing on three legs, the right foreleg bent daintily up to her chest, staring strangely at him. A look of confusion marred the beauty of her face.

"This shouldn't be happening," she whispered slowly. *"You shouldn't be back. You should be lost to us. What did you do?"*

Vilmar shuddered again and swallowed with difficulty. He felt he was going to pass out at any moment. He looked to his left.

The unicorn fawn was standing there quietly with a look of smug satisfaction on his young face.

"Are you all right?" Vilmar gasped out. He found his chest hurt, his throat burned and his voice was raspy.

The unicorn fawn smiled in his unicorn sort of way and nodded once.

Vilmar turned back to the doe and stag.

At the same time Bran burst loudly onto the scene. She looked in confusion at each of the unicorns and lastly at Vilmar, huddled shivering and weak on the ground before her.

Her green eyes went wide and she was by his side in an instant.

"Vilmar!" she exclaimed clutching him about the shoulders. "What happened?"

He ignored her question. Vilmar struggled to sit up and look at the unicorn doe. The effort made him shaky and there were sparkles in his vision.

"I found the risk to be worth it," his voice managed to croak out.

He uncurled his tense fingers and let Valynt's Dahla horse spill into Bran's trembling hands.

He heard everyone gasp in unison.

Bran stared speechless at the little figurine resting on her palm. Then she looked up into Vilmar's face incredulously.

She spilled the Dahla horse into her lap and took hold of Vilmar's face by the ears. Before he knew what she was doing, Bran had pressed her lips hard onto his. This was no gentle kiss. It was without warning, forceful and their teeth clinked roughly against each other. She then pushed his face back and without another word or glance, snatched up Valynt's Dahla horse and bolted away.

The voices in Vilmar's head had gone blessedly silent. He didn't want them to start up again. He was exhausted from the shock of his ordeal. He gave in to the shock.

Vilmar fainted dead away.

CHAPTER 43

Delkan sat in the midst of a large group of dwarves seated around the campfire. They were laughing and joking and passing a skin of ale about. The thoughts of the impending battle seemed far from their minds. Tonight they were alive and happy and bent on enjoying their memories.

Quite abruptly, the shadow of a loose pony appeared outside their ranks. Conversation gradually ceased as the pony came into their midst and was noticed.

It was Blueberry, Garn-Ithel's new Dahla horse. Blueberry wore a saddle and bridle but his rider was nowhere to be seen.

Blueberry looked about in confusion. No one made any move to catch his reins. His wide, intelligent eyes finally settled on Delkan and his confusion seemed to vanish. He made his way confidently to where she was seated on a log with some other dwarves. The pony put down his face to hers and nuzzled her with an affectionate nicker. Then he knelt and with a loud groan, deposited his bulk on the ground right in front of her.

Patiently, he laid there, legs curled up underneath him, looking expectantly at her with his great dark eyes.

Aldoin snorted and said aloud, "It seems the permission of your attendance has been requested. I think Garn wants to speak to you... alone."

Delkan glanced about the campfire suddenly feeling every eye upon her, even Blueberry's.

She shrugged as if it was nothing.

"Very well then," she replied casually and reaching out, grasped Blueberry's short mane and hitched herself, with some difficulty, aboard his broad back. No one made any move to help her. Blueberry lunged to his feet and stood there a moment swishing his tail and stamping his feet

"I'll be back soon," she said lightheartedly. "Keep the ale warm for me, will you?"

She spun Blueberry about expertly and headed away from the campfire at a smooth trot.

She didn't see the crowd of dwarves behind her nudge one another and start to smile and chuckle knowingly. Horns and mugs of ale were clinked together and quickly refilled.

Once away from the encampment, Delkan gave Blueberry his head and let him carry her wherever he wanted. The steel gray pony headed off at a swift canter through the dark woods, picking his way over fallen trees and around brush piles as if it were broad daylight.

Delkan's mind spun with possibilities. What could Garn possibly want? Had some new information been discovered about Savas-Zev?

Soon she saw that the pony was making for a clearing in the woods where a huge bonfire had been erected.

Garn-Ithel stood in front of the blaze. Blueberry trotted up to the fire and stopped.

"What are you doing alone out here and why did you build such a huge fire?" she asked totally confused. "Don't you know it's dangerous to do that? Savas-Zev's goblin army is so close. They might see."

"We're safe here," he assured as he came up to her. "The unicorns are standing guard."

"Well then what did you want?" she asked again.

"Well... it's just like this," Garn stuttered nervously, rubbing his neck. He looked very embarrassed.

How could a dwarf look embarrassed? Now the alarm bells really did go off in Delkan's head.

"I've been trying to talk to you for days... and... well... every time I go to, you're surrounded by people. You seem to have so many new friends nowadays, Delkan, my lass."

She threw back her head and laughed.

"New acquaintances I should say," she chuckled at him. "Comrades at arms. Kinfolk about to die beside me in battle. But not friends. Not like Bran and Vilmar and Iyorath," Delkan chuckled as she gestured. "And certainly not like you."

Garn heaved a great sigh and looked very much relieved. "That's a good thing to hear," he muttered quietly.

"Now. What's this all about?" she questioned. "What's so important you had to yank me away from my merrymaking?"

Garn began to shuffle and sputter uncomfortably again. Finally he was able to force out, "I made somethin' for you."

He handed her a thing tied to a leather cord then quickly stepped back as if stung and resumed his shuffling and nervous muttering.

Delkan took the amulet and examined it by the blazing, dancing light of the bonfire. On the cord hung a simple smooth wooden disk with a single dwarven character etched onto it.

It was 'brethe,' the dwarven rune of union and betrothal. Her eyes went wide in shock and surprise.

"Garn, does this mean what I think it means?" she asked breathlessly.

He met her gaze and a shy smile flickered across his face.

"I would like to marry you, Delkan," he quickly blurted out. "I know since the dwarves have been mustering, you and Bran have become quite popular. Bran seems uncomfortable with it but you've been reveling in it. I just wanted to put my request in before some other worthy warrior does."

He took a deep breath and continued on before she had a chance to say anything. "You've been the only one for me ever since I met you, since before you lost your legs. Since then the toughness, which has always lain dormant in you, came to the surface and I loved you even more when I saw it. Legs or no legs, you're a fine dwarf lady who any man would be honored to call his mate. I want to fight this fight beside you, Delkan. Live or die, I want to share my life with you and no other dwarf maiden. When I do die, I'll sing your praises to the Great Dragon so all will know Delkan of Fang-Tor province was the bravest dwarf who ever lived."

It was now Delkan's turn to stammer and be without proper words.

"You don't have to answer now," Garn rushed onward. "You can think it over for a while… or forever. I don't care. Just don't say no. Please, Delkan."

Delkan opened and closed her mouth several times before she trusted herself enough to speak the words she had in her heart.

"But I have to give you some answer now," she took a deep breath and said. "Okay, here goes. I think it would be very unwise of me to promise something fate might yet take away. Please give me until after this upcoming battle and then I will think on your request with more joy and happiness in my heart. Please understand me in this, dear Garn."

Garn dipped his head low and considered her words seriously for a long moment. Finally he raised his head and there was a hopeful light in his face. "You didn't say 'No,'" he retorted.

She gave him a careful smile.

Garn-Ithel nodded once and smiled quietly. "Good enough then," he said and patted her stump gently. She smiled again and laid her hand over his warmly.

She then turned Blueberry and headed back to camp. She watched Garn carefully out of the corner of her eye until she saw him turn his face back to the raging bonfire. Then she very quickly and quietly slipped the betrothed charm around her neck and hid it under her clothes. She smiled happily to herself and caressed its smooth surface over the rough fabric of her tunic.

Unbeknownst to her, Garn too had been watching her out of the corner of his eye. He had caught the motion of her donning his charm.

He turned his attention back to the bonfire. He smiled privately to himself and felt an inner peace and warmth, which had nothing to do with the fire.

CHAPTER 44

The war encampment of dwarves had emptied in preparation for the naming ceremony of the great obsidian spearhead Bran carried. They were all gathered in a field which contained a jumble of large, rocky boulders before an enormous blank granite face. This made an incredible, natural amphitheater within the wilderness. Those who were not dwarves but were also in the encampment had gathered out of curiosity to witness the ritual but they were careful to keep a respectful distance from the front of the crowd.

Vilmar and Iyorath were the only non-dwarves who dared to stand at the front of the outdoor stage. They watched the gathering crowd with some awe. The dwarven war bards had arrived early in the morning as their presence was a must at this ritual. They watched as seven great drums, as large as two full-sized wagons, were rolled ponderously downhill on their edge, guided carefully by thirteen of the shortest but most muscular, bald dwarves they had ever seen. They were preceded silently by an equal number of half-dwarven flute players. Iyorath had seen many instruments but he had never seen flutes like these. Each group of thirteen had a set of flutes which were shaped so they reared themselves up above the musician's heads. The flared ends of the flutes were carved in the likeness of the patron animals of each dwarven province. The stylized jeweled eyes of the flutes sparkled and glittered like live things in the dimming, orange light of the setting sun.

"I know nothing of dwarf rituals," Iyorath was saying to Vilmar. "I can't even speak their language."

"I'll translate what I can to you as long as they don't find it offensive," Vilmar replied. "But I know scarcely more than you."

"That's as it should be," Garn assured as he came up behind them. "Don't want you outsiders knowing too much of our ways."

Vilmar smiled in return but added, "But I guess if I did want to know, all I would have to do is ask one of the thousands in my head to explain it to me."

Garn snorted, unperturbed by this mild threat.

"Pah! They wouldn't tell you either, young pup," he assured in satisfaction and plopped himself down beside them with a grunt.

Bran found them just then.

"I've been looking everywhere for you two," she said. "I need to introduce you to Zul the High Priest."

She nodded before them to a very stately, impeccably groomed, older dwarf with a pointed black hat with no brim, who was making his way slowly toward them through the crowd. He was being stopped frequently by other dwarves.

"He looks like your father, Varg," Vilmar observed quietly.

His words took him back to the first time he had met Varg, the time when he tried to make her father believe he thought Bran was male because of her beard. It seemed years ago.

Bran's comment to this was to give an amused snort. "Zul is nothing like my father!" she said. "He's the High Priest of all the provinces and has many dealings with other races so he knows how to treat them. Compared to my father, Zul is quite cuddly!"

Zul had come within earshot by then.

"Who's cuddly?" he demanded gruffly. "Not me!"

His face then split in a wide smile displaying all of his bright, white teeth. Vilmar was amazed such a deep voice could come from such a little dwarf. His words sounded like large boulders sliding noisily down a steep incline. He clasped arms with Bran and Garn. He then turned to the elf and the dwarf and Bran made introductions. He clasped Iyorath's arms in a strong grip and did the same to Vilmar. But when he touched Vilmar's arms he suddenly stopped and refused to let go.

Vilmar felt his keen gray eyes peering closely into his marbled ones. But for some strange reason, he was not afraid. He immediately felt he liked this dwarf and could trust him with anything, whether casual or private. He felt a friendly smile in return being coaxed gently out of him.

"Ah, this is the dwarf friend you've told me so much about," his booming voice rumbled, still refusing to release Vilmar from his grip or his gaze.

"Yes, Honored Master. This is my friend Vilmar," Bran replied.

"He reeks of magic. But I can't quite tell whether it's druid or dwarf. A very strange combination," he mused as he scanned. "Tell me, boy, who is your teacher?"

"A unicorn," he returned obediently.

Zul whistled, very impressed. "A unicorn, you say? How old?" he inquired further.

Vilmar was puzzled. "I'm not exactly sure as to her age. I didn't think to ask, nor do I think it's polite," he stammered, unsure of where this thread of conversation was going.

"Probably right. Probably *is* rude," Zul replied.

Vilmar could feel him poking about in his head, scanning further but respectfully not going too deep.

"She feels very old, ancient even. You are probably her last charge before her melding. Well, that explains the druidic feel to your power. But why do you feel like dwarf magic, my son?"

He felt him probe further. Vilmar knew he could have stopped him easily. But he trusted him so he chose not to. "My stars! You've got an entire metropolis of souls within you! And they're all there willingly. Amazing! No wonder you reek of dwarf magic."

He let go of his hands and withdrew his mind from Vilmar's at once. Vilmar gasped in surprise and deflated somewhat. Zul considered him carefully as he caught his breath and reassembled his slightly scrambled thoughts.

"If the gods are willing and allow us to survive this great tribulation before us, then you may need my assistance afterwards. I can help you deal with the multitude in your head. You will need my help, young mystic," he offered pleasantly.

"Thank you," Vilmar said politely. "I would like that... I think."

Zul smiled broadly again showing all his white teeth. "I was wondering, can you do fire magic?" he asked the young human.

It was Vilmar's turn to smile and without replying, he snapped his fingers. Vilmar's fingertips sparked and little tongues of flames leaped out from them.

Zul clutched his wrist eagerly and examined the flames and the hand, which had produced them. He seemed quite pleased.

"Excellent!" he spouted in glee. "Your grasp of fire magic is formidable. Perfect!"

He stepped back and licked his lips in eagerness. "I was wondering if you might help me in the ritual tonight?" he asked.

Garn coughed in shock and Bran squeaked in surprise.

"But... is it... quite right? This is a dwarf ceremony!" he stuttered.

Bran sidled quietly up to him and casually stomped on his foot. "It's a great honor," she hissed to him in a scolding tone. "It would be insulting to refuse his Eminence!"

Zul raised his hand forgivingly. "I'm sorry. With all the dwarf echoes in your head, I mistook you for a taller dwarf. Let me explain myself," he took a deep breath.

"I will be expending a lot of energy in the ritual tonight. Any energy I could save would be a great blessing leaving me more strength to devote to other details. One of the magics dwarves can be born with and find extremely useful is fire magic. Could you, perhaps, make a large bonfire for me which consumes no fuel and seemingly feeds itself off of the air?"

Vilmar smiled a large smile, which seemed to go completely around his head.

"How big?" he retorted confidently.

Zul smiled in return and began to chuckle. Vilmar joined in. He nodded and returned quickly to his pre-ritual preparation. The sound of his laughter as he left was like an avalanche in the distant mountains in the dead of winter.

Bran gestured behind them, recognizing someone and they all turned. Delkan had entered the scene in certain splendor. Four dwarves were bearing her in a grandly carved, oaken chair. She giggled at them as her retainers set her down and seated themselves on the ground on guard about her.

"Excuse me," Bran exclaimed. "Where's the crown, your Majesty?"

"Aw! Push off!" Delkan retorted haughtily and stuck out her pink tongue at them. "I'm rather enjoying all this attention. Want me to tell them to scoot?"

"No, your servants can stay," Bran grumbled. "But just don't let them fight your battles or feed you grapes in my presence!"

"Hah! I wouldn't dream of it," she assured. "Fame is fleeting, my friends! I'm only enjoying it for the moment. I still plan on sweating and bleeding beside my dearest friends. Make no mistake!"

She arranged her frame in a more comfortable but not as dignified position in the chair and crowed, "So when does the fun start?"

"I guess as soon as everyone gets settled or the sun is completely down, whichever comes first," Bran said as she seated herself beside her on her right.

Dra-Oog suddenly appeared through the throng looking resplendent in all her war finery. She was draped in gold chains and her silvery white tresses and beard were braided in warrior locks. She wore an ornately gilded and decorated steel breastplate and a great, dwarven, broadsword at her hip. She looked ready to go into battle for the last time, uncaring of whether she lived or died. She made quite an entrance.

At the sight of her, Delkan sat up straight in her chair and motioned hurriedly to her four to scatter. They obediently complied, melting silently into the growing shadows.

Dra-Oog chose to sit right beside Delkan on her left and fixed her with a terribly judgmental and stern gaze.

"A throne, Delkan?" she asked quietly. "I don't believe there was any royalty in your family tree, vast though it was."

Delkan blushed deeply to her roots and hunkered down lower in her great chair trying to look very small.

Dra-Oog's narrow gaze met Bran's and a secretive wink was aimed at her. Bran did her best to stifle a chuckle. Dra-Oog meant no real evil to Delkan, she was certain from the look. But she knew her mere presence was enough to put Delkan suddenly on her best behavior. Dra-Oog was simply jerking Delkan's chain for her own amusement.

Garn strode confidently over to Delkan and seated himself in front of her on the ground. He aimed an angry glare Dra-Oog's way as if daring her to start something.

Dra-Oog inclined one silvery eyebrow the barest bit and turned her face away. But Bran caught the faintest hint of a smile of amusement.

"Pardon my ignorance," Iyorath spoke up as the human and elf took their places beside their dwarf friends. "But why does Zul need a magic bonfire?"

"To petition the Great Dragon, of course," Garn barked gruffly as if everyone knew and said no more.

Iyorath's fair skin wrinkled in further confusion and he turned to the young human for a more friendly explanation.

"The ritual cast tonight will stir up great powers. Their deities may take an interest in the proceedings. But rarely is anyone ever allowed to speak directly to a dwarven god. They consider it blasphemous. You must first petition the Great Dragon and he will pick a time when the gods are in a more generous mood to make your request known. No one but maybe Zul himself may talk directly to the gods and the cause must be great indeed. Dwarf gods have an ego which must be cautiously placated."

"Isn't this a good enough reason?" Iyorath asked. "I would think the impending battle that might end all their suffering would be at the top of the gods' list of worthy causes."

"Oh and it is," replied Vilmar. "But a dwarven High Priest petitions the gods privately, not openly. Also, we are here only to name a magical weapon. If they see fit to approve the ritual, it will be answer enough."

"Dwarven gods seem as taciturn as the dwarves themselves," Iyorath grumbled, shaking his head.

"And I suppose the elf gods are honey, love and goodness?" Garn challenged back.

"No, not all of them," Iyorath was quick to point out. "But I understand the adherence to certain rules when dealing with deities. Elf gods are so fond of their elaborate rituals."

"Sounds predictable for an elf," Garn grunted. "We dwarves like to be more direct about such things. Children can grow up while you're wasting time with all that embellishing!"

"Well, at the speed your children mature, I can certainly understand the need for this," Vilmar said and glanced at Bran with a chuckle.

"Quit your prattle," scolded Dra-Oog gruffly. "They're beginning."

The great dwarven drums began to murmur. They could all feel the rumble through the souls of their feet as the light quickly faded and the torches were lit.

There was a sudden sound as of the braying of a thousand mules as the flute players blew their opening blast. The drummers made their massive instruments rumble louder, smoothing the flutes' raucous sound. The drummers then began to hammer repetitively on the great hides, forcing booming voices out of the drums. The thunder from them rolled like an earthquake through the ground and made the air vibrate with its timbre. The notes of the flutes intertwined with the great beats turning empty air into a sound so loud it was nearly possible to see the music.

Iyorath thought if this was the dwarven way of petitioning their deities, then certainly it was not a very gentle one. It was more like pounding on the gates of heaven and loudly demanding an audience with one's favorite god. Such a thing would never be permitted to happen among the elven deities. He found the introduction very abrupt.

Vilmar caught Zul's gesture as the dwarven High Priest nodded in his direction. He took a large breath and sank his consciousness deep into the earth to find its molten, orange heart. He then brought it up into his body, into his fist, and standing up, cast it like a child's thrown ball into the natural amphitheater beside Zul.

There was a deafening crackle and boom like an explosion. An enormous bonfire blazed to life next to the dwarf High Priest. It was so sudden all the surrounding dwarves ducked and hid their faces. Even the dwarven musicians paused in their playing for a split moment before resuming their song with even greater fervor.

Zul alone remained steadfast at the sudden appearance of the huge fireball. He did cast a sly smile and approving glance in Vilmar's direction.

The huge bonfire hovered a scant three feet off the ground. It cast long shadows among the throng who had gathered and illuminated their expressions of wonder and amazement. So hot was it, the heat-hardened dwarves in the front row scooted their ranks away from the raging blaze to a safer, cooler distance.

"Can you feel it?" Garn hissed reverently to the friends gathered around. "The gods are here! Can't you feel them?"

The air had gone electric. It tingled with energy between the drumbeats like the air before a lightning storm. They could all feel it. It was as if the air itself were alive and watching the proceedings.

Vilmar's whirling eyes stared straight into the heart of the bonfire. He knew the dwarf's words were all too true.

He felt the soul of Fire itself smile at him.

Strange words spoke in his brain, words which hissed and crackled like the flames. *"I like these people,"* it said. *"I help them and they make beautiful things. They also are not afraid of a little danger. Their heart is lava and stone."*

Again he felt Fire's essence smile at him. Vilmar kept his thoughts to himself.

"Hear me, my people!" Zul cried out and the drumbeats died to a mere rumble. "I stand before you a poor cleric, the son of a long line of poor clerics, a line which traces back to the beginning of our people. In me the blood of the ancestors runs true and strong. Hear me as I speak the words long forgotten by most dwarves in the old tongue. Help me call forth the Great Dragon."

He turned to the raging bonfire and began to chant words no one knew. The surrounding dwarves took up the chant in their modern tongue.

"Come, Great Fire Serpent. Come, Fireworm. Come and hear our request."

Vilmar noted a changing of the spirit in the flames. It was melding into a form all could see. The fires dipped and flickered, seeming to struggle.

The great bonfire suddenly blinked out. But the light did not leave. Instead of a fire, there remained a huge ball of golden light. It bathed their upturned faces with a gentle glow. It then began to flash and glitter like golden quicksilver. The flashes then slowed and took shape. They realized the flashes were from golden scales as an enormous reptilian form took shape before them. It seemed to be curled into itself but then slowly unrolled. They all could see four legs like great tree trunks, the wings unfurled and stretched high into the night sky, the tail unwound into a forked tip and finally the long neck and head revealed from where it was hidden under a folded wing.

Vilmar's jaw dropped. He had never seen a creature so beautiful in all his life. Its scales glittered like gold coins encrusted with diamonds, its wings seemed powdered with gold dust which cast rainbow rays all about, and its eyes gleamed like highly polished red rubies.

It gazed around the assembled population of dwarves with a lofty air. Most of the dwarves fell on their faces as its glance passed their way. Its head circled slowly about the crowd, finally coming to rest on Vilmar.

Vilmar felt as though all breath had been sucked out of him. Some distant sensation told him what he was doing was extremely rude. One does not meet the gaze of an immortal, eyeball to eyeball without showing some sign of respect. But he was trapped. He could do nothing but stare into those fathomless red depths. He saw the wisdom of all the ages held there, silent and secret. He felt the incredible power of the beast and knew a warrior spirit slept just beneath the surface. And he felt so incredibly tiny and insignificant compared to the might and majesty of the creature he now faced. The Great Dragon was an ageless and timeless being of power. He was old without being aged, youth itself, although he had never been born but had always existed. The dwarf legends just gave this spirit the shape of a great golden dragon. And it would exist in spirit long after the world had forgotten there ever existed dwarves or dragons or unicorns. It was an immortal essence. To appear in person at this ritual was an honor beyond measure.

The Great Dragon finally removed its blessed glance from him and Vilmar nearly fell to the ground in relief. One does not lock gazes with an immortal and expect to be left totally unchanged by such a thing. Vilmar felt different, small and unimportant in the great scheme of things.

"I have come, Zul," spoke the Great Dragon and its voice rumbled like an avalanche of huge boulders in the mountains, through the air and the soles of their feet. "Speak your request but be cautious of your words for *they* are listening right now. They are very interested in these proceedings tonight."

"Great Lord, the world of dwarves stands upon a precipice. The outcome of this battle will decide our future. Either we succeed and prosper or we fail and fade out of all existence and knowledge. We ask your many blessings upon all which shall come to pass. We plead for your assistance in this war ahead. If this truly is to be our final days, then let us live it in such a way as to make our forefathers proud of their sons and daughters. Let great deeds be done and great honors be won. Let us make such an end as to be counted as the greatest of all the great heroes who have gone before us."

The Great Dragon inclined its head slightly at his words.

"Such a grave time is indeed before you all. The gods do not relish the thought of being forgotten and fading into the mists of time like smoke from a burnt-out fire. But Fate is ever fickle and changes its mind frequently. What have you done to insure the dwarf race will not die out?"

Zul brought forth a thing wrapped in a loving bundle of expensive cloth.

"My Lord, we have made a weapon to trap the enemy of our people within," Zul said with great eagerness.

The dragon reared back its head and its eyes blazed brightly.

"Yes, I have heard rumors of this weapon from the stones themselves. Show it to me," the dragon ordered.

Zul was only too happy to obey. He carefully untied the strings from about the bundle and unwound it. The dragon bent its golden head low, watching the unveiling process with great interest.

And then Zul had it uncovered. The spear lay there naked and shiny as a newborn babe. Zul grasped it by its base and held it up triumphantly.

The dragon reared back its head and took a step or two back.

"That weapon could trap a god!" the Great Dragon said in awe. It then stepped a bit closer to examine it better.

"I sense more than just dwarf hands made this," the dragon said and it swung its great head about and fixed Vilmar under his magical stare once more.

"You had a hand in this, young human?" the dragon asked.

"Yes," Vilmar stammered out.

The great red eyes glittered at him.

"Then please come forward."

Vilmar felt compelled to obey. He rose quietly to his feet and walked slowly to the dragon. He felt keenly aware every dwarf eye was upon him. He tried not to think about how large the dragon grew the closer he came to the great beast.

Finally he stood at the foot of the dragon. He fell to his knees at once, out of respect and refused to look anywhere but at the great golden claws of the dragon's right foreleg before him.

"You helped to make this?" the dragon asked.

"Yes, Lord. Daga and I, that is," he responded as politely as he dared.

The Great Dragon snorted and began to laugh a little. Vilmar shuddered at the sound of the Great Dragon's laughter.

"Ah, Daga, the great meddler of the dwarf race! I should have known his paw would be in this," said the dragon and, glancing up, Vilmar could see all of his sparkling white teeth. He quickly dropped his eyes again.

"But more than an aged dwarf and a gifted young green wizard made this object. Who else helped? You tell me, young human."

"My teacher helped—she, her mate, and young son," he replied carefully. "She is a unicorn."

"A unicorn!" the dragon breathed and smoke hissed upward from its nostrils.

Vilmar nodded and fell at once to his face, fearing he had said something wrong. Maybe dragons didn't like unicorns? There was a long silence in which Vilmar could hear his heart beat.

"I thought I sensed the presence of unicorns in this," the Great Dragon finally said. "Stand and look me in the eye, young human."

Shaking in fear, Vilmar immediately obeyed. What had he done? Had he said something wrong?

Slowly he brought his face upward and locked gazes with the Great Dragon. He felt himself falling into those great red depths of time. He felt the dragon's voice speak to him in the very same way as the unicorn's, in his mind.

"The unicorns and the dragons are linked, Vilmar. Did you know that? We are both sacred beasts. We were the first magical beings to ever exist. We exist to balance each other, the fire with the water, the healing with the war. We are kindred, dragons and unicorns. We are family. To have your progress guided by one of the first is no mean thing. And unicorns are not just attracted to any human. Wizard, you may be and so the sword is forbidden to you, but warrior you are also. And having a warrior spirit has attracted my attention as well. Also being especially blessed of the spirit of Fire does not hurt things either for you.

"Know this, Vilmar, young human, farrier's son. The grace of the gods is with you and their eyes are never far from you. You have nothing to fear from me. You are under my protection as well as the unicorn's. You walk forever shielded by grace. You need to know this for the upcoming battle. You will need every bit of strength you possess whether it be physical, mental or spiritual. Remember, you walk in grace."

Slowly, gently, the Great Dragon withdrew its warm presence from his mind. Vilmar looked about blinking, and then, quite suddenly, his eyes rolled back into his head and he staggered to his knees.

Zul caught him before his head hit the stone. Bran was there, in an instant, at her friend's side.

"He is not harmed, just overwhelmed by it all. He will recover rather quickly," the Great Dragon reassured.

Iyorath came forward to assist Vilmar's departure.

"Take him and free him from his blackness, Iyorath Asra. As you will free others from the darkness which chains them. This is your task in this life: to free the ensnared," the Great Dragon spoke to him.

Iyorath stared at the great dragon in shock, not understanding. Many dwarf eyes looked from the elf to the Great Dragon and back.

"Peace, young elf. Time will make sense of all my words," the Great Dragon replied.

The sacred serpent swung its massive head back to Zul the High Priest.

"It is amazing so many non-dwarves should have so many chores vital to the survival of your race at the end. The dwarves are truly not alone in this. Please do not forget this with the passage of time," it spoke to him and all gathered.

The golden dragon then swung its head about and its sharp gaze fastened on Bran. "The Blood Raven lives!" the dragon breathed and smoke issued forth in thin trails from between its teeth.

Bran fell to her knees and was unable to look away.

"Great Lord..." she could stammer at last. "I want to be no one's savior. I only want to avenge my family."

The golden dragon smiled gently down onto her. For a moment Bran felt her mother was looking down at her. The thought brought a lump to her throat and tears to her eyelids.

Then anger swelled in her heart, anger at the tears which hung on her face. She clenched her fists and dragged a sleeve violently across her face.

'No!' she said to herself. 'I will not cry. Now is not the time for tears. Now is the time for action. There will be plenty of time to cry for the dead when this is all over.'

She thought she had kept these thoughts to herself but to her surprise, she had clenched her fists and shouted them at the Great Dragon. By the gods, she had screamed at an immortal! How dare she?

But the dragon only smiled gently at her words.

"All too true, my dear," he spoke to her. "When this is over, we shall all cry rivers of tears for the brave lives which were cut short all too soon. And I myself will cry with you. Will you, Bran, daughter of Yaffa and Varg, catch my fiery tears in your strong, bare hands?"

"I am servant to the gods and to the Great Dragon," Bran replied almost without thinking. "I am yours to command. Use my life or take it if you wish. I am your servant."

The dragon nodded its golden head gravely. "And this is why you *are* the Blood Raven," it spoke reverently to her.

The Great Dragon then bent a foreleg the size of a large tree trunk and tucked its shining head next to its shoulder and bowed low to Bran.

The motion was mirrored by all the surrounding dwarves, even Zul the High Priest.

"Bran, you shall wield the spear in the battle to come against Savas-Zev," said Zul and he held out the spear to her.

Without thinking, she took hold of the shaft.

And the dwarves began to chant her name and pound their fists on the ground. The great, deep voice of the drums echoed their chant. Her name rose high into the night sky.

Her thoughts were whirling too fast for it to make sense. She felt she might faint... but no, not in front of everybody. Her legs felt weak and unsteady.

Zul was looking closely into her face. He saw the doubt and fear in her eyes. He wrapped a strong hand over her sweaty, shaking ones and gave a reassuring squeeze. His grip seemed to say, 'C'mon, little one. You can do this. It's just a ritual.'

She swallowed hard and took a deep breath. She nodded in return. Zul grinned widely.

He took the spear gently from her and turning to face the crowd, held it aloft for all to see. The drumbeats stilled and people grew quiet.

"And if Bran should fall, cut down in battle, who shall take up the spear and carry on the fight?" Zul shouted to the crowd.

Bran gasped in shock. She had just gotten her guts up to go through with this ritual and now he was talking about her dying? It was not a very reassuring thing to say to her right now in front of all these strange dwarves.

"I will!" shouted a voice from the left.

All heads turned to find who had spoken.

Delkan had raised her hand.

Zul wove through the crowds, Bran trotting along behind on his heels. When he reached her, he offered her the spear. She took it at once in her strong hands and clutched it tightly, making the whites of her knuckles show.

"I will take it to repay Bran for all she has done for me. I brought a lot of trouble into her life. It is time I make it up," she said and there was a fierce light in her eyes.

"And if you die?" Bran asked quietly, privately so only those near could hear her.

"If I die, it still will be worth it," she said vehemently and loudly. "I will be dying for the honor of my people, my family and my friends. It *will* be worth it!"

The Great Dragon nodded his head in approval.

"So be it, then," Zul said and declared in a loud voice. "If Bran, the Blood Raven falls in this conflict, then Delkan of Fang-Tor will take up the spear and the fight will go on."

A great cheer went up from those gathered about. People began to chant Delkan's name and the drumbeats rose higher. All the noise seemed to rouse the unconscious Vilmar from his stupor.

Bran stared at Delkan as if she didn't know her. Her friend had just sworn in front of all those gathered, she would die for her. There was such a jumble of emotions in her heart she could not make sense of. Her chest felt tight and her eyes were blurry. She swallowed with some difficulty.

Delkan smiled confidently at her friend and taking her hand in both of hers, clenched them tightly. She butted heads with Bran and whispered privately. "Don't worry! It'll all turn out all right. And I'm damn sure not letting some old codger of a wizard make mincemeat outta my friend!"

Tears hung on the edge of Bran's eyes. But when she heard Delkan's words, she just had to laugh. Delkan laughed with her and shook her shoulders hard.

Bran smiled and began to chant her friend's name along with the crowd.

Zul raised his arms again, motioning for silence. Slowly the bedlam subsided.

"And if Delkan of Fang-Tor province falls in battle, who will take up the spear?" he cried to the crowd.

"I will!" bellowed a deep voice behind them. "No one is taking away my bride and not getting some payment for it!" Garn promised in a loud voice.

Bran looked in surprise at Delkan. She only shrugged and grinned widely.

Zul wound his way over to him and Garn grasped the handle in a firm grip.

"If Delkan falls in battle then Garn-Ithel will take up the fight," Zul declared to the crowd.

"And woe be to any wizard who gets in my way!" Garn shouted in a loud voice.

The surrounding dwarves laughed and took up the chant again, the drumbeats blending in with his name.

Again the Great Dragon nodded and inclined his head in respect toward Garn.

And yet again Zul raised his hands begging for silence. He held up the spear again and intoned once more in a deep voice.

"And if Garn-Ithel shall fall in battle, who then will take up the spear?"

There was silence for a long while.

"I will!" said Dra-Oog and she came forward, her face grave and stern. The flickering firelight from the torches lit her silvery hair and armor with a warm glow.

She took hold of the shaft and declared in a proud voice, "I was friends with Bran's mother. We were as close as twin sisters. I believed Yaffa was really going to kill Savas-Zev and I would watch her back. But that never happened. Savas-Zev robbed my friend of her dream to rid our people of this menace. Since my friend is no longer here, I will take her place. I am Dra-Oog."

There was a long respectful silence.

Delkan started the chant for Dra-Oog. It was echoed by Bran. Then one by one, others picked it up until all the dwarves were thundering her name along with the massive drumbeats.

All those dwarves who had sworn to take up the spear surrounded Bran and linked arms, chanting along with the countless others. The drumbeats added their percussion to the raised voices. Some dwarves stomped their feet and clashed weapon upon shield, adding to the cacophony of sound carried high into the night sky.

Vilmar and Iyorath clapped and shouted with the rest as they watched their dwarven friends begin a frenzied bouncing dance about Bran, paced in time with the chants. They laughed as they chanted and danced.

"Look at them!" Vilmar had to shout to his elven friend. "Anyone would think the battle had already been won!"

Iyorath shook his head and nodded.

"Why did you not volunteer to take up the spear?" Vilmar asked suddenly.

Iyorath shot him a disbelieving look. "This is a dwarf affair," he explained above the bedlam. "The final blow should come from a dwarf, not a human or an elf."

Vilmar nodded in complete understanding.

"Besides," muttered Iyorath more to himself than to anyone else. "I will have plenty to do elsewhere."

His words were drowned out by the clamor of noise about them.

The Great Dragon abruptly spread his wings wide and roared loudly into the night air, silencing every dwarf's voice.

"Enough!" it declared in an authoritative and booming voice. "I have come to witness a great weapon's naming. It is time we get on with it!"

Everyone immediately sat down like obedient children, sternly reprimanded.

"Well, that was a very dwarf-like response," commented Iyorath in a hushed voice.

Vilmar hissed back to him for silence.

Zul took up the spear again and returned to front and center, beside the Great Dragon. He raised the spear on high where all could see, glittering like black water tossed by a midnight wind. He began to chant.

"I ask the gods' blessing on this spear of power. I ask they impart to me the name of this great weapon made to save our people from oblivion. I implore them to be wise in their choice of names. May my petition please the gods and save our people."

He then began to chant in the old tongue, long forgotten by those dwarves now gathered about. His voice started out soft and slow but gradually rose in strength and volume. Over and over he chanted the same words. All could feel the power building and gathering, like storm clouds about to hurl forth their bolts of lightning to stab at the ground from the sky. Vilmar could feel his ears trying to pop.

He suddenly gave a loud shout and the Great Dragon reared his head back and spouted flame over the entire assembly. All the dwarves gathered fell to their faces and covered their heads with their hands.

Then there was silence, a long eerie silence in which each person could hear his own heart beat like thunder in the mountains.

Slowly, fearfully, they all got to their feet and looked about.

The Great Dragon was gone. Zul stood there alone. But his eyes were blazing and Vilmar could see he was wreathed all about in power and magic.

"It is done," Zul said in a quiet but commanding tone of voice. "The name of the spear is, '*Shak-Kur*'."

The dwarves gathered about cheered. The drumbeats and the flutes started up again and everyone began to shout the name in exuberance.

Iyorath glanced at Vilmar and was surprised to see a look of great confusion on the young human's face. His brow was wrinkled as if he had been told a joke he didn't understand.

"Vilmar?" he asked cautiously.

The young wizard turned his whirling eyes to look at him.

"What is 'Shak-Kur' dwarvish for?" he asked.

"It means 'twig'," Vilmar said with a quizzical little smile.

Iyorath began to snort but quickly bit back his response, understanding it would be taken as disrespectful. Vilmar shot a private warning look his way.

Fighting to keep from laughing or even smiling, he replied, "I think we had better call it Shak-Kur, especially when other dwarves are about."

Vilmar nodded quickly and emphatically. His expression told the elf that his opinion of the dwarf name was the same as his own.

He gave a doubtful shake of his head.

"I guess some things are just lost in translation," he murmured quietly.

CHAPTER 45

Savas-Zev poured over his maps of the local land, trying to decide the best area to stage his first strike in the war to come. He was so totally engrossed in his task he didn't even raise his head when the guard at his tent door shouted he had a visitor. He supposed it was one of the scouts or lower-ranking commanders with news. He simply bellowed for them to enter.

There was a slightly muffled, strangled sound and then the guard fell dead, halfway in and halfway out of his tent.

This served to get Savas-Zev's complete and full attention. He straightened up and made to step around his table, quickly readying a protective spell. But he stopped almost immediately in shock.

A thin woman of a particularly striking appearance strode into his tent and stood quietly, letting him examine her with a small, fearless smile. She was tall, almost as tall as the wizard himself but thinner than he would ever be. So thin in fact there existed no flesh or muscle on her slight frame. The outline of every bone appeared starkly through her skin—even her face—and it was possible to see the blue, branching lines which outlined her veins. Her skin was so pale it seemed to take on an ashen hue as of a newly dead corpse. Her hair was long and straight and like her dress, was the color of darkness. Her eyes were set deep into the hollowed-out sockets of her face and they were the most riveting of all. They were all backwards. The pupils were white, like some dead thing and they were surrounded by the same blackness her hair and dress seemed to be fashioned from.

The wizard gasped and a small tickle of fear made his heart skip a beat.

The smile from her blue lips widened a bit. "You know me," she said, surprised only a little. A frigid wind rustled the canvas of the tent as she spoke.

Savas-Zev shivered and nodded. He swallowed with difficulty and suddenly found his throat had gone dry.

"You are... Death," was all he could say.

He had recognized her at first glance. She went by many names. To some she was called 'Lady of the Hourglass' to others it was 'Keeper of the Last Breath' and 'She Who Ever Hungers'. She knew the lifespan of each and every person of every race. She rarely walked outside the realm of dreams and when she did, it did not bode well.

She inclined her head in a small show of respect. She then approached him and her movements were as smooth as a hunting cat, confident of killing its prey.

He trembled but forced himself to remain where he was, rooted to the spot. An icy aura preceded her and caressed his arms with cold fingers.

"You have captured my interest, Savas-Zev," she said quietly. "I have fed well off of your schemes. It seems I am in for another feast quite soon. This is good for I am quite hungry."

She came nearer yet and leaned close, whispering in his ear secretively. He stoically bore the icy needle, which speared his inner ear from her breath.

"I am hungry, Savas-Zev. I am oh so hungry," she whined like a child pleading for a toy. "I am famished as you can well see. I will require many deaths to sate me."

She began to circle him, winding the influence of her voice in a seductive web about him.

"Feed me, Savas-Zev. I am so very hungry," her voice gently cajoled him and she breathed passionately on the back of his neck, raising a trail of goose bumps on his skin.

He felt his thoughts go stupid as if her very words had drugged him. The room seemed to spin as his eyes tried to follow her motions.

"What's for dinner, my love? Dwarf? Elf? Human? Or maybe wizard?" she hissed. "I serve those who feed me."

She breathed her words in a seductive tone.

His mind began to whirl as he latched onto how useful her last sentence could be to him.

Was she promising her assistance with the dwarves? He knew how well she enjoyed the death and mayhem battles would bring, especially if they involved dwarf or elf lives. Her blessing could prove quite advantageous to his designs.

She smiled a crafty smile, already anticipating his thoughts, and licked her lips as if she had just received a brief whiff of the heavenly odors from a busy kitchen.

"Dwarves live far too long anyway. There's no reason anyone should exist so many centuries. It upsets the order of things," she purred to him and her words appeared to make perfect sense. "Unless, of course, their life provides me with as much sustenance as yours has done."

Her previous words echoed through his brain, tantalizing him with the prospect of what might be had. *"I serve those who feed me."*

"You wish to beg a boon from me, I see," she said in a voice barely above a whisper.

He could only nod.

"You intrigue me, wizard," she said in a conspiratorial tone. She quietly breathed on a long-fingered hand and he saw it flush with a normal, rosy color.

"Dare to ask me anything, Savas-Zev," she placated. "You have pleased me so far. Ask. What do you desire of me?"

She stroked his face like a tender lover with a now warm hand. Her touch was intoxicating. She smelled of perfume and romantic promises. He desperately wanted to please her.

"Anything," she pleaded. Her voice promised imagined sensations and pleasures he had long ago discarded for ambition and power. "Ask me anything,"

"The wizard pup in their camp..." he started cautiously.

"Yes," she replied in a sultry tone. Her words wound about him like heady incense slowing the mind. "What of the child?"

"I want him," he replied confidently, vengefully.

She tilted her head and narrowed her eyes suspiciously. "You want him?" she repeated. "You want him how? Please specify, my pet."

He could refuse her nothing.

"I want you to spare his life," Savas-Zev said quickly. "I want him all to myself. I want to decide the time of his demise."

The Lady of Death had chosen to circle him as he said this.

"You wish to toy with him, like a cat with a mouse," she replied stepping behind him, her one warm finger tracing a line across his shoulders. The physical contact with her made a thrill of excitement race through his veins.

He tried his best to follow her with his eyes. But his vision had suddenly gone hazy.

"For this you dare to ask Death Herself to spare a life?" she murmured like the whisper of an approaching flood.

"You will still get him eventually," he hurriedly put in. "He is only human. I do not ask you never kill him, just let me decide when and how he dies."

"You wish to torture this wizard-child?" she hissed.

"Yes!" he returned at once and the eagerness in his voice was obvious.

"Yes..." she repeated in a hiss like cold water on a hot skillet. "Hmm. An interesting boon you beg, wizard," she muttered as she circled back into his vision. But she was still smiling smugly. He took this to be a good sign.

"But in order to spare a life, I will expect a certain payment from you," she said clearly as she circled again behind him.

Before he could think coherently about what he was saying, he burst out. "Anything! Just give me this."

"Anything?" she repeated. She was behind him again and he couldn't see her. His head felt very funny.

"Anything! I'll pay any price you ask. Just give me this one thing."

She had disappeared, dissolved like poison powder in red wine. He turned his head from side to side, his bleary eyes searching for any sign of her.

She was gone.

He sighed, obviously deflated. His head began to clear somewhat.

Suddenly, she was there, scant inches from his face, nearly nose to nose with him.

"I accept your bargain, Savas-Zev. Now you will accept mine," and her voice was no longer seductive but stripped of all tenderness and serious in its intent.

His head cleared a bit more. Too late he began to see the error in this arrangement.

At this very instant, her long fingers clutched onto his face and her lips latched onto his own in a kiss as passionate as it was forceful. He felt his teeth grind roughly together with hers, which were as cold as a glacier. He felt power being sucked from his limbs, life and warmth being drained from his body as her kiss drank it in like a vampire drinks lifeblood. He struggled and tried to wrest her hands away from his face. As he struggled, he saw her true form, saw her wither away to a rotting corpse which drained him, felt her fingers melt to bones and smelled her perfume shift to the stench of rotting flesh, crawling with flies. Was that her tongue in his mouth or only maggots wriggling greedily? He felt the bile of revulsion rise in his throat. He fought harder only to find his limbs no longer obeyed him, for every bit of strength was being sapped from his body. He wilted to his knees like a dried, brown flower, long past its prime beauty, an empty husk of spring's glory at the impending approach of winter.

She released him before the very end, before the last bit of his life had drained away. He gasped and crumpled, helpless to the earth, her laughter ringing in his ears, vibrating through every bone in his body.

"Wait!" he gasped. "What payment? What is this favor's price? Tell me!"

An icy wind blasted his weak form forcing him closer to the pale ground. Her mocking laughter wreathed his shrunken body and teased his pained and chilled ears.

"Payment has already been taken. Poor Savas-Zev!"

Vilmar's sleep was troubled. He dreamed ugly dreams, dreams of death and destruction.

He stood on a pinnacle overlooking a great battle. Black smoke rose thickly into the morning air, staining the sky dark as night. Beneath him he could clearly see the flicker of fires from torches and siege engines. He heard the yells of victory and the screams of pain and despair from the two warring sides. There were dead dwarves and goblins everywhere, even at his very feet. He could smell their last dying fears and the reek of blood and carnage was thick in his nostrils. A great raven sat on the limb of the nearest tree and stared impassively at him.

The raven was the color of blood from beak to tail tip. Even its eyes were red. The red bird turned and looked behind him. Wordlessly he followed the bird's gaze.

Barely a few steps behind him stood a woman. She was tall with long black hair and wore a black dress. The hem of her dress was soaked in blood and so were her hands. She turned to look at him.

Vilmar shuddered, his heart turned to ice and the blood froze in his veins for he recognized her.

She was the same woman he had met in the tunnels of Tor Ambroc before the great dwarf pox had come. He would never forget those chilling, backwards eyes.

But she looked somehow different this time. He peered closer to ascertain what it was. And then he realized how she was different. She was no longer skeletal but fleshed out and well fed. Her eyes did not swim in the hollows of her face; he could not see her collarbones or her shoulder blades through the fabric of her dress or her skin. Her body had the rosiness of health, the curve of muscle and breast as any woman's body should have.

But those eyes were still chilling and backwards.

She smiled kindly at him and it was then he noticed the blood staining her lips and teeth.

She had fed and fed well. She opened her mouth and spoke to him and when she spoke, a cold wind blew the hair back from his face.

"Why are you afraid?" she said. "I have not come for you."

He awoke with a start and found himself bathed in a cold sweat. He looked about and tried to remember the dream, which had bothered him so.

He found, to his shock he did remember it. He remembered the dream about the woman in the battlefield and the one before in Tor Ambroc. No wait! His mind was still racing. The one in the tunnels was not a dream. It had really happened! The battlefield dream had yet to happen.

Yet to happen...

Why had he remembered?

His face drained of all color as his mind connected the dots. He leapt from his cot and left his tent and bolted for the woods. He needed to speak with the unicorns. They could make sense of all this. They would certainly be able to answer his questions with all their sacred knowledge of fate. They could help. The unicorns would know what to do.

He had barely gone a few feet when he tripped and fell over a log around a campsite at the very edge of the forest, nearly landing in the occupant's campfire. Dazed, he shook his head and looked about, blinking.

There was an exclamation behind him.

Vilmar struggled to get to his feet and run away before whoever it was found him. But he was too slow.

A narrow, but strong pair of hands hoisted him to his feet by the back of his tunic and spun him about.

"Ah! The wizard-in-training decided to plop face first into my fire. Now why would he do that? Are hot coals and ashes good for the complexion?"

Vilmar snorted. "Like I spend many hours awake at night, worrying about my face with an impending war on my doorstep."

Iyorath shrugged casually. "Like I can fathom the things a human would obsess over," replied the elf. "Although I have been told most humans gifted with freckles, hate them. I thought maybe you were trying to get rid of them without anyone finding out how superficial you really are."

"Hardly," retorted Vilmar as he brushed himself off. He went to continue on his way and felt his left ankle buckle. Pain shot upwards from his foot.

The elf noticed immediately. "Maybe you better wait a bit before you go galloping off again. That ankle seems to be a bit angry at you for some reason," Iyorath said.

Vilmar shook his head. "I have to get to the unicorns. They can easily fix this," he said insistently.

He took a step gingerly and almost fell down again.

"Yes, but they shouldn't be bothered with every little ache and pain," scolded the elf as he forcefully wrapped Vilmar's arm about his own shoulders and helped him hobble back into his own camp.

"I can also fix it easily although it may take a few days more than a unicorn horn. Now sit," he ordered.

Vilmar painfully obeyed and seated himself on the nearest log. He tried not to wince as the pain from his ankle pounded and throbbed like a drumbeat. His whole foot was beginning to feel hot as it swelled.

Iyorath tossed more wood on the fire and stirred the coals vigorously, encouraging little tongues to leap up and devour it.

The elf returned to Vilmar and gently teased off his boot from the affected limb. It was still agony for Vilmar. Then the elf went and rummaged around in one of his packs and finally produced a wooden box with a strange, aromatic salve which smelled strongly of wintergreen. He smeared this heavily on Vilmar's bare ankle. He then gently took hold of the injured joint and closing his eyes reverently, muttered some words in elvish.

Vilmar felt a sudden flush of icy coldness infuse the joint, stilling the pounding pain in his ankle and soothing the agony at once. Iyorath then took some very large, waxy, dark leaves from his pack, which looked as if they had been freshly picked and wrapped the ankle. He wound a bandage securely around the whole ankle and foot. When he was done he gave the limb a critical eye and nodded.

"Keep it wrapped for three days without changing it and soon you will be good as new," he recommended.

Vilmar was fascinated. "What was it you said?" he asked.

The elf shrugged. "A simple elvish healing prayer. It helps with any wound. And yes, it works just as well on horses," he informed as he put the extra bandages and salve away. "Now leave the hero stuff to the heroes, wizard-pup."

Vilmar again remembered why he had come.

"I still have to get to the unicorns," he started and began to stand. But the elf gave him a warning look and with a frustrated groan Vilmar sank back down again.

"What is so important that you have to bother the unicorns in the dead of night? Do you think they're too magical to need sleep?" he inquired.

"I... I probably shouldn't tell you," he said.

Iyorath raised a feathery, high-arched eyebrow quizzically. "Indeed."

He set a kettle on the fire and brought out a second cup and a tin of dried peppermint. He then resumed drinking from the half-full cup Vilmar had earlier interrupted.

"And just *why* shouldn't you tell me? Some secret unicorn/wizard business?" he asked.

"No," replied Vilmar. "You'll probably think it silly."

Iyorath's slanted eyes narrowed. "Humph!" he snorted like a dwarf. "Try me!"

Vilmar sucked his teeth and chewed a lip for a long moment.

"All right then," he said abruptly as if accepting a dare. "Then try this one on for size. I had a bad dream."

Both feathery eyebrows rose at this. "Well now, young human. There are dreams and then there are dreams," Iyorath replied in a low voice.

Vilmar nodded grimly. "I'm aware of that."

Iyorath bowed his head in return. "And I believe even though you are a very young human, you have already been exposed to a great many things in your young life," the elf posed.

Vilmar nodded again and his look was grim.

"And..." said Iyorath slowly. "Having been exposed to said serious things, you have learned the difference between a mere nightmare and an important message the spirit world is trying to send you."

Vilmar again nodded and smiled grimly. "Exactly!" he replied.

Iyorath drained his cup without taking his keen eyes off the young man. He quietly reached forward and poured another cup of steaming hot water for himself and one for Vilmar. Without speaking a word, he filled the small metal tea strainers and plopped one in each cup.

He handed Vilmar his cup of peppermint tea and said, "Tell me of this nightmare."

So Vilmar began slowly and hesitantly. But then, as the elf listened without interrupting or his face betraying any sign of disbelief, his voice grew in confidence. He told Iyorath about his most recent dream and about the meeting in the tunnels of Tor Ambroc.

"Do you believe me?" he asked finally when he had finished.

Iyorath had finished his cup and was starting on his third. Vilmar's first cup had gone cool, untouched in his hands. Vilmar stared absently into its shadowed depths.

"Of course I believe you, young human," he said in a slow, very quiet voice. "I have had my own meeting with this woman."

"You have?" Vilmar said in surprise. "How? When?"

"Many years before your parents were even born. Would you like to hear the tale?"

Vilmar nodded eagerly.

"It was long ago when I was a young elf and had not yet reconciled myself to the notion that I would never be a wizard. You see both my parents were wizards. So were my twin brother and sister. The night before Savas-Zev killed—or rather imprisoned their spirits far from their bodies—I saw her. She was walking down the corridors of my parents' great house. I saw her and recognized her from a distance as being human and therefore an intruder for we had no human guests at the time. But because she was female and not dressed as an assassin, I chose to shadow her and find out what she was up to. I followed her all the way to my family's sleeping quarters. There she stopped in the hallway. My parents' bedchamber was the door to the right of her and my twin siblings' chamber was the door to her left. She clearly looked at my parents' door first and then my brother and sister's. Then she turned about and faced me as if she had always known I was there, following her. She looked as you have already described, clothed in a black dress, with long black hair, a skeletal body, and frightening, reversed eyes. She looked at me and laughed and a cold wind blew down the hallway toward me when she did so. She said she had not come for me—yet. And then she disappeared like smoke blown away on the wind. It was the word 'yet' which chilled me through and through. I fled like a child who had stayed up all night hearing ghost stories. I fled like a coward. The next night, Savas-Zev took my family away from me forever."

They were both quiet for a very long moment.

"Like your one time, I did not dream her. I encountered her so I know she is real," the elf informed him gravely.

Vilmar stared absently into the coals of the fire, his tea forgotten.

"Iyorath, who is she?" he finally dared to ask.

"She is the Lady Death. To dream or meet her is not a good sign," the elf said in a soft voice.

"What does it mean that she has appeared to me twice?" Vilmar asked.

"I do not know," Iyorath replied with a confused shake of his head. "But it seems the gods themselves are betting on the outcome of this battle. That is never a good thing."

CHAPTER 46

"The time draws near. Soon, very soon, I will leave this earth," the unicorn doe said quietly as if to no one.

"Do your mate and fawn know?" Daga asked her.

"My child has known since the day he was born. He has always known he would be the last of my children. He is fine with it. He knows and this is as it should be," she replied.

"And... your mate?" Daga continued.

The unicorn doe sighed and hung her head.

"It will be harder on him. It is always harder on the lovers, especially when one chooses a mate so much younger than oneself. So far, he has gotten along by telling himself this was far in the future, so far he need not worry about it."

"Well, the future has now arrived. He is on the threshold of the end of your time together," Daga said.

"I know. And he also knows," she replied.

They were silent for a long moment.

"Have you told Vilmar yet?" Daga said.

The unicorn was quiet for a long moment, mulling over her answer.

"No, and I don't think I will. He already has enough on his plate. And things will start to go very fast soon. It may be easier for him if he has no time to think about it until it happens. He already suspects I'm leaving. I've hinted it to him."

"Yes, but he also believes it's far off and will happen peacefully. He has no idea of this new road you are planning to take. The violence of it will shock him," Daga said.

The unicorn sighed heavily.

"There is no hope for it, I'm afraid," she replied. *"Mistress Death has stepped all things up a notch and now my feet are being forced to*

take a path I had hoped I could avoid. It would have been much easier had She not interfered. Deities are not supposed to do that. The balance is all skewed now."

"Requiring you to reciprocate in kind," Daga grumbled.

The unicorn nodded her pearly head.

"She has robbed me of my peaceful end. Now a great sacrifice is required to set the balance. I will not easily forgive Her this," and she stamped a delicate white leg angrily.

"Do you think She is doing this to get you?" Daga posed.

The unicorn narrowed her eyes, thinking deeply on this for a moment before she finally shook her snowy mane in denial.

"No. Death eats lives, not souls. She may chew on the rind of the soul but She has never tasted one," the unicorn informed.

"But maybe that is what She wants—to taste a soul. And what better than a unicorn soul? Like elves, unicorns normally pass on, they do not die. So She has never had one within Her grasp before," Daga asked her.

"She cannot touch me," the doe said confidently. "Unicorn souls are forbidden."

"That may be but don't think the thought hasn't occurred to Her," Daga said, worry etching his normally jovial face.

"If this is Her plan then She has undone Herself. She has allowed Herself to become greedy. So greedy others can see it. I can deal with this most easily, I assure you. Matters will be set right. I promise you, Daga," she stomped her other foreleg for emphasis.

"Oh, I believe you all right," Daga assured. "I just worry for you, that's all. Things will be very touch and go here in the next few days."

The unicorn's eyes softened and she stepped close to him. "Then thank you for worrying," she said and tenderly licked his forehead like a young fawn.

Daga grumbled but endured the contact, understanding where it came from. "Just take care, will you?" he fussed at her.

"Always," she replied "I am always most careful when nudging Fate."

Daga grunted in reply. "That's good 'cause we all know Fate can have big, sharp pointy teeth!"

CHAPTER 47

Savas-Zev was not feeling too well. Ever since the Starving Lady had visited him, he had felt weak and shaky as if he were only half alive. He avoided taking to his bed for as long as he could. But soon he realized he could no longer fight it. He barked orders and shouted insults at his underlings from a portable cot in his massive tent. He tried different brews and concoctions but nothing seemed to help. Even rest did not assist him in regaining his strength.

To make matters worse, he was brooding over the incredibly bad timing of this strange malady. Death, it seemed, had left him with barely enough strength to live, let alone command and influence the outcome of a major battle. This did not assist his healing or improve his mood in the least.

On the third day out from his meeting with Death, his guards told him of a peculiar goblin who was begging to be seen by him. He could tell, although his guards feared his wrath, they also dreaded the constant badgering by this little individual. He finally agreed to give an audience to this pest and relieve his guards of some of their harassment.

He was consumed by a fit of coughing when they ushered a little green goblin into his sanctuary. Savas-Zev struggled to control his voice and regain some composure before the goblin.

Instantly, the little fellow was at his side, offering liquid from a tiny flask secured to his belt. "Drink this, Master. It will control the fits for a little while," the creature said to him.

Savas-Zev glared at him as if the goblin were offering him poison. But the goblin persisted, seeming unaffected by his threatening stare.

Finally, he gave in and snatched the bottle away from him. He unstoppered the flask and wiped the mouthpiece thoroughly with his sleeve, grimacing in distaste at the thought of the last lips upon it. He sipped the dubious liquid experimentally. It tasted strongly of licorice.

"That will fix your throat and voice long enough for us to have a conversation, hopefully a very beneficial conversation," the little green imp said confidently.

It did soothe his throat and calm his coughs immediately. But Savas-Zev still eyed the bottle as if there were ingredients in it which were meant for more than just a cough and a sore throat.

He handed it warily back to the little green goblin without any thanks other than a curt nod.

"Who are you?" he demanded gruffly.

The goblin hopped upon the nearest chair and sat there with its legs curled underneath it on the seat, like a toad ready to spring.

"They call me 'the Frog', or Froggie if you like. Froggie will do," he introduced briefly. "I collect things."

Savas-Zev's eyes narrowed suspiciously.

"What sort of things?" he inquired.

"Oh, all sorts and kinds of things," he informed a bit too eagerly, bouncing a little as he perched rather than sat on the chair. "Pretty rings and things. Magical and non-magical jewels and chains. Decorated daggers. Things like that."

"So, you're a thief and a pick-pocket," Savas-Zev said with a wry smile.

Froggie shrugged as if the terminology meant nothing to him.

"Call it what you like," he returned. "Makes no never mind to me."

He began to examine his long fingernails as if they might get dirty in the space of time it took them to talk.

"I also collect... information." He said this last word with special relish and slyly looked up at the wizard over his fingernails. "I collect such things and store them in a safe place until I come across some situation which might make them useful. Then I bring them out," he explained.

Savas-Zev's smile increased. "So you're a spy as well, eh?" he muttered.

The little goblin named Froggie simply shrugged and grinned back at him. He then scratched his balding head and scrunched up his face in thought. "Now I've heard a few things here and there you might not know about."

Savas-Zev frowned darkly. "What kind of things?" he asked guardedly.

The goblin then scratched his beardless chin and settled himself a bit more comfortably.

"Well now, I hear tell you're gonna be fightin' a big war here soon. That's all well and good and my folk are always happy to oblige anyone with assistance in mayhem and murder. And there's no love lost between goblins and dwarves. The loot, too, should be quite good in this case—always a bonus with goblins if you take my meaning," the little goblin prattled on.

Savas-Zev gave a long, impatient sigh. "Get on with it, Toadstool!" he grumbled. He was in no mood for lengthy gossip.

Froggie blinked twice at the blatant mistake in his name but spoke not a word about it.

"Now every goblin enjoys a good fight. But, of course, you would know that! However, there seems to be a rumor going about that their chances of winning this war do not seem very high with you being on your sickbed. No troops wanna fight a battle they know they will lose. It's just plain bad for morale and a prime recipe for desertion, if you take my meaning."

"So far, Mr. Frog, you have told me nothing useful. I know I'm sick! I know the timing is rotten and I also know I don't seem to be getting better anytime soon. Do you really have anything good to say?"

"Patience, Lord! I am coming to the all important point," Froggie teased and then fell silent. He peered closely at Savas-Zev, wincing so all of his yellow teeth showed. He began tapping them with one long nail as he considered his next words.

"You know what you need? You need a unicorn horn! Yes, siree! A unicorn horn would have you fixed and as good as new, perhaps even stronger! Of course it would be even better if the horn was still attached to a live unicorn! Yes, this would be even better, my great Lord," he cackled as he said this.

The wizard gave a loud, derisive snort and rolled his eyes. "Of course I know that!" he fumed, completely exasperated. "Every wizard worth his wand knows that! But I don't exactly have the time left to me to go scouring the land to find one unicorn willing to give up the power of its horn."

As he spoke, Froggie's eyes narrowed and his smile widened until it threatened to wrap completely around his head. He laced his long fingers together and waited. He seemed quite willing to wait patiently until the wizard was through his tirade to speak.

All at once the warning bells went off in the wizard's head. "Wait," the wizard said suddenly. "What do you know?"

Froggie's smile now included all of his yellow, sharply pointed teeth.

"What if I were to tell you, my Lord, I know of not one unicorn, not two, but of *three* unicorns living quite close by?" Froggie almost whispered to the wizard.

There was a long, deafening silence.

"Where?" Savas-Zev could only mouth the word.

Froggie smiled wryly and nodded his head in a certain direction. "In the dwarf encampment. There's a whole family unit helping them. I know. I've seen them," he murmured slyly to the wizard and began to rock back and forth on his perch.

The world began to spin suddenly about Savas-Zev. His hands shook uncontrollably and he went pale in an instant.

It all now made sense. The magical aura he felt on their young wizard, the voice in his scrying bowl, all the fuzzy corners of the puzzle, which never fit before, now suddenly fell into place.

Three unicorns were helping the dwarves.

"Now what would such information be worth to you, my Lord?" asked Froggie.

Savas-Zev's eyes went back to the little goblin and they gleamed with renewed brightness and determination. He spoke in a low voice to the goblin, his voice now full of politeness. "Would it please you to bring me back a unicorn?" he asked.

The little goblin only grinned wider in answer. "Alive or dead?" the little green imp requested.

"Well, with unicorn power, alive is always better. Temporarily at least," Savas-Zev suggested craftily.

"Of course, my Lord!" replied Froggie. He then leaned forward, closer to the wizard.

"Do you want me to capture just one or all three?"

Savas-Zev leaned back comfortably into his cushions and his eyes narrowed in malice.

"Well, one is good. Three is even better. Why don't you surprise me, Froggie, and then we'll discuss a hefty payment which might suit you?" he offered.

Froggie grinned maliciously back and hopped off the chair. "Consider it already done, my Lord!" he assured and bowing low with a great flourish, he rushed out of the tent to do the master's bidding.

"Hmmm," Savas-Zev murmured quietly to himself. "This predicament might not be so bad after all."

Iyorath Asra sat alone in the darkness just outside the vast encampment of dwarves. His back was to a tree and he sat as still as a silent sentry. But he was not on guard duty.

His mind was a million miles away as he gazed at the flickering fires from a thousand torches and campfires.

"What did you think of the dwarves' ritual?" spoke a voice in his head.

So unexpected was it, he half jumped and half rose with his hand on his dagger. He spun about to look behind him.

The unicorn stag stood behind him, glowing like the moon on a shadowed night.

"I'm sorry. I did not mean to frighten you," spoke the stag in his head.

He shrugged and sat down again.

"But what did you think of the ritual? I am really curious to hear your thoughts," the unicorn repeated.

"I found it very abrupt and loud, just like the dwarves themselves. They don't mince words or time. They get right to the point of things as if they had the lifespan of a human."

"Some do," replied the unicorn. *"They live such a war-like existence that some live less time than most humans. They have learned to say what needs to be said because there may not be a next time."*

Iyorath nodded, mumbling his agreement.

The unicorn cocked his head slightly, like a curious dog, considering the elf. *"How many years have you spent with these people who are not your own?"* the magical creature asked.

Iyorath stopped and blew explosively at the thought. "I'm not sure, really. I haven't had time to think about it. Several years, I guess. The years pass so quickly to me," he said after a time.

The unicorn cocked his head in the other direction, still considering. *"Do you miss your people?"* the stag asked.

"I have no family. Remember?" Iyorath said and his tone was flat of all emotion.

"I asked about your people, the elves, not your family."

There was a long silence from the elf. The unicorn stag waited patiently. "I have no purpose with my people. Here I am needed..."

"And wanted?" the unicorn finished for him.

His silver-gray eyes met the unicorn's midnight blue orbs. "My own people didn't know what to do with me. Here, at least, I'm useful," he replied in the same flat tone, careful to keep from feeling the pain which lay just underneath the words.

"Still, it must be hard being so far from your own people, surrounded by a race with a different language and ways."

Iyorath said nothing for a long moment. He finally gave a deep sigh.

"If I die in battle tomorrow, at least there will be no one here to mourn me. And I will have died with enough honor to be well thought of," he said in a voice filled with self-loathing.

The unicorn tossed his head and snorted. The pearly mane floated about his shoulders and neck like wind-tossed snow. *"You can't possibly believe that,"* the stag replied.

Iyorath gave the unicorn an angry glance. "Why not?" he demanded. "I can believe what I want to here."

"Your friends may be a motley assortment of races but they have become your family, Iyorath. If you were to die, they would most certainly mourn you. They think you worth the tears. Accept it," the unicorn said, stomping a cloven hoof for emphasis.

The stag looked Iyorath narrowly in the eyes until the elf could bear it no longer and turned away. *"You're plotting something,"* said the stag suddenly.

Iyorath grumbled inaudibly and turned his back on the unicorn. But the stag persisted and circled around to stare him in the eye again.

"You're planning to throw your life away in a heroic act, aren't you?" it demanded of him.

"You know nothing!" Iyorath told him forcefully.

"Careful, elf," the stag teased. *"You're forgetting your perfect elven manners to never argue with an immortal."*

The unicorn met his stare and Iyorath found he could not tear his eyes away. He felt the blessed beast invade his mind and rummage about in his most recent thoughts.

"I see countless crystal globes and broken glass in your mind. I see streaming stars and screaming souls in your thoughts. I KNOW what you are going to do. You cannot hide it from me."

"Fine then," spat the elf at him and getting up, he stalked away. "You still can't stop me from doing it!"

But the stag trotted past and stood in front of him, blocking his passage.

"I have no intention of stopping you for it is a noble act which needs to be done," the stag told him. *"But I will NOT let you throw your life away on it. That's why I'm coming along to help you."*

Iyorath stared into the stag's ghostly white face in front of him.

"I will NOT let you kill yourself in this," the stag repeated. *"I will protect you and get you there undetected. It will be safer this way."*

Iyorath managed to blink a few times in disbelief. "But to do it you'd have to... disgrace yourself," he said in horror.

"The practice of I'Olana is a blessing not a disgrace," the stag corrected. *"There is no dishonor in having you ride me. But I know this is what elves believe. My hooves can get us there faster than your feet."*

Iyorath had no idea what to say. He opened his mouth a few times like a fish out of water, but nothing came out.

"Will you accept the assistance of an immortal in this venture?" the stag asked.

Iyorath Asra could only nod helplessly. He could refuse a unicorn nothing.

Vilmar sat quietly in Bran's campsite and watched her rummage about in a small wooden box for the supplies she would need to adorn his hair and beard like a dwarf. He had a large scrap of cloth thrown around his shoulders. Neither spoke much to the other. Bustling dwarf campsites surrounded them and yet they were completely apart and private, each in their own little world in their minds.

Garn and Delkan sat with some other dwarves at a neighboring campsite and were quietly observing the proceedings. One of the other dwarves puffed on his pipe and frowned at the goings on next door.

"Why is she doing that to a human?" he griped sullenly. "What's she trying to do, turn him into a dwarf warrior?"

"Leave them alone," barked Garn at the other. "He's the only human I've ever met deserving of such treatment. Let them be."

The other dwarf continued to grumble but in a lower voice. "The only ones who deserve that kinda treatment are heroes," he groused.

Delkan turned her eyes back to the two figures. "But Vilmar is a hero," she said in a reverently hushed voice. "They both are."

Back at Bran's camp, she had found the tools she needed and was quietly brushing the back of Vilmar's head.

"I never thought I would be contemplating death so soon in my life," he spoke quietly.

"Nor I," agreed Bran. "We're both just pups of our kind. When did our lives get so grim?"

Vilmar smiled and had to remember not to shake his head. "Remember when we dreamed about such things because they were exciting and adventurous?" he asked her.

Bran smiled in reply. "Oh, I remember quite well. It was only a few months ago. Life has gotten very adult all of a sudden."

She stopped brushing to reminisce. "I still would like to go on a grand adventure. Just not one like this where the fate of the whole world rests on my shoulders," she said.

Vilmar nodded.

"Don't do that!" she scolded and cuffed the back of his head. "Not when I'm just starting the braid."

Vilmar remembered to hold still. "You know, I don't think I want to go on if everyone around me dies," he said seriously.

He felt Bran's forge-calloused hands work deftly at tying off a braid.

"It is a distinct possibility," she replied. "But at least you've got some of your family still alive."

Vilmar's face screwed up in confusion. "I do?" he asked not comprehending. "Who?"

"Dwyn. We both saw her before you torched all those goblins," Bran replied as she came around to his front to work on brushing and trimming his beard.

Vilmar's face went dark and he shook his head dismally. "No. She's gone."

The shocked look in Bran's eyes prodded him to go on. "I went back later when my head had cleared and tried to look for her. I even tried to track her. She was gone. I don't know what happened to her. She could be alive or dead. I just don't know."

Bran was silent for a while, her eyes worried and sympathetic. "I'm sorry. Truly I am."

Vilmar nodded sadly. "She would have liked to see me become a hero. She was always like that, very romantic, a dreamer. Maybe, if we make it through this, I'll try to look for her again."

Bran smiled and nodded.

"And I'll help you every step of the way," she said smiling. "One needs to have their family about them."

Vilmar suddenly thought of something. "What about your family?"

"You know about my family," she replied her eyes becoming suddenly shadowed.

"I know you lost your parents. But what about further back? Did you have any brothers or sisters?" he inquired a bit too eagerly.

Bran turned her face away as she searched for more leather string to tie off the braids.

"I'm the last of five children," she informed in a flat voice. "I have three older brothers and one sister. They did not show up when the messenger hounds were sent out for this muster. I looked but I did not see any of them. They too must be dead, fallen prey to one of Savas-Zev's plots. But I don't know for certain."

Vilmar's face fell. He was silent for a long while. "I guess we both are truly alone in this."

She nodded and busied herself with his beard. "I guess."

There was silence again between them. There was no sound but the intermittent cracks and pops from the fire and the distant sound of other campsites around them.

Bran moved the lantern so she could see his face better.

"I don't want to survive this if you don't make it," Vilmar said suddenly.

Bran's eyes locked on his whirling marbled orbs instead of the chore of her hands before her.

At once Vilmar regretted saying anything. He blushed and hung his head.

"I... mean," he stammered, attempting desperately to take his foot out of the hole he had just stepped into. "You and I were there at the beginning, when we were just kids dreaming about adventure and this war was a long way off. If I lose you... there will be nothing left of my past. And I will have lost my best friend."

Bran looked deeply into his face. "I can die fast tomorrow or slowly as one by one all the dwarves I know and love are killed or poisoned by Savas-Zev and his schemes. Or I may not die at all. This must be done. The question of Savas-Zev must be answered before a lot of dwarves go on with their lives," she said.

Vilmar nodded still looking at the ground.

Bran took his chin and tilted it upwards to work on his mustache. Her eyes were shielded. He could not read the thoughts on her face.

"I just wanted you to know how I felt, that's all," he said lamely.

A hint of a smile teased the corners of her mouth. "Oh, I know quite well how you feel," she said, smiling only a little. "I also know how I feel about you."

Vilmar's eyes locked on her own. Bran's emerald green ones were shielded no more. He saw a genuinely private affection spark for one moment and then disappear, replaced by her normal stoic dwarvish personality. She smiled quietly at him and her thumb gently caressed his cheek. He took hold of her wrist and squeezed gently. His multicolored eyes misted over slightly. He smiled back.

There was no longer any need for words between them.

Savas-Zev staggered shakily out of his tent, his weight braced heavily on a tall staff. He felt frail and breakable, like an old man who had lived a thousand years. He snickered briefly at the irony of the thought. He *was* almost a thousand years old. He had managed to cheat Death so many times. He no longer felt quite so lucky.

His goblin minions were bustling about him, making ready for battle. Whenever his eyes touched one, the individual goblin worked a little faster, not caring to be singled out for abuse.

But the wizard had also noted the larger and stronger goblins failed to flee from his presence like the others. They sensed their esteemed leader had quickly grown frail and weak. They no longer found his presence quite so threatening.

He knew the signs of discontent all too well. It was high time to rectify it and put himself back on the pedestal where he belonged if they were truly going to follow his lead and fight this war for him.

"Froggie!" he bellowed, catching sight of the diminutive little figure scuttling away just out of the corner of his eye. The goblin jumped in fright and scuttled a little faster.

"Where is that blasted live unicorn you promised me days ago? We go to battle today. I need the horn now!" he shouted.

Like an unwilling dog on a leash, Froggie crept dejectedly up to the master wizard, cowering all the way. He groveled in the dust at Savas-Zev's feet and stammered something inaudible.

But it was then one of the larger goblins came up to the wizard's elbow and declared in a voice loud enough for all to hear, "My Lord, it comes to you now."

The goblin gestured with a muscular arm to the dirt trail which led to the wizard's tent.

Savas-Zev's heart leapt with hope. He straightened and peered eagerly downhill. A crowd of goblins had gathered and were gesticulating and talking loudly as they slowly made their way uphill. A glimpse of pristine white could be seen every now and then, contrasting sharply against the motley assortment of goblin figures.

Savas-Zev smiled and licked his lips hungrily, too eager to wait.

"Who caught the unicorn?" he inquired of the fellow at his shoulder.

"No one, Lord," replied the goblin. "It brings itself."

Savas-Zev stared at him in surprise but the goblin's expression remained impassive. The green-skinned creature merely shrugged and turned away.

The unicorn could easily be seen now as it advanced up the hill. The small crowd about it had swelled to a huge throng of loud, boisterous goblin kind. They stabbed threateningly at the unicorn with their crude weapons without really injuring it. But the gestures only served to annoy the creature.

It stopped and remained still a moment, glaring about at the goblins surrounding it with pinned ears, snaked neck and a hateful look. It then suddenly reared up and kicked out with a bellow like an ox. One goblin fell dead of a caved-in skull. The creature then plunged forward and, grabbing another goblin in its teeth, shook him savagely until they all heard its neck pop. The second goblin fell in a broken heap. It glared about again, warning them away with its expression.

Savas-Zev literally began to salivate. He could feel the unicorn's power even from this distance. It was intoxicating! Unicorns were similar to dragons when it came to power, the older the creature the stronger the magic. This unicorn was still about three hundred yards away and he could feel her power advancing ahead of her like a great tidal wave. The closer she came, the stronger he felt. She must be ancient! Maybe she was one of the first. His body began to tremble at the thought of absorbing all that power. He licked his lips again, hungrily.

The unicorn's deep blue eyes locked onto his own. She regarded him, silent and still for a long moment. Her expression was of a warrior about to go to battle, steadfast and resolute, not really caring of the eventual outcome. Then, slowly and purposefully, she marched up the hill and closed the distance between them.

"Savas-Zev, I presume?" she asked.

He nodded once.

"If you want my power..." she said slowly, defiantly, as if it were a dare, *"...you may have it."*

She bent one delicate leg and bowed low to him, tucking her small, beardless chin up to her pearly neck and gently touched the earth with the spiraling tip of her long lance. Her mane spilled about her neck like a frothy waterfall and her tail pooled on the ground behind her like spilled milk. She remained there, silent and still except for a slight trembling of her snowy flanks.

Savas-Zev could hardly believe his good luck.

"Someone get me a sword!" he demanded, his malicious intent plain for all to see.

The goblins surrounding him scattered like roaches to do his bidding.

CHAPTER 48

"Why are we even doing this?" Delkan complained as she sat on the rocking back of her Dahla horse. Sashay would not stand but paced in place, which was as still as he would ever be. The magic horse tossed his head and shook his cream mane in eagerness.

"We parlay because it is the right thing to do," insisted Dra-Oog resolutely. "We are not thieves in the night. We announce our intention like civilized people. Peace can still be brokered even at this late hour."

Bran sniffed grimly and growled, "The only peace I will accept will be Savas-Zev's head on a pike!" She sat cold and still on Valynt and her Dahla horse mirrored her demeanor.

"Everyone wants that. Some more than others," Garn muttered. His pony Blueberry swished his tail at an imaginary fly.

"I think it's safe to say the last thing any of us want is peace with that accursed wizard," admitted Iyorath. "But protocols must be followed."

"Hush, all of you!" Dra-Oog scolded. "The delegation arrives."

A small contingent of large orcs led by a hunched human figure on a tired horse approached. The human wore a long cape with a deep cowl hiding any of his facial features.

Bran sat up a little straighter in eagerness. She wanted to look into Savas-Zev's eyes just once to convince him she hadn't died. She had survived his torment and was alive and well. She wanted him to know this. And then she wanted to bury the spearhead deep within his gut. She felt Val pick up on this feeling and the Dahla horse trembled in anticipation underneath her.

Garn risked a quick glance to their rear. Behind and below the hill stretched their army. It was a vast gathering of men, a few elf tribes and thousands of dwarves from all the surviving Tors which remained. The

Golden Warriors were directly behind them, row upon gleaming row of armored cavalrymen and women ready to fight and die if necessary.

"It would be a shame for us to get all kitted up for nothin'," Garn muttered almost to himself. Delkan smiled wryly and nodded in complete agreement.

The figure on the tired horse halted in front of them. Bran leaned forward, unable to stop herself and peered keenly into the black recesses of the hood.

For a long moment the hooded figure on the horse did and said nothing. Then it seemed to straighten painfully and reached its hands up to the hood. They all noticed then the man's hands were striped thickly in dirty bandages, even the fingers. Burnt flesh peeped out from between the strips of cloth. The hood was slowly shoved back and they found they faced a man who was swaddled head to toe in bandages. His face was fully covered by a black mask. The skin which peeped out from around his eyes seemed burnt as well and if any were unsure of his malady, the wind then changed and the breeze brought with it the foul odor of singed flesh and smelly salve over top of putrid infection.

The horses snorted and stirred uneasily.

The masked figure on the horse sighed heavily as if the slightest movement was a sheer agony he had come to endure.

"What is you purpose here?" it said in a voice loud but muffled by the mask.

Dra-Oog spoke as she seemed to be the only one unaffected by the man's tortured appearance.

"We come to parlay with Savas-Zev," she replied. "Not his emissary. Where is he?"

The figure took a deep and painful breath.

"Master Savas-Zev is currently indisposed. You will treat with me instead. This is the way it must be," the figure said.

Dra-Oog seemed rattled by this admission but only for a moment. She recovered quickly. "There is no need to waste lives on either side. If some sort of peace treaty can be... arranged... then we can all live."

The figure laughed and turned his tired horse sideways.

"Savas-Zev wants no peace. He wants all of you to die, especially every last stinking dwarf. Please commence your glorious battle," he said and turning about, started to leave.

"Wait!" called out Iyorath and he urged his horse forward a few steps.

The hunched figure paused and looked at him.

"You're hurt," he began hesitantly. "We could help you. We've got healers. Please let us help..."

The figure was silent for a long moment. Then he gave a short explosive laugh, which died almost before it had begun.

"I am beyond all redemption. Death is my great healer and I pray She comes soon. I am weary of this world and all its empty promises and lies. It is too late for me."

The figure paused a moment more and then inclined his head back to those gathered.

"You want to stop this war? Give Savas-Zev the magical apprentice who has caused him so much grief. Then none of you need die. Give him the fledgling wizard and you all can go home. Do not, and you all will die this very day. This is his wish."

The figure turned away and headed back down the hill, orcs following behind him.

"Well, that was certainly useless and uncalled for!" Garn snorted to all gathered.

"What do you mean uncalled for?" asked Delkan.

"I don't stink!" he explained. "At least not as bad as the wizard. I just had a barrel bath last week!"

Vilmar started as Iyorath stepped without warning into his tent.

"What do you want?" he growled as he partially turned his attention back to the tome which lay open in front of him.

The elf regarded the young human for a moment. He was pouring over Savas-Zev's grimoire. His young face was furrowed in concentration. He was agitated. This seemed strange to the elf. A person reading a book is normally calm and relaxed, not agitated.

"You are unsettled," he observed aloud. "What is it?"

Vilmar sighed and reclined his spine into the back of his chair. He rubbed his face with both hands.

"This damned accursed book!" he growled in frustration. "I've been pouring over this thing as much as possible trying to find some clue, some reason, some source of Savas-Zev's power. Something, a*nything* which will help us."

He sighed and closed his eyes. He inclined his neck backwards in great fatigue.

"And?" Iyorath prodded.

Vilmar opened his eyes and threw up his hands in a gesture of futility.

"Nothing!" he fumed. "I've found nothing but spells of destruction and black magic, how to turn hateful thoughts into vengeful deeds with extra power. Nothing that can help us right now."

He cast his gaze out of the door of his tent. Battle had been joined. The air was full of the cries of warfare. The dwarf drummers hammered battle plans to different contingents on their great kettledrums. The air was full of smoke and they both could smell blood from the wounded and dying masses.

"We're running out of time," Vilmar said so quietly only an elf could hear.

Vilmar turned back to Iyorath and repeated again in a much more polite tone of voice, "What did you want?"

Iyorath only shook his head. "You have already answered my question. I wanted to know if you had discovered anything new which might be helpful."

Vilmar shrugged uselessly. "How is Bran doing?"

"She frets," Iyorath told him with a wry smile. "Her people are fighting and she wants to be in among them. She doesn't understand why she is sitting here doing nothing while the rest of her countrymen are dying."

Vilmar smiled and shook his head. "Did you explain we can't risk her being taken out by a lucky shot from them? We need her fresh and strong for when the final blow is delivered."

Iyorath snickered and rolled his eyes in frustration. "Have you ever tried explaining anything to a fidgety dwarf with battle lust in her heart? Might as well scream at the mountains to get out of your way. It won't do any good."

Iyorath fell silent and became suddenly withdrawn. After a time he said, "I also came to say goodbye."

Vilmar was startled for only a moment. "What... Where are you going?"

Iyorath nodded his head behind him to the battle beyond the tent. "Out there. To meet my destiny."

Vilmar shot to his feet and came at once to his side. "But... I thought you were going to sit out this fight."

Iyorath sniffed. "No. Never! I'm just not going to be in pitched battle, that's all."

Vilmar's expression told him he did not understand.

"Subterfuge!" the elf declared lightly and then his tone and expression became grim. "Bran said Savas-Zev had soul cages, lots more soul cages. Those spirits need to be freed. If I can't be a wizard, then I want to free the souls he's kept trapped for so many countless generations. That's my part in this war."

He paused. "Of course there's no guarantee I will return from this venture. Just like anybody else, I guess. So I thought I should come and say goodbye. Just in case..." He couldn't finish the sentence.

The next thing the elf knew he was being crushed in a bear hug from Vilmar. He hesitated one moment only and then returned the hug.

"Promise me one thing," Iyorath said as he pushed the human back to look him in the eyes.

"Anything," Vilmar said.

"Stick close to Bran. Not just during this battle... but after. Especially if you both survive. Bran needs you, Vilmar, and you need her. You're good together."

Vilmar smiled. "Next time make me promise something more difficult," he laughed.

Iyorath took hold of Vilmar's face and closed his eyes, pressing his forehead to the green wizard's and whispered something in elvish. He then let go and stepped back with a peaceful smile on his pale face.

"What was that?" asked Vilmar.

Iyorath shrugged as if suddenly embarrassed. "A sacred blessing. It says something about protecting my brother of heart not blood when we are apart and in danger. Good luck."

Vilmar nodded. "You too. And I will see you again."

Iyorath managed to muster a quick smile. "I sincerely hope so, my friend."

Then, without another word, he turned away and left the tent.

Vilmar sighed sadly. He stood in silence for a long moment. The sounds of the battle outside were distant to his mind as his thoughts spun miles and years away.

And then a completely unrelated notion flitted through Vilmar's brain. His brow furrowed in confusion. He went at once back to Savas-

Zev's grimoire and turning the page, his eyes attacked the words before him with newfound vigor. His finger stopped on a certain passage. He read it over and over, making sure he understood the words clearly.

"By the Great Dragon," he whispered in horror to himself. "That's his source. He's a leech!"

CHAPTER 49

"I will get you unseen to the wizard's lair and stand guard outside," the unicorn stag told Iyoarth. *"But afterwards the rest is up to you."*

The elf nodded as he strapped on the belt with his short sword. "I suppose it's safe to assume the soul cages will not be left unguarded this time?" As he said this, he slid a small dagger into his boot.

The stag shook his head setting his white mane to dancing. *"Anything is possible with Savas-Zev."*

Iyorath shrugged his head into a lightweight elven helm. Next he strapped a belt across his chest lined with small but lethal throwing knives. "Why isn't your mate helping me with this? Why you? You've a youngling to protect."

He said this while fussing with the buckle on his chest. But it took the unicorn so long to respond, he finally looked up.

The stag was perched on a rocky outcrop facing the battle with his rear to the elf. When he finally did reply, it was the softest whisper in his brain. *"Her duties lie elsewhere."*

Iyorath shrugged and supposed it meant she was helping Vilmar. He turned to face the unicorn stag. "I'm ready. I'Olana?"

The stag turned and faced him, nodding his milky head. *"I'Olana,"* the stag repeated and there was a fierce light in his deep blue eyes.

Iyorath took a deep sigh and muttered a prayer. He then bowed respectfully to the unicorn before throwing a leg over the moon white sides and taking hold of a handful of silky mane. The unicorn reared with a loud bellow, flinging its battle cry to the wind. The minute its cloven hooves touched the earth they were off in a smooth gallop.

The unicorn stag aimed its charge down the rocky incline toward the battle below.

Iyorath clung to its smooth back as tightly as he was able. The white mane stung his face in the wind of their speed as its delicate but powerful legs churned the ground beneath them and yet never left a mark. Faster the magical beast ran and faster, until Iyorath was certain no mere flesh and blood horse could have caught them. The scenery about them began to blur and the unicorn glowed with magic. Iyorath felt suddenly sick to his stomach from the speed.

The stag noticed. *"Close your eyes,"* it instructed him. *"This is why two-legs do not ride us—not because it shames or diminishes us but because our true speed sickens your kind. Close your eyes. I will tell you when we reach the wizard's lair. Trust me."*

Iyorath did as he was bid and closed his eyes. He could hear they had entered the field of battle. The sound of fighting was all about them, the clash of metal on shield, the cry of anguish as soldiers were hit, the roar as others rallied their comrades to try again. He could smell the blood-soaked mud beneath their feet. He could smell the sweat and tears of those around them.

He worried suddenly the unicorn would run them straight into a stray arrow.

"Do not be afraid," the stag consoled, picking up on his thoughts. *"As long as I glow, we are invisible to their weapons and those around us. An arrow or a spear could pass right through and never harm either of us. We are only partially here. The rest of our being is on the plane of the magical beasts. They cannot harm us. Do not open your eyes."*

Iyorath squeezed his eyes shut all the more and clung to this ghost creature he had strangely become one with. Iyorath realized he could feel everything the unicorn felt. His senses were sharper. If he looked with his inward eye using the unicorn's vision not his own, he was not sick. Galloping at this speed wasn't really running to the unicorn. It was breathing normally and its heart beat at resting speed. It was more like projecting a magical bubble around oneself instead of actual movement and then adding direction to the bubble with a brief puff of breath.

He borrowed the unicorn's vision and looked about him with his inward eye. They ran through the thick of the fight, passing like an unseen ghostly phantom. He could feel the straining bodies of both sides, smell their sweat and their blood, feel their physical and mental anguish as they were cut down before the cruel barrage of weapons.

"Do not interfere. We can do nothing in this state," the unicorn instructed.

"Which side is winning?" he asked with a thought for he feared words would break the protective spell they were under.

"Both sides are evenly matched. Just when the dwarves attain some high ground in the battle, their advantage is taken away. All the traps we have set for them, they seem to know about and avoid. Or worse they turn our traps against us. The wizard is giving them an unfair advantage," the stag informed.

"Is it time for Bran to launch her strike against Savas-Zev?" Iyorath asked.

The unicorn was silent a moment and the elf felt him separate and pull his consciousness away momentarily.

"Soon," the stag said simply. *"Very soon. We must be done with our chore before then."*

Iyorath turned his inner eyes ahead along their path. He saw where they were heading.

They had left the pitched battle and were now galloping unseen among the encampment of the enemy. It was easy to tell the two encampments from each other. The dwarf camp had white linen tents with dwarven runes and block artwork framing the tent doors. The tents of Savas-Zev's troops were mostly made of skin and hide rudely stitched together. In places some tents were even fashioned from the skin of fallen comrades.

The elf shuddered and looked away.

They were approaching the largest tent, pitched in the exact center of the camp. It was woven from white linen and had magical runes etched all about the entrance, which seemed to flicker and shift like live things, protecting what was inside.

The unicorn slowed its pace to a more normal walk. Its glow increased. *"It is easier for me to shield us both when I am moving quickly. Standing still and making us both invisible, especially after you dismount, will be difficult for me. I can only do it for a short amount of time."*

Iyorath dismounted and approached the door of the tent. It was not guarded. He stopped there. He was loathe to touch it. The magical runes undulated before his eyes. The entrance was trapped, he was sure of it.

"Savas-Zev is not home," the unicorn stepped to his side. *"It is sealed with illusion only. Whatever springs out at you will not be real. Trust me."*

This did little to reassure Iyorath. He looked about. There were some tough looking human, goblin and orc soldiers moving all around the tent, not guarding but also not looking at him.

"Proceed! They cannot see you so long as I am with you. Now hurry!" scolded the stag.

Iyorath took a deep breath, drew his short sword and reached for the tent flap.

There was an eye-dazzling sparkle, which stunned him. His vision went blurry. Slowly it cleared. It seemed he had large thick ropes coiled around both his hands. Then the 'ropes' moved and his vision sharpened.

Not ropes, snakes! Vipers!

Four large serpents had coiled around his wrists. One had reared itself up to look him in the eye. It struck at him and gaped open its mouth. Iyorath could clearly see the long fangs as they unfolded and venom dripped from them. Another snake was slithering up his arm to his face; still another had buried its fangs in his arms as he watched.

Iyorath struggled not to cry out. He almost dropped his sword in fright.

And then a long spiraling lance slapped across the snakes and they turned to dust in an instant.

"See? Just an illusion made to stop you. Now go inside! Quickly! I will stand guard here," the unicorn told him.

"You're not coming with me?" the elf asked.

"I cannot. This is your battle, my friend. Now go!" and with this, the unicorn stag shoved him bodily through the tent's door with its muzzle.

It was dark inside the tent. Iyorath stepped forward cautiously, holding his sword out ahead of him.

There was a hiss and a sputter and lanterns magically sprung to life. Iyorath jumped, startled. Then he realized they must be magically charged to do so at a living presence.

He took a deep breath and tried to calm his pounding heart. He made his way further inside. The tent seemed to be divided into four separate rooms. This first one was obviously a library. Iyorath moved through it quickly. He pushed aside the flap to the next room and breathed a sigh of relief it wasn't trapped.

Again the magic lanterns fizzed and sprang to life. The light reflecting off of many shiny things temporarily blinded Iyorath's eyes. He threw up his arm over his face until his eyes adjusted properly.

And yet he knew he was in the right room. He could hear the screams from millions of souls echoing in his brain. Slowly, he lowered his arm to behold a dazzling sight. He was surrounded by glass bubbles with stars whirling about inside. They were everywhere, piled on the ground, suspended in front of him by magic, floating in the air above his head; everywhere there were glass globes. He couldn't even see the back wall of the tent there were so many of them. And they were all screaming, crying, wailing for help.

For a moment he was too dazzled to know how to proceed. He looked at his sword and decided it was not the correct tool for the job. He needed something like a club.

He muttered an apology to the souls in the room and promised them he'd be right back. He stepped out into the first compartment of the tent, the library. He searched wildly for something club-like.

Then his eyes landed on the wizard's staff leaning up against a bookshelf.

'How appropriate would it be to free the wizard's prisoners using his own staff?' he thought to himself.

He snatched up the staff, not bothering to think why such a powerful wizard had left something so valuable behind. He felt it begin to hum in his hands.

Iyorath ran into the next room. He took a deep breath, and brandishing the magic staff like a club, gave a powerful swing and a yell. The first soul cages exploded into a million tiny shards. This created a chain reaction. Large pieces of glass began to fly about the room, colliding with other soul cages and shattering them. The first break snowballed into more like an avalanche. Iyorath fell into a huddled ball on the floor, covering his eyes and shielding his face with his arms. Glass was shattering everywhere around him, shards were falling about him like rain. Stars were growing brighter and zipping around the room like fireworks gone wild. The cries for help in his mind changed to yells of triumph. They were deafening. The light of the souls ripped holes in the ceiling of the tent, racing to freedom. They shrieked with joy and laughter. The air was full of broken glass and blinding bright lights.

Iyorath didn't dare move from where he crouched in a heap on the ground.

Some dim sense in his mind told him he still had hold of the wizard's staff and it was humming ominously. He knew he should let it go, or break it in half. But he couldn't move.

He could hear the sound of tearing fabric as the escaping souls increased in number and began to shred the linen of the tent. Although his face was covered, he became aware of a brighter light than the souls issuing up from the ground.

He risked a look up through his fingers. What he saw stopped his heart from beating.

The fleeing souls had shredded completely the dividing wall to the next room in the tent and it collapsed away as he watched. There was something lying on the ground in the next room, something large and white and glowing, splashed with blood. He recognized what it was with a gasp of horror.

Then a great sob was torn from his chest and tears sprang to his eyes. He prayed to go blind from what he looked upon. He prayed this was an illusion too.

"Gods help us!" he moaned in anguish.

CHAPTER 50

Bran had been pacing her tent all morning. Guards were appointed to keep her inside, and the magic spear had been taken away so she wouldn't be tempted to run off. Delkan had been trying to talk sense into her but she'd finally given up. She just glared and growled as Bran walked a trench into the ground of her tent.

Then the door flap was flung aside and Dra-Oog stepped in. She was dirty from fighting, her armor dented and splashed with blood, and she smelled like death itself.

Both dwarves looked up hopefully.

"How goes the battle?" asked Bran not even giving the elder dwarf time to say anything.

Dra-Oog frowned. "Badly," she informed. "We are too well matched in numbers. Just when we gain the high ground, it gets taken away again."

"Then give me the spear and let me go!" Bran demanded. "How long are you going to have me wait?"

She started to argue the point when Vilmar stepped inside, ducking to get through the door. On his face was the grimmest expression anyone had ever seen. And he had the spear in his hand.

"It's time," he said. He untied the leather sheath from around the spearhead and handed it to Bran.

Dra-Oog turned a stormy look to the human wizard.

"Since when does a human child countermand a dwarf army captain?" she fumed.

"Since now," Vilmar told her tartly. He then turned his attention to Bran. "Get Valynt. We ride at once to battle."

Dra-Oog sputtered and fumed but they ignored her. Things passed in a fog for Bran. Her thoughts seemed to have slowed down and yet everything had become very clear. She blinked and found herself on Valynt with Vilmar beside her on his Blink mare. She didn't remember leaving the tent. She didn't remember mounting up or gathering with Delkan, Dra-Oog, Garn and a handful of other eager dwarf volunteers. She looked behind her. Delkan was there on Sashay, Garn right beside her. Dra-Oog followed them red-faced, sullen and still fuming but silent.

"Where's the elf?" Bran asked Vilmar.

"Busy," was his curt reply. He didn't look at her.

"Vilmar, what is it? What has happened? I've never seen you like this," she hissed.

Vilmar turned to look her in the face and Bran shuddered with abject dread. His eyes since the change had always unnerved her. She had never been more afraid of them until now.

"I found the source of Savas-Zev's power," he told her quietly. "Whatever happens next in the moments to come, do not become separated from me. He will try to part us. Don't let him. This won't work without the two of us. We stay together. Understand?"

She nodded. "I understand. But what..."

He didn't stay to hear her finish. He spurred Blink on and the great horse headed downhill into the chaos and the din of battle. Bran had no choice but to follow.

Valynt moved surely and confidently beneath her. Bran looked at Shak-Kur and noticed the obsidian was glowing from within. She could feel the power within the spear awaken and travel down the wooden shaft to her hand. Its magic saw her and recognized the strength in her. Bran could almost feel the essence of the spear smile in a friendly way.

Shak-Kur was hungry.

She looked ahead of them as they approached the field overrun with warring people. There was a whistling roar from the air in front of them. Bran looked up and her eyes widened. She let go of the reins and reached for her shield.

The air before them was black with whistling arrows.

Vilmar spoke a word and swung his arm in a deflecting gesture. Instantly all the arrows bounced in midair as though they had hit a wall and fell tumbling end over end uselessly onto the battlefield. Their horses' churning hooves chewed them into splinters.

The drumbeats from the dwarf bards on the hilltop altered pitch announcing the arrival of their heroes. As one the dwarves cheered them on.

At the sound of the dwarven drumbeats, the goblin army changed. They grew still, quiet and stopped fighting. As one they turned to face Vilmar and Bran as they charged headlong to greet them.

And they parted ranks silently.

Bran and Vilmar checked their horses' speed. Bran gave the hand signal to those following to slow.

The goblins glared at them but did not attack. They parted ranks allowing the mounted company to pass uncontested.

They slowed their horses even more.

"What's up?" Bran hissed to Vilmar. "I never thought I'd ride to meet my destiny at a walk! What are they doing?"

"Ushering us to the wizard," Vilmar said seriously.

"This feels like a trap," Delkan called up to them.

Vilmar refused to look anywhere but ahead of him. "To anyone who is not me... it is."

This made all the dwarves sit a little taller in the saddle.

Vilmar continued. "It's me they want. The rest of you are battle fodder. Remember what I said. Guard your backs."

Bran gripped Shak-Kur tighter. The spear sang in her hands. It wanted to eat magic.

They were being herded—funneled in a great spiral, step by hooved step into the very center of enemy territory. Dra-Oog who took up the rearmost position cast a suspicious eye over one shoulder. The orcs were closing ranks behind them, cutting off any hope of escape. They smiled maliciously and fingered the blades of their weapons already dripping with battle gore. They were determined not to let any of them escape.

Dra-Oog turned her eyes forward again and set her jaw. She vowed not to make it easy.

Their procession finally came to a halt on a large area of ground already churned into mud by many feet and blood. The goblins and orcs had formed a large circle about them bordered on the inside by their biggest and toughest looking orcs.

Vilmar was silent a moment. Then he dismounted and dismissed Blink with a soft word and a fond pat.

Bran started to protest but Vilmar held up a hand to stop her. She felt returning the Dahla horse made him weaker. Vilmar obviously disagreed.

Dra-Oog yelled a brief command and all the dwarves who were still mounted formed a circle, horses' noses and dwarf weapons out, hindquarters facing in. They glared fiercely at the surrounding horde. The orcs only sniffed. They did not seem worried in the least.

Bran faced the same direction as Vilmar. He took three steps into the very center of the goblin's circle, stopped and waited. Everything was quiet save for a horse's snort now and then.

Bran thought how very helpless he looked standing there. He bore no weapons on his belt and no armor. He wasn't even dressed like a wizard. He wore a simple green hunter's cloak, tunic, leggings and brown boots. He still looked like a blacksmith. And save for the white beard and strangely marbled eyes, he still looked like a mere man-child. What could he possibly do?

A slight breeze tickled Vilmar's red hair, revealing his freckled face.

"He is here," Vilmar said quietly.

No one dared to ask who he meant.

A dust cloud formed from where there was no dust just five steps ahead of Vilmar. It grew in size and shape until there was a man-sized twister of black smoke before them. Then with a *poof* it disappeared, leaving a person behind.

He was a tall, thin man, dressed in what looked to be black robes. But the robes shifted color when they moved so the eye was confused. The man looked both old and young. His features were sharp and pointed. He was balding on top but what hair he had left flowed in gray waves down past his shoulders. He had a sharply trimmed beard and mustache.

His eyes glittered like deadly mercury at Vilmar.

"At last we meet," Savas-Zev said and he smiled. "I have been so looking forward to this."

"Savas-Zev, I presume," said Vilmar.

The tall wizard began to circle him quietly.

"I'll admit you don't look like much," he said as he scrutinized Vilmar up and down from all angles. "I expected something a bit more dramatic in appearance. Not... this."

The wizard turned his eyes to the others who accompanied him.

"And how nice of you to bring along your retainers. You will find them quite useless in the end but it was good of you to get your friends to chip in on this venture. They will find what I have to say most interesting... before they die."

He came around to stand in front of him again.

"Did you enjoy reading my book?" he asked.

Vilmar smiled quietly to himself for a moment. "It told me everything I needed to know."

"Did it now?" he cajoled. "And what exactly did you need to know about me you could not ask me yourself?"

Vilmar's smile increased a bit more. "I found the source of your power."

This gave Savas-Zev a pause. "You think you know, boy?"

Vilmar nodded.

"Well then, tell me. Tell everyone here where you think it comes from," the black-robed wizard crossed his arms in front of him smugly.

"You steal it from people," Vilmar said. "Every life you take, every soul you cage, you take their life force. And it makes you stronger, younger, and helps you extend your own life. That is how you were able to live so long. By killing others and feeding off their energy like a tick."

"And you mean to squash that tick, eh?" the wizard asked.

Vilmar nodded. "You are not immortal, Savas-Zev. I'm here to remind you of the fact."

The black-robed wizard began to chuckle. He took a few steps back. Vilmar felt the power in him begin to swell and gain strength. Immediately the green wizard threw up his own defenses.

"Not an immortal, eh?" said Savas-Zev. "What if I told you I am now?"

For the first time in this conversation, Vilmar looked confused.

"What do you mean?" he asked. "You cannot become an immortal from mortal. Not unless..."

Savas-Zev reached his right arm down straight to the earth beneath him. Something began to slide out of his cavernous sleeve through his extended fingers. It was long, like a pike shaft. But it was not wooden. It was like a lance, which narrowed gradually to form a pointed tip. It was as long as the tall wizard's arm, white and spiraled toward the pointed end. And it glowed with a pure light from within.

"Unless I absorb the power from an immortal... which I have. A unicorn's spirit is quite rejuvenating."

He paused to observe the effect his words had on the green wizard.

Vilmar could not take his eyes off the sparkling white lance which was gripped in Savas-Zev's claw. He felt the magic emanating from it and recognized it. He knew the wizard was not lying this time.

Savas-Zev had killed his unicorn teacher and taken her horn as a grisly souvenir.

Overcome with emotion, Vilmar fell to his knees in grief.

Savas-Zev only laughed. "Nothing and no one can harm me now. I am all-powerful."

Bran brought up her spear to bear. "Steady, Vilmar," she encouraged. "Use your anger. Time for tears later."

Savas-Zev turned his cruel gaze upon the dwarves. He unmasked his true hatred of them.

"And these ants which follow you are no match for what I have become. They annoy me."

He gestured as though he were swatting away a fly, "Be gone, pests! My soldiers will have you for dinner!"

At first Bran thought Valynt was rearing. Then she realized she had been struck by a wind with the force of a great battering ram. She clung tight and found herself and Valynt and every other dwarf with a horse who had come with them were flying through the air like toys tossed by a giant child. She clung to the spear in one hand and grasped the Dahla horse figurine around her neck. With a word she dismissed Valynt before she hit the ground again just in the nick of time. A large boulder smacking her was the next thing she remembered. She tumbled down a small hill and finally came to rest against another rocky outcrop.

"Don't black out, don't black out, don't black out," she told herself frantically. She didn't want to be like Delkan and wake up with no legs.

Dazed as she was, she tried to jump to her feet. But the arched breastplate of her armor had been bent backwards and when she took a breath, her lungs exploded in pain. Her vision spun as if she were still tumbling downhill. She flailed about and looked for Shak-Kur. To her relief she found it was still clenched in her hand. But the long wooden shaft had snapped off leaving her a spearhead with only some pole end, about the length of a short sword. Shak-Kur hummed and throbbed. She felt a jolt from the wooden handle and her immediate pain and dizziness were gone. She took a deep cleansing breath in relief and sprang to her feet.

Where were the others?

CHAPTER 51

"Ah good!" Savas-Zev cackled sadistically. "I've made you angry! Now let's see what you're really capable of, young pup!"

An angry wind had started to blow about both wizards. Vilmar staggered back to his feet. His marbled eyes were whirling so fast he could feel it. He could feel the voices in his head shouting in fury at what the wizard had done.

Savas-Zev had killed a unicorn and not just any unicorn, a firstborn. The punishment for such a crime must be great indeed.

The wind whipped his sandy red hair and blew it into his eyes. He did not care. All Vilmar could think about was the last time he had seen his teacher. He did not know it was truly the last time. He wished he had done more, said more, paid attention more.

And now her murderer was standing across from him, mocking his anguish. He felt a white-hot rage blaze inside of him. Fire leapt to the challenge, begged him to use it. He accepted.

He reached out with one hand, gesturing. The next instant Savas-Zev disappeared in a blazing pillar of white-hot flame. The flames twisted and roared, shaping themselves into a storm of heat.

But the next moment, Savas-Zev floated above the fire, completely untouched.

"Nice try. I'm still here though," he laughed.

Vilmar levitated into the air until he was eye level with Savas-Zev. He looked below him and gestured once. The gathered goblins and orcs burst into flame with one unified scream.

"Impressive!" the older wizard admitted. Then he shrugged. "I can always get more."

Vilmar's eyes focused on the unicorn's lance he still held. The wizard noticed the direction of his gaze and held out his fist.

"You want it?" he teased. "Come and get it."

Somehow Bran's short sword had survived the magical toss through the air without a scratch and she drew it now. She looked about, desperately trying to figure out where she was, where Vilmar was and how quickly she could get back to him.

She had been thrown uphill onto an outcrop of rocks. 'Plenty of cover to hide me should I need it,' she thought. She clambered nimbly like a goat atop the nearest boulder to look about and get her bearings. Far below she saw the clearing. Vilmar and Savas-Zev were floating in midair and she could literally smell the magic crackling in the breeze even from this distance. She gasped when she saw what lay beneath them. The ground was blackened and scorched, littered with the burnt skeletons of orcs.

"Vilmar," she whispered. There was no question in her mind who had killed the orcs.

She looked about for everyone else. The only one she saw was Delkan. Still on Sashay, they looked none the worse for wear. She had a shield in one hand and her sword in the other. Sashay was galloping at a good clip and Delkan was slicing down every foe she met fearlessly with a yell of triumph.

"Go, Delkan!" Bran cheered. "Give 'em hell!"

It was then she noticed movement among the rocks below her.

"Damn!" she muttered and dropped down behind the boulder for cover.

Why didn't she keep her stupid mouth shut! There were at least eight goblins and orcs making their way up to her vantage point, probably more she couldn't see. She needed a bow and arrow. A quick glance told her they weren't heavily armored. If she had a bow she could have taken them out one by one before they got to her. But she had no missile weapons, just a sword and a broken magic spear.

"Damn!" she whispered again.

There was scuffling on the other side of the rocks. Bran grew very still. She strained her ears to try to figure out where they would come from first.

The spear hummed in her hand. There was a sudden jolt and a scene flashed into her head the next instant. It was as if she were a hovering hawk looking down on herself crouched behind the rocks. The closest and biggest orc was doing his best to creep directly over the top of the stone she was hiding behind to pounce on her. The next closest was going to circle around the boulder to her right, the other to her left. There was a sudden flash of light behind her eyes and the picture was gone as quickly as it had come.

The spear was trying to help.

Bran stilled her breathing and readied the spear.

There was a sudden roar from above and a shadow fell across her. Bran yelled and stabbed upward with the spear. At the same time she spun out and to the side. There was a satisfying *chunk* as the spear struck home and a shriek of intense pain. Bran jerked out the spear. A gout of black orc blood followed her hand and splashed her face. She leapt backwards to keep from wrenching her wrist as the orc's dead weight fell straight down. She sidestepped and spun as the next jumped out at her. The very same instant she stabbed upwards at the one on her right, she ducked then slashed the kneecaps of the one on her left with her sword. As she yanked the spear out of the second orc, she twirled it about, changing its angle in her hands and slashed the crippled one a fatal blow. They both fell dead.

Bran staggered against the nearest rock and panted. The spear was doing strange things. It was humming so violently her hand shook. Then she gasped and fell to her knees as something struck her from inside. Her discomfort lasted only seconds.

She took a deep breath and climbed carefully to her feet. She felt strong and confident. She stared incredulously at the spear. It had taken the orcs' physical strength before they died and funneled it into her.

She stared at the magic weapon as if she had never seen it before.

Shak-Kur was definitely trying to help.

Dra-Oog and Garn had landed somewhat in the same vicinity and quickly paired up, back to back, to face ten goblins who fell on them almost immediately.

"Are you okay?" Dra-Oog shouted at him as she fended off three goblins at once wielding a short sword and dagger with practiced efficiency.

"Never better!" laughed Garn. "Daga used to toss me about like that all the time when we were pups. Er... when I was a pup!"

Garn had just lopped the heads off two goblins with his battle-axe and swept the legs out from another one.

Fighting and talking came easily to both battle-hardened dwarves.

"Where's me fiancée?" Garn bellowed.

Dra-Oog gestured with a jab of her chin since her hands were busily spinning death at all who came near.

"Oh, she's fine!" Dra-Oog informed between stabs and slashes. "Horse landed on its feet in soft mud. They shook it off and are galloping death now."

Garn shouted with laughter. "That's me woman!" He was so relieved; he chopped the legs off another advancing goblin and spat at him. "There! See how you like it!"

Dra-Oog rushed past him and put the stricken goblin out of its misery with a quick slash to its throat. "Enough!" she scolded. "Where's Bran? We need to get her back to Vilmar and quickly!"

Their immediate adversaries dispatched, they stopped and looked about while catching their breath. They did not see her. Then Garn cast his eyes up into the rocky hillsides.

"Oh no," he muttered.

Dra-Oog followed his gaze upward. They saw Bran fighting three enormous orcs on a rocky outcrop. But what Bran could not see or know was the entire hillside below her was teeming with goblins and orcs all creeping their way up to her vantage point.

"Like fleas on a wet dog," muttered Garn. "And they're all crawling for the head."

Dra-Oog shook her head wearily. "We need more men than just the two of us. Or the three of us if we can flag down Delkan," Dra-Oog muttered. "We need an army."

"Or one wizard," mused Garn.

They both looked in Vilmar's direction.

"Wizard's busy," Dra-Oog growled.

"We can't just leave her!" Garn said and a note of desperation crept into his voice.

"We're not," assured Dra-Oog. "Even if it kills us."

They exchanged the same grim look. They did not speak what they thought. A look between warriors was enough to tell each they had come to the exact same conclusion. They clasped hands together in fierce determination.

"Sound your horn," Dra-Oog directed. "We may get lucky and there might be some of our lads close enough to lend a hand."

Garn nodded. "Worth a shot at least."

Garn took up his horn, which swung mute and unnoticed from his belt. He placed it to his lips, swelled his lungs with air and blew a great ringing blast. Over and over he blew his horn as he and Dra-Oog made their way to the rocky outcrop where Bran was pinned down.

Far away in the dwarf encampment, the great kettledrums stilled briefly into silence. And then they too took up the call for aid, booming their great voice over all the battle. Every dwarf fighter heard the drumbeats in the air. They felt it through the soles of their boots. As one force, the dwarves changed direction and all began to fight their way toward Bran.

CHAPTER 52

Vilmar floated in the air above the scorched and blackened remains of the orcs below. Savas-Zev hovered across from him extending the unicorn's lance toward the green wizard.

"You want it, take it," he taunted. "If you can."

As angry as Vilmar was, the unicorn had taught him not to trust his anger. Savas-Zev's offer made him suspicious.

"Why?" Vilmar said at last. "The deed is done. You've killed her. I cannot bring her back. Nor do I think she would want me to."

Savas-Zev lowered his arm. "You do not want the unicorn horn?"

"Without the unicorn it once was attached to, it is useless to me. Why would I want it?" Vilmar replied.

The tone of complete calm in his adversary's voice confused Savas-Zev momentarily.

"I will not resurrect her. She is dead. Her power is gone forever," Vilmar said quietly as the winds around him continued to tug and whip his clothing.

Savas-Zev only smiled. "You really are a babe in the woods if you think her power is completely gone. It lives in me. And I can use it as I will!"

As he said this he rotated the lance in his hands until the pointed end was facing Vilmar and he spoke one word. Lightning exploded from the lance and arced toward Vilmar before he could do anything to stop it. Pain ripped through his limbs, lanced across his bones and teeth and sent every nerve ending into revolt. He felt his body convulse to resist the pain.

And then he remembered what the unicorn had taught him.

Water and wind made the lightning. Therefore the lightning was a part of an element. And he had received its blessing. He stopped guarding himself against the pain and accepted the attack, accepted the lightning, accepted its essence in him. He went limp. His mind went numb.

Without his concentration to control what he was doing, he tumbled out of the air and hit the ground. He rolled twice before coming to a stop. Vilmar lay perfectly still.

"Humph," sniffed Savas-Zev as he gracefully alighted on the ground once more. "Too easy."

He slipped the unicorn's horn up his sleeve and turned to depart.

"We are not done here," said a firm voice behind him.

Savas-Zev turned about to see Vilmar picking himself back up from the blackened earth beneath him.

"I haven't finished with you yet," Vilmar told him. "Did you really think it would be so easy?"

There was a long pause. Savas-Zev turned to face him. "Yes, I did. Obviously I was mistaken." He looked the young wizard up and down with new eyes. "What are you?" he said at last.

Vilmar took a deep breath. "I am the lightning," he told him. "I am the rain. I am the storm. I am the ice and snow. I am the fire. I am the earth. Nothing of these things can harm me. Do your worst, Savas-Zev. I can take it."

"Ahhh!" breathed the elder. "You are a green wizard. That explains it." He laughed soft and brief. "I still do not fear you. There is a reason why there are no more green wizards. I am that reason."

Vilmar seemed unmoved by this revelation. "I don't care," he replied. "After all you have done to hurt and kill people... dying while trying to stop you is quite acceptable to me. I simply don't care anymore."

As he said this, far behind him a horn started to sound. It blew and blew and blew. And then the dwarven drums began to hammer out a new rhythm.

Vilmar paused momentarily, his attention diverted. Then he turned to face the sound of the blowing horn. A small fireball grew within his hands. He cast it in the direction of the ringing horn. As it hurtled away, it grew quickly in size. It smashed itself against a distant outcrop of rocks and boulders, lighting up the sky with flames before it finally dissipated.

He turned back to Savas-Zev. The elder wizard had taken careful note of his action.

"You just incinerated fifty of my troops," the wizard stated quietly.

Vilmar shrugged. "You said you could always get more."

"You incinerated fifty goblins and orcs," he repeated. "*Only* the goblins and orcs. No one else. You must really hate them."

Again Vilmar shrugged. "You taught me to hate them," he said.

Savas-Zev's eyes glittered and he narrowed them to peer closely at Vilmar. "You said you do not care anymore. But obviously you still care about something. Or should I say... someone."

Vilmar was silent.

Savas-Zev smiled. "And now I have found the source of your power. Love!" he laughed and clapped his hands. "That's it? That's all it is? Oh, but it is so simple! I can kill love so easily. Love can quickly be turned to hate. And once I have accomplished that..."

He rubbed his hands together and smiled so wide it threatened to completely envelop his head. "Then I can turn you. Even if you do vanquish me through some rare stroke of luck, it won't matter. Because in order to kill me... you must become me. And I'm sure you don't want that, do you?"

Vilmar was staggered by this logic. He tried not to listen but the wizard, seeing he had pricked a nerve, went on.

"Power abhors a vacuum. You cannot just kill me and then have paradise. Utopia is a lie! If I am the most evil thing out there then some equally great evil must raise its ugly head to take my place. The most likely candidate is the one who destroyed the evil before. That means you, my boy!"

Savas-Zev came close and clutched Vilmar's tunic with both hands.

"So here's your chance to be the big hero and save the day. Go ahead and kill me. It's what you came for, isn't it? Finish me off and have done with it."

Savas-Zev's face twisted with madness. He spouted froth as he spoke and it hit the young wizard in the face.

Vilmar grabbed his clawed hands and tried to force them off. But he clung too tightly. "You're insane!" he told him as they grappled.

"Am I?" Savas-Zev cackled with glee. "Yes, I must be mad. Completely, blissfully out of my head crazy. Take a good look, boy! This is where you'll be someday. This is what awaits the great hero. Insanity! There's my revenge. I will die laughing because I know someday you will be here too, just as mad as I ever was."

As they twisted and turned, Vilmar's eyes caught a glimpse of something which didn't belong.

About a hundred yards behind Savas-Zev stood a woman. She had long black hair and wore a black dress. She was very thin and pale. Blood dripped from her mouth, her hands were soaked in it and her bare feet and the bottom of her ragged dress were stained in the blood of the dead and dying. But her eyes stopped him. He had seen those crazy reversed eyes before.

Death had come to watch their final struggle.

She smiled and her teeth were sharp and stained with blood. "Feed me," she whispered.

And then the young wizard twisted, trying to spin, yanking his attention back to what was right before him. Their legs became entangled and Vilmar lost his balance. They both tumbled to the scorched and bloody earth.

Somehow, in all their struggling, the unicorn's lance became dislodged from the elder wizard's sleeve. Savas-Zev saw it and made a wild grab for it. So did Vilmar. Their hands clutched it at the same time. There was a white flash and something—some alien power—shook both of them to their core simultaneously. Vilmar caught a glimpse of everything within Savas-Zev's mind. There were vast hordes of people inside him, empty husks which used to be souls, drained of their life and hope filling the recesses of his consciousness like a huge pile of corpses.

Savas-Zev laughed at him and Vilmar realized the cruel wizard had glanced inside at all he had hoped to keep hidden.

"Look and see what I have found," the wizard declared in triumph. "A multitude of souls within your mind. And yet you have not fed on them. You could have defeated me easily had you known. But you haven't. In what ways are we not alike, you and I?"

Even as Vilmar fought to break free, he felt the wizard cling tighter. He felt Savas-Zev's free hand on his neck, choking him. They rolled about and Vilmar found himself suddenly pinned down. Savas-Zev was on top of him holding the unicorn's lance lengthwise against his chest to keep him there. Vilmar could feel the claws biting into the flesh of his neck as Savas-Zev slowly strangled the life out of him. His vision began to grow fuzzy. He couldn't breathe.

"Since you don't know how to properly take advantage of a person's life-force I will teach you. This is your first... and last lesson. First I drain all of the souls you carry within. Then I drain you along with them. Thanks for all the power, infant!"

Vilmar could hear the screams of the dwarf souls he carried as they were sucked out of him, like bodies caught in a whirlpool. He tried to stop Savas-Zev but he could feel himself growing weaker. He gasped for air. His lungs burned. He couldn't breathe.

Was it all in his mind or was the ground beginning to tremble? No, it was real. The rumble was the vibration from many hooves.

Something black sliced into his fading vision and hit Savas-Zev directly in the chest, scooping him off. There was a shout overhead.

"Vilmar! Get up! I can't do this without you!"

It was Bran.

Vilmar gasped and coughed, flooding his lungs with air once again. Dwarf hands clutched him roughly and put him back on his feet. He staggered, still lightheaded. Short bodies caught him and steadied him.

"He's drained him!" a dwarf voice he used to know but couldn't quite place just now, spoke.

A forge-hardened hand patted him encouragingly on his back. "Hang in there, lad. Not much more to do. Pull yourself together for one final push. Then you can rest. Bran needs you now. Help her."

Vilmar gasped and his vision cleared somewhat. His eyes found Bran and Savas-Zev.

The wizard was laughing maniacally.

"A spear?" he shrieked still laughing. "You kill me with a spear?"

Bran smiled in sadistic satisfaction. "No," she said still smiling. "I kill you with a *twig!*"

So saying she added an extra thrust to Shak-Kur. The spear began to pulsate and hum.

There was laughter coming from inside Vilmar's head. *"You think you've won? Never! Even if you kill me I will still control you. My words now will shape your future. We are twins, you and I. What part of you is not like me?"*

Air! He needed air. Blessed air. His throat hurt too much to speak. He replied to Savas-Zev in kind. *"The part that has friends!"*

But the reply was only more laughter. *"That will change. Pare down hatred and what do you find at its core? Love. Hatred is love transformed. And I have transformed you. You just don't know it yet. I still have my revenge even as I die."*

"No!" Vilmar shouted.

He snatched up the unicorn's lance and hurled himself at Savas-Zev. Bran had him pinned to the ground by his chest with the spear Shak-Kur. The spearhead was glowing and humming. It shuddered in her hands to the point where she had trouble holding it. She could have held it better if she had the full shaft length. But it had snapped off and was shattered, the end splintered. Her hold on the wooden handle was awkward. She braced herself against the lance and the stirrups on Valynt. "Hurry!" she called to him.

Vilmar thrust the unicorn's lance into Savas-Zev's shoulder with an enraged yell. A shock wave shook all of them. Bran and Vilmar refused to let go. Vilmar could feel the souls within them both hurling themselves at the gates, which restrained them. With a roar of internal effort he flung the mental gates wide open.

"Fly! You're free!" he commanded.

He nearly let go of the unicorn's horn in the wave, which hit him as they all surged out.

He gasped again and opened his eyes to look at Savas-Zev.

The elder wizard's face was not twisted in torment. He was laughing. Savas-Zev met his gaze and his eyes glittered one last time.

"We are the same!" he hissed.

And then he sagged limp and the spirit rushed out of his body.

Vilmar gave one shuddering deep breath and collapsed in a heap on top of the dead wizard. He knew no more.

CHAPTER 53

"Vilmar!" Bran shouted. "Get up!"

Shak-Kur was still throbbing in Bran's hands and she was beginning to lose her grip on it. She fought to hang on, twisted in a strange position because the shaft was shorter than it should have been. She prayed the girth on Valynt's saddle wouldn't snap from the strain.

Just then Delkan rode up. Sashay had an arrow sticking out of his hindquarters but other than that was untouched.

"Did you leave me any?" she grinned. Her sword blade was red and the front of her armor was splattered with blood.

Bran shook her head briefly. "Just the clean-up. Although I could use a hand. This spear is going to shake me out of the saddle."

"I'll take the dead wizard," a voice spoke in their heads. They all looked up.

Mayhem was galloping to meet them. The white flames blazed brighter about his body than they had ever seen before.

The white horse with a black head stopped in front of Bran. It reached out its long neck and touched the shaft of the spear with its muzzle. Immediately the buzzing stopped. Bran sighed in relief and withdrew Shak-Kur.

"My herd is forever in your debt for helping us with this matter. Call on us whenever you have need and we will come." Mayhem turned his blue eyes to the body of Savas-Zev. An angry light sparked there. *"The wizard is only mostly dead. I will take him and return to my plane. He has much to answer for with my people. The remainder of his spirit will never escape us."*

Mayhem reached down and took hold of Savas-Zev by the shoulder. With a powerful swing of his neck, he slung the limp body over his back, turned and trotted away from them. He leaped through a magic portal which appeared in front of him, and both horse and wizard were gone.

Delkan smiled and said, "What do you want me to do with your fiancé'?"

Bran gave her a sharp look. "I said nothing about..."

Delkan's laugh cut her off. "You didn't need to. Any dumb fool can see where this is going to end up."

"But... he didn't say anything about it," stammered Bran.

Delkan kept laughing. "Of course he didn't! He's been too busy and preoccupied with the weight of the world. But now it's all over so... in case he gets all human on you and forgets... you better do the asking."

"But..." Bran licked her lips in apprehension and looked to the other dwarves making their way to her. She lowered her voice to Delkan. "Did you have to be so loud about it?"

Delkan snickered. "If you think people will protest because he is a human, don't worry. They won't. Everybody knows. Except maybe you two. And everybody thinks he's the most dwarf-like, honorable human that's ever been so it's okay. And the best part is we can have a dual wedding!"

Delkan then turned her eyes to where Vilmar lay sprawled out and unconscious on the ground. "Although I think you'd better wait until he wakes up to ask him."

"Get up, elf. All is not lost," a gruff voice said right above Iyorath's head.

He was shaking in grief. His hands gripped the staff so tightly, his knuckles had gone white. He couldn't let go.

"Here, let me hold it for you," the voice offered helpfully.

Dwarf hands took hold of the staff gently. There was a twinge in his nerve endings and he suddenly rolled backwards, his hands free. He looked up.

Daga stood in front of him. The staff towered over his head. Iyorath was immediately concerned for his well-being. The staff hummed and sang with power. It had belonged to the wizard who had tried to exterminate Daga's whole race. But Daga did not seem concerned in the least.

He turned the staff over in his hands. "Your master is gone," he told the staff. "You are no longer needed. Disperse and be free."

Iyorath literally felt the air between them sigh in relief. A black cloud began to pour out of the tip of the staff. It raced high into the sky and was gone. The air felt lighter.

"Did you just release an angry spirit?" Iyorath said.

Daga smiled wryly. "The spirit was angry, but not because it was evil. It was angry because it was trapped. It is now at peace."

Daga's eyes turned to the staff. "It's just dry kindling now. Nothing more. Burn it when you get the chance. That would make the oak spirit happy."

Both their eyes went to the body of the maimed unicorn before them. Daga turned and went to the unicorn, kneeling and stroking her silken sides.

"I loved her as a sister," he mused quietly. "She alone understood what it was to be so old as I, the first of my kind. We helped each other all throughout our lives."

Iyorath said with a sob, "We should have saved her."

"No!" Daga said looking up at him and the light from his eyes was angry and fierce. He then turned back to the unicorn and softened his tone. "No. Everything happened, as it should have, as she wanted it. This venture we started, this evil we sought to eradicate... it needed a sacrifice to work. Otherwise the dwarves would have all died. She volunteered to be that sacrifice. It was by her design and her choice she died. The gods approved."

Daga heaved a heavy sigh and stood up again. "She interfered in all our lives just to save us. She knew the cost and she was more than willing to pay it. We need to thank her spirit. Not regret her loss."

His dark eyes turned back to the elf and he smiled grimly.

"You did well. We all did. My people are saved. It was worth the loss. Weep for her but be glad she helped. The world would be a much darker place today if she hadn't. Let the tears flow. They are not evil. They are just proof of how much you loved her."

The sob grew in Iyorath's chest and he buried his face in his knees and cried.

CHAPTER 54

Someone was poking him. Vilmar opened his eyes. He was in Bran's tent in a human-sized cot and she was jabbing him with a stubby finger.

"You pass out a lot!" she commented with a grin. "Is it the human blood or the magic that does it to you?"

Vilmar did not laugh. He didn't even smile. His face was blank of all emotion. He dared not move. He could feel how much the fight had taken out of him. He knew if he moved, everything would hurt. So he lay still.

Bran tried again to pull a smile out of him. "Your eyes are back to normal."

"Yes," he replied distantly. "The spirits have left. They are free."

"Good!" Bran said smiling wider. "Then everything is as it should be!"

But Vilmar continued to lie there, not smiling, not showing any emotion whatsoever. He stared blankly at the tent's ceiling.

"Vilmar, what is it?" Bran said. "It's all done. You saved the day! Savas-Zev is dead and everyone is free to live their lives again. Everyone is celebrating except you. It's like only half of you came back. What's wrong?"

He sighed heavily. "Savas-Zev said I would become as evil as he someday, that I would take his place as the new great dark power in the world."

Bran laughed a real long, loud belly laugh. And then she slapped him hard across the face. "And you believed him? You're more stupid than I thought!"

Vilmar stood on a rocky outcrop with Daga. They overlooked a plain dotted with funeral pyres. It was four days after the battle, a day typically reserved by dwarves for mourning their new dead. Smoke curled into the air and from time to time the sound of chanting came to their ears.

Vilmar's face was dark and serious. Daga had never seen the young human look so grim.

"You are the strongest wizard I have ever seen, pup. Not many could have done half the things you have done and at your tender age," Daga told him.

Vilmar was silent.

"I'm sure she wanted to say goodbye but couldn't. To do so would have ruined what little advantage we had. She loved you a great deal, I know. And she was quite proud of you. She told me often."

He was talking about the unicorn. Again Vilmar did not speak, but his eyes became glassy with unshed tears.

Daga sighed. He then broached the topic he had been avoiding. "I know what *he* told you. Savas-Zev, that is."

Vilmar nodded. "He said I would become just like him."

Daga sniffed. "Do you want to?"

For the first time emotion crossed Vilmar's face as his brows wrinkled in utter revulsion. "No, of course not! Hell no! A thousand times no!"

Daga smiled broadly. "Well then, there you have it," he said spreading his palms apart and shrugging with ease. "Then don't."

"But..." began Vilmar but Daga cut him off wagging a scolding finger at him. "Savas-Zev cannot control you beyond the grave *if* you don't let him. This is your life, not his. You have free will here. Live it as you wish. Bran and Delkan and Garn and the others will keep you on the straight and narrow when you stray. Never forget your friends or lose them. That is where Savas-Zev went wrong. He alienated every friend he ever had until he had none. After that, his slide into darkness was swift. There was only one place to go for him and it was down."

Daga took Vilmar by the arms—because he couldn't reach his shoulders—and patted them reassuringly. "Dwarves will always tell you when you're behaving like an idiot! It's our twisted way of saying how much we care. When we scold you, pull us closer, don't shove us away.

That's when we need you the most. It is no mean thing to be friends with a dwarf."

Daga turned his eyes to the encampment and thought a minute.

"You know, our kind usually finds humans silly, weak creatures with no sense of honor. Familial bonds between dwarves and humans almost never happen. We usually have impossibly high standards for our mates. But..."

He waggled his head as he chose his next words. "I think we can make an exception in your case which even Varg would approve of."

Vilmar looked at Daga with confusion for a moment. Daga smiled wide and gestured with his eyes toward the encampment. Vilmar followed his eyes and then comprehension dawned on his face.

Daga patted him on the arm again. "It's time for some joy and it's time for us all to get on with our lives. Now go down there and get her before some other dwarf does!"

The dual wedding feast of Delkan and Garn and Bran and Vilmar went on long into the night. There were mounds of food and rivers of mead for all the guests. They had decided to marry before the troops dispersed for their homelands so their weddings were attended by several thousand people.

Sometime in the late evening darkness, Vilmar staggered off to relieve himself. He woke up some hours after. He had tripped on a tree root coming back and fallen asleep in a drunken stupor. His head roared and there was grass in his mouth. He moaned in pain from the hangover. It had been a long time since he had felt truly safe enough to let himself get thoroughly and completely toasted and now he remembered why. The discomfort the next morning was definitely not worth it.

He tried to get up and his limbs screamed in revolt. There was amused laughter above his head.

"Here, friend. Let me help you up," offered a female voice from above.

Thin graceful hands laid hold of his arms and gently but firmly, lifted him off the ground. His head roared and his vision spun. He looked down at the feet of the person who had come to assist him. The feet were large, bigger than dwarf feet and bare. They were caked with dried mud. The hemline of her garments was tattered and black.

Something was wrong, he remembered thinking. Her feet were not caked with mud. It was darker and the wrong color for any variety of mud. It almost looked like...

He gasped and snapped his head up to look in the face of his mysterious Samaritan.

The eyes were reversed with white pupils surrounded by black. He would never forget those eyes.

He uttered a yell and was suddenly crab-walking as fast as he could back and away from the person who stood in front of him. He scrambled until the sturdy bark of a tree stopped his progress. All thought of any hangover had miraculously left him.

"Shout all you want," Death told him. "No one will hear you from all the noise. Which means I finally have a chance to talk to you in private."

Vilmar's blood was racing and his heart pounded. Few people ever had a real live encounter with the Starved Lady herself. It did not bode well for those who did.

"Relax!" she reassured. "It is not your time yet. I just want to talk. Really."

With an effort Vilmar tried to control his fear. He did not feel he was doing a very good job of it.

He barely recognized her. She looked so much different than when he had last seen her. She actually looked well fed. Her eyes were not sunken, her cheeks were round and smooth with a rosy blush. Her bones did not stand out in sharp contrast all over her body. She even seemed to be a little round and curvy in places and attractively so. She filled the dress out nicely this time instead of making it look like a black feedbag draped over a wooden frame. Even her skin had the pink of health rather than the blue-veined tint of starvation.

She allowed him a moment to take in her appearance thoroughly before she spoke.

"Yes, I have changed quite a bit. I see you've noticed," she said to him, smiling. He also observed the lack of an icy wind blowing when she spoke. "Wars tend to feed me well. I will not need to eat again for some time."

She tilted her head, considering his reaction to her words before she continued. "Life is not my enemy. She is my sister. She is only my opposite. Without life, I would starve. We need each other to survive. But right now I hunger no more."

She approached closer to him, stepping with confidence. "I will eventually hunger again, rest assured. And when I do, you will be the first person I come to."

She squatted next to him.

"Why?" he gasped. "Why come to me?"

She laughed and stroked the side of his face gently with the back of her hand. "Because you fed me so well in the past. A pet will always return to the person with the best food."

"You're... my pet?" he asked.

Again she laughed. "No, silly mortal. It was just a comparison, nothing more."

Vilmar's thoughts whirled in desperation. "What Savas-Zev said... will I really become like him?"

She smiled and her eyes glittered. She leaned in close to his face. "I certainly wouldn't have a problem with that." Then she withdrew and stood up. "I am Death, not a soothsayer. You will become like Savas-Zev only if you want to. You are in control of your own future. For now, live and celebrate life. My hunger is satisfied."

She turned to leave.

"But know this, green wizard. I will hunger again someday. And I will return. You can be sure of it. Enjoy yourself and your life until then."

He sat on his worn-out horse in the dark. Behind him on another poorly used animal sat another hunched figure wrapped in a tattered blanket. They were in a small copse of trees overlooking the dwarf encampment. Flickering light from many torches and campfires lit the valley below. The sound of much celebrating rang loudly into the night air.

"It sounds like a wedding feast," a tremulous voice shivered from behind him. "I love weddings. Can we go? Please?"

He sighed. She was going to take a lot of work, this one. He hoped she would be worth it.

"I think the crowds would only upset you, my dear," he told her.

"But my brother... I want to see my brother again. Please, Dask," she asked hesitantly.

Dask pulled the hood lower over his burned and mutilated face. "I told you... your brother is dead, Dwyn."

He turned his horse around and picked up the lead for the following horse.

"Besides, even if he was alive, your brother would not want to see you in this condition," he told her. "Come. I will take care of you. You now belong to me."

They both turned away from the celebrating army and headed down the hill, into the shadows. The darkness consumed them.

The End

Among airmen there is a saying, "There are old pilots and there are bold pilots. But there are no old, bold pilots."

However, there was one bold pilot I know of who was lucky enough to live a long life—and that pilot's name was Douglas Bader.

He was a young British kid who had a passion for flying and was a natural with biplanes. He joined the RAF in 1928 as an extremely promising young recruit. As a pilot at the age of barely two decades, he loved doing low-level acrobatics above the ground and it almost cost him his life. He nearly became one of those bold but short-lived pilots on a cold day in December 1931. He survived the crash but lost both legs. I'm sure some doctor told him he would never fly again.

Now I'm not a pilot. I'm an equestrian. I'm sure someone telling Douglas Bader he would never fly again would have the same physiological impact on him as someone telling me I'd never ride horses again. The doctors did not take into account the strength of spirit which resided in Douglas Bader.

At the tender age of twenty-one, his country pensioned him off and assumed that would be it for the young pilot. His glory days were done. He recuperated and learned to use his prosthetic legs, all the while biding his time for a chance to fly again.

Then came World War II. Britain desperately needed pilots. Bader stepped up and volunteered his services to train new recruits. Legless, he was still one of the better pilots Great Britain had and soon the commanders offered him a position flying missions over Germany which Bader was only too happy to accept. They put him to work flying Spitfires and Hurricanes.

Then disaster struck him a second time. August 9, 1941 he was flying over Le Tourquet and collided with a Bf 109. His plane went down and he was captured by the Germans. They took away his prosthetic legs and put him in a hospital. He promptly escaped only to be captured again and thrown into high security Kolditz prison whereupon he proceeded to escape again! His determination impressed his German captors.

He returned home to his family as a highly decorated soldier and was knighted by the Queen.

Through the creation of this work of fiction, *The Legend of the Blood Raven*, I discovered Douglas Bader's story. The character Delkan is based on his struggle and triumph.

Wars create heroes. They expose us to the best we have inside of us... and the worst. These stories have the power to move and change lives—if you let them. Let these stories be told and let them inspire others to strive for the best.

And may that best in each of us change the world for the better and bring hope to the future.

ABOUT THE AUTHOR

D.C. McLaughlin grew up in Delaware on the Tony Florio Woodland Beach Wildlife Refuge. She is a veterinary technician and has spent most of her life working as a race and show horse groom. She now resides in York County, Pennsylvania, with her husband of many years on a small farm with three Haflinger horses, a flock of chickens, several cats, a retired greyhound and an assortment of corn snakes. When not caring for the animals, she participates in historical re-enactments and studies Middle Eastern dance.

OTHER BOOKS BY THE AUTHOR

DEADLY CONVERSATIONS

Book 1: Zan Miller meets Mykhalo, a 300-year-old Bavarian vampire. She tries to keep the relationship casual but suddenly finds herself beset by problems only he can solve. Complicating matters further is her teen-aged daughter Bree who questions her faith and battles the gift of magic inherited from a very old power. Bree holds the secret to ending Mykhalo's torment... but at what cost to her mother?

WHISPERS OF LIFE

Book 2: "Two can keep a secret if both of us are dead." Zan and Bree travel to Germany to tie up loose ends. It was only supposed to take a week. But Zan discovers more secrets surrounding her—ancient secrets. Mykhalo's enemies are now targeting Zan for a sinister goal. Bree's heart is on the line and Mykhalo still has more to say. A lot more! All the while the bodies around them keep piling up.

WANDERLING'S CHOICE

Once upon a time lived a farm girl who dreamed of having adventures and didn't want to get married... EVER! So she acquired a fine horse from a mysterious trader and ran away to find that exciting life. Abducted by a cruel young king and held hostage in his large castle filled with soulless servants, Rhiannon has only two options for escape—marry the tyrant... or become a zombie slave.

Available in eBook and Print

www.ingramcontent.com/pod-product-compliance
Lightning Source LLC
Chambersburg PA
CBHW071643260626
47170CB00001B/209